Pocketful of Names

Other Books by Joe Coomer

The Decatur Road

Kentucky Love

A Flatland Fable

Dream House

The Loop

Beachcombing for a Shipwrecked God

Sailing in a Spoonful of Water

Apologizing to Dogs

One Vacant Chair

Pocketful of Names

❧ ❧ ❧

Joe Coomer

Graywolf Press
Saint Paul, Minnesota

Publication of this volume is made possible in part by a grant provided by the Minnesota State Arts Board, through an appropriation by the Minnesota State Legislature; a grant from the Wells Fargo Foundation Minnesota; and a grant from the National Endowment for the Arts, which believes that a great nation deserves great art. Significant support has also been provided by the Bush Foundation; Target; the McKnight Foundation; and other generous contributions from foundations, corporations, and individuals. To these organizations and individuals we offer our heartfelt thanks.

Published by Graywolf Press
2402 University Avenue, Suite 203
Saint Paul, Minnesota 55114
All rights reserved.

www.graywolfpress.org

Published in the United States of America

ISBN-13 978-1-55597-461-9
ISBN-10 1-55597-461-9

2 4 6 8 9 7 5 3 1

Cloth Edition: ISBN 1-55597-423-6

Library of Congress Control Number: 2004116115

Cover design: Christa Schoenbrodt, Studio Haus

Cover photograph: Lawrence Sawyer, iStockphoto

for Beverly Woodward Hutton,
of Walpole and the World

Pocketful of Names

Prologue

*H*ere was a dog swimming in circles on the surface of the wide and empty sea. In the beginning there was only the splash, his mouth fringed with seagull feathers, his body immersed in a froth of air and water both powerful and without substance, his effort ineffectual in a porous maelstrom of wake. He simultaneously breathed and drowned. His legs were his own yet disarticulated. Then his skin seemed to collapse upon his organs and he knew there was cold layered in his fur, and his body broke buoyant on the water and he felt pressure on the webbing between his toes and he was swimming. The white boat he'd jumped off was streaming away like the white bird he'd just missed. He swam after the yacht for a few moments, whining, the wake melting before him. Then he turned away, and held the turn till he met his own wake in the deep green water and tried to climb up on it, held to the turn hoping to climb up on his own solid back.

There was water in his eyes, pooling on his snout, gurgling in his ears, and he tried to wash this all away with more water. It made him angry that water was always less supportive than it looked from above, and so he snapped at it, bit it and tore at it, but the water remained water with such obstinance, the way a windowpane remained glass, the way no meant no. His forepaws slapped at the surface. The feathers in his mouth slipped down his throat in brine and he coughed and vomited and then swam through it. Water cleared from his eyes at last and he could see the blue day far above him, birds wheeling. There were small buoys nearby and he made for the closest and tried to climb up on it, but it was too small, too slippery beneath his chest. The buoy rolled and popped away. Another gave the same result. He tried to drag one away but it wouldn't come with him. Ahead was a floating bird, a black bird bobbing on the water. The bird watched him, but did not move. The dog pushed air through his teeth, and bubbles pulsed from his jowls as he swam harder. The bird, a dozen feet away, did not fly, but dove. The dog stuck his head under the surface of the sea and followed the bird's flight beneath his own paddling feet. Here was a bird flying under water. He barked. Within the bark, the bird disappeared and the dog watched the bubble of his voice, his bark made visible, wobble out of him and away, rise in a globular meandering to the surface.

He coughed once and again, finding that he had to keep his mouth open a bit to get enough air. He let the sea wash over his tongue but would not swallow. Small whirlpools broke off the curling fur of his back.

From time to time, in the slip and splash of the waves, he heard his name being called, and turned in the direction of the voice ready to forgive, happy to forgive. He came across a stick and mouthed it eagerly, thinking this was only a game after all. But when he turned there was only the empty water. Still, the stick was comforting, and so he held it in his mouth, sank his teeth into the soft wood, and swam.

There was something dark in the distance, no more than a cloud, but it was something to aim for. He could hear more than he could see: a motor beyond the curve of the water, the croak of the birds that could swim and fly. A swell lifted him above most of the world for a moment, him and the reach of water he swam in. The darkness on the horizon approached more quickly than it should have, more quickly than he could swim toward it. He vomited again, unable to keep all the water out of his throat and stomach. And soon he wished he no longer had to swim. He was tired of carrying the stick. On the next swell he saw that the darkness was a piece of land in the water. It seemed the water was colder than before, too cold, and he wanted to bring his legs up against his body, tuck his snout under them. His swimming slowed, and he brought his paws beneath his chest and stomach, but his body began to roll. He barked again, the roll so abrupt, his fear so sudden, and he swam. For a time he swam from buoy to buoy, point to point, as if they had been left for him to follow.

The island grew larger. There were buildings on it. It seemed like he might be able to stop swimming there. If he could only shake the water from his fur. It made him too heavy. It was harder to keep his head up, to blow the water from his nose. But he could see the tall trees swaying in the wind now, saw individual rocks on the sloping shore. It was easy to understand how he could make it there. The sun reflected off the broad, pink rock, and he knew it was warm, that he could lie there while the water drained away.

But something else was happening. He reached a point where no matter how hard he swam, he came no closer to the shore. He began to roll again and yelped at the rolling. He swam forward but moved sideways, along the shore rather than toward it. He was being washed past buoys that tugged to follow him. He made an all-out burst to reach the island before he was beyond it, kicking himself forward, shoving the water behind. But it was no use. The island moved away from him at the same rate he swam toward it. There was so much water. It made him sleepy, thinking about the water, and confused, thinking about why he was adrift in the first place. His paw came up and knocked the stick from his mouth, and he stopped paddling and slowly rolled, rolled reluctantly with fatigue. The water was cold on his back, on the top of his head, but the sun was warm on his belly. He could feel the water draining from between the toes of his paws. He was holding his breath, waiting to sink. He turned once and saw that the bottom of the sea was only a few feet away, but he was too tired to reach it, too tired to even walk to the island. He held his breath against sinking, knew that when he exhaled he'd never have the chance to inhale again. He made one last quick attempt to breathe but a wave washed over his snout and he breathed in only water. He kicked himself over and snorted fiercely into the sky and swam on a few weary strokes. The air he sucked in was full of spruce and guano. The island was almost above him, the water calmer here. But he let himself roll again, felt himself rolling. At last he was tired enough to die. His ears lolled in the water, and he let go his last breath, and sucked in feebly, unable to stop himself from drawing in whatever was there. He was surprised to find it was air, that his nose did not burn. He breathed again, opened his eyes. His eyes were only an inch or so below the surface, his snout a few inches above. He saw his willowy paws bent into the sky. He was making no effort. His body was not his own. He'd died, but had no memory of his dying. When he exhaled he sank a bit, and when he inhaled he rose a bit. He found that he and the surface of the sea existed at the same level when at rest. He found that he did float. This notion made him so comfortable that he soon became drowsy. If his fur had pockets his paws would have been in them. Floating seemed to fit him and the moment the way his tongue fit his mouth. The incoming tide and the current washed him around Ten Acre No Nine Island and into the abandoned granite quarry where he came to rest on a ledge, paws up, fast asleep.

Part One

*T*he first thing Hannah said to the dog: "I don't know if there's enough room for you on this island. I'm already here."

She'd come to the quarry to see what the afternoon's high tide had brought. This was the first time it had delivered a dog. The quarry acted as a weir, yet in addition to trapping herring it collected all the driftwood, cut buoys, and floating debris carried in the currents around Ten Acre No Nine Island. Dead gulls, the occasional prop-slashed seal, the carcass of a basking shark had all washed in before, but never a breathing dog. She'd examined him for minutes before concluding he was alive, before telling him there might not be enough room. The dog did not wake. He lay on his back on a granite ledge in the quarry. His four paws hung from the sky as if on hooks. The second thing she said to him: "You're a fat one." Still he did not wake. There were bits of feather glued to his gums, seaweed looped around his tail. Blue mussel sand crested on the waves in his fur. There was no way to know as yet whether he was a biting dog or a licking dog. A nice brown leather collar, but no tags. His breathing caught on his own starched tongue. The feathers he'd used for gills were drying out. The tide had left him on the ledge and had now dropped a couple of feet or more, so that the next step down in the quarry was visible.

The quarry, a little more than an acre cut from the center of the island, was shaped like an amphitheater whose stage was a pool of seawater. The slab steps were irregular, some only a foot high, while others required a ladder or a circuitous route that reminded her of an Escher print to reach their bases. At times it was seventy-five feet from the crest of the quarry to the surface of the water and at times it was eighty-five feet, depending upon the state of the tide, which rose or fell ten feet every six hours. Below the dog, the granite was carbuncled by barnacles. Lower, moss and seaweed clung to the sheer surfaces, and far below, where there was always water even at the low, lay a rich field of urchins and cold-water starfish and mussels. The pink granite, like that quarried in most of the islands off Stonington, Maine, had gone to government offices and churches in Boston and New York, to the Brooklyn Bridge, the Metropolitan Museum of Art, Grant's Tomb, Sing Sing. The afternoon sun broke off the upper walls in flat sheets of light. All shadows were angular, every cut sharp and square, but the mouth of the quarry, where the water flowed in and out, was a ragged tear of splintered stone and boulders. Her great-uncle had a part in this, working with a case of dynamite during a storm, enlarging the entrance so his narrow lobster boat could slip inside, making a safe sea harbor.

While she waited for the dog to stir, she fished a short plank with faded remains of blue paint from the water, then a bit of twisted root, a small Styrofoam net buoy, and a red cap with "Seavey's Lobster Co-op" stitched in yellow. She could carry these things up the steps and ladders with her, but the dog was a different matter. She'd have to use the derrick and boom. When bulkier objects floated in, a log or wooden box or enough driftwood to bundle together, she would use her great-uncle's lift. The derrick itself was iron, left by the quarrymen, and the boom an old mast. Although she'd seen him use it several times when she was young, it had taken her weeks to get the hang of operating it when she came back to the island alone six years ago. The winch on the lift was powered by an old V-8 Ford engine that lived under a tin roof on the rim of the quarry. It sounded like Armageddon when started, as the muffler and much of the exhaust manifold had long since rusted away, and every fire of each spark plug collected in the huge funnel of the quarry and was from there sent forth across the waters like repeated dynamite blasts. She'd received complaints about the noise from Crotch Island, whose quarry was in operation once again, and from Stonington, whose citizens were reminded of her great-uncle's illegal explosions. She knew the sound of the engine might worry the dog, so she first let the cable and the carrying trap freewheel off the winch down into the quarry. The idea was to get him into the basket, an old wire lobster trap, about two feet by four, before she started the engine. She climbed back down into the quarry and swung the trap around to the ledge below the dog. The dog's eyes were now open, although he still lay on his back, unmoving.

She watched him watch her push the trap against the stone beneath him. The third thing she said to the dog: "Good dog." He responded with a brush of his tail across the granite and a groan. He rolled over slowly, turned his head toward her, and vomited salt water. Bending over, she pushed on the stiff fur of his back and slowly slid his body over the rim of the rock shelf. His legs dropped in the trap first and supported him enough so that his fall into the bottom of the cage was more of a crumple. He put his snout on his forelegs, too weak to lick the vomit from his jowls. She tied a pair of straps over the top of the cage, looping one through the dog's collar. After climbing back out of the quarry, she brought the cable up taut with a hand crank, then hit the starter button for the winch engine. The engine came to life like a bear from a cave. She shifted the winch into gear. The dog was trying to rise up out of the trap but was restrained by the straps. As the cable wound round the drum, the dog rose higher, suspended in the hollow quarry, sunlight catching him fully now. He was surrounded by the reflection of light off flecks of mica and facets of quartz embedded in the granite face. As the dog cleared the rim, his forepaws patting the floor of the basket, she shut down the engine. Tugging on the long boom with a line, she brought the dog over soft ground, moss and spruce needles and dark shade. The trap settled on the earth and she unfastened his collar. He stepped out, walked unsteadily to the nearest tree, and raised his leg.

"So," she said to him, "life starts over again, eh?"

🐚🐚🐚

She craved isolation, and thought an island the most productive place for her to work as an artist. Focused. Find a center and stand there and work in place. The natural barrier of the sea would not only keep her in place but repel others, all those who felt the need to praise or critique her work, to talk about art rather than live it. It was an efficient existence. Her isolation ensured her devotion to her work, and all her materials were at hand, or were brought to her by the action of the tide and current, or by the deliberateness of birds searching for a nesting site and a nice piece of granite to drop a mussel on. Though wary of the sea she'd come to trust it to keep its place, at least to a range. She knew she couldn't fall asleep below the level of the highest tides in summer, though the warm granite slabs were inviting: the water would take her. And she knew that in winter the waves could reach beyond the bare rock and into the spruce forest: great driftwood logs lay yards inland, and spruce limbs faltered under the weight of their own burls, barked hives of growth caused by salt stress.

If the margins of the island shifted, it was large enough to support a calm interior, a forest at the northern end, a meadow at the south. Hannah tended a garden in the meadow, near the foundations of an eighteenth-century farmhouse and barn. The soil was thin over the granite and occasionally gave way to outcroppings, but there was enough dirt to support onions and lettuce, tomatoes and beans. There were wild blueberries and blackberries among the rock, and still, next to the granite threshold, lilacs and irises bloomed. Working in the shallow furrows between the house and barn foundations, ground she assumed rich with chicken droppings, she'd from time to time find a button or shard of early pottery and remember again that she was only the latest of many to lose something on this island. Somewhere, in a crevice in the granite or perhaps in the garden soil as well, were the pocketknife her great-uncle had given her as a child, and a fine porcelain butter pat she'd used for a watercolor paint tray. Both had fallen from her kit over the last six years, as she crossed the island looking for a subject.

She produced watercolors so faint they looked like the bled-through seepings on the next page in the pad, or like the blottings of a real painting when it was almost dry. Yet these thin, severe renderings, little more than water and paper mixed, when committed to sculpture found opacity and weight. The watercolors rarely left the island, the sculptures and her larger oil paintings, always. She packed each piece in dried meadow grass and cardboard boxes, tied the box with lobster warp that had washed up on her beach after storms. The address labels were provided by her gallery in New York, and for a return she wrote her name in water. If they didn't make it to New York she didn't want them washing up on the island again.

In the summer she wore short-ankled boots and cotton socks, flannel shirts and khaki shorts, so that her legs were brown and berry scratched, her knees hairless where she bent down on granite. In the winter she wore calf-high boots and wool socks and flannel shirts and fleece-lined pants from L. L. Bean because, like the feathers she used in her sculptures and the driftwood she burned in her stove, her wardrobe had to be delivered. Catalogs and mail order consumed more of her time than she liked to consider. She was ashamed that after all these years, isolated as she was from other people, that clothes and fashion and her personal appearance still stole part of her productive life. She read the words cotton and wool and linen and craved that texture between her fingers, across her bare back. The words themselves seemed to reside beside others like bark and granite and sand. She believed so stringently in natural fibers that the comfort and warmth of her Polartec made her feel as if she were a backslider, a plastic heretic. It seemed faithless to wear something next to skin that would melt rather than burn, burn like her own skin would if it caught fire. But a kayaker had left a fleece jacket hanging from a branch of one of her trees. It was a cool day, and she was at the far end of her island. She put it on, and wore it while beachcombing home, and wore it through the afternoon and fell asleep in it, and saw no reason to take it off the next day. It was as if someone had left a religious tract rubber-banded to her doorknob and in an instant of weakness she'd read it and become intrigued. She'd ordered fleece pants and sweaters and even blankets, but hid them in her house like pornography, and then put them on like robes of sin, allowing her body to be warmed and fondled by petroleum.

Once a week she called in an order to the market in Stonington. In the winter she ordered enough for two weeks in case the boat couldn't get through. The delivery boat motored into the quarry, leaving her groceries and mail, taking her sculptures and paintings. The delivery boys, the only people she had regular contact with, seemed to change from tide to tide. In the summer, the boys came in open Whalers or skiffs. In winter, they arrived in boats that had something to break the wind and spray for the helmsman, an old lobster boat or a skiff with a house cobbled out of plywood and canvas. They gave her a blast on the horn as fair warning when they came into the quarry, but still her mail and crates of food were often left there on a ledge, the boat gone before she could arrive. She didn't think the boys were unfriendly, only on schedule. There were dozens of islands in the Merchant archipelago, few inhabited year round, but in summer the channels were busy with the boats of residents and tourists.

She was long past caring about men or even companionship. Her last romance ended a year before she came to the island. Her work was what mattered now. It was more than enough on a day-to-day basis, but she wanted, on her last day, to look back and see a body of work that not only pleased others, but made worthwhile a privileged life by the sea.

🐚 🐚 🐚

She guessed he was a spaniel or Labrador of some sort. She'd had little contact with dogs. In the midst of his leg-lifting he'd fallen over like a suitcase. Hannah picked him up, though he was easily sixty pounds, and carried him down the trail to her house.

It was a small cape, another early farmhouse. The clapboards had weathered gray, but she'd painted the door and window trim periwinkle blue. She never ceased to be pleased with its aspect, returning from either end of the island or the quarry. There was another small house, built entirely of granite block, nearer the shore, and beyond that the old man's boat house, built on an incline just above the high-tide mark. A rusty set of rails led from the boat house over a smooth run of granite into the water. His old lobster boat was still inside. She considered it past use. It was a wooden boat, and its seams, since the old man had died six years ago, had opened up.

She'd come to the island twice as a child with her mother to visit her great-uncle. He picked them up in Stonington with the old boat. He seemed old from the day she met him, but a dozen years later, when she came back to work for him, he seemed no older. He took her hand for the first time when she was eight years old, and holding his own cheek with the other hand, told her, "Don't be afraid of me, young one. The islands wear a face. I'm still soft as you on the inside." But his hands were rough and there was stubble beneath his chin and he smelled like fish. For a time his only family was his brother, Hannah's grandfather. Then there was her grandmother, her mother and father, Hannah herself, and then they began to die in that order, so that by the time Hannah was twenty she was his only family.

She swam those first two visits, but had no memory of the water being cold. She remembered her mother wearing a deep blue one-piece swimsuit, sitting on a slab of pink granite at the water's edge. And her great-uncle sitting in a red steel lawn chair at a distance. They both watched her jumping off the short granite pier at high tide and dog paddling back to shore. She cut her knee on a barnacle and the three of them walked back up through the grass to the house for a Band-Aid. She remembered the blood, thinned with salt water, trickling down her shin to her foot and onto the island.

Her mother had told her not to expect too much from him. He was poor and didn't talk much. But on her second visit, when she was ten, he took her out one day to haul his lobster traps. The stench of the bait was almost unbearable, but the old man lost his silence. There were dozens of other lobster boats in the myriad channels cutting through the islands. He stopped alongside every other one for a chat. She realized she didn't have as many conversations in a week in New York. When he asked if she wanted to band the claws of the lobsters, she put her hands in her back pockets.

"They don't bite, much," he told her, then held out his left hand. His middle finger was a section short.

Her jaw dropped, but she asked, "How much does the job pay?"

"Sternman, a good one now, gets part of the catch. Might mean ten dollars a day to you."

"I'll want gloves."

He nodded. And so she bagged bait, banded keepers, and hosed down the boat for the final four days of her visit. He'd tried to round off her pay to fifty dollars when she was leaving, but she'd returned the ten and told him, "You'll need that to pay my wages next summer."

But she didn't return the next year, or the next. Her parents had been divorced when she was nine. And while her mother managed well for several years, by the time Hannah was twelve an afternoon glass of wine had evolved into a bottle. She died in an auto accident two months after Hannah's seventeenth birthday. Hannah lived with her father, who'd remarried, for the next five months, sharing a room with her half sister, Emily, who was eight years her junior. The day after high school graduation, she left for Bennington College in Vermont. Her father died in her sophomore year of an aneurysm. Emily and her mother moved to Texas, and Hannah rarely heard from them.

She found herself with no home to go to that summer after her father's death. She'd never been close to his parents, and they lived in California anyway. Her mother's parents were gone before she was born. But a week after school was over she received a postcard from her great-uncle. She hadn't seen him since her mother's funeral. It stated simply, "Sternman needed. Apply 10 No 9 Island. Good wages for top man." He closed with, "See Arno Weed," as if there were anyone else on Ten Acre No Nine Island. Bennington was an expensive school. She had a partial scholarship, but there were still costs. She jotted back a card: "No others need apply. Commercial pier, June 2nd, close of day. Hannah Bryant." She sketched beneath her name a pair of lobsters, one boiled and orange, the other rare and blue.

Her paint-splattered clothes she packed in one bag, and her easel and art supplies in another. Most of her friends were going off to New York or Boston to work in galleries or design studios for summer internships that would pay little or nothing. She understood from the beginning that if she sold her time for too little she'd never make a career of art. If her art itself wasn't going to pay, the work she did to support it had to pay well. The most productive of her friends were going to paint houses over the summer, in order to paint freely at school for nine months. The least productive would sit in someone else's gallery, and think about opening their own someday. The deaths of her parents gave her the resolve to pursue the life she wanted earlier rather than later.

🐢 🐢 🐢

Halfway to the house, the dog over her left shoulder, she spotted fresh dirt. Between a big spruce and an erratic boulder was a hole a foot and a half deep and half again as much in diameter. It was the first fresh soil she'd seen in more than nine months. When she moved to the island after Arno's death she thought the holes were animal burrows, a wood-chuck, or a fox chasing a field mouse, or a raccoon looking for grubs. But not once had she seen any animal larger than a mouse, other than a deer, on the island. The holes were always uniform, dug near some feature, a large stone or a big tree, the corners of the houses. And they were usu-ally dug at night. She knew she'd surprised someone a year earlier when she woke early to take photos of the sunrise and found a short-handled shovel in a new hole by the quarry engine. Someone was looking for something, and had been, however sporadically, for at least six years. Hannah filled the holes back in, and realized that the mess the house and boat shed were in when she arrived might not be the result of an old bachelor's bad habits. As she always did when she came upon one of the diggings, she paused and scanned her immediate surroundings. The dog made efforts to keep his eye on the hole. He moved his head from one side of her neck to the other.

"Be still, Driftwood," Hannah said.

Nothing. She could hear a lobster boat out in the gut between her island and Saddleback. But all around her was only wind, only the air funneling between leaves and needles and fur. She kicked a little dirt, the color of burned leather, back down into the hole. She wondered if anything had been found at the bottom of these holes, or if they were all dry, if the digger were a glutton or incredibly persistent. A month after she came to the island she posted "NO TRESPASSING" signs on trees at every conceivable landing. They'd all faded to ciphers or blown away over the years. In their place she constructed warning sculptures, dead, debarked eruptions of driftwood from granite crevices, boards tied together with faded warp and festooned with seal bones, the feathered skeletons of seabirds, hollow urchins. The bitter ends of rope blew in the wind, and when not bitter they were knotted nooses, hanging sticks and stones and long-billed caps. These warnings almost fenced the island,

and a storm from any quarter always damaged at least one. She called her repair of them stormwork, her ability to repair them proof of their power. Still somehow, the digger managed to slip through, slip past.

The dog plainly wanted down in the hole. She let him slip free and watched as he sniffed his way to the hole's edge and slid in. He took so much interest in the very bottom that Hannah, after one more quick scan of the nearby woods, the meadow, and the rim of the quarry, bent down, too. She lay on her stomach and sniffed. Nostril to hole, it smelled of dirt and dog. She took a handful of the loose loam, some of the very latest dirt produced on the planet. It was thin and rare here, every inch requiring decades to accumulate. That someone had disturbed it made her mad.

"Driftwood," she said, the sound of her own voice unfamiliar.

The dog climbed out of the ground. She pulled and pushed the soil back into the hole, trying to replace it level for level, as it had come out. She flung spruce needles over the bare soil, tried to pat down tufts of moss, and finally blew across the dirt, all to apologize and start things over again.

🐚 🐚 🐚

Arno picked her up at the close of day in *Break of Day,* his old lean lobster boat. There were so many new wire traps aboard, hanging over port and starboard rails and the stern, that she had to throw her bags on the forward deck. She squeezed into the open pilothouse beside him. He didn't say "hi" or "hello" but, "Ought to be able to run a few more traps with a good sternman."

"I'd think so," she said.

"I was sorry to hear about your dad. My dad died when I was ten and I still miss him. It won't get any better for you. I'm full of sympathy."

"Thank you, Uncle Arno." She took his hand for a moment. "It makes me feel good to know I'll always miss him. I'd hate to forget. How old are you, Uncle Arno?"

"Well, your grandpa would be seventy-nine. That makes me eighty-one."

"I'm twenty now. That gives us over a hundred years of experience."

"Yes, it does," he said. "I hope that's enough." He smiled, leaned out of the wheelhouse and flipped a line off a cleat, his hand twisting and turning as if he were chasing a minnow in an invisible bucket.

Arno didn't look any older than the first time she saw him, but *Break of Day* did. In place of the support for the wheelhouse roof was a weathered broomstick. Short lengths of green garden hose replaced the wooden spokes on the wheel. The exhaust stack was scaling with rust and every pane in the windshield was cracked. The engine sounded strong as he pulled away from the pier, but there alongside the compass were cans of starter fluid, Fix-a-Leak, and fifty-weight oil.

"How's *Break of Day?*" she asked.

"She takes a little longer to swell up every spring it seems. I don't haul in the winter now, so she sits in the shed and weeps till May. We had an awful dry spring, too. You could read a newspaper through the port seams. I caulked that good, though. Bilge pump works fine. You'll leak, too, someday."

"Why did you remember me, Arno?"

"Pull in that fender there. I can't count the sternmen who've come and gone. I need somebody who'll stick to something. I want to see if you're that kind. There won't be no pay the first week. But if you're around at the end of the second week, I'll double that."

"You'll double nothing?"

"I'll double the usual pay."

"I have to go back to school at the end of August."

"That's sticking to something, too." He bumped the ball of the throttle stick with his closed fist. There was a gap in the knot of his hand where the joint of finger should have been.

"Your finger," she said, "it's still missing."

He held his spread hand up before his eyes. "I'm yet to trap Moby Claw," he said. "I'll get him someday and get my finger back. The albino bastard."

She smiled, glad that he'd remembered the story made up for her years earlier.

They motored through the moored lobster boats of the harbor, across the Deer Isle Thorofare and into the huddled islands. Half-tide rocks were beginning to show, the foreshore of each island lengthening in the late afternoon. The granite glistened with wet seaweed. Quartz crystals reflected a slanting light and every barnacle cast a small dark shadow. Spruce trees capped each dome of rock, dropping cones and needles into the sea. A seal watched them pass by. And even then she thought, here's the place where rock turns into life, where water polishes rock into a slick sheen of living.

They rose at five in the mornings to work a calmer sea. Arno had three hundred traps out and hauled one hundred and fifty every day. By two in the afternoon they were usually back in Stonington for fuel or bait. If the day's catch was good, Arno would drop it off at the co-op, too. If they'd caught little but shorts and females with eggs, he'd put the few keepers in his own lobster car moored in the quarry. The last half hour of each day was spent scrubbing down the deck and washboards, rinsing the gurry off the bait barrel, off their own overalls.

They were followed by gulls. Arno would find the buoy, motor along-side, gaff the warp and drop the line over the pulley and around the hydraulic pot hauler. When the rectangular wire trap broke the surface, they'd both wrestle it to the washboard where Hannah would sling off the seaweed, open the trap door, and throw out the crabs and shorts, measure the near keepers and band the keepers. Then she'd remove the mesh bait bag, sling what was left overboard to the gulls. They'd descend upon it in a frantic thrash of hunger, the air torn by wing beat and open beak. Somewhat fresher dead herring went back into the bait bag. By now Arno was working on the second trap in the string, and the work was always this rush of next, another, now. When the last trap of a string was baited, Hannah stood back while Arno gunned the engine. The warp at her feet ran out over the stern, following the brick-laden traps overboard. The coils of warp at her ankle gave her nightmares. A string of traps was heavy, and if her foot were lassoed by the line and she were yanked overboard she didn't know if Arno could save her. When she asked him what the plan would be if one of them fell overboard, he smiled at her and said, "I've heard of dragging a line off the stern. Wouldn't do it because it would just bother. But if you had that line and if you went over and thought quick you could swim over and grab that line whizzing by. If you could swim."

"Can't you swim, Arno?"

"Never learned."

"You've never fallen overboard in sixty years?"

"In eighty years. Wouldn't be here if I had. Once an uncommon wave hit the boat while I was leaning out for a . . . for a bit of relief. My feet left the deck and my hands were occupied. Closest I've come. My heart beat some that day. Even if I could swim I wouldn't have lasted. Water's too cold. Wearing all these clothes and boots and apron. Oh, I could splash about a bit, I guess. Maybe one of the others would come along."

"I could teach you how to swim, Arno. The water in the quarry warms up. Nobody would see us there. You ought to know how to swim. I'm going to start swimming there in the afternoons. Someday you cut off a pair of your dungarees and come down and join me."

"Oh, I couldn't do that, Hannah girl," he said.

And she thought he was referring to the swimming, but it was only the cutting up of the dungarees that he refused to do. She saw him at the rim of the quarry the first few times she swam. He pretended to be working on the derrick or the old winch, but as she swam from one ledge to the next, or around the lobster car and its suspended crates, she felt him following her. At first he only watched, but then she noticed he bobbed his head at each stroke. Later, she looked up and he was sitting on the rim of the quarry, his arms doing slow strokes out into the free air. When he finally came down, fully dressed in khaki pants and long-sleeved shirt, Hannah pulled herself up and stood by him, water pooling at her feet. She wore a bright red one-piece, whose straps crossed over her back.

Arno said, "Seems if I fall overboard it would be I'd do it in this outfit. I guess I ought to learn to swim in it."

She looked down at his feet. He wore an old pair of brown sneakers, small dead seals, to match her purple, rubber-soled dive moccasins.

"You could at least take off your cap, Arno," she said.

"All right." He laid it down on the rock. The top half of his skull was as bright and translucent as a freshly cut onion.

She squeezed the water out of her hair. She was cold now, exposed to the air. "We'll start out slow, waist deep."

And so their classes began, by a slow chilling immersion, standing side by side at the bottom of the quarry, practicing at first the strokes of the dog paddle. Hannah was warmer, reimmersing, and Arno colder. "I am eighty-one and still surprised by the coldness of this ocean."

The first time he crossed overhand from the granite to the lobster car, Hannah swimming alongside, he arrived completely breathless.

"It's OK to open your mouth and breathe as you swim, Arno, when your face is out of the water," she told him.

He held onto the float, his shirtsleeves tight against his slender arms, and told her, "Lobster larvae, top few inches of the water, molting."

She never opened her mouth again in Maine waters.

They swam every afternoon the sun was out, but for no longer than ten or fifteen minutes. Even in the enclosed quarry the water was too cold.

Arno dried his swimming khakis on the line behind the house. Hannah painted them there in gouache one Sunday morning, after they'd dried and blew freely in the breeze. The shirt swam into the wind, one sleeve forward and the other back, and the slacks streamed behind. She stood the painting on a windowsill in the kitchen to dry, where Arno saw it for the first time. He peered into the picture while he washed his hands, looked at it from one side and from below, as if he were trying to see behind it, where the wind came from. He turned to her.

"My swimming togs," he said. "You've captured them while they were blowing in the wind. They're still blowing. They'll blow forever now."

"I never thought of it that way before. I guess they will."

"I didn't know you could do that, Hannah."

"It just takes practice. You didn't know you could swim, either."

"It's easy to start something. Sticking with it is the hard part. That's what you're learning how to do in school?"

"Yes."

"Make a living at it?"

"Probably not."

"But that's what you like?"

"I live and breathe for it."

"Then you stand by it. You'll do all right. Can't stand a quitter."

If the fog was thick, they wouldn't go out. Sometimes it hung on for days. If the weather built up, they didn't go out. But they hauled in rain, hauled when the fog was intermittent, hauled in a chop so steep they couldn't find many of their buoys. Hannah was never so tired. Her feet were sore from constantly shifting them on the tilting deck. The muscles in her forearms and back were painful to touch, and her hands were blistered and cracked. The corner of a trap caught her on the cheek as it came aboard, and left a scrape, bruise, and a welt under her eye. But she found to her relief that she didn't get seasick, even in greasy water, and Arno never felt the need to admonish her, only offering factual advice from time to time. While the work was ongoing he spoke little, only nodding his assent, or holding up his hand when he wanted to move the trap to another location. But again, when he came near another boat, he chopped the throttle and held a chat across ten feet of water while the other boat worked traps. He never introduced Hannah to any of the other lobstermen, but they all seemed to know who she was. She'd hold up a rubber hand and wave and they'd wave back, but never had anything to say to her.

"Why don't they ever speak to me, Arno?" she asked.

"Oh, you're from away," he said.

"But this is America, we're all from away. Don't they ever go anywhere on their vacations? Do they get ignored when they go there?"

"They're just shy. It's all I can do to talk to you and we've got blood between us," he said.

"But why?"

"I don't know. All of a sudden it comes over me that I've got very little important enough to say out loud. I hate to burden people with my thoughts."

"You talk to these fellas."

"They're used to me."

"Hmph," Hannah snorted.

"See there, we've talked too much already."

Arno kept a big vegetable garden. It produced far more than the two of them could eat, so Arno packed cucumbers, tomatoes, and beans into plastic bags and then paper bags, sealing them with tape. He'd take a few bags along every day and pitch them at the boats when he came alongside for a gam. The sternmen would catch them, peer inside, and often as not, pitch back a bottle of beer, usually a Shoal's Dark Ale, Arno's favorite. He'd never drink while working, but sipped a beer every evening before supper.

They took turns cooking. She was always hungry, found herself wandering in the garden for plunder, found the doors on the kitchen cabinets impediments to quick feeding. They ate early in the evening, just after their swim. Arno would nap then, or walk down to the boat house where he'd mend a trap or paint a buoy. Hannah used this time to document the island with her camera and to collect bits of it in a shoe box. She had in mind a project for her sculpture class the following year: to stagger the photos and the island stuff in a kind of shadow-box maze, whose entrance was a picture of the entire island from a distance, and whose center was another photograph that she weathered on the beaches of the island all summer, tucking it into the crotches of spruce limbs and rifts in granite, letting the tide wash over it till it was shredded and cracked, more paste than paper, photographic sand. The path to the center would be littered with shell, lichen and bark, shards of granite and cropped photographs, close-ups of her own hands and Arno's, feathers and wild iris blossoms. She was a painting major at Bennington and kept up with her sketching and studies, but was repeatedly drawn to the texture of the island rather than its reflection, to the nubble rather than the shimmer.

Arno went to bed early. There was a TV, but the generator had to run while it played and this seemed to make it doubly irritating. So Hannah would read in the late evenings, or rearrange her rocks and shells and bones on the kitchen table and play solitaire among them, allowing the random placement of flat card and rounded stone to tell stories and fortunes. She could hear Arno snoring in the room above, a soft kind of flutter that reminded her of someone slowly buttering toast. By the time she went up to her own bed at eleven, to a room wallpapered by her great-grandmother eighty years earlier, the night was full of such fluttering, inside and out. The window remained open all summer to the consistent shoveling of water onto rock. Seals occasionally broke through the wind in the trees with a sharp bark, but the gulls quieted in the night. If it were foggy, the horn on Mark Island or Halibut Rocks parted the curtains like fog itself rather than sound. If it were clear, there was a loom over Stonington in the distance, and the light on Halibut Rocks, faint as her own pulse, slipped into her bedroom every six seconds. When she heard Arno downstairs making coffee it seemed as if he'd somehow passed her on the stairs as she'd come up to bed. But even at 4:00 a.m. it was daylight out, and gulls were already screaming over lobster boats that were gunning from one string to the next.

Over her toast, buttering it slowly in a raspy snore of blade across bread, she asked Arno, "Why'd you never marry, Uncle Arno?"

"No one would have me, I suppose. When I was young I wasn't as handsome as I am now. I had a few girls but none of them wanted to come out here. It's hard for a wife out here. It's a deep lonesome."

"I'd move out here in a minute."

"Oh, it's all right for a while, but the winter's dark and cold. If I could have power over anything it would be to make the wind not blow. It's the cold wind that ages me. I never knew a more insistent creature, just to blow and blow and blow, and me and the trees and the rocks and the water all shriveling and crying out to no use. It's not the ocean that does away with most of us fishermen, but the wind over it. I'd kill my dog to stop the wind blowing."

"You don't have a dog."

"It's a hopeless situation, I agree."

After a month of work he said to her, "It looks like you're going to stick with it."

"My hands don't hurt anymore," she told him.

"I don't haul enough traps to keep a good sternman. The good ones want their own boat. The bad ones want their own boat, too, but want someone to give it to them. When someone doesn't, they quit. They're just boys. I knew you'd stick."

"How could you have known?"

"Those four days you worked before."

"I was a child then, playing on a boat ."

"Young maybe, but you were old for your age. You're old for your age now. We may be one hundred together, but I'm not certain who's older. Where's your boyfriend this summer?"

"I don't have one."

"Pretty girl like you must not want one," he said.

"I don't think I'll marry either, Arno. Your life doesn't seem so bad."

"You can't say you want to be a lobsterman."

"No, but I like having my own way, choosing where I'll go next, what I'll do."

"Well, as you can see it didn't get me very far, still sleeping in the room I was born in."

"You were lucky enough to find yourself here. No reason to move on."

"I'm like one of these big boulders the glacier left on the island. Too much inertia to go someplace else. But it pleases me that you're fond of the old place."

"I'm gathering up a box of the island to take back to school with me."

"People have been chipping away at this island for centuries. I heard of one lighthouse keeper's wife down on Boon Island who'd carry a pail of topsoil back out to that forlorn rock with every trip to the mainland so she could have a little garden. Time and again the sea washed it away, but she persisted till the day she died. That's real brave, working against the elements, against time."

"Why is it Ten Acre No Nine Island, Arno?"

"It used to be called High Island. They changed the name around the turn of the century, when they changed Green's Landing to Stonington. It wasn't so high anymore after they quarried the dome of granite away."

"I thought maybe they measured it at low tide and got ten acres, and then measured again at high and found it was nine."

"That's a good explanation but from what I heard it was a bet between one of the quarry owners and his surveyor. They gambled a week's salary on the measurement. That night, the owner had some boys blow a gate out to the ocean with black powder, flooding the lower portions of the quarry, turning a freshwater pond into ocean. The owner won his bet."

"I thought you did that, Arno."

"I just made the opening large enough for *Break of Day* to enter. Had to do that at night, too. Couldn't get permission from the town or the Corps of Engineers so I blew it out during a thunderstorm. There's government bureaucrats in hell right now still mad at me for that. My daddy bought this rock in 1920, when the granite business lost out to concrete and steel, and we've owned it since. I figured it was mine to do with. The government's been trying to get this place for years. Taxes go up all the time. The summer people will pay anything for these islands, and they do, so then my taxes go up. It's more than a lobsterman can pay. They say sell but why should I have to do that? They force folks into unspeakable positions. Even the summer people are worried. Out to Isle au Haut and over on Long Island they're giving young families places just to keep the schools and a year-round community. I'm not worried about it anymore, though. I've got enough to last through it and when we're all gone these old rocks will still be here, or they'll be underwater, or under a slab of ice a mile thick. But damned if I don't hate the government for forcing your hand. Why should I have to give up my family place because some rich fella wants to live on the island next door for two weeks a year?"

There was fog the next morning, so he took a jar of ammonia and a brass wire brush, and told Hannah to follow along. He led her to the edge of the meadow, where a little graveyard was sheltered by over-hanging spruce limbs. There were two gray granite tombstones, low and arched. The names of her great-grandparents were on them. Both died in the early 1960s. Next to these was a taller, narrower, more ornate stone of the island's own pink granite. The Virgin Mary was carved in relief over the date and name: 1887 Primo Palatucci.

"One of the Italian stone carvers brought from Europe," Arno explained. "They brought hundreds of them here to the islands during the granite boom. Come all this way to die under something heavy."

Beyond this were two large round beach stones, with smaller stones at the foot of each grave.

"Who are they?" Hannah asked.

"Before memory's time," Arno answered.

He plunged the brush into the jar and began to scrub his parents' headstones. Bits of lichen clung to the wire bristle.

"Have to do this every year or you can't read them. I want you to make sure I go right here. Not next to my mother but three feet over. The government might give you trouble. They say there's not enough topsoil here, according to state regulations. You put me here all the same. How's this old island going to get any more topsoil if we don't bury ourselves in it, put back what we took from it?"

She put her hands in her pockets and backed off a step or two, not sure of what to say. I'm not a sternman, she thought, I'm the undertaker.

"I won't know what to do, Arno," she said.

"I'm not ready just yet. I'm talking of the distant future. I'll leave instructions."

"Why three feet over?"

"Susie's there next to Mother. She was born between me and your grandpa. Only lived a day or so. Mother never wanted a stone over her, but Dad kept track by this spruce. She's there, so have me three feet over."

"Why didn't she want her marked?"

"I don't know. Dad didn't know. It's all right not to understand some things."

Hannah had found it best to be blunt in her life, to ask all the questions that came to mind without fear of the consequences. At six: Don't you love us? At twelve: Where is the bottle? At sixteen: Is love only temporary then? At eighteen: What makes you think I want to live here another day? And so it was easy to ask Arno, "What kind of stone do you want?"

With the wire brush he pointed in the direction of the quarry. "You've seen that half-finished fleur-de-lis up on the east rim."

She nodded. It was a huge stone, three feet square, with a roughed-out carving in one face. There were many stones like it on Vinalhaven, Hurricane, and Crotch islands, half-finished carvings intended for the pediments of buildings in Boston or New York. It was as if the quarries failed overnight. Granite eagles, columns, and gargoyles lay overgrown by the grass and blueberries like an American version of the Roman Forum. The three links of the Oddfellows, the all-seeing eye, and the Mason's tools were all bound in the roots of spruce, having never served. Lesser stones, meant for paving or foundations, were piled in heaps at the water's edge and still waited on a schooner. Lavabos and fountains would never hold water because they were still full of pink granite. All these stones lay where they were last carved or where the oxen left them a hundred years earlier. They were too heavy to move without equipment or beasts. It would take a crane on a barge and a forklift to get the carved flower to Arno's grave site.

"But how . . ." she began.

"I don't want that one. Beyond it, where the spruce is leaning out over the water, there's eight or ten blocks just under the water at low tide. There's several with carvings. One's got a little flower on it. I'll bring that one around someday. Pick it up with the boat and haul it around to the landing."

"But how will *Break of Day* pick it up? The pot hauler won't lift a stone."

"Like moving a mooring, Hannah. You tie the boat onto it, tight, at low and as the tide comes on, the boat has enough buoyancy to lift a great stone. Then motor slow around to the landing. Use the winch in the boat house to drag it ashore, and the winch at the rim of the quarry to drag it up there. The graveyard is lower than the quarry rim so it ought to be easy to roll it down here on a set of poles."

"Nothing about it sounds easy."

"I'll grant there'll be plenty of opportunities to give up. But it seems awful silly to buy a piece of granite with so many close by."

The fog eddied between them.

"It doesn't seem like summer on a day like this," Hannah said. She crossed her arms over her chest.

"Until you taught me how to swim, this is as close as I ever came to being underwater," Arno said. "People always say they get lost in a fog. I always thought I was real easy to find: nothing else to look at, the noise of the world hard to hear. You get caught up in a fog and the only thing for it is to sit still and listen for what's not there. You've got to hold your own hand."

When he'd finished cleaning the three headstones and pushed himself up off his knees, Hannah told him, "I promise, Arno."

"Oh, you didn't need to say it out loud, Hannah. Me and you, we're like that Mark Island horn. It bleats every fifteen seconds around the clock, but you only hear it when you need it. I know you'll be there when I need you." He turned away and walked back down through the water-laden grass toward the house. She waited next to the stones and watched him disappear.

🦋 🦋 🦋

By the end of the summer she'd saved more than enough for the remainder of her tuition. Beyond her pay and her cut of the haul, Arno had given her all the proceeds from the extra traps they'd fished that her presence had enabled. There'd also been little opportunity to spend money. Stonington had a grocery, a dress shop, a few gift shops, and a couple of small bookstores, but she rarely had time to visit. Arno always seemed to have the engine running on *Break of Day* as she ran into town from the commercial pier. There were several galleries in the village, but she was convinced that her own career would produce better work. She toured each exhibition and took in what she could, but never purchased a work. At these times she reminded herself of her mother, who rarely bought herself an outfit, always returning to the phrase, "I can make that for half the price." With art, Hannah thought, she could make it for one-hundredth the price. The difference between her and her mother was that her mother denied herself the dress, but then never went home and made it. Hannah not only had her cash at the end of the summer, but a portfolio of sketches and finished works, and enough raw materials from the island to supply a year of projects at school. Her bags were full of rocks.

"Can I come back next summer, Uncle Arno?" she asked him on the pier.

"Don't need to ask," he said.

He put out his hand to shake hers, and instead she took it and placed it on her cheek and held it there. "I know you didn't learn to swim to save yourself," she told him.

"So old for your age, little girl," he said. "Make a lot of art while it's cold. We'll play again when it's warm." He tried to put a wad of cash in her hand.

She put it back in his shirt pocket. "Never pay me for something I haven't done yet. You'll turn me into a quitter."

She looked over her shoulder. There were two young men wearing orange bibs, standing on the pier. Jesus, she thought, it's taken them all summer. But they didn't ask to carry her bags, or if she needed any help at all.

"I'll be with you in a minute, boys," Arno said.

"My replacements?" she asked him.

"No, it's just me from here till next June." He whispered, "I've given up on all the young men that know me."

She picked up her bags and portfolio. Even though they were stuffed with rocks they felt like half the weight of a lobster-laden trap. It pleased her not to need help. She felt her biceps push against the fabric of her shirt.

"Thanks, Arno."

He nodded.

She pushed past the two young men without looking up.

🐚 🐚 🐚

Over the fall, winter, and spring she sent Arno photographs of her art-work and he answered with postcards of one line:

"Lobsters at $4.69/lb."

"Lost two traps off Colby Ledge."

"*Break of Day* in the shed."

"Quarry near froze over."

To her questions he replied:

"Generator down but firewood holding out."

"Ed Gross from Billings fixed generator and we had pie."

Then as spring came:

"Caulking *Break of Day*. That last painting was a good one."

"*Break of Day* over."

"First seal pup in the quarry."

"Chanced a short swim today. Water some cold."

"Set 100 traps this week."

"Pilot whales in Merchants Row."

She found herself lonely at art school, surrounded by students who wanted to live as artists but who rarely put anything down on paper. They were all talented but few were dedicated. She spent her winter internship at a foundry in upstate New York, learning to cast wax sculpture in bronze, to weld and braze, to do enough woodworking to build bases for sculptures, and to finish the bronze in a variety of patinas. The men and women she worked with had never trained as artists, and looked upon their work as work, as a skilled craft, but it was a rare sculpture that left the foundry looking worse than it came in. Most were improved. She took from her two months there a willingness to spend eight hours a day on art, to make a job of it. And she left there all fear of working with weight and fire.

She met a sculptor who'd lost several of his molds in a fire before they were cast, who told her that the only important thing about art is making it. The lost molds didn't concern him. The only art lost is the art not made. It's a hard thing to remember, he said, because you have this competing desire to impress others and be appreciated. Rarely does that make your art finer. What made your art better was being impressed with your own turnout, then dissatisfied with it, so that you felt the desire to start the process over again. If someone tells you they like something you've done, you can't help but make the same thing again. I always try to start my next piece before I show the last one to anybody, he said.

But she'd seen one of this man's sculptures and didn't care for it. It seemed unfaceted, simple. She asked the foundry owner if he was a successful artist and he told her they'd never cast more than one of each sculpture. She knew if other people didn't appreciate her work and buy it she couldn't live as an artist. Commercial success was really the only way to keep score. It would be fine to continually impress yourself if you were independently wealthy and didn't mind living in a void of competition. It was self-serving to avoid the market, a selfishness born of fear and lassitude, and if it didn't support you then most likely your art was little more than an indulgence, little more than a hobby, simple masturbation.

It was unacceptable to lose work or time. If an artist loses a piece she is far more injured than the owner or insurer, as it was the only artifact capable of recording and explaining that period of her life, the transitions in a career. She felt sorry for the sculptor who'd never regain the months lost, but also felt his carefully mounded complacency marked a shallow career.

The last postcard Hannah received before setting out on the eight-hour drive to Stonington at the end of the term stated, "Lobsters unwary. Artist needed quickly."

🦞 🦞 🦞

She arrived at low tide. The receding water left Stonington harbor mud-ringed and ledge-bound, defining the channels that the boats followed whether low tide or high. Even though it was late afternoon, few lobster boats were on their moorings. Arno was late. She'd expected to see *Break of Day* at the pier, piled high with traps, engine idling. The pier was crowded with trucks, parked at odd angles. She had to park in town and carry her bag and easel down. Beyond the parked trucks a group of about a dozen people, mostly women, were huddled around the door to the harbormaster's office, listening to a VHF radio. A woman turned to Hannah as she walked up and said, "They've found the boat, but no one's aboard."

"Shhh," the others said.

It sounded as if there were a dozen fishermen trying to find room on the same channel at once. They kept chopping each other up, rolling over each other's voices like waves in a confused sea. Suddenly their garbled transmissions were overridden by a clear, young, modulated voice, where silence existed between words rather than the sound of a roaring engine. It was the Coast Guard out of Southwest Harbor.

"*Razor Blade*, please switch to two-two."

And immediately a fainter call, "Switching two-two, Coast Guard." A young woman leaned over and turned the channel selector.

"*Razor Blade, Razor Blade*, Coast Guard Group Southwest Harbor."

"I'm here, Coast Guard."

"Please repeat your position, *Razor Blade*."

"We've found the boat about three miles southeast of Isle au Haut, over Grumpy Ledge. She's circling at a pretty good clip with no sign of anyone aboard. There's two more boats out here with us now."

"*Razor Blade, Razor Blade*, can you give me lat and lon coordinates?"

The voice responding to the Coast Guard was clearly an exasperated one, an older man. "Look at your chart, son. Grumpy Ledge, three miles southeast of Isle au Haut. I'm going to try to put my sternman aboard."

Another voice: "Coast Guard, this is *Break of Day*. I'm off *Sweet Paula*'s port. *Razor Blade* is kind of busy. *Sweet Paula*'s in a pretty tight circle and she's dragging at least one trap behind her and a couple of buoys."

"We've got a boat en route, *Break of Day*."

"*Razor Blade* is coming along on her starboard. There's a pretty good wake. If there's anybody aboard *Sweet Paula*, I can't see them."

"*Break of Day*, this is Coast Guard Group Southwest Harbor. Be advised to keep a lookout for people in the water. Is the crew on *Razor Blade* attempting to board?"

"They're alongside now . . ."

"*Break of Day*, this is Coast Guard Group Southwest Harbor. Can you provide lat and lon coordinates?"

"If you'll stop walking on me, Coast Guard, I'll tell this story. He's aboard! Goddamn, that was a wicked good jump, Coast Guard."

"*Break of Day*, this is Coast Guard Group Southwest Harbor."

"68.31.22 by 43.58.06, Coast Guard. She's under control now. That boy's got her settled."

There was a pause in transmissions. The radio seemed to vibrate on the desk. Then Arno's voice broke through again. "There's no one aboard, Coast Guard. He says there's no one aboard. We're going to leave the boat here, Coast Guard, and keep on looking. *Break of Day* out."

She heard Arno's voice a few more times that evening as the search continued. Every lobsterman in the area was crisscrossing Jericho Bay and the waters off Isle au Haut, wherever *Sweet Paula* ran traps. There'd been only one man aboard, Sonny Thurlow, the boat's owner. His stern-man had called in sick the evening before. The boat was named after Sonny's daughter. He'd been expected at the pier by two and when he hadn't shown up by four, the radios had started chattering. By four most of the lobstermen were done for the day, but almost all remained out or headed back out when Sonny hadn't shown up. Arno pulled into the dock at ten that night, out of fuel. Hannah threw her bags aboard.

"Sorry I'm late, dear," he said.

"It's OK, I heard you on the radio."

"We're going to pull around here and fuel up. Have you got some warm clothes? We might be out all night."

"What happened, Arno?"

"Don't know, don't know. I saw him, spoke to him, about six-thirty this morning. He was fine. Threw him a little jar of that blueberry jam I put up last summer. Didn't eat as much of it over the winter as I usually do. But he wasn't on his boat. Awful eerie to come upon a boat in the ocean with no one aboard. I've searched every ledge and buoy and light that you might climb up on. So has everybody else. Maybe he's ashore somewhere, but I'd think he'd have let us know by now if he'd swum ashore. The Coast Guard's taken the boat to Southwest Harbor to see if they can come to some understanding."

It was a clear night, infrequent clouds scudding beneath a sliver of moon. The sea was calm, but cut like a rasp.

"What if he's not onshore, Arno?" she asked.

"These boats are out here searching for a body, dear. Little hope now, but no boat here wants to be the first to give up."

"Did someone look in the string of traps *Sweet Paula* was dragging?"

"Sure. Sure we did that. You want to run that spotlight for me? Keep it out on the starboard bow. That's right."

"Arno?"

"Yes, dear."

"Every lobster buoy looks like a person."

"I know. Light up every one you can."

"Yes, sir."

"When he was lost, the tide was going out," Arno said. "But it's coming in now."

They motored slowly against the tide, cut between Russ and Green islands off the Thorofare, swung east between Potato and Little Camp, then ran beneath Camp and Devil islands, hugging their shores. The spruce above them was dark and silent, the small waves breaking onshore white and narrow. Turning south again, Arno slipped between Spruce and Millet islands and rounded Ten Acre No Nine.

"Don't often come up on her in the night anymore," Arno said. "Used to a lot as a young man. She's pretty, isn't she?"

"There's a star at the tip of every tree," she answered.

Arno, rather than heading out to sea, kept turning around his island.

"Not as dark as it once was," he said. "So many lights in Stonington now, the loom carries this far. Shine the light up on the old house."

"Shouldn't we hurry, Uncle Arno?"

"Dear, that boy was only cold for a little while, forty-five minutes, an hour. He's not cold anymore. It won't be us that finds him by looking. The tide and the current will either bring him home or take him farther away."

He made a slow circle of the island. Both houses and the boat shed were dark rectangles against dark fields, dark forest. But the granite of the foreshore was as brilliant and complete as a priest's collar.

"You forget about the waves working against the rock all night long, too," he said. Then he throttled forward. "Let's have a look over in Toothacher Bay. Those boys never set a trap there, but they always wanted to. And the tide don't care where they fished. Snap that light off. It's blinding me."

"It seems dangerous," Hannah said, "all these boats out here in the dark."

"We're not looking for that boy anymore, we're looking for the sake of his little girl and her mother."

"How old is she?"

"Well, Thurlow named his boat after his daughter when she was born. I'd say she's three or four now."

Break of Day swung around the flashing light on Halibut Rocks and glided into Toothacher Bay on its own wake.

"You can turn that light back on, Hannah. We'll work our way past these ledges slow, then slip out to Heron and then to sea. I suppose any-place we look is as good as any other now."

Hannah played the light among clustered buoys and along shore. A seal on a ledge lifted its head as they went by and she audibly gasped. Every bird call sounded human, the lap of the water against the hull like a desperate swimmer trying to climb aboard. By four in the morning when the eastern horizon began to lighten, *Break of Day* was far at sea, tilting over broken waves. There was little to look at. The water was too deep for lobster and so there were no buoys. Driftwood and even sea-weed were sparse this far offshore. They came across a Styrofoam cup, a Clorox bottle, an empty five-gallon bucket of motor oil. As the sun broke the surface, Hannah asked Arno if there was anyone on the planet farther east than they were.

"I guess we've come far enough," he said, and turned the boat about. "We always kid each other about being lobster bait some day. I guess we only do it because it's true."

"Yuck, Arno."

"Some rightness to it. We take and we take and some we have to give back. If we were hunting lions it wouldn't be any different. You've seen that postcard they sell, the big lobster with a boat in his claw? He's mad."

"What's he mad about?"

"Us eating all his kin, I guess. Maybe just the ghost traps."

"What's that?"

"Before we had these new traps with the panels that rot away, you know. If you lost a trap it would sit down there on the bottom catching lobsters for eternity. First lobster would crawl in, eat the bait, then die of starvation. Next lobster'd crawl in to eat him. Long chain of lobsters eating lobsters. Ghost traps."

"It sounds like an art gallery," Hannah said. "They do the same thing to artists in New York."

"You still going there after you graduate?"

"Yes, we all are. It's the only place they feed artists regularly."

"The same way we feed lobsters, till they're big enough to eat? You're sure the whole town's not a ghost trap?"

She just smiled at him.

Arno's two radios were tuned to different channels. On 16 they listened to the regular request from the Coast Guard, asking all boaters to be on the lookout for a missing fisherman off Isle au Haut. On 74 they listened to the somewhat muted chatter of the other lobstermen.

"Are you on this one, Eric?"

"You out there, Steve?"

Some calls were answered, some not. The owner of one boat told another he'd found one of his buoys floating free, had tied it onto another so he wouldn't lose it. Details of the story washed back and forth till they were smooth. There were questions whose answers got lost in the troughs of waves: Was the gaff still on board? Was the pot hauler running? Who was going to haul Sonny's traps? By the time Hannah and Arno slipped into the quarry and tied up along the float, the sun was over the trees and the radio was silent.

Sonny Thurlow's cap was found four days later on Great Spoon Island. His body never surfaced. The Coast Guard reported they'd found drugs on *Sweet Paula*: a small bag of marijuana and several amphetamines. Arno attended Sonny's funeral. When he returned to the island, Hannah asked how it went. He didn't answer, just changed from his old black suit into his work clothes, picked up the hoe that always leaned outside the door. She let him have fifteen minutes alone in the garden before going up. When she arrived she saw that all the young plants had been cut off, the lettuce and bean sprouts turned over, the transplanted tomatoes hacked to pieces. Arno was at the end of the garden, dismantling cucumber mounds.

"Arno?" she asked.

"No garden this year, Hannah."

"But why?"

"I'm too old for it. I don't eat enough to bother the earth."

"But we give away what we don't use."

"I'm too old, I said."

"I'll take care of it, Uncle Arno."

"This is still my island, young lady. Not yours yet."

They didn't fish for three days. Arno sat in his room upstairs, fully dressed, but wouldn't put to sea. Midmorning he'd walk down to the boat house and sit there till lunch, when Hannah would bring him a sandwich. He'd nap in the afternoon, then crank up the generator and watch TV for a few hours in the evening. On the fourth morning, Hannah woke Arno. When he'd turned on his bedside lamp, she told him, "I'm hauling traps today. There's lobsters been in some of them for days now. *Break of Day* needs fuel. If you'll help me take her into the dock, I'll bring you back here. I know you're not feeling well."

"Close the door and I'll get dressed," he said.

They took the boat into the dock, fueled up, took on bait. Arno still wasn't speaking unless spoken to. But instead of steering *Break of Day* back home, he headed for their first string, and Hannah gratefully gaffed the warp beneath the first buoy. She assumed Arno knew she was bluffing, but it was an out, and he'd taken it. When they met other boats, they all asked where *Break of Day* had been, and instead of answering, Arno just waved. One sternman called out, "Nothing for me this week, Arno?"

"No garden this year, boys. I've give it up."

He did begin to introduce Hannah, turning from the garden to her, saying, "This is my niece, Hannah Bryant." Hannah was so stunned all she could do was wave her gloved hand.

Once she told Arno, "I'd like to know their names, too."

But he simply blinked and said, "I can't remember them all. They're too young."

They didn't put out as many traps as they had the year before. By midsummer he'd replanted a few onions and tomatoes, but just enough for their own needs. Hannah bought him a new set of binoculars for his birthday, and to show his appreciation he sat in his rusty lawn chair and picked out birds on the rocks with them. He told a story for each bird. How an osprey on Russ Island had screamed at him as he walked the beach. He knew he was within a couple hundred feet of her nest, but he wasn't threatening it in any way. The bird made passes, lower and lower, over his head. Finally, he heard the sucking flap of her wing beat directly above him, and ducking, caught the sharp splat of her shit full on his back. Then her mate came around and tried to shit on him, too, but missed by six or eight feet. Surprising, he said, the quantity of material in a single osprey passing. He said it felt like she'd hit him in the back with a twenty-pound cod.

He'd seen a seagull, a big Black Back, yank a baby crow from its nest and drown it before eating it. "Just protecting its territory," he replied to Hannah's wrenched face.

"We used to shoot the seagulls. Carried shotguns on the boat just for the sport of it. They knew which boats had guns aboard."

When he was a boy he'd brought up a shag as a pet. He'd tie a string around its neck, loose enough so it could breathe, but too tight to swallow. They'd fish together, boy and bird. The shag would dive off the bow of the dory and return with a small fish in its throat. "A little massaging would bring it right up," he said. Arno would use the little fish for bait and go after cod. "He'd get a big meal then. We were a good team."

Yet there were days during the summer when Arno, without warning, would refuse to get up. Hannah would rise and start breakfast but he'd never come down. She'd knock lightly on his door and he'd tell her to take the day off, or say he wasn't feeling well. She hung around the first few times this happened, but he didn't really seem sick, just ornery. He wouldn't string more than two words together all day.

"We have to go out tomorrow, then," she'd say.

"I know."

"Do you want to go into town with me?"

"No."

"Do you want anything?"

"Some beer."

She'd take the skiff the three miles into Stonington for the day, visit the galleries and bookstores, have lunch, pick up a few groceries. Or she'd go three miles north, tie up to the rocks below Haystack Mountain School of Crafts and visit the classrooms. On clear days she could stand on the seaward deck at Haystack and just glimpse Ten Acre No Nine through the gut between Saddleback and Millet islands, and wonder what Arno was doing. He didn't seem old or even tired, but acted as if he were being harassed by a flock of crows. Even when they were out lobstering, his gams with the other crews were getting shorter and shorter. When the vegetable and beer bartering ceased, it didn't take too long to trade viewpoints on the steepness of the waves or the thickness of fog.

In Stonington she was simply another tourist, one less stunned by the extreme tides. At Haystack she was another head stuck in the door to the teachers, but the other students noticed her. They knew she was and wasn't one of them. The young men there, potters and weavers and poets, pulled up chairs for her, offered segments of oranges and halves of tuna sandwiches at lunch. They were so much more confident than the sternmen she'd met on the commercial pier. It was the difference between men who recognized her and those who didn't. The boys at Haystack all wanted to show her their work and see hers, but she had no desire to take them out to Ten Acre No Nine. She thought the things she made there weren't ready yet. Besides, in his present state, Arno might throw one of them off the rim of the quarry. But one boy was persistent, a ceramic artist from Hawaii, a boy who bounced a soccer ball on his knee between classes, Mark. There was always clay beneath his fingernails. He wore baggy shorts and socks without any elastic left in them. His blond hair fell over his ears and eyes so that he was constantly moving it for better sensory perception. The bodies of his pots were curved and sensual, the lips and rims always pinched as if they were upset. He used earth-tone glazes that he allowed to slip around the vases as he twirled them in midair. She met him the first day of August, during the first of his three weeks at the school. By the end of the second week she was taking the skiff to Haystack every evening after work. They made love in his car, and in the woods, and beneath the raised wooden sidewalks. His hands were smooth and supple and he moved them brusquely over her body. His body seemed as hard and smooth as driftwood. During his last week, she asked Arno for a day off, then another. She came back to Ten Acre No Nine after dark in the skiff one night, and Arno was starting up *Break of Day* to search for her. The next day she brought the boy back to the island. Arno told her he could sleep in the granite house or down in the boat shed.

"Then I'll have to sleep there, too, Arno," she told him.

"So be it. We still fish at five."

"I want to bring him along."

Arno stood there, the back of his hand on his cheek. "It isn't a side-show or a tourist boat," he said. "It's our work."

"I'll put him where he won't be in the way."

"Well, there's no such place on a narrow boat, and you know that. You've had two days off this week already. We're behind. It's not just silly having a guest on board, it's dangerous. I hired you because you weren't like these other sternmen around here."

"I wasn't helping you just for the money, Arno," Hannah said.

"Well, let's be honest, you weren't helping just to be helping, either."

"Mark's going to be gone in just two days," she pleaded.

"Has he made plans to come back?"

"No, not yet."

"Then best let him go and get to work on your own life."

"It's none of your business, Arno."

"*Break of Day* leaves for work at five tomorrow morning. If you're not there, we'll just call it a season. If you want to, we'll try again next summer."

"OK," she said. "If I'm being irresponsible, you're just being stubborn."

"Call it what you will. At least you know you're being irresponsible."

"Arno, I might be with him the rest of my life. I'm still young. If a few lobsters die in the traps, they were just going to be eaten anyway."

"I think you've made up your mind," he said. "Come back next spring when you finish school and we'll start over. If the boy's still around, we'll teach him the work."

"Arno, please don't make me pick between you and him."

"I just want you to pick yourself over him, little girl. I'm not mad."

"I can still help next week."

"No, you spend all the time you can with this boy and then go on back to school. I'll be out all day tomorrow. You be gone when I get back. Leave the skiff at the commercial pier. I'll miss you."

And with that he went to bed.

Hannah packed her bags, and she and the boy spent his last three nights in his room at Haystack. She sat in on his classes, but while he worked in the studio he asked her for some space. She stood on the deck at the water's edge and gazed out toward the islands but there was haze at a mile, obscuring everything but the boats working off Stinson Neck. It was maddening to her that Arno was so incorrigible, so jealous, that he couldn't see beyond his own needs. Mark followed her back to Bennington and stayed with her and her roommates for a week, but then he left to meet another friend in New York for the long drive to California, where he planned to sell his car and catch a flight back to Hawaii. She called him a few weeks later when she decided he wasn't going to call her. When he answered, she began to drown in his voice, and could think of nothing more to say than, "I love you, I love you." A week before Christmas she received a postcard of aqua water off the coast of Molokai. He wrote in block print, "SORRY." She turned the card back over. The ocean there seemed oddly empty. There were no lobster buoys. It was the last she heard from him.

🐦 🐦 🐦

"C'mon, boy," Hannah said softly. The dryer he became the older the dog looked. There was gray at his muzzle and chin, and the hair on his tail reminded her of Spanish Moss on a dead branch. Hannah was always uneasy for days after finding one of the freshly dug pits. There seemed to be a permanent presence in her peripheral vision. The island was noise-ridden, the ocean scouring the gravel on the beaches suddenly overpowering, mimicking footfall and cough, a skiff dragging over the rocks, even gunshots and chain saws. She knew the only thing that would allow her some calm and the ability to return to work would be to circle the island on foot. The dog didn't seem up to this and so she took him down to the house, set down a dish of water, and left him there. When she was twenty feet away from the door she heard his insistent bark for the first time. She paused on the grassy path that led down to the boat shed when she heard the bark, began again, and stopped once more at his second bark. It was more wail than bark. It was the first time she'd been missed in almost six years. It felt strange to turn back on her own tracks, to answer a call. The dog was leaning on the door when she opened it. He staggered back on his hind feet, dropped down, and rushed forward to smell her shoes.

"I didn't get very far. Not much new there," she told him.

There was a puddle of water around the dish, and drips leading to the door. She wiped this up with a sponge. Once again, it felt odd, wiping up a spill she hadn't made. It wasn't annoying, but unusual, as if she'd had to do something twice for no reason.

"Are you hungry?" she asked, realizing that just because she wasn't hungry didn't mean the dog wasn't.

He looked at her and banked his head slightly as if her voice had come out of the floor. There was little meat in the house, but she thought an egg might pass. She fried two, breaking the yolks, on her propane stove. The dog watched, still listening to the floor.

"You're going to get a crick in your neck that way," she said. "I hold my head that way when I paint and it's always sore the next day."

He sighed.

She put the eggs on a saucer, after patting the oil off them, and set them on the wood floor. The dog approached, picked up an egg by its edge, and carried it away flapping at his chin. There was a small hooked rug before the hearth. He hooked his nose under the edge and shoved the egg beneath it.

"No way," Hannah said. While she retrieved the first egg, he carried the second to her overstuffed armchair, and dropped it behind the seat cushion. "No, no, no," she told him. He watched her put the two eggs back in the dish and the dish on the stove. Then he went back to the rug, lifted it up with his snout, and crawled under it, sniffing for the egg. "We eat out of dishes here," she said, incredulous. Plainly someone had lost a very weird dog.

She opened the door, and he shot out between her legs. He skidded to a halt ten feet away and turned to wait for her.

"I'm not ready yet," she said, and picked up her cell phone. For years she'd had to give the list of groceries she wanted for the coming week to the delivery boy when he arrived with the previous week's order. Now there was a cell tower in Stonington and Ten Acre No Nine was just within range. She called the grocery and added a ten-pound sack of dog food to her order. It would be delivered that afternoon.

She pushed the phone into her jeans pocket, and then they set off at an old dog's pace. At first it was irritating to walk slower than she was accustomed to, annoying to wait for him to catch up. But halfway around the island she realized she'd forgotten to be afraid. She wasn't looking behind every rock and tree with trepidation. Instead, she was turning around and walking backwards, looking for the dog. He had a burst of speed that never lasted more than fifteen feet. It seemed to take him five minutes to recuperate from this effort, then he'd put on another display, scampering up a steep granite incline, or chasing a gull. If he stood still he seemed to become disoriented, his legs would begin to vibrate, then a general wobbliness would manifest itself in his hips, as if he were attempting to learn the hula. After six years on the island alone, Hannah still put her fingers over her mouth when she giggled.

"You're still on your sea legs," she told him.

He turned to her when she spoke and this pleased her. How many times had she spoken to someone in school or back in New York when they'd never bothered to turn and look at her, when they couldn't even offer eye contact?

She sat on a smooth expanse of pink granite on the seaward face of the island and let the dog catch up. The ocean was a few feet away, licking at the rock politely but steadfastly, content with its work of the millennia, reducing stone to sand one calm wave at a time. Twenty thousand years ago these rocks lay under an ice sheet two miles thick. Perhaps nine thousand years later the melting, receding ice, and the rebounding land settled on a coastline approximately where she was sitting. She thought the ocean was so erodingly persistent because it knew sea level was only temporary. Before long, Ten Acre No Nine would either be the tip of a mountain or another net snag on the bottom of the sea. She made this realization, too, in New York six years ago, understanding there was only so much time to get to the beach in one life.

Driftwood caught up and sat down next to her, throwing his hip against hers as if he'd known her for years. He licked the back of her hand once, then seemed to scan the horizon.

"Anything out there you recognize?" she asked.

He turned to her and yawned.

"We're probably never going to understand each other," she offered.

He acted as if this didn't matter.

"No tags. I can't decide what kind of dog you are. Collie, Spaniel, Labrador mix? Some Poodle thrown in there for the downsizing? I'll call in an ad to the Island Ad-Vantages. But it won't come out for a week. Did you fall off a lobster boat? I've never seen you on one. Did you swim out from Stonington one island at a time? I doubt it."

He groaned in lying down, placed his head in the notch between her stomach and raised thigh. She could feel his warm breath coil into her navel through her cotton T-shirt. He closed his eyes. She sat there silently for a few moments, her own eyes repeatedly following the thin sheet of receding water after each wave. When she came to she realized the dog was asleep. His paws paddled the granite softly in a dream of swimming. She couldn't move. That was odd. She'd always been able to move before. She felt bolted to the rock. The dog's head seemed to weigh as much as a tombstone. She tilted her own head to see if there were some alternative. There was a short board bumping against rocks at the water's edge. She would have liked to retrieve it, but could only watch as it worked free and floated out to sea inches at a time, the tide carrying it away. Finally, the dog woke and lifted his head. Hannah popped from the rock as if on springs. The dog looked up at her, slowly opening and closing his eyes.

"Christ," Hannah said, examining the surface of the rock impressed in her palms. "Christ," she said again. "You just took twenty minutes of my life."

Driftwood yawned and set out once again in the direction they'd been traveling. This time he took the lead.

🐾 🐾 🐾

She finished her senior year at Bennington College and with three friends moved to New York. To Arno's postcard in the spring advertising for a sternman, she sent back a long letter telling him he was right about Mark, but that she had decided to spend at least a year in the city, trying to make a career. Maybe next year, she wrote. But one year became two, and two, five.

The first year was a struggle. She and her friends carried their slides or portfolios from gallery to gallery, but were repeatedly turned away. They showed their work at artists' cooperatives, but had to wait their turn, and then would only get to hang one or two pieces. They survived by selling an occasional piece to friends or family, and working as waitresses and hostesses. Their apartment had only one window and it faced a concrete wall. The light, filtering down from eight stories above, was the color of muddy water, and changed little from dawn to dusk. Hannah refused to paint in it. She took her backpack easel and worked on the street and in Central Park, constantly under the gaze of pedestrians or in the flight path of Frisbees. Using a second easel to hold a mirror, she painted self-portraits en plein air, always including the gawkers over her shoulder. Their faces were fuzzily morphed, as they only watched for a few moments at most, and were then replaced by other onlookers. Her roommates were disturbed by these paintings, a disfigured monster always looming behind Hannah as she painted, her own face crisp and clear.

Her three roommates and four other artists rented a white space in Brooklyn and held their own exhibition. Hannah sent Arno an invitation, knowing he wouldn't come. Their paintings were up for a week. Not a single work sold until the last day of the show when a woman in a business suit came in and bought two of Hannah's paintings for just under a thousand dollars. She was a dealer from a gallery in Chelsea. She gave Hannah her card and asked her to bring her portfolio by sometime.

"I'll be there tomorrow," Hannah told her.

"Tomorrow's Sunday. I won't be there. Call Monday and make an appointment," she said, and left once the canvasses were wrapped in heavy brown paper.

Hannah's friends gathered around her, looking at the business card.

"I've been to that gallery," one said.

"What did she say?" another asked.

"She said Hannah's paintings were nice."

"Nice?"

"Congratulations, Hannah."

"Yeah, we got back half of what we paid for the space."

"Hannah got her portion back," one of her roommates said. "The rest of us are still out three hundred bucks apiece."

"Yeah, it's going to be awhile before I can do this again."

"I'm not going to do it again. We paid two thousand for about, what, a hundred walk-throughs. That's twenty dollars per looker we paid."

"Sidewalk's cheaper."

"I'm going back to school."

Hannah held the check in her hand. She'd make a copy of it before cashing it. Subtracting the space rent, and the ads they'd placed, and the cost of the paint and canvases, she'd made a little over five hundred dollars. She thought momentarily of offering this profit to her friends, paying twice her portion so they wouldn't be out so much. But then she realized she could buy more canvas with it, a better grade of paint, perhaps rent a booth at an art show. She'd taken on as much risk as they had.

She looked up at her friends. "I didn't even ask her if she bought them for herself or to resell."

One of her roommates squeezed her upper arm, and smiling, said, "Hannah, you are so lucky."

Hannah smiled back, but at the same time thought that lucky was an unfair word. She doubted she'd have used it if one of them had made a sale. She worked as hard or harder than they did.

The gallery put her off for more than two weeks. She showed her portfolio to the same woman who'd bought her paintings earlier, Gwen Waashen, the owner of the gallery. It was a small space, but well situated in Chelsea. There were three rooms, one behind another, separated by short hallways. Gwen's office was off one hallway, a restroom off the other. A receptionist sat in the first room. The exterior wall was sandblasted brick, the other plastered and painted off-white. Gwen paged through a file of small watercolors, flipped through a book of photographs of larger works, and stood back from two canvases that Hannah let lean against her own knees. She showed no discernible emotion.

"How old are you, Hannah?" she asked.

"Almost twenty-four," she answered.

Gwen smiled for the first time. "You're already old enough to drive, old enough to see R-rated movies, old enough to drink, dear. You don't have to use 'almost' anymore."

"No, ma'am. I'm twenty-three."

"Where did you go to school?"

"Bennington College, in Vermont."

"I can give you this hallway for one month in the spring and one in the fall. We'll see how it goes after that. The lighting is terrible, I know." There was a niche in the wall, about twelve by eighteen inches, opposite the bathroom door. "A telephone used to sit here," Gwen said. "You can use the space for one of your small stone sculptures. I'll let you pick. There's room for two large paintings or four smaller ones. We'll decide together how much to ask for your work. The gallery earns 50 percent initially, 40 percent later if you have some success. How does that sound?"

"Good. It sounds good," Hannah said.

"I can't promise you a single thing, except that it won't cost you anything to show here."

"I understand. Where are the two paintings you bought in Brooklyn?"

"They're both gone. They sold last week."

"Really?" Hannah beamed.

"Don't get the big head yet. I made very little on them. Come back on the first with two more of your paintings. Bring another self-portrait and that landscape of the farmstead in Vermont. And one of your little rock sculptures."

"Thank you," Hannah offered.

"It's your lucky day."

"Yes," Hannah said.

Before she left, Hannah looked at the paintings in the other rooms. They ranged in price from two to eighty thousand dollars, mostly abstract pieces in muted tones. She signed a commission contract, and Gwen asked her how things were going generally.

"I work at a Starbucks knockoff thirty hours a week," she told her, "but I was only there long enough to meet you."

"Don't quit the rent-job yet," Gwen said.

"Are you an artist?" Hannah asked her.

"Once, long ago."

"Why did you stop?"

"I found I really liked looking at art much more than making it."

"I think I'd make it whether anyone looked at it or not."

"Really?" Gwen said. "But you're young. When I'm eighty and you're fifty, we'll have this conversation again."

"I'll tell you the same thing then."

"Then you don't want to know who bought your paintings?" Hannah was caught short, realizing she'd boxed herself in.

"No," she answered. "It doesn't matter."

Gwen smiled.

"It's very difficult to take on emerging artists. The cost of this space won't permit it. We're lucky to have found each other."

"But it's not luck," Hannah said. "I've worked very hard to make these paintings. And you've worked hard to build your gallery."

"Hard work doesn't always guarantee success. Let's call it providence, then." Gwen hooked her hair behind one ear, as if clipping the idea into place.

"Preparation and care with maybe some God thrown in?" Hannah said.

"Something like that."

"I'd rather it was just me and you."

"You've got more confidence than I do," Gwen said. "At any rate, you've got to do your part before I can do mine. Canvas and paint, get to work."

🐢 🐢 🐢

By the time Driftwood and Hannah worked their way around the north side of the island they could see a small wooden boat entering the quarry. A young girl stood at the console helm, her red hair as bright as a new buoy. The forward part of the boat was stacked with boxes and grocery sacks. Neither the boat nor the girl usually made Hannah's weekly delivery. The girl waved enthusiastically when she sighted them. Hannah ran ahead to meet her, showing her where to bring the boat alongside a shelf in the quarry.

"Took me fifteen minutes to find the opening," she yelled up. "And I even had a chart." She threw a short line to Hannah. She wore a green ball cap and a jacket with a high collar to protect her skin, but her nose and cheeks were faintly burned. The white skin at her neck pearled into the pink burn of her face like a single petal of a tulip.

"You're new," Hannah said.

"Yeah, that's what everybody keeps telling me. But I'll be old by the end of the summer." She began to hand small boxes of groceries to Hannah. "Here's your mail. I know your name. My name's Zee Eaton. Zee's short for Zinnia, which I despise. I'd much prefer to be the last letter of the alphabet than a flower."

"I'm Hannah."

"Yeah, it's on your mail. It's just you out here?"

"Yes."

"You and the dog?"

Hannah looked up. Driftwood hung over a tier of granite, gazing down. "Did you bring the dog food?"

"Oh yeah, it's here. Somewhere. Here." She pulled the sack from beneath another of cat food.

"Have you seen this dog before?"

"No, but I've only been in Stonington for a week. My dad and I just moved here from Jonesport. My grandpa's in a nursing home here." She took a handmade business card from her wallet and handed it to Hannah. "That's my number. If you need anything else, any time of the day, give me a call. I'll make a run for twenty. I've got the grocery contract till school starts. But I'll still make runs in the evenings and on weekends."

"OK," Hannah said. "But I don't need much usually."

"Well, anytime. This sure is a hole. You ought to rent it out for parties."

"Zee, I ask all the delivery people not to talk about the quarry, or tell anyone about it. I like my privacy."

"OK, sure. No problem." She looked uneasy for the first time.

"What is it?"

"My dad may cover for me every once in a while."

"That's OK, you can tell him, of course. And if you hear of anyone in town losing a dog like this one, let me know."

"I'll do it. He just showed up, uninvited?"

Hannah nodded.

"I've seen kayakers carrying dogs. Hope we don't have a missing kayaker, too."

Hannah pitched the line into the boat. "See you next week."

"You can call me on the radio, too, channel 9 or 16," she said, clicking the outboard into gear. "The boat's name is *Z To Go*."

🦑 🦑 🦑

Despite Gwen's advice, Hannah did quit her job and devoted her time to painting. She couldn't wait for her roommates to leave the apartment for the day so she could paint without distractions. After she picked a subject she'd spend weeks defining it, moving from one canvas to the next as all possibilities narrowed to the one she could abide. By the time her first show arrived, she was completely broke, having borrowed paint from friends and painting on cardboard and Masonite salvaged from the street. Gwen sold six small paintings and five larger canvases for almost thirty-two thousand dollars. At the end of the four-week exhibition, she presented Hannah with a check and the three paintings left in the hallway. "I'll see you in five months," she said.

"I don't understand," Hannah said. "Weren't you satisfied with the sales?"

"Of course. But that hallway belongs to five other artists as well. They've got to make a living, too."

"Would you be upset if I showed my work somewhere else in the meantime?"

"You should enter juried shows. I'll see what I can do to help with those. But I hope you'll understand that I took a chance with you, and that you won't compete with me at another gallery. And I hope you'll honor your commitment to future exhibitions here. If clients return asking about your work, I'll send them to you, of course. In the meantime, I want the pictures you bring me next spring to be of the same quality as these were. Our prices will go up accordingly then. Did you make enough to get by till that time?"

"Yes. I never expected so much."

"Good. Please don't acquire a drug or alcohol problem. I mean, don't let this go to your head. You're a wonderful artist and you work hard. You need both qualities to survive. Don't let anyone distract you. They'll try. Your most valuable asset is your time, and that's what they'll want. Don't let them have it. You won't be able to be nice about turning them away. But choose the art. It will last and they won't."

Hannah left the gallery that day with a vague notion that she now owned something to defend rather than celebrate. But by the time she made it back to the apartment even her smile couldn't be contained. She showed the roommates her check and they spent half the night at the pub on the corner, calling in reinforcements when they ran out of ideas to extol the virtues of art. She showed the check to friends of friends who'd never seen one of her paintings. They made copies of the check, and each of her friends decorated one at the bar. A dog tore at the corner of one. Balloons carried another away. Van Gogh wept at the dollar sign, and a de Kooning figure stared angrily at the name of the bank. Hannah, drunk on wine and congratulations, saw the sea in the check's wavy background, and drew orange lobsters standing on their tails, claws clasped overhead in victory. From a tiny *Break of Day* a lasso shot out and tugged on a giant flipper. Another lobster gripped a minuscule potter, and broken vessels littered the bottom of the ocean. The party only cost her three hundred dollars and a day of hangover: a few sketches, the time it took paint to dry.

🖋🖋🖋

Carrying her groceries and mail from the quarry to the house, she passed the fresh dirt of the hole again. Whoever it was must have come to the island in a small boat or must have been dropped off from a larger vessel. The second option would require an accomplice. Lobster boats didn't tow their dinghies. They were left on the mooring so they wouldn't become fouled in the string of traps trailing off the stern of the boat. Whoever it was must have been more frightened of her than she was of them. At least this was so in the past. It was the future she was uncertain about.

She stored away the perishables in her gas refrigerator. It didn't hold a great deal of food, but was very efficient. Most of the year she had the whole outdoors for an icebox. Then she took a cart back up to the quarry rim for the ten gallons of springwater. There was no fresh source of water on the island, only a cistern carved into the granite and covered by a stone vault. It was fed by the rain gutters running off the roof of her house. She didn't mind washing dishes and bathing with this water, but didn't want to drink it. It had a mildly acidic flavor, as if bugs were sucking on her taste buds. Hannah noticed, as she rolled back down the path toward home, that Driftwood hadn't followed her. She found him on the hearth rug, asleep once again. She put the water away after filling another bowl for the dog. Then she took her sketch pad and made a half-dozen quick renderings of her new model, in case he should disappear at any moment. Perhaps, when he woke, he might find himself back where he belonged. Perhaps, she, Hannah, and this island were only a dream for him. She always lived inside her art, whether her subject was another person, a dog, or a rock.

ᕯᕯᕯ

Each exhibition brought her more success. Everything sold, whether painting, sculpture, or preliminary sketch. She bought better equipment, rented a studio, searched farther for materials and ideas. One by one her roommates left, and Hannah took up their shares of the rent. None of them were able to make a living with their art. They moved farther out from the city center, looking for cheaper rent, or moved back home. They took full-time jobs in galleries, or as teaching assistants, or preparators for other people's artwork. By the end of her third year in New York, Hannah found herself alone in the apartment and found that she liked it. There'd always been an undercurrent of jealousy, almost resentment, at her success. If she took an afternoon off to go to a museum and asked friends to go along, they often replied with a smile, "Hannah, I've got a real job."

It was irritating to go to an exhibition with someone else anyway. They moved too quickly or too slowly. They spent more time in the gift shop than the galleries. They couldn't afford to eat in the museum buffet.

Once a month she spent a day at the Metropolitan in the permanent collection. "Here is a line that has lasted," she told herself as she memorized a piece. "Remember what the varnish and two hundred years have done to the color blue." "If I took the sky from this painting, and the contour of the thigh in that sculpture, and the abraded gilding of this mosaic, how could I make them mine?" Often she found herself alone in a gallery, alone in a museum, at closing, a guard touching her shoulder. Her vision was blurred, her hands unable to grasp. She walked to the exit in a fog of habit, then would find herself at home without memory of the subway ride, or the walk, or her key in the door. Then her own paintings, hanging on the walls around her, would blend with those of the museum and she felt so much pride in her work, in the very smell of fresh oil paint, and pride in her place in the long history and tragedy of art, its human making, its human misunderstanding. Never did she come to this moment with another person at her side.

🐚 🐚 🐚

Two days after it arrived, she began to pick through her stack of mail. It was a mild morning. The windows were open and flies flew into and out of the house freely. She could smell the foreshore, a raw mixture of seaweed and rotting crab, a slush of life and death draining off stone and filtering down through sand and mussel shell. There was no mud around the island. Low tide didn't stink. Water and stone alone supported that life which could grip or cement itself to rock, or which could swim faster than the tide. Only for twenty minutes, twice a day, at slack tide, did the water pause and the current falter, allowing the dead to drift to the bed of the sea. Hannah had come to be able to sense this time, long before she could see it. She could sense it in bed, in the middle of the night. It was strong as coffee boiling. The island seemed to go slack itself, as if it were falling out of orbit. The wind held too much sway. It always reminded her of the time she once watched a flower, which had been buried in shade, turn willfully to the sun. The sweet gurgle of the current slipped into silence, and the clarity of the water, especially at high tide, made it seem breathable. A small boat suspended at the surface balanced on its reflection, and made Hannah realize that when you rowed on the surface of the sea you also rowed on the surface of the sky.

She'd worked all the morning, wrapping popplestones, round, sea-worn rocks, in wool. She'd ordered the yarn from a man on Swan's Island who raised his own sheep. It came bleached, and she'd experimented for some time with dyes, finally arriving at worn colors she was satisfied would make people think the sheep had been licking the island's lichens. She'd wrapped the stones till their coverings made them soft and muted. They no longer cracked with a report when she dropped them in a basket. The wool whirled over the surface of the rock in endless striations and each strand invited following, till it disappeared under another or ended in a knot of interlocking color. It was like the root of an entire forest, or the filaments of a mind, birds in a dense copse.

Now she rested in an overstuffed green mohair chair by the window, the arm near the window faded to brown. Her mail was in her lap. There was a deposit slip from her bank in New York. Gwen deposited her sales directly now. There were *ArtForum* and *American Art Review* magazines, the local weekly paper out of Stonington, a couple of paperback novels she'd ordered from Barnes & Noble, seed catalogs, art-supply catalogs, the calendar of exhibits from the Metropolitan Museum of Art in New York and the Farnsworth in Rockland, a bill from her propane supplier, a bill from the grocery, and one from the man who'd delivered three cords of firewood six months earlier. He'd come in a landing barge, beaching it next to the granite pier in calm seas, and then drove his truck full of firewood right up through the field to her house. It was a curiosity of Maine that bills for services often arrived months after they were performed, as if no one requested payment until they needed it. There was also a letter from her half sister, Emily. Hannah hadn't seen her in fourteen years. They exchanged Christmas cards every year but letters were infrequent. It had been sent overnight, but had sat in her Stonington post office box for almost five days with her other mail.

After their father died, Emily moved to Texas with her mother. They seemed to have moved around for a few years, then Emily's mother got remarried to a minister in Abilene. Soon Emily's cards were lengthy testaments to her love for Jesus, how He'd changed her life. After she graduated from high school she immediately joined a religious order Hannah had never heard of before. She wasn't Catholic, but she and her sisters practiced celibacy and wore garments symbolizing their marriage to Christ. Their spiritual guide was an elderly former nun who'd left the

Catholic Church. Several men were members of the order as well, but weren't allowed to live on the grounds of the ranch outside Cleburne that had been donated to the group by one of its sisters. To support themselves they kept honey bees and leased their land to local ranchers for grazing, to deer hunters in the winter. Gas royalties provided the rest. Some of the members had children from their previous lives. Emily was their teacher. She was twenty-six years old now and had been a member for almost four years.

Hannah opened the letter with a palette knife. She thought perhaps Emily's mother had passed away. Her penmanship was so ordered and regular that it seemed copied from a blackboard. Under the simple heading, "Devoted to Christ," Emily began:

Dear Sister,

Our hot season has begun here. The new field of sweet clover for the bees is blooming and they swarm over it eagerly. I am also well. My students are finished with their studies until fall.

I have thought to send one of them to you. Please respond as soon as possible. He is seventeen. He is bright and curious, and is beaten by his father, one of our brothers. The boy intends to run away, and I hope you can provide him with a destination. He needs a place to finish his last year of high school. He has run away twice before and his father has brought him back to me, once with a broken arm, once with many bruises. I fear for his life. I am sure he would be safe with you, so far away, so remote. I can put him on a bus to Bangor. I know we were never sisters in the closest sense and that we only share our father's blood. But we share Christ's blood too, and I plead with you to accept and protect this child till his father can be healed. If I had anywhere else to send him where he wouldn't be found, I would. I know you are alone there on the island. Isn't there room for two? Time is of the essence. The boy's father returns in one week from a business trip and Will intends to be gone before his father returns. You can call me here at the home at any time.

Your sister in Christ,
Emily

🐢🐢🐢

At each succeeding spring and fall exhibition, fewer of Hannah's friends showed up for the opening. At last she didn't attend them either. She dropped the paintings and sculptures off at Gwen's gallery and let her decide how best to hang them. It was the last she saw of her work. Everything sold. She wasn't one of Gwen's major artists, but she made more than enough to support herself for the coming year. From time to time she'd run into someone from school and they were routinely stunned by her success. With each of these meetings, she became further distanced from her old friends, from the give-and-take of artists in a community. She traveled back to Bennington on two occasions to see her professors and even they were mildly affronted. No, she told them, she had no other work outside of her art. No, she didn't need to teach to supplement her income. She wondered if they'd like her to come and speak to classes. "From the trenches," she said. They turned her down, politely, saying her case was unusual: most artists didn't make a living from art, or even get much recognition until they were in their forties or fifties. Come back when you're older, they said, and then they'll believe what you have to say.

She began taking graduate courses at NYU in various media: printmaking, pottery, marble sculpture. Here she met Jalendu, a teaching assistant in art, two years her junior. They saw each other for a little more than six months, until Hannah decided the relationship would go no further. A month afterwards, when she stopped answering his calls, Jalendu was found in the Hudson River, downstream from the George Washington Bridge. His distraught sister, when she arrived from Calcutta, knocked on Hannah's door to ask how Hannah could not love her sweet brother.

🦋 🦋 🦋

Hannah folded Emily's letter and replaced it in its envelope. She stood unsteadily and the remaining mail in her lap fell to the floor. She stepped over it and closed the window. Driftwood lifted his head and watched her cross the room. She looked up the phone number of the order, finding it on a three-year-old Christmas card. She asked for her sister. She heard the phone put down and footsteps fade away on a stone floor. Hannah waited. There was a dense quiet. Suddenly, out of the silence, Emily said her name. Hannah almost dropped the phone. Emily must have come across the stone floor on bare feet. She snuck up on Hannah from more than two thousand miles away.

"I just got your letter," Hannah said.

"He's . . ."

"It would be best if he didn't come here."

"He's already on his way," Emily said. "I paid cash for the bus ticket. There won't be a record. I'm sorry. He's on his way."

"I don't know what to say," Hannah said.

"There was no time. I'm sorry."

"He can't stay here."

"Why not?"

"I don't have to answer that question. How dare you send him without getting my OK?"

"He's taking the bus to Bangor. From there he'll get a taxi to Stonington. I showed him your island on a map of Maine. If you can't keep Will, don't send him back here. He won't come anyway. I just hope he makes it there. He had to make bus changes in Louisville and New York. He won't be there until tomorrow."

"This is unfair," Hannah said.

"It's true that I wasn't thinking of you. But you took so long to call, and I had to send him somewhere. He was in danger here."

"How do I know his father won't come here?"

"He doesn't suspect I'm involved. The last two times Will ran away, the father didn't come to me. He doesn't even know I have a sister, much less one on an island in Maine. He's being beaten, Hannah. He's a good boy. Please give him a chance. I don't have access to much money, but I'll send some whenever I can."

"It's not the money."

"He'll be eighteen in May, and the father won't have control over him."

"That's a year from now."

"Yes, I know. He's a good student. He wants to finish school. You should enroll him under your last name. I made up a set of transcripts so he couldn't be tracked. He may have to take placement tests, but he'll do fine. In the meantime he's willing to work at a summer job to help pay his way. He's not asking for anything more than a place to sleep and study."

"I live alone here. I'm busy. I'm not on vacation. This is where I work."

"He only needs a place to hide. Haven't you ever been afraid?"

Hannah put down the phone, walked across the room, and walked back. Emily was still on the line.

"When will he be here?"

"The bus arrives in Bangor at ten in the morning. Then he'll have to find a taxi or another bus."

"Tell me what he looks like. I'll go to Bangor and pick him up. But I won't promise anything beyond that."

"Thank you, Hannah."

"You've grown up, Emily. I hardly recognized your voice."

"You sound so much like Daddy," Emily said. "Do you miss him, too?"

"When you live alone, you don't miss anybody."

"How strange, I'd think you'd miss everybody. But maybe you're right. I don't miss Jesus. I feel him with me always. Maybe you feel the same way about everyone you've lost."

"Maybe," Hannah said.

Emily described Will. Hannah said she'd call when the boy arrived and gave Emily her cell number. "Don't ever call me from the order," Hannah told her. "My number would show up on the phone bill there."

"I won't," Emily said. "God bless you, Hannah."

🐚 🐚 🐚

After Jalendu's death, her painting faltered. The loss of luminosity in his face on the morgue table drained the light from her palette. Brushes did not snap between her fingers but felt as alien as pipe wrenches. She dropped them, full of paint, to the floor between her feet. Her empty hand, suspended in the air before a blank canvas, seemed to be signing to its two-dimensional shadow. It was the sparest of languages, whose only word was her inability to begin, its only response a fainter echo of agreement.

She thought she had failed at love in both ways: by being in the first instance somehow unlovable, and in the second by loving too little. Jalendu had complained to her about the powerlessness of his love, whether its object was woman or God. "You and God treat my love as if it is nothing more than my hobby. I give it freely but it has no takers. How can something so strong within me have so little value?"

"I'm sorry," she said. "I know. I understand how you feel, but I still can't help you. I'm sorry."

And she thought again of the work time lost to him, of the time being lost apologizing, of work yet to complete. She'd been to enough restaurants, enough movies. She stopped answering the phone, answering the door, until the ringing and knocking halted. Then, at a softer knock, she thought to answer the door again and it was Jalendu's sister, his face gone feminine, his tears, his regret. And all the work she had planned seemed suddenly to forget her, as if it were now ignoring her, not answering her knock. It had been eight years since the young woman had seen her brother. She'd been eleven when he left for America, and now she needed Hannah to help identify his body.

For months Hannah walked the city. She'd wake early, cower under a peacoat and head out, crisscrossing Manhattan Island, wearing out a pair of sneakers every few weeks. When she couldn't walk any farther, she rode each subway to the end of the line and disembarked, but never left the station. She saw no one she recognized. It seemed she'd gone as far as she could physically go. She'd bring her colors and canvas along, but was always too cold to start. It was as if she'd quit smoking but still carried a pack of cigarettes.

When the winter finally ended, she hung up her filthy coat and began to draw again, portraits of Jalendu. She drew and painted from the perspective of the seafloor or riverbed, Jalendu's body above her, floating facedown on the surface, a blanching light behind him. His face was altogether passive. He seemed as weary as she. She painted her mother, her father, Mark, all in the same attitude, spread-eagle against the sky, their bodies and expressions as flaccid as their undulating clothing. In the final form, in the canvas she took to Gwen, all these people became one, the features of each, including her own, hidden in one mystified face. She burned all the preliminary work. The collected ashes, staples, bits of fabric and wood, she poured into the confluent waters of the Hudson and East rivers in lower Manhattan on an ebbing tide.

She didn't know what her next step would be, what subject needed her. It was then that she received notification from the lawyer in Ellsworth. Arno had died, and left her everything.

🐢🐢🐢

When she first moved to the island after Arno's death, a friend or two from New York and Gwen asked if they might visit. Hannah dissuaded them all. The only visitors she'd ever had were either service people or delivery men. She'd never relaunched *Break of Day*. Arno's skiff was still serviceable, but the outboard had frozen up years before. Hannah relied totally on the launch service out of Stonington. It was inconsistent in the winter, but there was always the Isle au Haut ferry or a lobster boat in an emergency. She'd never had an emergency. She often thought of buying a new outboard for the skiff, but the boat rowed well enough if abandoning the island ever became necessary. As it was she preferred the launch, preferred having someone else in the boat.

When she called to schedule a pickup, a man answered.

"I'm sorry," she said. "I'm calling for the launch service. Zee Eaton?"

"You've got it. I'm her dad."

"I need a pickup early tomorrow morning, about six-thirty."

"Gosh, that's early for Zee, but I'll make sure she's up. Where are you?"

"Ten Acre No Nine. She knows it."

"You're the woman with the dog."

Hannah had never been described this way before. "Yes."

"Zee's been asking around for you. No luck yet. That must be some dog to swim all the way out there. I guess he island-hopped."

"I don't know," Hannah said.

"Your place was about as far as he could go without crossing Jericho Bay."

"I guess."

"I was going to have Zee ask you the next time she carried out your mail, but since I've got you now, I'll do it myself. I've been looking for a boat to fix up so I can do a little lobstering. The harbormaster said you've still got an old boat you aren't using."

"It's not for sale," Hannah said.

"It's a shame to let a nice old wooden hull dry out. Harbormaster said it hasn't been in the water for six years. She might be gone already."

"If you could just have Zee here at six-thirty," Hannah said. "I want to go to the commercial pier."

"OK, sure. She'll be there."

"Thank you."

She couldn't lock Driftwood in the house the next morning because there was no keyed lock on the old door. Only a hook and eye on the inside. The door latch was strong enough to hold the dog at bay, but not his howls of abandonment. She thought about tying him up outside, but didn't know how long he'd be there, how long this trip would last. She still wasn't sure she'd allow the boy to come to the island. The dog was so old he'd lost control of his sphincter muscle. At first she thought he wasn't trained, but she'd watched him defecate in his sleep. His stools were relatively firm so far, thank God. She'd picked up most of her throw rugs and spread the *Island Ad-Vantages* before the hearth and stove. He seemed so ashamed of his turds inside the house. He'd wake up, or turn around and see them issuing, and race to the door. As he watched Hannah pick them up and throw them outside, he lowered his face to the floor.

She could hear him howling all the way to the rim of the quarry. To her surprise, Zee was already there, fifteen minutes early.

"Sorry I needed you so early," Hannah said.

"Nothing makes my father happier than waking me up at five in the morning," she said. "You made his day. This is your first ride with me so I'm going to play the good captain. Can you swim?"

Hannah nodded.

"The life jackets are under this locker. The fire extinguisher hangs right here on the console, and if I fall overboard the kill switch to the engine is this big red button."

"Got it," Hannah said.

"Do you mind going fast?"

"No," Hannah said.

"That's the only speed I know," Zee said, but she motored slowly out of the quarry and didn't push the throttle forward till they were between Millet and Spruce islands. The skiff pulled up on a plane quickly. Hannah thought Zee handled the boat well. She stood at the console with one hand on the wheel and one on the throttle, her long bright hair streaming out underneath her cap.

"You keep a car at the fish pier?" Zee asked.

"No, at the ferry landing, but I want to go to the fish pier. I'll walk around."

"OK. I've been asking. Nobody's missing a dog yet."

"Thank you."

"Have you named him yet?"

Hannah didn't want to admit she had. She shook her head.

Zee went on talking above the engine. Hannah thought everyone on the islands they were passing must be able to hear her. "Waiting to see if you get to keep him?"

"He's somebody's dog."

"My dad wants me to apologize."

"For what?"

"He said you were short with him, about your boat, and he wants me to apologize."

Hannah nodded, noting that the girl wasn't apologizing.

"I'm just not ready to sell it," she said. "I was surprised that he knew about it. It's locked in my boat shed. You can't see it from the water."

"People talk about you. My dad's a sweet old guy. He didn't mean anything."

She was going to apologize, too, but also decided against it. "How old is your dad?"

"He's thirty-six, almost," Zee said. "He's gonna do some lobstering if he can get in with somebody around here. He figures he'll have to work out of the skiff, before he's able to buy a boat."

When they reached the pier, Hannah handed a check for twenty dollars to the girl and thanked her. "I'll be back sometime this evening and I'll need a ride."

"Just call me if I'm not here at the float."

Hannah left her there, tying up the boat.

The harbormaster's office was at the head of the fish pier. The door was open and he was at his desk, an elderly man retired from fishing. His cap lay askew on his head, as if he'd just crawled out from underneath something. Half of each piece of paper on his desk lay beneath another piece of paper, none of them seeming to have precedence. There were two young fishermen in the office, too, pouring one five-gallon bucket of clams into another.

"I'm Hannah Bryant," she told him.

"Al Hutchinson, harbormaster."

"I own Ten Acre No Nine. I'll thank you not to tell people what I have in my boat shed, or in my house or on my island. If I have something to sell or want to buy anything, I'll post a notice on the board here. I don't need to go through you."

He let his mouth hang open so long that Hannah felt guilty. Finally, he answered, "You're a pip, aren't ya? I've received your message, yes, ma'am."

When Hannah turned, she bumped into Zee. "Crowded on Deer Isle, ain't it?" Zee said and pushed on past her.

It was too late in the morning to see many fishermen on the pier, and too early to see many tourists on the sidewalks of Stonington. Her walk around the harbor to her car at the ferry landing didn't require her to recognize or say "hello" to anyone. But she loved this village, the way it merged with the sea, its houses and shops ebbing into the harbor, and the way the harbor seemed to flow uphill into town. The houses of Stonington were pinned and scotched over the granite the town was named for. It raised up in smooth outcroppings in gardens, erupted from foundations. Stonecutters had brought their trade home from the quarries, using their off time to cut paving blocks out of their backyards and basements. There was no lack of granite scrap for seawalls and sidewalks, hitching posts and doorsteps. The houses were mostly from the turn of the century, clapboard-sided with steeply pitched gables or Mansard roofs. They shouldered in among one another and the rock like an entire family in one bed. In the pockets left by the removed paving stones, and in the natural hollow places of the glacier-scarred rock, grass grew in sheets as smooth and contained as the surface of a pond. There were few trees able to support themselves in the shallow soil, but roses and perennials grew in profusion, exploiting every fissure in the stone. The shingles and clapboards of some buildings were salt-weathered and worn, paint-splattered and lichen-scabbed. Others were freshly painted, most often white, so that when the fog crept in, the houses seemed to merge graciously with the gloom, like boats slipping into water.

There were few people in the windows of the Harbor Cafe, and although she'd already had breakfast, the smell of butter on toast creeping along Main Street made her all but swoon. There were new photographs of homes and property for sale on the board outside of Shepherd's Real Estate. Although Stonington and the waters beyond were always ranked in the top three producers of lobster in the state, real estate values were outpacing the salaries of fishermen. Many were selling coastal property and moving inland. There was a new art gallery above the Grasshopper Shop, and she was glad to see that the Granite Museum would reopen in a couple of weeks. If you didn't earn your pay fishing year-round here, you earned it during the summer tourist season. Happily, the façade of the newspaper building hadn't been restored, and Main Street hadn't been widened to four lanes to accommodate the summer parking problems. There still weren't any trolleys in town, and there was only one ice-cream stand. William Muir's bronze statue to the quarrymen was weathering nicely, the cap of the granite carver festooned with gull droppings like every other high point in town, as if every gable and dock piling were high enough to hold winter snow through the summer. Two cars sat in front of Bartlett's Market, where Hannah phoned in her weekly order. It had changed hands recently and there were year-to-year fears that it would close, as the hardware store had earlier. Although the seasonal population was growing, the numbers of those staying through winter were shrinking. The population of the whole state of Maine was tidal, ebbing in the fall, flowing in the spring. It was a short walk down Seabreeze Avenue to the Isle au Haut Company, which ran the ferry service to the island.

Her car was stored in the old cannery building here. It was coated with six months of dust and bird droppings. Only the eight-finger sweeps on the hood, where the mechanic had lifted it to charge the battery and check the fluids a month earlier, showed that the car was white and not gray. She used it perhaps a half-dozen times a year. The car started smartly after one or two preliminary coughs, and once she'd rolled off the flat places in the tires, it seemed to run well. Driving was always uncomfortable. She'd rarely driven while in New York and only did so now under duress. Living on a small island month after month made the rest of the world seem obscenely large and wasteful. Any speed over five miles an hour was disorienting. There was only one way off Deer Isle, so cars and trucks began to line up behind her on the twisting two-lane road. She pulled over twice to let them by. But by the time she reached the causeway between Deer Isle and Little Deer, she felt herself under control again. She took the same shortcuts across the curves of the causeway that the telephone lines did. The climb up and over the steep and narrow Deer Isle-Sedgewick Bridge was always exhilarating, as though they'd built a carnival ride instead of a bridge in 1939. She always felt she was falling out of the sky when she left or returned to Deer Isle. The bridge spanned Eggemoggin Reach, a half-mile-wide valley flooded by the sea. A lobster boat moved up the Reach as if it were pulling a long zipper, the water "V"-ing open behind it to reveal a white lacy foam of underwear, that soon enough washed blue again, embarrassed by the sun. How quickly, Hannah thought, the natural world returns to its own order after we've passed through shouting our names.

Beyond the bridge, the earth rose up in forest and hay field. From Caterpillar Hill she looked back over blueberry barrens to the dark green islands suspended in cobalt. She could see the bridge below, Deer Isle, Isle au Haut, and all the way across Penobscot Bay to the Camden Hills. Her own island was out there, in an opaque haze, waves still washing its fringe of granite beach even though she wasn't there to witness it. It was foolish to go so far as two hours away, insane to bring another human back. Her work would suffer, and her work was all that mattered, the daily process of understanding the world by moving her hands over stones.

She was at the bus station in Bangor ten minutes before the bus arrived and watched its passengers disembark from the safety of her car. She didn't know if he would be expecting her, if he'd called Emily since she'd spoken to her. Probably not.

He seemed tall, stepping down out of the bus, but when he reached the ground he seemed small. His hair was black, and though very short he kept running his hand over it as if it were once long. He wore jeans and sneakers and a tan corduroy jacket over a T-shirt. His face was pale against his dark hair, as clean and pale and polished as the interior of an eviscerated urchin. He didn't look up when he came off the bus, made eye contact with no one. He stood with four others who waited while the driver pulled bags from beneath the bus with a gaff. His was the last, a suitcase covered in yellow and brown fabric in a herringbone pattern. It must have been fifty years old. Hannah watched as he carried it to a bench. He sat down and pulled the suitcase up on his thighs and opened it. He looked inside and patiently moved objects from place to place. He refolded two shirts. He opened a small cigar box and looked inside for a moment or two, then replaced it, too. When everything seemed to be ordered to his satisfaction, he closed the suitcase again, but stretched his arms across its surface and continued to hold it on his lap. He didn't look across the parking lot or up and down the bus concourse. He didn't seem to be waiting or looking for another bus or the taxi stand. It was very annoying. Hannah honked the horn lightly. He didn't look up. Several others at the station looked at her, but he didn't. She beeped again. If he heard the honk, he knew it wasn't for him. The very sun was climbing into the sky while this boy sat motionless. Finally he took the change out of his pocket and counted it. This, Hannah thought, promised some action. Yet he replaced it as well, seemingly impressed with his current financial worth and his situation in life. Hannah got out of the car and marched up to him. He looked up from her feet to her face as slowly as a flower turning to the sun.

"I'm Emily's sister," she said. "Are you Will?"

He nodded in assent, but only once. He didn't smile or suggest there had to be any other action taken from this moment onward.

"Did you know I'd be here?"

He shook his head.

"Were you just going to sit here for the rest of your life?"

"I was deciding," he told her. He was quiet for a moment. "I'm sorry."

Hannah raised her arm to push the hair out of her eyes and the boy winced. She held her hand motionless then, as if she'd just seen a bird light on the rim of her teacup. He looked back up at her, blinking. She knew the sun wasn't over her shoulder.

"Have you had breakfast yet?" He shook his head. "Come on. We'll go eat. There's a cafe just down the street. We'll put your suitcase in the car."

"We shouldn't do that yet. I'll take it with me. Not till we decide."

"Decide what?"

"Whether we'll stay together."

Hannah looked at him and tilted her head. She'd assumed it was her decision to make alone. It never occurred to her that he might turn her down.

※ ※ ※

He left everything to her: the island, *Break of Day*, and seven thousand in savings, barely enough to pay the taxes on the island that year. She flew to Bangor and rented a car for two days, fully expecting to return to New York as soon as things were settled. She stopped in Ellsworth to pick up a package of documents from Arno's lawyer. Inside was a letter addressed to her. It had been written two years after she'd last seen him.

Dear girl,

I've had a bum winter. So I'm going to get this down on paper now. I am sorry that you are burdened with my leftovers. Hope the island will be some comfort. You will find my remains at the Deer Isle Funeral Home. I chose an urn over a casket. It won't require so deep a hole. You know where I want to go. If I do not see you before I die—well, I have seen you before I died and it made me happy and real proud to know who you are. I never had a better sternman or artist. Take care of the old island. If you decide to lobster they will respect our family territory. I'd be honored if you used my buoy colors. The traps off Colby Ledge still produce the best. Maybe you can catch old Moby Claw for me. If you do, let him go. There's a little bit of me in him. Ha Ha

> *Your Uncle,*
> *Arno Weed*

She'd never gone back to visit because her time with him seemed part of her childhood, never went back to visit because she'd never forgiven herself for letting him down, never went back to visit because it was the place where she'd met Mark, never went back because Arno knew who she was, where she came from. Everyone she met from college onward knew only what she allowed them to know. Arno knew more. He allowed for her past and forgave. He forgave and forgave without ever saying I forgive.

She claimed his ashes, and the harbormaster carried her out to the island on a brisk spring morning.

"He made it through the winter," Al told her. "We had a cold one here, too. Several of us wanted him to come in off the island and live in town but he wouldn't hear of it. It's been awhile since you've been here, hasn't it?"

Hannah nodded.

"Old Arno's been sort of reluctant for five or six years."

"Reluctant?"

"He liked to stay by himself. Used to he'd come into town for town meetings and to vote and even to church once in a while. What are you going to do with the island?"

"I don't know," she answered. "At the funeral home they said a fisherman found him."

"We all knew he was out there. We didn't forget. Jimmy Haskell was working a string off the island and he saw your uncle. He was lying on the foreshore. He'd been painting his buoys up at the house and was carrying a bunch of them down to the boat shed. You could tell something overcame him because he'd dropped one buoy up near the house, a couple more a little bit farther on, and then he'd just dropped them all in a heap and gone on without them."

"Gone on?"

"Jimmy said he'd gone off that little trail that leads down to the boat house and made a beeline through the grass to the water. It's lucky Jimmy saw him. I mean, Arno was already gone, but it was low tide. If he'd lain there overnight, we might not have found him. The tide would have taken him. We never would have known what happened."

Hannah looked down into the water curling off the bow of the harbormaster's boat. She remembered the lobsterman lost years before, the face of Jalendu's sister, the loss of her mother and father. We don't know what happened still, she thought. We don't know what happens.

Someone had picked up the buoys Arno had dropped on the way to the boat shed. They were piled next to the granite doorstep. But they'd left the door open. She pushed on it slowly and stepped into what looked like the remains of a party lit by Chinese lanterns. All the furniture had been pushed to the walls. Newspapers covered the floor, and over them hung several strings of freshly painted lobster buoys that crisscrossed the house from kitchen to living room. The newspapers were speckled with paint. Hannah had to duck three times to make her way to the staircase. Here she put down her suitcase and the urn. She sat between them. Before her, Arno's red brush still sat in a jar, the mineral spirits evaporated. For the first hour she cleaned his brush.

🦐 🦐 🦐

He slid his suitcase into the booth first. He didn't speak to the waitress but pointed at the menu. When his pancakes arrived, he looked at them for a long while.

"What's wrong?" Hannah asked.

"There's no blueberries."

"Sure there are. They're inside. They put them in the mix. Those purple stains are blueberries."

"Oh. You can't play with them that way."

She'd imagined that a seventeen-year-old boy would eat quickly, but he did not. He measured each forkful. When he put his utensils down they were always in perfect alignment with the edge of the table and each other. He put them down as if each were a piece in a puzzle.

"Are you always this quiet?" Hannah asked.

He looked at her directly for the first time. His eyes seemed to be pieced together. There were triangles of green, shards of blue and hazel, scraps of black velvet. Three individual eyelashes were white, as if they'd grown from a scar.

He said, "You look like your sister."

"I haven't seen her since she was twelve."

"She's pretty," he said.

"I live on an island. It's very small. There's no one else but me and the water. I work there. I can't be bothered while I'm working. Are you a person who can entertain himself?"

"I'm an only child. I don't need anybody to play with." He said this without any hint of sarcasm or regret. They were both silent for minutes. "I know you didn't expect me," he said.

Hannah said, with a sigh, "I think everyone who owns a cottage in Maine gets more visitors than they expect. I guess it's my turn."

"I can pay for my breakfast, but I'll need to get a summer job."

"Do you know anything about boats, anything about the ocean?"

"I've never seen the ocean. I might have seen it on the bus, I'm not sure. I used to go fishing with my dad in a bass boat. He didn't let me steer."

"Can you swim?"

"Yes. I like to swim."

"The water's too cold here to swim."

"Are there icebergs in it?"

"Icebergs?" She smiled. "No, it's just cold. I have a small skiff. The motor needs work. If we can get it fixed, you can use it to go back and forth to Stonington. You might find a job there."

"How far is Stonington?"

"It's two hours from here, but only three miles from my island."

"So I'd have to go to school that way, too?"

"And it's cold in the winter. The water is dangerous. Sometimes it's so foggy you can't see. There will be times you can't get to school. You might feel trapped. Or you might feel like me: safe."

He nodded.

"I need to ask: will your father come looking for you?"

"I don't think there's any way he could find me."

"But he found you when you ran away before?"

"Because . . ."

"Because what?"

"Because I let him. I thought if he knew I was serious about leaving he would change. But it didn't change anything. Things got worse. What are you hiding from?"

"I'm not hiding from anything," she said.

He simply said, "Oh." Then he withdrew a sheet of paper from his suitcase and passed it to her. It was a high school transcript, showing he'd completed three years of college preparatory classes with straight A's. His surname was the same as her own.

"Emily made this up for you?"

"Yes."

"I'm too young to be your mother. I'm only thirty-four."

"My mom was seventeen when I was born."

"All the same, I'm your aunt."

"OK."

"Did Emily make up the grades, too?"

He smiled for the first time. "No."

"I want you to know: I've tried people. They didn't work."

He looked at her the way a squirrel would if startled. He said, "Me too."

🐾🐾🐾

She fully intended to go back to New York after Arno was buried, after the house was cleaned, after the weekend, after the summer, after her first winter. But after never seemed to arrive, always followed before. There was always something to be done on the island before she could leave, and New York was the best city in the world at waiting. It would always be there, would treat you the same whether you came home tomorrow or in ten years. If you missed a Broadway show or a museum exhibition there would always be a revival, a return. It was the most consistent place she knew. There were so many offerings, so many variables, that it changed little from decade to decade. Whereas the island changed drastically every day, because she was the only person on earth to witness it. She was in charge of noticing everything.

It was startling to find a tuft of grass and the soil beneath it washed away after a storm, and she tried to replace it with bags of topsoil brought from the mainland. She piled rocks in front of other small vulnerable headlands of soil. There was one oak tree on the island at the edge of the spruce stand. Crows occasionally carried off its acorns. She chased them off with a stick. Arno had been growing seedlings in the house, and there was nothing ethical to do but plant them. They required hoeing and eventually harvesting. Driftwood built up in the quarry, choking it. One corner resembled a beaver dam. She learned to use a chain saw and cleared it away. This work took a week. Afterwards, the quarry needed to be tended every day to avoid another pile up. Before she went back to New York, the house and boat shed needed to be painted. Then she realized someone had to live in the house to protect it over the winter. It hadn't been empty since it was built.

She buried Arno soon after she arrived. Below a shallow layer of humus, the soil was at first sandy, then packed with popplestones. The beach had come this far at one time. She pulled the rocks out one at a time and examined them, as if they were individual bones. At three feet down she found a smooth table of pink granite. It was as far as she could go. She left Arno there, to find what purchase he could. He'd never dragged his carved headstone from the sea.

She kept three of the smooth, heavy popplestones she pulled from the grave, in recompense for Arno. She washed them in the ocean, let them dry on a windowsill. They sat there for months, waves of wind sweeping over them, the sun and moon taking turn providing light and shadow. Finally, she wrapped the first in white linen, the second in scraps of a multicolored quilt, the third in burlap. Then she painted their portraits, framed by the window with a background of blue sky. She sent the painting and the three wrapped stones to Gwen, asking her to display the stones before the painting, to let people pick them up. The piece sold almost immediately, for twice the price she'd ever received.

At first she used Arno's skiff to retrieve her groceries and mail. Most of the lobstermen seemed too busy to wave, much less say hello. They roared by in their boats, kicking over a bow wave that the skiff climbed before diving into the trough. They were working, she knew, but they came too close. They did the same to cruising yachts. The skiff was almost swamped once by a following sea that was further confused by a lobster boat coming up on her stern. The crew stopped to ask if she needed help, but her legs were so cold, and she was so busy bailing that she never even looked up at them. They went on. When the market started a delivery service in the summer, she signed on. When the market couldn't or wouldn't deliver, she hired a boat to bring her supplies and mail out to the island. Eventually there seemed little need to make regular trips ashore. Almost everything could be done by mail.

Rarely did any of the many boats that worked around her island actually approach it. She watched the people on board through binoculars, keeping track of those who came close. She knew which boats went with each buoy within a half-mile. When summer kayakers pulled their boats up on her rocks, she sent them packing. When yachts anchored offshore, she made sure beachcombing on her island wasn't one of their vacation stories. She watched them go ashore on neighboring Spruce,

Millet, and Saddleback and fill their dinghies with shells and driftwood and round stones, as if they were the first discovery mission to ever land there, as though the little boats needed ballast to return to Portugal. She'd found that island stuff wasn't merely a souvenir, something to fade in a closed box under a child's bed till it was dumped in a city landfill, but rather the debris of art, nature's art, that could be recomposed to testify to the span of time between a glacier and her own mind. Too much had been taken away by foresters and then quarrymen and now tourists. Anything else that left the archipelago had to carry more weight than natural resources or even memories. It had to replenish the soul: her own, and others' who came in contact with it.

She hung Arno's freshly painted buoys over *Break of Day* in the shed. She pushed closed the many drawers he'd left open. She refilled a half-dozen holes around the house, and wondered what trees he'd been planning to plant until she found more holes, freshly dug, in the following months and years. Despite the holes, the island seemed the safest place on earth for an artist, the most conducive to creation. The world could well have begun here, she thought. It could again.

🐚🐚🐚

Will didn't speak on the drive back to Stonington, except to say, upon arrival, "I had to wait until they invented boats to come here."

He didn't want to hand his suitcase to Zee, but she wouldn't drop her outstretched arm. She took the bag and asked, "What have you got in here, rocks?" Then she told him, "Soft-sided bags are better for boats."

He looked at her, Hannah noticed, as if she'd imparted her innermost secret to him, as if he were embarrassed that she'd tell him so soon.

"How long are you here?" Zee asked.

"He's here for a while," Hannah answered for him.

"I'm gonna put the bags forward and both of you in the stern. There's a little chop built up this afternoon. There'll be some spray." She turned to Will, who stood in the center of the skiff. "You can sit down now." He did so, smiling uncertainly. He leaned over the side and put his hand in the clear water and quickly jerked it back. He looked at Hannah as if the water had bitten him. Zee stood at the console and started the engine. She paused to put her hair in a ponytail and guide the tail through the hole in the back of her cap. She turned to Hannah and asked, "All set?" Then she turned to Will. "Don't be lookin' at my butt."

Before he could respond, she ducked around and gunned the boat away from the float. She slowed as she passed through the mooring field, taking an oblique line on the short, steep waves to minimize the spray. Hannah gripped the coaming with one hand and the fiberglass seat with the other. When she saw Will watching her, she told him, "Don't be afraid."

"Why?" he yelled.

Zee looked back to see if anything was wrong.

"I don't know," Hannah said. "I thought you might be afraid."

"Are you afraid of drowning?" he asked too loudly.

"Isn't everybody?" she yelled back. "I wasn't when I was young, when I was your age."

He didn't respond. They both ducked as spray arched over them. When she looked up she saw he was waiting, that he was ready to speak. "What?" she yelled.

"Maybe I'll be afraid of it when I'm old, too."

"What a strange thing to say," she shouted. "I'm not old."

"You're twice as old as me," he said. "Don't you think that someone who's sixty-eight is old? They'd just be twice as old as you."

"Zee," Hannah yelled, "Will is looking at your butt."

"I knew he would," Zee yelled back without turning.

She hung close to the northern shores of Russ, Camp, and Bold, as the wind was out of the southwest and the islands provided some protection. But between Bold and Millet they had to cross open water, vulnerable to the waves to starboard. The skiff knocked up sheets of spray, flinging them away from the boat, but the stiff wind brought them back aboard. By the time they reached Ten Acre No Nine they were drenched. Zee motored slowly into the quarry, wiping water from her face.

"Sorry about that," she said. "I guess I could have slowed down some."

Driftwood barked from the quarry's rim. He put his feet on the top rung of a ladder.

Hannah yelled up, "Don't you dare!" He'd gotten out of the house somehow.

The dog jumped back and the ladder clattered from one ledge to the next.

"He's repelling the invaders," Zee said.

"You have a dog," Will said. "You didn't tell me there was a dog."

"Why?" Hannah asked. "He doesn't bite. Are you allergic?"

"No, but it makes you a different person. I would have thought differently of you."

Hannah's heart was still pounding. She'd been sure Driftwood would fall off the ledge, that he'd almost tried to climb down the ladder.

"She's only had him for a few days," Zee said. "He's a stray."

"Oh," Will said, and Hannah thought that Zee had taken something from her unfairly.

"What do I owe you for carrying Will out?" Hannah asked her.

"Oh, first trip is free," Zee said and smiled at Will. She handed him his suitcase and put her hands in her back pockets as the boat drifted slowly away from the granite landing. "But he'll be back, and then it will cost him dearly. I never charge anything for taking people out *to* an island."

🐚 🐚 🐚

She missed no one on the island but Arno. There, his absence seemed as staggering as the loss of millions of people in New York would be. Al came by after she'd been on the island for a few weeks and said, "Some of us were wondering if there was going to be a service."

"No," Hannah answered.

"I guess I mean to say that we're going to have one, and you're welcome to come."

"I've been to too many funerals."

"There won't be many people there. It's a time to give thanks and forgive, dear. Most of his friends are gone. He outlived them."

She didn't go. She read about the memorial service two weeks later in the paper. Six men had attended. Hannah thought it sad that no women were there. If she'd gone there would have been at least one. But she also knew that she'd come too late, and that attending the service would have been the height of hypocrisy. She felt the six years she'd been away, and Arno's death, left her without rights to the community, to his friends, even to *Break of Day*. It seemed proper to be isolated. She seemed to deserve being cast away, to be alone.

How could six years have passed so quickly? She missed him most in the early morning. Waking, she'd invent the small sounds of his movements in the kitchen, brace herself for the smell of coffee and toast slipping under her door. She wished he'd left notes on every appliance, telling her the secrets of the toaster, the refrigerator, the hot water heater. The engine on the rim of the quarry baffled her for months, although she could remember watching him operate it and the crane dozens of times. She knew that every step she took on the island was in his tracks, that she grabbed no limb where his hand had not been, leaned against no stone where he hadn't paused a thousand times to rest. The narrow worn trails across the island weren't made by rabbit or deer, but by a single man following himself again and again, for decade after decade, sure that the path he was on was the right one. Hannah had no such instinct. So she followed Arno's trails and looked for worn footfalls and burnished handholds as if they were blazes, cracked twigs and cairns made by yesterday's scout. She used the tools and utensils that showed the most wear. The teeth of the bread knife had been filed down by a multitude of loaves. His silver-plated spoon had been stirred to brass. The bone handles of his fork and knife were taped to the tines and blade. Wooden bowls were patched with sheet copper and boat rivets. Pencils an inch long were wired to old pipe stems, glued to rulers, anything to make them long enough to hold, to use to the nub. The many chips in china cups had been sanded smooth so that their rims were almost serrated. The back feet of Arno's kitchen chair had rocked sockets into the soft wooden floor. So she baked bread, drank tea, sat at the kitchen table, and fed herself three times a day. Instead of lobstering she drew and painted and carved. She did not feel his ghost around her, but knew the same smells came up from the sea, and the wind that blew over the house could not be told from that which blew over it when Arno was there.

She left *Break of Day* as Arno had left her, in the boat shed on her cradle, which sat on iron axles and wheels that rode rails into the fore-shore. Twice a day the tide crept beneath the big doors of the shed and lapped at the boat's keel. The lower four feet of the shed were granite, laid on sloping granite bedrock. The upper walls and the roof were shingled. There was a tin weather vane on the seaward end of the gable, a foot-long *Break of Day*, that imitated the yawp of a gull when it turned. There were usually a half-dozen seagulls standing on the ridge behind the vane, who always answered its change of direction call, turning and facing the other direction as the vane did. All the tools in the shed were broken or rusted beyond use. Paint in half-used cans was solid. The only requirement Arno had to hang something on the walls was that it be beyond all hope of further use. Cracked life rings, split gaff hooks, strings of shriveled toggle buoys, rotten netting and various bony rem-nants of fish, jawbones, vertebrae and leathery flukes were nailed to the studs and joists. Dust and the powdered and granular feces of birds and mice covered everything above the lower granite walls except Arno's freshly painted buoys, which seemed all the more colorful strung as they were among the dark rafters. But below all this, on the lower courses of the stone foundation and covering the granite floor a few feet inside the boat-shed doors, lived a spotty layer of life: barnacles and patches of slippery black life. Crabs scuttled beneath the cradle and along the rails. Occasionally, Hannah found tiny mussels living in the boat shed having latched onto life in the wrong place, where water didn't stay long enough to support them. She came here, too. She stepped inside having been away for a week or a month, but it always seemed years. Spiderwebs stretched between *Break of Day*'s hull and the shed walls. As layers of paint cracked and peeled off the boat, revealing yet further layers, she liked to think the old boat was, if not growing younger, then slowly breaking free from its chrysalis. She made her way aboard by Arno's rough-hewn ladder, whose rungs were as delicate and worn as the front stretcher of an antique Windsor chair, or the withered arm of a cripple. She wanted to leave the old ladder where he'd last descended it. He'd left *Break of Day* scrubbed clean and pickled for the winter. There was actually a wool blanket tucked around the engine. But the boat, like everything else Arno owned, was worn to the point of snapping. He'd worked so hard, for so long, wearing wood and steel and cloth down till it could all be seen through. His life had been as persistent as the waves working on the granite shore. It seemed he'd accomplished little more than feeding himself and paying his property taxes, barely maintaining the hold on what his parents had left him. His life made her wince. She teared up because his life seemed so dissimilar to her own, yet they'd both arrived at the same place. It was the only place she ever cried, sitting in the stern of *Break of Day*, rotten netting and a split life ring over her head, a narrow view of the tidal zone beneath her feet visible through the drying planks of the old wooden hull.

🐚 🐚 🐚

Will didn't ask, but she told him the dog's name. "He's some mix of German Shepherd and Beagle and Dachshund," she said. "I don't know what he is or where he came from."

The boy bent to the dog but did not put forward his hand. Driftwood smelled the suitcase first, then entered the crouch of Will's body as if it were a den. Only the dog's hindquarters were visible, his tail conducting a distant adagio. He snorted once, backed halfway out, then went back in. Will looked up at Hannah as though he were a bird in a nest.

Hannah said, "Driftwood, leave him alone."

"It's OK," Will said. "He's just doing what we did at the cafe."

When the dog was satisfied he led them down the path to the house as if it were something he'd just discovered. He cantered, looking back as if to make sure they weren't getting lost. When he reached the granite slab at the front door he sat on it and barked once.

"Yes," Hannah said, "you led us through the jungle safely once again. What would I do without you? How did you get out?" She turned to Will. "There's the garden. That granite building down the hill was built as an office for the quarry. Down on the shore there, that's the boat shed. The skiff is in there. Come on in, I'll show you your room." She opened the door and Driftwood squeezed in first. Will stepped past her with his suitcase and she smelled him for the first time: a pillowcase left on the clothesline through a rain. He stopped three feet inside, so she left the door open, and the wind followed them up the stairs. She took him to Arno's bedroom. She'd put clean linens on the bed, but she noticed now two dead flies on the windowsill. There were dark water stains on the wallpaper just below the ceiling cove molding. The bare bulb that hung in the center of the room had a dust tonsure.

"Do you smoke, Will?" she asked.

"No, ma'am."

"Are there any drugs in that suitcase?"

"No, it's just heavy with my books."

"Well, you get settled. If you need to wash any clothes, bring them downstairs and I'll show you how that's done here. I don't have a washer and dryer."

It occurred to her then that they would both have to get over seeing each other's underwear hanging on the line. In the winter she dried her clothes on a folding stand in the living room before the stove. She'd have to close her bedroom door now when she changed, close the bathroom door.

"Is it all right if I walk around the island?" he asked.

"Of course. It won't take you long. Be careful, some of the rocks are slippery."

"What kind of snakes do y'all have here?"

"I've never seen a snake on the island."

"No water moccasins?"

"What's that?"

"A bad snake that lives in the water."

"This is salt water. There aren't any snakes in it."

"Oh."

"There's nothing out there to be afraid of but the water. Just don't fall in. Is there anything else you want to ask me?"

"No, I'm sorry."

"Why are you sorry?"

"I don't know. That I can't think of any questions."

"I'm putting you up because I want to, Will. No one has forced me to. It was my decision. We'll just have to see how it goes."

"Yes, ma'am."

"My name's Hannah."

"I'm sorry."

She went back down to her work, but found herself pausing to listen. He moved lightly across the floor above her. Whenever he approached the closet a board creaked. The top drawer of Arno's old dresser burped when opened. She heard him stacking something on the floor next to the bed. Books? What kind of books did he read? For the first time in six years, she heard the springs of Arno's bed yawn. Where was the dog? The dog must be up there with him. It was past lunchtime. What would he want for lunch? He finally came down an hour after she'd left him. Driftwood came down, too.

"Would you like some soup for lunch?" she asked him.

"Oh, I already ate. I had a sandwich leftover from yesterday in my bag."

"Oh."

"Can Driftwood go?"

"Sure."

They walked out together, boy and dog. She would have to eat alone. It seemed incredibly inconsiderate. He'd sat on his bed, eating a day-old sandwich. She looked out the window and watched him follow the trail down to the foreshore. Then she went upstairs. His door was closed.

He was gone for hours, from one hunger till the next. It only took half an hour at most to walk around the island. Finally she decided to make dinner, enough for two, but she wouldn't wait for him. She finished her meal and still he was not there. She went outside and called the dog. Driftwood came running from the direction of the quarry. Smoke was tangled in his fur. She followed the smell of the smoke back up to the rim of the quarry, moving from a quick step to a dead run. Will was on one of the lower levels, his pants rolled up to his knees, tending a small driftwood fire. He had a half-dozen fish skewered and roasting over the flames. Hannah climbed down into the amphitheater by ladder, while the dog ran to the seaward edge and traversed the quarry a dozen times before reaching the bottom.

"I had dinner ready an hour ago," she told him. "Where have you been?"

He looked up at her as if he were embarrassed to answer a question that only had one answer on an island. "Here," he finally said. "I'm sorry, at school they ring a bell for dinner."

"You had dinner at school?"

"Yes, after Bible study."

"Well, this isn't school. I have dinner around six. I don't ring a bell. You're not a dog."

"Do you want some fish?"

"How did you catch these?"

"When the water was real low awhile ago there were thousands of them in here. I scooped them out with my hands and Driftwood bit them. The hard part was building the fire. Finally I found an old bird's nest for tinder."

"Will, I would have fed you. I'm not poor. You've got full room and board here."

He nodded, then lowered his head. "I like fish," he said. "I never saw so many fish in my life and every one of them the same size."

She bent down and picked up one of the skewers. The tiny fish was gutted and splayed across the forked stick. "They're herring," she said. "They get trapped in here at low tide. They swim along the shore and come in here and just keep making a circle, sometimes for hours. They're following each other, see. Usually when the tide comes in and makes the opening broader, they work their way out. Driftwood comes in that way, too, circles in an endless eddy. I gather it up for my artwork and to burn through the winter. You're going to eat these after the dog has bitten through them?"

"Yeah, I'd feel bad if I killed them and didn't eat them."

"OK, when you're done, put out this fire. Kick the whole thing into the water. And never start another one unless you ask me. I don't have a fire department if a campfire gets out of hand. There's about a couple dozen islands along the coast of Maine named Burnt Island. I don't want this to be one of them."

"I'm sorry."

"Your foot is bleeding," she said.

"I stepped on something sharp in the water."

"Probably a mussel shell. I've got medicine and Band-Aids. Bring your foot with you when you come home."

"OK, Hannah, I will." He said this as if it were possible to leave it behind.

"That was a joke, Will."

"I know, Hannah. You're funny," he said, without smiling, without the least hint of malice or satire.

☙ ☙ ☙

He rarely asked questions. Instead, he made a statement. "I saw a bird today flying underwater." Then he waited to see if she'd refute him.

"That was a cormorant. They catch small fish. Some people around here call them shags. Arno had one for a pet."

"I walked up on one unexpectedly and he pooped and puked at the same time before flying away."

"You scared him. Probably getting rid of the extra weight before lifting off."

"I felt real bad about scaring him so."

"Sometimes," she said, "they fly over the island in the evenings in a group of five or six, and they all have their mouths open, flying with their mouths open."

"They're not talking?" he asked.

"Nope, just flying with their mouths open."

"That's a mystery we'll never understand," he said.

"The fishermen don't like them because they shit on their boats. But I like to see them standing on a rock or mooring ball with their wings spread, as if they're selling watches. They're not like a duck. Water doesn't roll off their backs. They have to dry their wings in the air."

"Your sister says people who use that word taste it in their mouths."

"What word? Shit?"

He nodded.

"It's a lovely word. It doesn't taste bad at all. It starts off so innocently and sonorously and ends abruptly with that sharp spit. It's one of my favorite words. So few words really mean what they say. Shit is honest."

"You could say 'poop.'"

"Poop is a good word, too, but that's what a baby rabbit does. A shag shits. I thought you said you saw one?"

"I did. It was pretty awful, coming out of both ends at once that way."

"If you don't use the right word, you're pretty much powerless. Even a dog won't listen to you. Emily's kind of talk will one day reduce us all to the same dozen words, and we won't understand anything, won't be able to communicate at all. You'll try to tell me a bird's flying over and I'll think God broke wind." Hannah looked at Will and frowned. "That's the longest speech I've given in six years. My throat is sore."

"I'm sorry. You don't have to explain things to me. I can be more quiet."

"Don't be silly."

"You have a nice voice, Hannah," he said.

He seemed to offer compliments as offhandedly as he might pluck a blade of grass, as if they cost him nothing.

※ ※ ※

They pulled the outboard out of the boat shed the first week, and Will and Zee took it into Stonington to be overhauled. The skiff itself, lapstrake cedar, was dry but sound. At high tide they sunk it near the shore so the planks would swell. After three days the skiff held water, which meant it might also float. While Hannah walked the shoreline holding a long painter attached to the skiff's stem, Will took his first row around the island from the boat shed to the quarry. He'd never rowed before and lost his left oar overboard twice. But once in the safety of the quarry, Hannah turned him loose. Soon he could spin the boat in either direction, and row sitting or standing for a few strokes, before the oars leaped from the locks.

"It won't be as easy out in the ocean," she told him. "You'll be fighting the wind and the waves and most of all the currents."

"Won't they be going with me half the time?" he asked.

"That may be reasonable to expect, but it seems to hardly ever happen."

He practiced for days in the quarry before venturing out. Hannah followed him twice around the island on foot, cell phone in hand. She made him wear one of Arno's old kapok life jackets, crushed and faded as it was. He was thin, but his muscles were long and seemed tireless. He always seemed to be concentrating, worrying over the physics of each stroke, constantly looking over his shoulders.

"I know it's hard to believe," Hannah yelled out to him, "but if you'll row directly away from something on the horizon, you'll also row directly toward something else. Point the boat where you want to go, then pick a point directly behind you and row away from it. You won't have to turn around so often."

"It's hard not to look."

"Trust the diminishing point. Every time you look you lose half a stroke. If you can see clearly behind yourself, you'll know where you're going."

"But I'm going in a circle around this island."

"OK, there's Millet Island. You're pointed right at it. Now, look at me and don't stop looking at me till you run into that island."

Halfway across the channel Will stopped and pulled his T-shirt over his head, then found her on the shore and began to row again. She recognized the moment, his shirt taut as a sail between his two upraised arms, his pale torso curving into the wind, as one she wanted to paint. When he reached the shore of Millet, he stood up in the skiff and waved. It took her several moments to realize she should wave back.

❦ ❦ ❦

While he waited for the outboard to be repaired he roamed the island with a book. After breakfast he'd pause on his way back to his room and look at whatever Hannah was currently working on, but never offered comment.

She found she couldn't take her eyes off him while he studied her paintings and sculptures. She decided she wouldn't push him for a response to
her work, that she'd probably be disappointed when he did. She couldn't
expect a seventeen-year-old to understand what she was after when she
didn't often get it herself. It pleased her enough that he always turned
to her and smiled afterwards, even if it was uncertainly, as though she'd
caught him looking at nudes. From there he'd go back upstairs and come
down with a book under his arm, and he and Driftwood would set out for
some place to lean. His absence in the mornings left her disconcertingly
free to work. She found it difficult to concentrate on a product for the New
York art market with this boy roaming around her island. He'd return for
lunch with polished stones, shells, feathers, a morning's beachcombing,
and she felt she'd somehow missed out. He arranged them on the kitchen
table around his soup bowl as she'd done years earlier.

"There are tons of these little guys," he stated.

"Periwinkles."

"Maybe you could eat them."

"I think you can, but nobody does. Maybe when they run out of lobsters and urchins there'll be a periwinkle industry."

"It must be hard to be an artist here," he said.

"Why?"

"There's so much to look at and so much to do. I just think it would
be harder to be an artist here, where everything already seems to make
sense."

"What do you mean?"

"I don't know. But if you look in the shallow water you can see all this
simple stuff going on."

"Like what?"

"Just eating and sleeping and fooling around. Up on the island it
seems drowsy and warm, like I'm on a perch looking down on the world
and can see how simple things really are."

"Maybe you just feel safe here."

"I feel like I haven't slept in years and I'm trying to catch up."

For the second time in as many weeks, Will stepped back inside the house just after leaving and asked Hannah if it was all right to go out.

"Of course," she said.

"I don't know when to ask for permission," he said.

"This isn't a jail. I'm not a warden."

"But you've gone through my stuff while I was out," he said.

"No, I haven't." Hannah stood up and stared at him till he looked down. "Do I need to?" she asked.

"No. I'm sorry. My dad always went through my stuff."

He stood on the threshold, one hand turning the knob of the open door back and forth.

"My room's clean," he said. "Everything's put up and in its place."

"I don't care if your room's clean or not. You're the one sleeping in it," she said.

"You'll tell me if I'm doing something wrong." This wasn't a question.

"I will. I told you not to burn down the island."

"That's a big thing. You'll tell me about little things, too."

"I might not. I might just live with them, the way you do."

"I'm going out now," he said.

"Can you take the trash when you go?" she asked.

"Yes," he said. "Yes, I can."

🦋 🦋 🦋

"What are you reading, Will?"

"*Boon Island*. Your sister gave me all the books in the library on Maine. This one's about this ship that wrecks on Boon Island in the winter and how the survivors have to eat each other."

"I guess we better call about that outboard then," Hannah said, "before winter comes. You like to read?"

"Yeah. You can be alone even if you're in a roomful of people."

"I always thought of reading as never being alone. You know, you don't have to leave the house in the morning because of me. I can work with you around. You're not any more of a distraction than Driftwood."

"Driftwood poops on the floor. It smells really bad," he said.

"OK, you're less of a distraction."

"It's such a little island, but I keep finding new things."

"I still find it new after six years."

"But I won't be here that long. I've got to use my time. Do I have to get a license to fish?"

"Only for lobster."

"I could catch some fish for us."

"As long as it's bigger than a herring."

"Zee said there are stripers and bluefish. We have stripers in the lake in Texas, but she said these can be two or three feet long."

"Why are young men so interested in bringing down game? I've started a garden. It's slower, I know, but more sure."

"I'll help with the garden," he said. "We had a garden at the order. Have you planted the okra or muskmelons yet?"

"I don't think you can buy seeds for those here. Okra?"

"You dice it up and batter it and deep-fry it."

"You do?"

"Yeah, it's good," he said.

"It sounds Southern."

"Well, I'm Southern. It's just food. It's not insects or anything."

"We'll see."

"Why don't you have any chickens?"

"It takes me a month to eat a dozen eggs."

"I like chickens just to watch them. Even if they didn't lay eggs, I'd like them. I'd have a chicken."

"You're less quiet than you used to be," she said.

"It seems funny to me, too. That's the first time I've spoken that chicken opinion."

🐟 🐟 🐟

In the afternoons Will would volunteer for some chore. He patched the roof on the granite house, and swept it clean. He replaced the rotten bottom boards on the boat-shed doors. Together they built a scarecrow for the garden from driftwood, nets, and foil pie pans. He hoed up turf for a row of okra, then more for cucumber and cantaloupe mounds. He took over Hannah's daily ritual of gathering debris from the quarry. She'd often go looking for him and find him asleep in the middle of the field or on a slab of granite at the edge of the sea. He told her once that a wave had woken him up, the first time that had ever happened in his whole life.

When the outboard was finally ready, Zee towed the skiff into Stonington behind Z To Go. She promised to see Will back out to the island safely. The two of them were gone all afternoon. Finally, after three hours of pacing, Hannah called Zee's number. Her father answered.

"I think they took the truck over to Brooklin to the Marine Supply," he said. "They got the motor on your skiff, but you needed a new gas tank, an air horn, a good life jacket, and an anchor and some line. Zee wouldn't let him go out without all that stuff. You'll need to get the boat registered sometime, too, now that there's a motor on it. It might not be a bad idea to get him a handheld VHF if you can afford it. Maybe I can rustle up an old one."

"I wish Zee had called and told me what they were doing," Hannah said. "I've been waiting."

"Well, yeah. But they're kids. I guess you could blame your boy for not calling, too, though. Zee's doing him a favor, taking him to Brooklin. You don't want him out there without a horn and good life jacket. If he loses that engine, he'll need an anchor to set so he doesn't get carried out to sea."

"I know that."

"Well, don't go off on Zee. I'll have them call soon as they're back. You know, this is a losing deal for her. Soon as you have your skiff, she'll lose you as a client. Don't think she doesn't know that. She's that kind of person."

"The skiff is for Will. He'll go to work in it."

"Well, I can understand that. I'm looking for a boat to go to work in myself. I'll have 'em call when they get back, before they leave for your place."

"Thank you."

"Nothing to it."

🐢🐢🐢

The first thing Will said when he came in that evening was, "I got a job."

"What?"

"We went over to this place called Billings Marine. Zee had to talk to a guy there. She told him I was looking for a job and he took me upstairs to this office and they hired me on the spot. It's on the water. I can take the skiff right to work."

"But what do you know about working on boats?" she asked.

"Not a thing. I get to clean up and sweep and move stuff around and they're going to show me how to sand boat hulls and paint the bottoms. I start at seven tomorrow morning."

"Tomorrow?"

"Yeah."

"Do you want to start that soon?"

"Yeah. You won't have to buy me stuff anymore. Zee's house over-looks that little harbor that Billings is in. The skiff runs great. I've got to use my first paycheck to pay Zee back for the life jacket and horn. The guy who fixed the engine said not to use your old steel gas tank. It had rust in it. So we had to get one of those, too, a plastic one. Zee's dad gave me some chain to put on the anchor."

"That guy's trying to get his hands on Arno's boat," she said.

"Who?"

"Zee's father."

"He doesn't have any hands."

"What?"

"He doesn't have any hands, Hannah. He's just got two hooks. Zee said he lost them in some machinery on a big fishing boat a couple years ago."

"I guess I'm supposed to feel sorry for him now."

The boy paused. He stopped talking and looked down at the floor.

"What?" Hannah snapped.

"When my dad was mad at me he just hit me. At least I knew when he was mad."

"I'm not mad."

"Are you mad at Zee or her dad?"

"They can help you all they want. I don't care. You shouldn't borrow money from them."

"I won't take their help anymore unless I ask you," Will said.

"Don't be stupid."

"My dad would just hit me. He didn't try to hide it. At least he was honest."

"OK," Hannah said, "OK. You can't bring that up just to win an argument. If you use it now you'll use it for the rest of your life. This is what people do when they don't hit. You're going to have to learn about this form of interaction, too. I'm sorry. I was worried. You didn't call. You went off in a boat and you didn't call. I thought you were coming right back out. I'm not practiced at this."

"At what?"

"At living with other people. It's not just me. The damn dog was worried about you, too. He stayed down in the quarry all day. I had to take his dinner down there."

"It's OK, Hannah. I'm home now."

She realized her voice was vibrating, that she was short of breath, as if the wind were blowing too hard from behind her, drawing words and air out before she was ready to let them go. She walked across the room to the kitchen and bent down and put her hand on the dog.

"Are you hungry?" she asked the boy.

🐢 🐢 🐢

She hadn't risen so early since her lobstering days. But both Will and the old dog slept through the alarm. Every morning she had to go into his room and physically shake him to wake him up. His bare shoulder was as warm as the sun on stone.

"It's time," she'd say.

"OK, Hannah, thanks." Then he'd roll over, his eyes closing again as he rolled, and fall asleep once again. She'd go downstairs, shake the dog to wake him, and get either the woodstove or the propane heater going, depending on the type of heat she wanted that morning. The second waking usually took. While the kitchen warmed, she started breakfast. Will came downstairs, still dressing, and always paused at her worktable before coming to the kitchen table. Then, before his first bite, he asked what she was going to do while he was gone. The first time he asked this she answered, "What I've always done." But he asked again the next day, and the next.

"Why do you want to know?" she finally said.

"Because I like to think about where you are, what you're doing."

"I don't know that I like to think about you thinking about me while I'm doing something."

"Oh," he said. "I'll be sanding the bottom paint off *Tricia Gayle* this morning. It won't bother me if you sometime pause and think about me doing that."

"They give you gloves and a mask when you do that kind of work?" she asked.

"And goggles, too. So think of me with all that stuff on, and my cheeks and forearms and my whole body red with dust. I look pretty funny."

"I guess I could think about that at some point."

"What are you going to do today?" he repeated.

"I'm going to clear up this mess, feed the dog, and have a bath. Then I'm going to work at that table most of the morning. After lunch, I thought I'd work in the garden some. The mail comes today. That should fill up the rest of the afternoon."

"I'll think about you in the bathtub," he said and smiled.

She was shocked. She'd almost forgotten he was male.

"You will not," she said, hesitantly.

"Some of the guys at Billings said you used to garden naked." He smiled again, and put a spoon in his mouth.

"What do you think of men that spy on women with binoculars?"

"But you look at the lobstermen with your binoculars all the time," he protested.

"But they're at work. I'm not spying on them at their homes."

"So you really did garden naked?"

"I didn't know they could see me. When the winter comes you'll appreciate the feel of the sun on your skin, too. The summer is short here. I used to try to gather it all in."

"Boy," he said. "You and your sister sure are different. She lives where the sun always shines and never goes out in it unless she's covered up."

"Do the women wear some kind of shroud there, Will?"

"No, just clothes, but they go up to the neck and down to the ankles and hands. Sisters aren't supposed to tan."

"Why not?"

"They're married to Jesus and only he's supposed to see them. The sun is a heathen God."

"Jesus," she said.

"Right," Will said.

"No, I'm saying 'Jesus' in exasperation. How much of that stuff do you believe, Will? How long have you been going to that school?"

"Since I was twelve. I stopped believing in Jesus when I was nine or ten."

"Really?"

"Yeah, I went to the sisters' school because Dad joined their church. All you have to do is repeat what they say and they leave you alone."

"So you don't believe in anything?"

"I believe I gotta go to work or I'm gonna be late, Hannah."

He spooned oatmeal onto a piece of toast and folded the bread over. He put this in his shirt pocket. She walked him up to the rim of the quarry and stood there in her fleece housecoat with the dog until Will got underway.

And so she began to tell him at length what she planned for her day. It was hard at first, because she'd never thought of her days as having any structure or order. She could not plan her work. It seemed to happen spontaneously rather than step by step. It seemed to happen as she came upon it, the way one rock or tree appeared after another as she walked along the beach or through the woods. But she tried to give him a general sense of her hours now that they'd been returned to her. The skiff's, and Will's, wake left her as she once was, alone to pursue the island.

🐚 🐚 🐚

She'd seen him before, then, Zee's father, lobstering from a small boat among the islands. She had three of his buoys, black rings over a yellow body, hanging on the walls of the boat shed. They were brand new and had been cut free with a sharp knife. No propeller slashes scored the Styrofoam. She found this kind of buoy regularly on her beach, signs of territory wars among the lobstermen. Arno himself tied knots in lobstermen's warp, just below the buoy, to warn off encroachments on his fields. Occasionally, if the knots and cut buoys didn't work, boats were known to sink, or burn at their moorings. Arno had told her once, "It's better now, but not so long ago we didn't carry guns just to shoot seagulls."

So she'd seen him then, Zee's father, working slower than most, alone in a small cabinless boat, using not a short gaff to snare the pot warp, but the hook on the end of his arm. She'd thought it strange that he never put the gaff down, even when he opened the traps and pulled out the lobsters. He wore the standard Day-Glo orange bib overalls and a dark blue sweater. The baggy sleeves went all the way to his wrists. His boat had no name, or the outboard engine obscured it. He had to work among the islands: his boat was too small to go far offshore. He was from Maine, farther downeast, but even if he'd come from Swan's Island across Jericho Bay he'd be from away, at least where lobster territory was concerned. She knew the locals were just protecting their livelihood. He'd have a hard time breaking in, hands or no hands.

🐚 🐚 🐚

When Will came home in the late afternoon he was always freshly showered. He wasn't fond of baths and didn't want to bring all that bottom paint out to the island anyway, so he scrubbed himself in the marina showers after work. With his first paycheck he paid Zee, bought himself a fishing rod and tackle, and gave Hannah a hundred dollars toward his upkeep.

"You don't need to do that," she told him.

"I know. If you don't want it, put it away for me. I need to start saving for school."

"School's free, Will. It's a public high school."

"College."

"Oh, of course."

"Did you go to college?"

"I did. It seems like it was a long time ago," she said. She didn't say, "Me too. I want to go, too." Instead, she put the money in her wallet. "We'll open a savings account," she said. He'd only been with her a few weeks when she realized she'd miss him. It would be more than a year before he'd go, and she already missed him. And she wasn't able to put this aside, that he, too, would leave, and so there were days when she ignored him, acted as if he weren't there, as if he were already gone.

For ten days in a row she'd make his breakfast and a sack lunch, wash his clothes. Together they'd mend one of her island guards, or fight some stretch of erosion by piling up rocks that had washed down into the intertidal zone a hundred or a thousand years before. Then, some days, she wouldn't wake him and he'd go off to work late, without breakfast or lunch. She'd get up when she heard him leave. She thought about sending him out to the little granite house to live, so she wouldn't hear him breathing heavily in his sleep across the hall, so she wouldn't expend so much effort on waiting for him to return from work. Her own work was suffering. The hours of the day and days of the week used to flow uninterruptedly. Seasons had merged imperceptibly. Now the world hinged on his schedule, when he left and returned, the free weekends. She found herself stealing hours from her projects to plan a meal or sit with him while he fished. He seemed to inhabit his body and life so effortlessly. Even when he was late to work, he was able to forgive himself rather than forgiving her. Every slight she intended he deflected with his own apology. They'd be sitting on a slab of granite, the boy's fishing line stretching into the sea, the sun and waves filling seamlessly the pauses in their conversation, when the thought of lost hours would fill her with bitterness. She'd get up without a word and leave him there as if he were a stone left by the last glacier to pass through. Back at her worktable, she'd pick up scissors or a brush and the tool would feel lifeless in her hand, as if it had no discernible purpose. She worked, but found the things she'd say with wool and stone and impasto redundant, unable to sustain her. She realized that everything she saw through him was new, and everything she saw alone seemed as worn as her own reflection in a windowpane.

She wrote to Emily occasionally, sending her letters through Gwen, to tell her how Will was getting along. Emily's replies were terse and infrequent. She was glad the boy was doing well. After two weeks of searching alone, the father had reported Will missing to the police. The father and the police had questioned Emily but neither seemed suspicious that she was hiding his whereabouts. She dealt with the father on an almost daily basis in her community and felt Will had made the right decision for now.

🐢🐢🐢

Hannah gave Zee her father's buoys. "They've been cut," Hannah told her.

"Yes, I know," Zee said. "Thank you. Daddy's lost quite a bit of lobstering gear this summer."

"It's not easy to work into a new area."

"But he has rights," Zee said. She handed Hannah her mail and the week's groceries. The sun was low, whitewashing the upper walls of the quarry. "My grandfather fished here. He's in a nursing home in Deer Isle now, but he fished here for years. He stopped lobstering ten years ago, but he has a right to pass his grounds down to Daddy."

"Does your father know who's cutting his buoys?"

"No, it could be anybody. They do it in the fog, or at night."

"Why did your dad leave here to go downeast?"

"My mom's parents live up there. And Daddy and Grandpa never got along until now. We came back here after my mom left and Grandpa got sick."

"Tell your Dad," Hannah said, "to watch for a boat named *Poppa's Pride*. Fog's not so thick out here, dark's not so dark."

Zee put her hands on her hips. She started to say something, then stopped. Then she said, "Thank you, I don't know that I'll tell him."

"Why not?"

"He might kill them."

"OK, I'll let you decide."

"Why am I still here?" Zee asked. "I mean, coming out here? Will comes into town every day. He could bring this stuff out."

"He won't be here forever. I need a regular service. I can't depend on him."

"I can't get him to look at my butt. I've wanted him to since I told him not to. The kids at school are going to roast him over that accent."

"He won't care."

"I know. What's that all about?"

"It's just Will. I guess I don't have to ask you to watch out for him when school starts."

"No, I can't keep my eyes off him. He is your nephew, isn't he?"

Hannah focused on Zee's eyes and said, "Yes, why do you ask?"

"It just seems like he'd rather be out here with you than anywhere else."

"Don't be jealous, Zee. He loves the island. He feels safe here."

"Why does he need to feel safe?"

"That's for him to tell you someday, if he wants to."

As Zee left the quarry, Hannah realized Will must have rebuffed Zee many times over the summer. He had spent almost every evening and day off on the island. He's spent them with me, Hannah thought. She couldn't deny the satisfaction this gave her. It had cost her very little to return the buoys and tell Zee who she'd seen cutting them. She'd been rewarded with this peculiar sense of overcoming. It was just as well that he wasn't interested in her. Every indiscretion and contact he made put him at risk. Besides, he was going off to college in a year. Of course, it wasn't Zee's fault she loved him. She felt a little sorry for her. Hannah had seen in Zee's eyes the first recognition of Zee's own inadequacy. As capable and smart and hard-working as she was, as beautiful as she was, it was still possible not to succeed. Zee was clearly unnerved by this realization. Hannah could remember it. It made her sick to her stomach still, her inability to understand why all relationships came to this pass where only one person could squeeze through at a time.

❧ ❧ ❧

"I want you to pose for me," she said.

"What?" he asked.

"I want to paint you. I don't get many opportunities to do portraits. You'd have to sit still for several hours."

"Could you do it while I'm fishing?"

"No, I need to control the light. You'd have to sit inside."

"Could I read?"

"No, you'd need to look directly at me."

"I couldn't look at you that long unless you were naked."

"In your dreams. Aren't you a church kid?"

"We're the worst. OK, Hannah. I'll do it. Do I get to keep the painting?"

"I sell my paintings for several thousand dollars each. You can't afford it. You might not like it, anyway."

"Why not?"

"Not everybody likes the way I present them," she said.

"Are you going to make me look like a troll?"

"No, you're going to sit in that chair by the window. You'll have to sit without your shirt."

"I have to be naked, but you don't?"

"Just no shirt. I'm going to paint you from the waist up. It's about painting. It's not about you. It's about the figure, not Will."

"Thanks a lot. That really makes me want to pose," he said.

"The best thing about art is that it's indifferent. You have to be brave enough not to care."

"Care about what?"

"Whether you're beautiful or not."

"I'm not scared."

"Hmm," she said, "I always am."

"But you're pretty, Hannah."

"Thank you, but I'm not concerned about that. It's the art I'm afraid of, whether I can make it or not."

"But you've been successful, I guess," he told her.

"I have. But that success is always in the past. It never bumps into tomorrow. There's always today in between."

"I'll pose for you. Do you want me to flex my muscles?"

"You are so seventeen," she said.

Will posed for eight days, every afternoon after work, until Hannah thought the sun had changed its angle, moved too far toward fall. Work at the shipyard had altered his body since she'd first seen it two months earlier as he rowed toward Millet Island. His muscles were defined now and cast shadows that were curved rather than angular. His skin was more red than cream, and between his ribs the hollows held a deep mauve, as if the bones bruised the spaces between them. His hands hung off his wrists as carelessly as flags. She had him rest his arm on the high back of the chair, so she could paint his armpit, and so his hand would drift in the sunlight through the window. The old green armchair cast reflections on the underside of his arms and the narrow folds of his stomach and made the skin seem almost translucent. When he blinked, she blinked. When he scratched his neck, her own itched. He touched his cheek once, and later, in the mirror, she noticed she'd touched the same spot with the end of her brush. If he began to sweat, she ended the session. If the mohair armchair became unbearable, she ended the session. Of course, he can have the painting, she thought as she worked. He can have everything I have. He can't have the painting, ever. It's mine. But she'd found a way to work again. At least for the in-between. She'd work through Will. Whether it was her sculpture, her painting, or the island collages, she'd just think of Will while she worked, in the meantime. She'd do whatever the work required.

🐚 🐚 🐚

The island grew larger in the fog, became Sixteen Acre No Fifteen Island in August. Warm air flowing over cold water lifted the very sea into the sky and all transparency was lost. Birds emerged and disappeared as if flying across a stage. The shore of the island, appearing only a periwinkle at a step, seemed endless. Trees were more numerous, and the known path took twice as long to reach its destination. Driftwood barked at the fog when it moved. Mark Island Light moaned for a moment every fifteen seconds, becoming suddenly audible although it sounded continuously, fog or no fog. The first thickness of the season set in on a Friday evening and lasted for four days, morning, noon, and night. They walked around the island on Saturday afternoon, straining to hear the outside world. The waves were dampened by the fog and seemed to climb up on the shelving granite as if they were being pushed from behind. There wasn't enough wind to shake the pendant droplets from spruce needles. The diesel engines of lobster boats beat on the fog as if it were a rug suspended from a clothesline. Occasionally voices other than their own emanated from the rocks at their feet. A cormorant climbed up out of the ocean clapping. He clapped so enthusiastically it seemed the rest of the auditorium would join in imminently. They walked halfway around the island again before they realized it. Here Will stopped. He looked at Hannah and smiled.

"We're lost. I didn't know I could be this wet and still breathe."

"Should we turn back or just go round again? The dog has already quit us."

"Let's just keep going."

They paused at the entrance of the quarry. "We can walk around the lower level again or just wade across the entrance. It's only a foot and a half deep now, at low tide."

"I can't get any wetter. Let's wade," he answered.

They left their shoes on. The footing was unsure over a bottom of loose mussel shell and rockweed. She reached out and they locked hands at arm's length. The water was searing in its coldness. She could see starfish clinging to rock, a dead urchin tumbling in the current. His hand was warm and wet and unyielding in its support, as if she were holding onto a steel bar. One foot slipped and she put her arm down into the water up to her short sleeve before steadying herself. As they reached the far side of the entrance, she let go of Will's hand and pushed a strand of wet hair behind her ear. They were both wet from the upper thighs down. Her jeans felt heavy. She grabbed a fistful of denim at her knees in each hand, and bending over, trudged up the steep shelf of granite. Water flowed from her pants and shoes. Will came up behind her and shoved her up the bank by her butt, saying, "Come on, you can make it," and laughing. The cold water had taken her breath. When she reached the crest of bare rock she paused where a crust of lichen-frosted soil had lifted from the underlying granite. It looked like a bad toupee. She was reaching back to take the hem of Will's shirt in her hand when she saw the pale blue dinghy lodged in an eroded dike just below. It hadn't been there a half-hour earlier.

"Wow, look at that," Will yelped and scuttled down the slope to the small boat. It was barely six feet long, built of plywood. It looked as if it had been floating for years. The bottom was hairy with growth, all of which was still alive. The painter was no more than four feet long. A rock pinned its end to the island. The oars were aluminum and plastic, off some other more recent creature.

"Is there a name on its stern, Will?" Hannah whispered.

"No," he said. "Can we keep it?"

She dropped down into the vacant dike and pushed Will further up into its recesses. A softer stone had intruded into the granite at some point, and the sea had chiseled it out again, just in time to hide the dinghy.

"Be quiet," she shushed.

"Why?"

"This boat didn't wash up here. That painter is under a rock." She pointed. "Someone's here on the island and they just got here." Wisps of fog moved between them and up the dike to its head where a clutch of beach irises clung to the thin, salty soil. "This boat's been hidden."

"Do you think they're up at the house now?" he asked. "Maybe they've just come for a visit."

"In this weather?"

"What do you want to do?" he asked her.

"Someone has been digging up my island for six years. I've found deep holes."

"What holes?"

"Holes, here and there, around the buildings, beside big rocks."

"When?"

"Every few months, ever since I came here, after Arno died. I almost caught the guy once."

"What's he looking for?"

"I don't know."

"Well, let's find him and ask," Will said. "We'll take his oars with us. He won't be able to get off the island."

Her heart began to flutter dryly, as if blood were draining from it. She'd been waiting for this moment for years.

"Well?" Will insisted.

"I don't know if we want to trap them on the island with us," she said.

"It's 'them' now?"

"I don't know who or what or how many."

"The boat is too small for more than one."

"We need to be careful, Will. I don't want either one of us to get hurt."

"It's not so bad, Hannah, getting hurt. Thinking about it is worse. This is our island. We've got to defend it."

"It could be your father," she said at last.

Will paused. "No," he said finally. "He couldn't find this place in the fog. He wouldn't sneak here. He'd come with the police. The law is on his side."

"OK, we'll take the oars and go straight back to the house and call for help."

"We'll have to stop in the quarry and take the oars from our skiff, too. And the key to the outboard."

Will picked up the short aluminum oars and handed one to Hannah.

They cut back through the quarry. Hannah kept her eyes on its rim, sure that someone was watching them. It seemed a disadvantageous place to be. There was nowhere to hide with only water below and escarpments above. If someone kicked down the ladders they'd have a much longer walk to get out. Or they'd have to leave by water. Will pulled the skiff in from the mooring on a haulout. He pocketed the key and put the oars on his shoulder. Hannah thought about leaving in the skiff, but the water and the fog seemed doubly dangerous. They had no compass. She'd rather face the mole. They climbed out of the quarry and stopped. The field leading down to the house was white with fog. They stood quietly, listening.

"We need to get down to the house," Will whispered. "He could be going through it right now. We need to go now."

"OK," she said.

Halfway down the trail to the house, Hannah started beating the two aluminum oars together. The metallic ringing reverberated through the fog.

"What are you doing?" Will shrieked.

"If he's in my house, I want him out of it before we get there," she yelled. All the same, Hannah stopped clanging the oars. In the silence that followed, they heard footfalls, boots on wet dirt. Then Driftwood began to bark.

"C'mon," Will said. He threw his oars into the deep grass and began to run down the path to the house. The fog immediately swallowed him. Hannah ran, too, trying to look ahead, to stay focused on the swirling mist that was Will's wake. She heard him burst through the front door and caught him there, breathing hard in the living room. The fog came into the room behind them.

"I don't think he's been here," Hannah said.

"He's gone back to his boat. I thought I heard him running in front of us. He must have been running away. I've got to check my stuff." Will bolted up the stairs.

"I'm calling the sheriff and the Coast Guard," Hannah yelled. Before she found her cell phone, Will was back downstairs. He carried a sawed-off, double-barrel shotgun in his hands. He looked at her briefly, lowered his head, and left the house. She screamed after him. He'd disappeared by the time she made it outside, but she could hear him running through the grass. Somewhere up on the heights of the island, the dog was barking. Her legs were so heavy. As she ran it seemed she had to breathe all the fog before her, make it pass through her body before she could proceed. Every spear of grass grabbed at her shoelaces. The air was as dense as the pages of a bible. She knew the shortest route to the blue dinghy lay through the stand of spruce. She knew Will would know this, too. But the fog put her fifty feet off course and she had to go around an outcropping of granite. Even in the middle of the island it was covered with the bleached and eviscerated remains of crabs. A seagull screamed above her head and she ducked as she ran. In the woods at last, it seemed as if all the trees ran with her, as if everything on the island, the brush and grass and lichen, the stones themselves, was rushing toward the little blue boat. Driftwood began to bark furiously and then howled, as he'd once done at the sun in a fog, confusing it for the moon. The last twenty yards were through a dense growth of rugosa roses. She fell twice but never stopped moving forward as she was going downhill now. Will caught her with one hand as she burst out onto the smooth ledges of rock above the water. His face and arms were scratched and bleeding, too. The dinghy was gone from its hiding place. Driftwood was in the water, swimming back toward them.

"There he goes," Will said, pausing between each word for breath. The boat and its lone occupant were at the farthest extent of her vision. He wore a dark shirt and faded jeans, a ball cap. She couldn't see his face. He was in the bow of the dinghy, hunkered forward, paddling the boat canoe style with the scooped blade of a short-handled shovel. Will let go of Hannah's arm. She put both hands to her brow to block out the harsh glare of the sun reflecting off the atmosphere.

"We could take the skiff and catch him," Will said.

Just then they heard the deep muffled thrum of a diesel engine open up in the channel, but they couldn't see the larger boat.

"He's got a partner," Hannah said flatly. Then the dinghy was gone, too, dissolving into more fog.

The blast of the shotgun almost knocked her off the slab of granite. She crouched as closely to the earth as she could and covered her head. Will stood above her, the gun at his shoulder pointing up into the fog. A moment later he let go the round in the second chamber, and the flash in the fog turned his face the color of raw yellow wood. Hannah's lower lip began to tremble. The dog tucked his tail between his legs and ran toward home. Will followed the blast of the gun and its smoke a few feet farther, till he stood at the very margin of the sea. She could barely make out, through the ringing in her ears, his shout. He yelled across the water, "Remember the Alamo!" He stood there, seemingly waiting on a response, smiling. The larger boat gunned its engine. Moments later its wake reached Will's feet and he turned to Hannah, grinning.

She didn't smile back.

He shrugged his shoulders, as if to say, "What?"

She pushed herself up from the rock, queasy and disoriented. The noise of the gun still filled her skull. She walked slowly toward him. He was as handsome as she'd ever seen him, a pink scrape below his eye, another bleeding cut on his cheek. She took his free hand and gripped it firmly and with her other hand slapped him across the cheek and its running cut. He tried to jerk his hand from hers then, but she wouldn't let it go. Tears started to form in his eyes and she said, "Don't ever scare me like that again." Her own eyes started to burn.

"You can't hit me," he said, leaving his mouth open. "You can't hit me." He tried to wipe his cheek with his forearm, but the muzzle of the gun bumped into Hannah's side. She flinched at the heat of the barrel. With the heel of her hand she pushed the gun out of the way and brought him close, hugged him. She rubbed the tear and blood off his cheek.

"I'm sorry," she whispered.

"I don't want you to hit me anymore."

"I'm sorry. I'll never hit you again. It was the gun. I've never been close to one that went off." She wetted her thumb on her tongue and washed his cheek.

"It's for my dad."

"No, it's not. It's mine now." She let go of him and took the shotgun.

"It won't go off again, will it?" She held it away from her body, at arm's length.

"No, it only has two shells," he said. "I was just trying to tell them not to come back. It's your island. People will take your stuff if you let them."

"Come on, let's go back to the house. This isn't the Alamo. Everybody there got massacred, didn't they?"

"Yeah, that's what I'm trying to tell you. At least now they know we've got a cannon," Will said.

"Yeah, now maybe they'll bring back an army."

"We need reinforcements."

"This island is full," she said.

🐚 🐚 🐚

She felt it would be ridiculous to call the Coast Guard or the sheriff to tell them she'd had a trespasser. The summer brought thousands of boaters to the archipelago. The islands saw trespassers every day. Few of them meant any harm.

For the rest of the weekend, Will acted as if the slapping hadn't happened. Hannah put the gun in her closet. She asked him for the shells and he gave them to her as well. On Sunday evening she apologized again. "I'm sorry. It was done before I knew it. I was so mad at you for having the gun. And you scared me when you chased after them. I was just starting to breathe again when you fired. If there'd been someone else there to hit you, I would have let them do it, but there was only me. I was afraid you'd fall in the water after I hit you so I held onto your hand. I don't ever want you to put yourself in harm's way like that again."

He touched the cut on his cheek. "So I should stay away from you," he said.

Hannah paused. "That's not what I meant, but you could be right."

"It didn't hurt," he said.

"It hurt me. It still hurts. I'm sorry."

"If you hit me again, I'll leave," he said. He'd been looking away, but he turned back to her when he said this, to make sure she understood.

Hannah nodded. "OK, that's fair. And if you touch that gun again, I'll kick you off the island."

He nodded. "It was my dad's gun. I couldn't get it in my suitcase so I sawed off sixteen inches of the barrel. I left the piece of barrel on his kitchen table so he'd know I had the rest of it with me, so he'd know I was serious about leaving."

"What is it about you Texans and guns?"

"It's just a hunting gun, for dove and quail."

"It's for knocking birds out of the sky?"

"Uh, yeah."

"It'd be less horrible if you described it as a gun for killing people," she said.

"Do people become artists when they decide to hate everything else?" Will asked her.

"No."

"It's like you think the only honorable life is locking yourself up and gluing shit together."

He frowned and looked beyond her to the window, then brushed past her as he walked toward it. She was so furious she didn't turn to watch him. Suddenly he was behind her. His arms wrapped around hers, and one palm bumped across her breast as he locked his hands. He lifted her off the floor and set her back down. She struggled, but he was laughing. He asked her, his laugh hot in her ear, "Would it have been better if I'd said, 'gluing poop together'?" Then he jumped back, let out a whoop, and ran out the door. Before she could catch him, the fog had swallowed him whole, everything but his fading giggle.

In the morning the fog still clung to the island. The only place they could see twenty feet unhindered was across the living room and into the kitchen. When she saw he'd put on his work clothes, she said, "You can't go to work today."

"Why not?"

"You can't see from one end of the skiff to the other, Will."

"I can make it from island to island. I'll go slow. There's been fog before."

"Not like this fog. No, you'll just go in circles. Everything's different in the fog. I've brought the compass in from *Break of Day*. You need to learn to navigate with it and a chart and your watch."

"Do you know how?"

"Yes."

"Then go with me today."

"No. I'll show you and you can practice on a clear day. Besides, that boat could be out there in the fog. They have radar and we don't. It wouldn't be anything for a lobster boat to cut you in half, especially since they probably think you've been shooting at them."

"You couldn't keep me here if I wanted to go," he told her.

"Don't be a child about this."

"They expect me at work. Everyone else will be there. I have a job."

"I'll call in for you."

"Why won't you go with me?"

"Because I won't."

"You haven't been off the island since I got here, Hannah."

"I don't like to leave. But I'll go in with you on the first clear day. I want to look for that blue dinghy."

"I can't stay here every time it's foggy. School starts in a week. I'll have to be able to go."

"You can go in the fog when you learn how."

"I won't be afraid to live here," he said. "Teach me how to navigate."

They sat at the kitchen table. The fog made the room dark. Rather than run the generator, Hannah lit an oil lamp and used it to hold down one of the corners of the rolled chart: *Approaches to Blue Hill Bay*. The chart was foxed and stained. Coffee rings bit at each corner. She'd retrieved it from the overhead rack on *Break of Day*. Black mold clung to the outer edges.

"This chart is forty years old," Will complained.

"The rocks haven't moved," Hannah replied. "This chart will be good till the next ice age. Sit down."

He sat down, sighed, put his hand in his hair.

She looked up. "OK, so you're good at school. This is more important than that. Everything you've learned, you only learned so you can learn this. That's what my great-uncle Arno told me when he sat me down here to learn this. It may sound like math but it's really your life, OK?"

"Yes, teacher."

"God, how did Emily stand it?"

"What?"

"I mean, if you were one of the smart ones."

"Well, she didn't invoke the 'Great-Uncle Arno, Knower of All Things' ghost. OK, I'm sitting still and I don't have any gum in my mouth. Teach me. I'll be better at it than you in a month." He folded his hands on the chart and looked down at the parallel rule, the pencil, the dividers. As she began to explain the compass rose, she reached across and covered his clasped hands with her open palm and let her fingers drift down slowly over his, as though she were covering the mouth of a jar. He did not move his hands again till she asked him to measure the distance between Ten Acre No Nine and the mainland.

🐚 🐚 🐚

She hadn't called, but later that afternoon a Coast Guard officer knocked on the door. Hannah and Will were both startled. The dog barked. It was the first time someone had knocked on the door all summer. Hannah looked out the kitchen window before opening the door. It was odd to see him standing there in a uniform with a clipboard in his hand, encircled by a thick fog, as if he'd materialized from it. Even Driftwood seemed confused. Soon she realized another man stood ten feet back, the button on his leather holster popped open.

"I'm sorry to bother you," the officer said and introduced himself. "We're investigating a report of shots fired a couple days ago in your area." His uniform was so crisply starched, so white, it seemed brighter than the fogged sun. He put his cap under his arm as he spoke to her, clamping down on it tightly as if it might squirm free. He stood as square and solidly before her as a new refrigerator.

"Reported by who?" Hannah asked.

"A group of kayakers off Spruce Island. They were peppered by shot-gun pellets. No injuries. They thought the pellets were falling from the sky. They heard two blasts immediately prior."

"We heard them, too," Hannah said. She turned to Will and Drift-wood, as if the dog had to be hushed as well as the boy.

"Could you tell where they came from? One of the islands, a boat?"

"Foggy," Hannah said, and nodded toward the fog. "It could have come from anywhere."

"Do you own any weapons?" he asked.

"Yes," Hannah said. "I'll get it." She turned and looked at Will. She pointed toward the kitchen table. "I want you to figure a bearing from the west end of Devil Island to the southern end of Camp Island, figure the distance, and then how long it should take you to make that dis-tance at six knots." She walked across the room and went upstairs. When she came back down, Will was at the table working. She handed Arno's old deer rifle to the officer. He slid open the bolt.

"Did you know there's a cartridge here? It's frozen in the chamber."

"Yes. It was my great-uncle's gun. That bullet's probably been in there for twenty years or more."

"It might be safest to leave the bolt open until you get that out of there." He handed the rifle back to her. "Do you have any other weap-ons?" he asked.

"No," she answered.

"Thank you. If you hear or see anything that might help, give us a call. The kayakers think the shots came from a lobster boat. The boat came through their group pretty quickly. The speed and the fog didn't let them get a good look at it, but it was towing a small blue tender."

"If you find out who they are, I'd like to know," Hannah said. "I've had some trespassing problems."

"Any losses or vandalism?" he asked.

"No, just digging. Somebody's digging holes on the island."

"Well, a little clamming . . . "

"It's not clamming. They're digging on high ground."

"For?"

"I don't know."

"Truffles?" he smiled.

"I don't think so."

"Maybe they're taking young trees."

"No, sometimes the holes are in the middle of the field or in my garden."

"Hunh. Would you like me to have the sheriff come out and take a report?"

"I already did that several years ago."

"They've been digging that long? Maybe they're looking for artifacts, Indian artifacts, or bottle dumps, old bottles."

Hannah shrugged.

The officer shrugged. He seemed to defrost with the termination of his duties. His shoulders rounded and his jaw became slack. The man behind him clipped his holster down. Off in the fog, a radio chirped. The officer leaned around Hannah and spoke to Will. "Don't forget to allow for current, young man." He smiled.

Will said, "Yes, sir."

"My gosh, where are you from, son?"

"Texas, sir."

"Me too. Grew up on shrimp boats and the Coast Guard has me up here freezing to death." He leaned back and smiled again. "Call if we can be of any service, ma'am."

"I will," Hannah answered.

They moved off through the fog toward the boat shed. When they'd completely evaporated, Driftwood barked once.

"Shh," Hannah said.

Will came up behind her again. "You didn't have to lie for me," he whispered.

"I think they would have called it reckless endangerment and you would have been back in Texas inside of forty-eight hours."

Hannah closed the door. Driftwood sat halfway up and barked again, only once. Just as he did, a little turd shot out about two inches onto the wood floor. He curled around and sniffed it, snorted the smell out of his nostrils. Then he sniffed it again. Satisfied, he lay back down and closed his eyes.

"It's your turn," Hannah told Will.

The retaliatory gunfire came two weeks later, a few days after Will started school. They were sound asleep, but the first bullet woke them both. It tore through the bottom of the front door and splintered the sixth riser of the staircase. The second shot shattered a pane in the kitchen window and exited the house just below the ceiling cove molding. The reverberation of the rifle fire hung over the house for moments afterwards like prelude rather than echo, as if it were lightning and thunder was yet to come, or as if some great tree had broken and was still falling toward the earth. Will called her name calmly, and when Hannah didn't answer he was at her door and then at her bedside.

"Listen," she said from her bed.

"What?"

"Listen."

"Can I get my gun?"

"No, they're not here. They're out in the bay, on a boat. Can you hear the engine?"

"No."

"It's very soft. They know we can't see them. It's too dark, no moon. They're just idling away, waiting to see if we turn on the lights. I wish you'd make a smaller target of yourself."

Will squatted next to the bed. "How many shots did you hear?"

"Two. That's how many you shot at them. Eye for an eye."

"Jesus, don't they know the difference between a shotgun and a rifle at distance?" he asked. "I'm going downstairs and call for help."

"No," Hannah said. "No more police or Coast Guard." She got out of bed. She knew it would startle him, watching her cross the room in a T-shirt and panties to her robe on the back of the door, even as dark as it was. "It's just two shots from sea," she said. "They're too afraid to come ashore. It was just revenge. Let them have it. I don't want to risk losing you."

"I wasn't going to call the Coast Guard," he said.

He followed her downstairs, where they both stopped suddenly when the dog whined. Driftwood was standing at her knee, shivering.

"Is he OK?" Will asked.

She bent down and brushed his fur with her hands, moving over his back, along each side and down each leg. There was nothing too warm, too liquid.

"He's just afraid," she said.

"I'm going to call Zee," Will said.

"It's three-thirty in the morning."

"She only lives a block from Stonington Harbor. She could go down and see if any boats come in during the next few minutes."

"That boat isn't going back in. It's going out for the day. You can't include her. You can't include anyone. This has got to be between us and them. Whatever it is they want, they can have it."

Early that morning they strung twine from the bullet-entrance holes to the staircase and molding. Both trajectories pointed toward open water, perhaps a couple hundred feet off the granite pier and boat shed.

"They almost came right up in our front yard and shot the house," Will said.

When he left for school that morning, she told him, "Not a word."

Will turned to the dog, who was already moving up the path toward the quarry, and told him, "Not a word."

She watched them both till they fell over the rim of granite. The dog would be back as soon as Will's skiff was out of sight. She could see more than a dozen boats from her stoop, each of them busily working their traps, as disinterested in her as bees. It was maddening. She knew the only thing hidden on this island was its future, an artist's vision. What could she have, what could Arno have had, that would drive some

lobsterman to risk murder? The only thing she could think of was the
island itself. But to steal it a bucket of earth at a time? A glacier moved
more quickly.

🦞 🦞 🦞

Twice during the early fall they put a second life jacket in Arno's skiff
and searched for the blue tender. Will already knew that it did not live in
Stonington Harbor. Almost all the lobstermen there docked their service
boats at the commercial pier and he'd never seen it there or at Billings in
Allen Cove. But there were literally hundreds of other coves and inlets
on Deer Isle or Isle au Haut where it could hide. They took a picnic and
searched during the middle of the day, when they'd find dinghies in plain
view, on moorings, rather than at a dock or pulled up on a beach.

September was her favorite month, when the islands still held their
summer warmth, but most of the tourists and their yachts were gone.
The very air was ripe, so crisp that the wind cracked on her nose. She
wanted to pick up everything and rub it on her cheek, spruce needles
and maple leaves, stones from the beach. The seagulls by this point
seemed to have learned to rest on drafts of warmth; flight looked little
more stressful than sleep. With every breath she tried to store heat like a
stone, to cache memories of basking like acorns. It was strange that the
air could approach body temperature and the ocean be so unaffected.

She was nervous about going out with Will. It was the first time she'd
been in such a small boat without a definite destination in years. He was
eager to have her aboard. With all her longing she wanted control of the
tiller, but found a way to thwart herself by holding the field glasses, using
both hands to survey the horizon. As long as the boat was moving, lacer-
ating the surface and its ability to reflect, she was fine. Only in the calm
inlets, when they were surrounded by their own images, did she feel as
if she were being watched. Will wanted to turn off the engine in tidal
coves and let the skiff drift while they had their lunch, but she couldn't
abide this. They beached on deserted peninsulas of rock and shell and
ate onshore, feeding the crabs and gulls with their scraps.

On one Saturday they searched all of Southeast Harbor and Greenlaw Cove. On another they worked the western inlets of Deer Isle: Burnt, Crockett, and Goose coves, Southwest Harbor, Smalls Cove, and Northwest Harbor. Late in September, after school had begun, they took a Sunday to Isle au Haut, motoring slowly through Burnt Island Thorofare to Moore's Harbor and Head Harbor and around the high island itself. They tucked behind York Island, raising the engine twice to scrape over rockweed-shredded ledges. There were too many places to look, among the Merchants themselves, west to Vinalhaven and North Haven, east to Swan's Island, through Casco Passage to Blue Hill Bay.

Perhaps the little boat had even been sunk, since they knew she knew what it looked like. It certainly didn't seem like a boat in regular service anyway, so overgrown and weathered, as if it had been used for a mooring ball, a float to mark the location of something below.

But she enjoyed the time with Will. He seemed pleased when she chose a direction. He'd come to operate the skiff with skill, entering shallow water cautiously. The day never seemed long enough for him, although he allowed each moment its full breath. The name of every bird seemed important and no wave existed separately from the ones around it, his hull, or the look on his face. The blue tender was their white lobster. Whether it existed any longer was unimportant. She knew when she was eighty, and Will was approaching retirement in some distant city, she'd write him to say she was still looking for the weathered blue tender in hopes of finding something she'd once lost.

🐚🐚🐚

For her November exhibition at Gwen's gallery, Hannah began a series of new paintings. She painted only the shadows of things. The series began with tabletop arrangements under strong light, objects whose shadows made them easily recognizable. She proceeded to the shadows of mullions across the carpet, the shadow of the house across grass. From there the simple rich color of shadow took control, the casting form indiscernible. Swathes of blue impasto swept across the canvas in waves of darkness, deepening in black pools that cowered at the margins of the panel, where a faint red light seemed to pulse at the end of brush strokes. She tried to paint the dark areas of a radar screen, just as the sweep blinked out.

☙ ☙ ☙

Through the fall she made her usual preparations for winter. Full propane tanks were delivered, along with several cords of wood. Will carried and dragged all the driftwood they'd collected from the quarry and the seaward beaches up to the house and cut it to stove length. Full of salt and pockets of seawater, this wood hissed and popped when it burned, spit out storm fumes and squalls of green flame. She ordered in extra canned goods, and beans and rice and flour in bulk. She stocked new brushes, extra paint, glue, linseed oil, rolled canvas. She winterized the engine and winch at the crest of the quarry. Never able to suffer stapled plastic over her windows all winter, she and Will screwed large sheets of clear Plexiglas over the entire window frame. The house didn't breathe anymore, but it stopped the incessant whistling and rattling of the sashes in winter winds. When Will saw her order a case of flashlight batteries, he asked, "Does the ocean freeze over?"

"Of course not," she answered. "At least not since I've been here. There's pictures of people walking from Stonington to Crotch Island though, in years past."

"How cold is it going to get?"

"Not as cold as it does inland. The ocean moderates the weather. Unless there's a hurricane."

"It just seems so placid now," Will said.

"I know. It's not the cold, Will. It's the wind and cold and the dark."

"When the winter starts," he said, "I always think of the calves born in the spring. I know they can't understand what winter is. They must think their whole world is collapsing."

"No, they don't. Mom is still there."

"If they're lucky."

"What happened to your mom?" Hannah asked. She was gluing leaves to an oblong stone, layer after layer, leaves from the single oak on the island. It was the only tree that seemed to participate in fall. She didn't look up at him when she asked. He was across the room at the kitchen table, writing a classification essay on toothpicks.

He answered her by saying, "I've got the flat, utilitarian toothpicks, useful for building forts and other crafts. And the frilly, skirted toothpicks, to make unsavory burgers look savory. The common pick, for dislodging food. And colored toothpicks for cheese and meatball parties."

"There's flavored toothpicks to use in place of after-dinner mints," Hannah suggested.

"That's good. I'll use that."

"My mother died when I was seventeen," Hannah said. "She was a drunk. I was old enough to know better, but I still felt like she abandoned me. I thought I was prepared for the world but I wasn't."

"I'm sorry," he said.

"You had nothing to do with it."

"I can still be sorry."

"I don't need or want your pity. I've got my art. It heals everything." She pressed the midrib and veins of each leaf down with her index finger, then used a bone to press flat the interstices. Each leaf overlapped the next. There were so many layers, and the binder she was using so pliable, that the stone within its cocoon shifted when moved as if it were alive.

"She left me with him," he said finally. "When I was seven. I haven't seen her since."

"Did he beat her, too?"

"I don't know."

"Are you mad at her?"

"No. Yes. I mean, I wish she'd taken me with her."

"It's going to get cold this winter," she told him. "But not so cold that we can't survive."

"You're not so different from your sister," he said. "She believes in Jesus and you believe in art."

"Art's got a longer track record. And I don't just believe in art. I believe in my art. And enough other people believe in it for me to make a living. What do you believe in?"

"I believe it's going to get cold."

She didn't respond, but listened to his pencil on the single sheet of paper. It was like a dry leaf sliding slowly down a tin roof.

He looked up later and asked, "Would you say the flavored toothpick is the peak of toothpick technology?"

"I wouldn't say it three times fast," she said.

Then, while she was smiling, he told her, "Zee invited me to the Homecoming Dance. It ends pretty late, so her dad said I could spend the night at their place."

She was going to title the piece *"Leaf Borne Rock."* She first came to the idea when she noticed that the oak tree had picked up a fist-sized stone in the crotch of a branch and carried it six feet above the planet. She knew that years from now, the leaves in her sculpture would decay and the binder weaken. The stone would eventually split free and fall to the earth. The time between now and that event was what she was selling.

"That sounds fun," she told him.

"I haven't said I'd go, yet."

"You know she likes you."

"I don't like the idea of leaving you out here alone."

"I'm alone all day."

"But not at night."

"Will, I was here for six years before you arrived."

"It's so hard to believe, though," he said. "It's hard for me to believe that you existed before I came here."

"That's a rather self-centered view of the world. Just go to the dance."

"You could go, too, if you wanted. Zee's dad is going to be a chaperone. They were asking for more chaperones. All the parents are going to make us breakfast at midnight."

"I think I'll pass."

"You wouldn't have to dance."

"I can dance."

"Do you want to read my essay?"

"Sure."

He gave her the three handwritten pages. She rested them against the leaves while he walked to the window and looked out into the darkness.

"There's only one 'l' in 'utilitarian'," she said, without looking up.

He answered, "If the ocean froze over between here and the mainland, would we own the ice to the midpoint of the channel? Would we even be an island anymore?"

She didn't know what to say at first, but finally hit upon, "There is no way on earth I'm old enough to be your mother. I'm going to bed."

☙ ☙ ☙

Dear Hannah,

Another letter to you to inquire about Will. I hope he is at home in his new school. I still see his father quite often. I have tried to console him by saying that Will soon will be eighteen, and will be his own man anyway. He has asked God for forgiveness. I find myself tortured at times by my part in all of this. This man seems to be sincerely grief-stricken, and worried night and day about Will's welfare. Does Will, too, have second thoughts about leaving his father? I feel like an adulterer, a home breaker. The solace I offer this man seems petty and hypocritical. Perhaps this long break has lessened the danger to Will. His father offers apology after apology to his sisters and brothers, to his church and God, but cannot reach the one person he wishes to prostrate himself before. Every week he leaves for a day or two and drives to distant cities to look for Will. Each day he is more hopeless than the last. I have not forgotten, however, the bruises on Will's back and arms, his silences. But was the relationship hopeless? Have we made it so? This father's tears have fallen on my hands and with them I grasp yours. I leave it to you whether to speak to Will.

Your sister in Christ,
Emily

Emily,

    This man's wife left him. Now his son has left, too. If he's remorseful, he deserves to be. Will is wonderful. He's happy and doing well in school. If he wanted to return, he could. You worry me with your pity. Hold your tongue.

    Hannah

Hannah, as usual, sent the letter in another package for Gwen to mail, so it would carry a New York postmark.

๛ ๛ ๛

The night of the Homecoming Dance Hannah worked late, packaging her paintings and sculptures for delivery to the gallery. She cut foam to fit closely around each object, and used flotsam for crating, completing a cycle of cargo lost and found. The knock of the hammer and stroke of the handsaw added notes to Mahler's Fifth Symphony, which played loudly on the boom box. She swung the canvases and larger boards around the room and into place in a traditional choreography, a rite of spring and fall. The seasons had produced another crop of art. She swung the paintings as if they were caught in wind, as helpless before it as leaves. Rectangular shadows warped into trapezoids and parallelograms on the walls as she spun and dipped. The flames in half a dozen lamps flickered as each work of art cartwheeled overhead, and windows caught a revolving reflection of canvas and flesh, paint and shirt, image and eye. I can dance, she thought. This is dancing. She looked at each piece one last time before nailing it into the dark. At midnight she made herself sausages and eggs and had them with half a bottle of red wine. She went to bed at three, leaving the lights burning, and didn't wake till noon, when she felt Will's hand on her shoulder.

"Don't you want to see me in my tux, Hannah?" he said, leaving his hand on her shoulder.

He was back. He'd left for school the morning before with his tuxedo in a plastic bag.

"I have Polaroids, too, of me and Zee. They took them at the dance."

When she sat up in bed, dragging the quilt over her groin and legs, the ax at the back of her brain sliced all the way through and lodged between her eyes. She put her hands on her forehead to keep the blade inside her skull.

"What?" Will asked.

"Headache."

"Do you want something?"

She looked up. He was still in his tuxedo, black with a white shirt and red cummerbund. He backed up and twirled. She lowered her head quickly.

"You're a stud," she said.

"Do you want to see the pictures?"

"Maybe in a little while."

"Do you want some aspirin or something?"

"No. I think I'll just lie here a little while longer."

"Gosh, Hannah, who's in high school here, me or you?"

She frowned at him. She'd used that line on her own mother once.

"OK, I'll shut the door."

"You're a stud, my Will."

He closed the door. Jesus, she thought. He looks twelve years old in that monkey suit. Christ, my head hurts.

❦ ❦ ❦

In the fall the scattered blueberry bushes on the island rose up like isolated outbreaks of fire, burning scarlet among the rocks. It took weeks for them to burn out.

After she'd followed a wooden crate, floating ten feet offshore, a third of the way around the island, she cut back across the meadow for rubber waders and a boathook. The water wasn't much colder in the fall than it was in the summer, but the air was. She didn't want to get wet again. Will followed her, without asking why. It wasn't the usual smashed lobster crate. This box still had a lid, and rode the waves fully half out of the water. He let her wade in and reach out, drag and spin the crate into the beach. There were no markings on the unusually white wood.

"It's heavy," Will said. "How can it be so heavy and still float?"

"Fat people float," Hannah said. She inserted the blade of her pocket-knife under the lid, perhaps a quarter-inch thick. It pried up easily. Inside were twelve smaller crates covered with plastic mesh, Clementines from Spain.

"Oranges," Will said.

"Sixty pounds of oranges," Hannah said.

"We're saved. No scurvy this winter," Will said.

"Oranges float," Hannah said, as if it were a new scientific discovery.

She cut through the mesh and they each took an orange the size of a plum in their fists. They peeled as easily as candy bars, the skin brilliantly pungent as it was torn. Each orange wedge fell from the other like lips parting.

"Do you think they'll be salty?" Will asked.

Hannah placed one on her tongue. It had the same texture as skin, as a nipple before it hardens. She bit across its full length and immediately had to hold her cheeks to her teeth with her hand.

"What?" Will asked.

Her jaw wanted to break away from her skull. It was like color in her mouth, a deep expanse of pure color straight from a new tube of paint. It was so surprisingly sweet, so orange, that she felt it was the first time she'd tasted an orange, finally understood what all the fuss was about. She took her hand from her mouth and told Will, "This is the best orange I've ever had in my life."

"No way," he said.

She put four wedges into her mouth at once. Why not? She owned sixty pounds. The juice rolled over her lips and down her chin. After she'd swallowed and wiped her face, she said, "This is a gift from the Gods."

Will put a wedge in his mouth and smiled. He put in others.

"It's hard to believe, isn't it?" Hannah asked.

"Let's carry it to the house," he said. "We won't tell anyone about it."

They hadn't gone twenty feet before she caught his eye with her full gaze and asked, "Do you remember when we found the oranges, how sweet they were, how good, just us?"

❦ ❦ ❦

By late November, Will had spent several nights at Zee's house, when the water was too rough to return to the island after school. He slept on the couch in the living room of their small home.

"Doesn't her father mind?" Hannah asked.

"Why should he?"

"Well, you and Zee."

"We're just friends. He doesn't mind. He likes someone being there with Zee."

"I don't understand. He's not there when you sleep over?" Hannah asked.

"He's there when we're sleeping. But he has a second job and he doesn't get home till midnight some nights. He does maintenance at school."

"Maintenance?"

"He's a janitor. He does the floors three or four nights a week."

"And then lobsters at five in the morning?"

Will nodded. "He's not having much success. He still hasn't found a good boat he can afford."

"So you and Zee are there alone till midnight sometimes?"

"We're not alone. There's the two of us."

"I got that part."

"We've got three classes together. We study."

"You ought to get some of that, Will. She's pretty."

"Christ, Hannah, it's none of your business."

"Well, what's wrong with her?"

"Nothing's wrong with her."

"Then, what's wrong with you?"

"I can't talk to you about girls. There's nothing wrong with me. My father was always telling me who and who not to like, too. I like who I like."

They were sitting on the sofa in front of the woodstove. Will faced the grating, his legs crossed and stretched out toward it. Hannah sat on the cushion next to him, her legs drawn up beneath her.

"He tried to tell you who to date?"

"He told me who to see and who to stay away from. Some of the fights started that way."

He was throwing bits of bark into the fire.

"You always lost the fights," Hannah said.

"Always. But just the fist part. The fist part always started because I'd already won the word part."

Hannah turned her body to him, and clasped her arms around her own torso.

"You don't want Zee because you like me," she said simply.

He turned to her, waited a moment, then said, "I couldn't believe how much you look like your sister."

"What does that have to do with anything?"

"I was in love with her, I guess, and so was my father."

Hannah pushed herself up from the couch slowly.

"She's only eight and a half years older than me," Will explained. "She's you, but years younger."

She turned back to him from the foot of the stairs. "Wait a minute. You're not here because you and your teacher, you and my sister, had . . ."

"We didn't have anything," Will blurted. "It was my father. She liked my father. I told him to stay away from her. I knew how he'd treat her. And every time she refused his advances, I used to laugh at him. He'd come home all depressed and I'd laugh. She believes in being pure. She does. She's so beautiful, just like you, and he tried and tried to touch her. It made me sick. She'd chosen her life and he was trying to wreck it and I told him so. Every bruise I got I'd lift my shirt and show her. I'd go directly to her and lift my shirt. She was pure. She wasn't something to take."

"You left her with him then. Aren't you afraid for her, leaving her with your father?"

"I was, but she wanted me to go. I begged her not to send me away."

"Then why are you here?"

"Because she told me she loved me and she told me she loved him, too. I told you it made me sick. I mean, that she could love both of us. I was happy to go then. And now I've found you. I don't think about her anymore. I mean, I do but not in a way that makes me crazy."

"Will, I'm too old for you."

"I know that."

"You do, really?"

"Of course. Your sister has her religion and you've got your art. Neither of you needs anybody."

"Listen, I like you being here. I didn't think I would at first. But I do. And for some weird reason I get jealous. Jealous of Zee, and the people you worked with this summer, jealous of the island even because you like it so much, and now I'm jealous of my sister."

"It's weird," Will said. "People say stuff about you in town and I just want to cave in the side of their head. The harbormaster called you a New York Shewitch and Zee had to tell him to shut up before I killed him."

"Zee told him to shut up?"

"She says she has a sullen respect for you because I like you. She says y'all could be friends in another life."

"That's encouraging," Hannah said softly. She turned to him directly, "You sure are a messed-up kid."

"Takes one to know one."

🦢 🦢 🦢

Two days later, he asked her if Zee could come out to the island for the weekend. Her father was going up to Jonesport for the night.

"She could sleep in my room," Will said.

"And you'll sleep on the sofa, right?"

"Yes."

"Her father doesn't worry about you two at all?"

"He's as suspicious as you, but he said he'd rather Zee have sex than run away from home. Zee sure blushed."

"I just hope you're using condoms," Hannah said.

The blush on Will's face spread from the creases along his nose to his cheeks and forehead. It was the first time she'd seen him blush.

"Wow," Hannah said, "let me get my palette and try to match that."

"C'mon, Driftwood." He and the dog left the house at a run.

Zee's father brought her to the island. They motored into the quarry just after noon, as Hannah and Will fought the bark-stripped skeleton of a spruce onto a granite ledge. The root system, broad and flat, wouldn't allow them to slide the tree ashore. Zee and her father tied up the boat so they might help.

She'd seen him only through binoculars. It was odd to see him so close, life-size, as if he'd rushed up the long tube of a telescope. His long sleeves were buttoned at the cuff, but the steel hooks were plainly visible. His hair wasn't red, but he moved like Zee, the same gait of someone used to stepping over obstacles. There were wind channels across the skin of his face, and erosion where the sun ran into his eyes. Smooth, glossy pink areas at the tip of his nose and at the ball of each cheek seemed to have been left there by the constant nuzzling of a baby.

Hannah held to the branches of the driftwood tree so she wouldn't have to shake hands.

"Let me help," he said.

"Oh no, it's OK," she said.

But he reached down anyway, into the tangle of roots, and slipped both hooks into separate forks. Zee clasped a branch closer to Will.

"Altogether now," her father said, and they pulled the wet carcass up on the ledge. The trunk was moss slick, the roots strung with monofilament. Pot warp weaved through broken limbs like a yellow vine.

"There's an old warrior," Zee's father said. He slung the dripping water off his prosthetics and hid them in his pant pockets.

"Thanks, Mr. Eaton," Will said.

"Yes, thank you," Hannah added.

"Nothing to it. I'm glad we've finally met face to face. Will's told us lots about you. I'm Tom Eaton."

This was where he would have taken his hand from his pocket and offered it to me, Hannah thought.

"Hannah Bryant," she said, and wiped her own mucky hands on her pants, as if they were too dirty to shake anyway.

"Thank you for keeping Zinnia. I've got to go to Jonesport about a couple of boats. Ought to be back by tomorrow afternoon. I don't like her staying in the house by herself."

"Would you like to come up for some coffee, Mr. Eaton?" Will asked. Will looked at Hannah.

"No, I've got to get going. It's not a long drive but I've got lots to see."

Hannah put her own hands away, behind her back. "I'm sorry. At least Will knows how to be hospitable. I wanted to thank you for letting him sleep over, feeding him and everything."

He grinned at her. His face was so randomly creased and windburnt that his even, white teeth seemed incongruous there, like something manmade on a beach. His eyes were the same color as his hair, brown with flecks of gray at the temple and iris. He wore loose corduroy slacks and a blue linen shirt under a bone white jacket. He looked more like a pilot than a lobsterman and janitor. Hannah was cold, now that the wrestle with the dead tree was over. She zipped up her fleece coat. Driftwood had been working his way down from the rim of the quarry. He leaped off the last three-foot ledge and ran to Tom Eaton's crotch.

"Driftwood," Hannah snapped.

"It's all right," Tom said. He reached over Driftwood's back and picked up one hind foot. The dog immediately stopped sniffing and turned to find out why his foot was in the air. "Works every time. Dogs are never worried about being friends first. Takes a lot of courage. If you'll come get this foot, Ms. Bryant, I'll back away a bit."

Hannah stepped over and took Driftwood's foot. The metal of the hook was cold as the sea. The dog stood awkwardly between them, jerking on his leg.

"I wanted to thank you, too, for the return of my buoys," he said. "I didn't get much satisfaction from those boys. They denied cutting them loose."

"But . . ." Hannah said.

"I know they did it. I stopped losing so many buoys after I talked to them. That's how I know."

"Good," Hannah said.

Zee and Will were already climbing ladders out of the quarry. Hannah let go of the dog and he shot across the granite, taking the long route to catch Will at the rim.

"You be good," Tom Eaton yelled at his daughter.

"I'll be real good, Daddy," she sassed back and laughed.

He turned back to Hannah. "You see, she's left her books and home-work in the boat."

"I'll take them up," Hannah said.

"He seems like a good kid, your nephew."

"He's had some family problems, but I think he's OK, too."

She followed him back to the boat and took the canvas tote of Zee's books. As he untied the line from the rusty iron ring embedded in the granite ledge, he told her, "I know I'm not supposed to know, but I thought you might be interested. There's an old blue tender in one of the salmon pens off Pickering Island. Sits in there all the time. I think they feed from it. Arnold Johnson owns those pens. He's about a hundred. He says that tender goes missing from time to time but always comes home. Says it's the most loyal boat he's ever owned."

"Will must trust you," she said.

"He knows I despise pirates." He didn't lift his arm to wave at her as the boat pulled away, but simply nodded.

As she took the long way out of the quarry, she tried to reconstruct the visual memory of how he'd untied the line from the iron ring. The hooks separated and closed. He used the point to pick at the knot. It seemed to fall apart as if he'd been knitting and suddenly withdrew the needle. It made her shiver, the sudden thought of losing her own hands.

At the house she found the dog and a fresh turd on the kitchen floor.

Will and Zee's jackets straddled the back of the couch in an abandon of humping.

"Where are you guys?" she called.

"Up here," Will yelled. "We're studying."

Hannah put Zee's bag on the kitchen table and climbed the stairs slowly, stamping on each tread. Zee was sitting on the end of the bed. Will was at his desk, his hand lazing in the crotch of an open book.

Hannah folded her arms and leaned against the casement. "Wouldn't it be nice if Zee could follow along in her book?"

"Oh, shit," Zee said, raising her hand to her mouth.

"I brought them," Hannah said. "They're downstairs on the kitchen table, where you two are going to study this weekend."

She didn't wait to see if they'd come down. She picked up Driftwood's pellet in a wad of toilet paper and carried it and a shovel to a slight depression near the boat shed. Driftwood followed. The ground wasn't yet frozen. She scooped out a shallow divot, deposited the pellet, let the dog sniff her work, then she patted the ground back down.

"There's a little battle against time's erosion won, eh, Driftwood?" she said. "It'll take the wind a little longer to blow us away now, the sea a little longer to wash us down. We'll not be forgotten so soon."

She leaned the shovel against the cedar shakes of the boat shed. She had to lift the old door off the sill to open it. It was warmer inside. Driftwood scouted the perimeter, began biting barnacles off iron rails near the sea doors. He tested their hardness and was able to break down a few. The crunch of his canines on the shell made Hannah's teeth hurt. "Those are going to sting coming out," she told him. "Maybe you'll know when you're pooping now." He stopped chewing for a moment, as if to consider this, when a thin wave washed under the doors. As it retreated over the granite, the dog chased the sea back out of the shed. Then he waited, watching the bottom of the doors, for the wave to return. It came suddenly, swifter, and this time an inch high, wetting his paws before he could back away. He sniffed his feet, looked back over his shoulder at Hannah, and continued chewing the barnacles.

There was a row of Arno's old brown beer bottles, many still full, leaning against the windowpanes. The afternoon sun shot through the empties and made ochre patterns against *Break of Day's* hull. Inside each dark-rimmed bottle shadow, the light seemed to split into a multi-celled organism. She wondered if the old beer was any good. It was at least six years old. The silver labels that remained on the full bottles were tattered and dull. Cobwebs strung the gold caps. There were, what, seven full ones? If she drank all of them in a row, that would make her how drunk? She decided against it simply because she didn't like to pee every fifteen minutes. She'd spent twenty-five hundred dollars three years earlier on a gas toilet, had it and a sink and tub built onto the back of the house because she'd found herself in her midthirties peeing too often to walk out to an outhouse. How had Arno done it, winter and storm, summer and rain, holding his pee till he was almost ninety? The gas toilet incinerated its waste. Very little of what she ate and drank stayed on the island. Instead, the wind carried her away a little bit at a time. Not to say that she didn't have a pee on the foreshore every once in a while, when she was far from the house.

She climbed up into the stern of the boat. Flakes of rust and paint rained on the granite floor. Driftwood watched her climb, then settled down, chin to forepaws, to wait. She sat on the bare wood of the washboard, clasped her hands and pressed them between her crossed legs.

So Will had loved Emily. And he had loved her. And now he was in love with Zee. It was plain to see, and impossible to understand, how his affection was so embracing, so encompassing, and so malleable. His heart seemed to be so easily restored. She knew that she herself held grudges for years after the end of a relationship. She revisited diaries, letters, and even greeting cards in attempts not to understand old failures but to relive them. There was nothing to be resolved, no transforming catharsis in memory. Time did not heal old wounds. The hurt persisted, and like pearls, the pain survived deep in a center that had to be continuously swathed with yet another layer of forgetting that only soothed until the next remembering. The boy at Haystack, Mark, his name a crystal she cut her tongue on each time she said it. It was the first time in her artistic life that art seemed unimportant. She just wanted to bury her face in his neck and lie there forever. It was more important that she watch him create. And Jalendu, who was as lost in love as he was in New York, and who tried to hide from love and the city in her. How could you not love my sweet brother? It was easy not to love him. She had no other choice. After months of desperately trying to be in love with a man she admired, who made her laugh and cry with his tenderness, a man who found the world around him strange and mystifying and full of beauty, who regarded her as its zenith, she'd given up. "It's not that I don't want it to be there," she'd told him. "It simply doesn't exist."

"Perhaps it will be born later," he suggested.

And from that point on she could not meet his eye or hear his voice. It was all part of the world she already knew and did not need. When they separated she did not miss him. After he was gone, there were times when it was only as if he'd moved back home to India. He was safe, at home in his culture, surrounded by comforting, close reflections of his own face. "I will die if I cannot be with you," he said. And he did. And he was right about love, too. It was born later. She came to the understanding that this was a man who would have been a companion. There were worse things than being adored. She saw him in a glass of water, in puddles on the street, the rain sweeping down her windshield before she switched on the wipers. His sister came and took his remains back to their parents' home on a sandbar in the River Hooghli. Sitting there in the stern of *Break of Day,* she suddenly realized that both men, Mark and Jalendu, had lived on islands. It was troubling. Is that why she'd come here? Or was it only coincidence? Arno had left her an island, not a farm in Nebraska. In fact, she'd only moved from one island to another. Manhattan was an island, too. If you wanted to be direct about it, every land mass on earth was an island. The only thing that differentiated every human, every island dweller on the planet, was their individual distance from the water.

A flake of white paint, hanging from the pilothouse overhead, caught her eye. She took its edge between her fingertips and peeled it away from the layer of paint below it. It resembled a leaf. She looked down at the sole. More flakes had fallen there. She gathered them up and arranged them in her hand, and rearranged them, till they took on an aspect that pleased her.

🐚 🐚 🐚

The leaves' downward hurry left the sea's surface fall-spattered and tannin-drunk. Waves raked the leaves ashore and piled them in undulating winrows of color on the pink granite. There they dried and blew brittle across the island, cartwheeling in yellow and orange across brown spruce needles, screaming *do you see me?* Zee and Hannah and Will chased them out of the woods and into the tall grass where the leaves hung momentarily like shirts coming off hangers

"Why are we gathering leaves?" Will yelled, breathless.

"Because," Zee and Hannah yelled simultaneously, then looked at each other and dissolved into laughter. Zee's father hadn't found a boat in Jonesport, but had found a weekend job. She'd been spending all of her weekends on the island. By the time they'd run up to the graveyard, each had a fistful of maple leaves.

Will put his in their laps.

"But they're valuable, Will," Hannah said.

"Not to me."

"The maple leaves are the rarest. They have to come here in the current from the mainland."

"Just because something's rare doesn't make it valuable," he said, and sat down on the stonecarver's headstone.

Hannah turned from Will to Zee. She was looking at the boy as if he'd just outwitted Socrates.

"Don't let him sway you just because he's pretty," Hannah told her.

"But he's so pretty," Zee said.

Will smiled and held his arms out as if to say, "And here I am."

"Oh, God," Hannah moaned.

"The leaves are pretty, too," Zee said.

Will dropped to one knee in front of her. "But they're not prettier than me, are they?"

"Kick him now, while he's down," Hannah suggested.

Zee began to decorate his dark hair with leaves, sliding the stems behind curls. Hannah placed leaves on his shoulders like epaulets and in his shirt pockets like medals.

"Pretty is as pretty is," Hannah said.

"I'm going to get my camera and take a picture of him," Zee said.

"No, you're not," Will said.

"Yes, I am. I'm going to do a whole series of photos of you in leaves and moss and bark and brush for my art project."

"What art project?" Hannah asked.

"For school. In the spring we're having a big art show and auction to raise money for an art wing at the high school. You could donate something, Hannah. All the artists on Deer Isle are donating paintings and sculptures. Some of the teachers at Haystack are donating pottery and glass and baskets. We're going to have a kiln in the new wing and a print shop with presses and all kinds of neat stuff."

"When will it be built?" Hannah asked.

"We have to raise the money first."

"I could do something," Will said.

"But you guys are seniors," Hannah said. "You won't get to use it."

"No," Zee said. "But it's fun. The kids who use it years from now won't have had the chance to help build it, either. And they're going to have prizes at the art show."

"I could do something," Will said.

"What could you do?" Hannah asked. "There's been art supplies all over the house since you've been here. You've never touched them."

"I'll do some rock art like you," he said. "You know, stuff nobody can understand."

"Ha ha. I understand it," Hannah answered.

"You know, Hannah," Zee said, "most of the other artists on Deer Isle, they don't even know you're an artist. A couple of them have been to New York and seen your work, but most everybody in Stonington knows you say you're an artist, but that's all. I mean, you don't show or sell your art here."

"I have a relationship with a gallery in New York. They sell everything I can make."

"Still, you take all your materials and your inspiration from here. Seems like we should at least get a chance to see your work before it leaves forever."

"I'll think about it, Zee."

"I know what I'll do," Will said. "I'll take some of the island beach stones up to Ellsworth, to that tombstone-engraving place. I'll have him cut words into the rocks."

"They already do that," Zee said. "You can buy them at the Grasshopper Shop, little oval rocks with 'Peace' and 'Love' and 'Friendship' carved into them."

"I know," Will said, "but my rocks will say 'Bitterness' and 'Envy' and 'I'm only a rock' and 'Lie.'"

"Will," Zee said, and wilted.

"Lovely," Hannah said.

"You guys don't appreciate art," he answered.

"I'll come up with something, Zee. You put my name on the list," Hannah said.

"Great, now you guys are friends," Will said disgustedly.

"What's wrong with that?" Hannah asked.

"I've seen it before," Will said. "Now you'll stop talking to me. You'll talk to each other. You'll say things about me behind my back and go quiet when I come in the room. You won't let me be one of you, now that there's two of you."

"You're just the center of our world, Will," Hannah said, and reached over and put her hand on his cheek.

He drew back, stood up, and walked away from both of them. "Outcast," he said as he moved away. "Plague. War. Women."

🐢 🐢 🐢

By late November the mornings were so cold that vapor rose off the ocean's surface and it seemed the island was a peak rising above a vast expanse of clouds, the archipelago a mountain chain embedded in a thick winter. Above the white vapor, the sky was phthalo blue, ocean thinned with air. North winds blew pollution from Boston and New York far out to sea. Zee stood before windows in her pajamas on Sunday mornings and said, "I can see Nova Scotia," or "I can see Ireland."

"You can not," Will said from the kitchen table.

"Let me see," Hannah said and shouldered in beside her.

She'd heard them, the two of them the night before, downstairs. She could feel the house shift when Zee left her room. The stairs screamed, and she heard the dog lift his head. Then she could feel the weight of two on the couch as surely as if they were both on top of her own body.

Hannah put her hand on the small of Zee's back as they looked out. It was smooth and still warm. Will's hands were recently there. Her pajamas smelled of French toast. I don't have to let her stay, she thought. I don't have to let either of them stay. I've been alone in this house before. I shouldn't have to be alone in it with them living here. I pay for everything. It's my house. My work pays for everything.

"Look," Zee whispered to her, "it happens in an instant. The sea smoke is swirling up off the water. It turns into sky while we're watching. Nature just doesn't care. It will do anything in front of you."

"Why are y'all whispering?" Will asked. "Do you see a school of fish?"

"He loves fish," Hannah whispered.

"Why do men love to fish, Hannah?"

"Because when they catch a fish, bring it from the dark ocean into the clear day, it's like seeing a woman naked for the first time. But they get to do it over and over. They'll never see us naked for the first time again. Every nibble they get is like an electric shock of hope. There's something that's always been clothed and they're about to undress it."

"Maybe the fish likes it, too."

Hannah's voice rose, "Zee!"

"I'm fish-flopping on the bank in love," she whispered.

"You can't breathe, you mean."

"That too," she said.

Hannah didn't speak. She took her hand off Zee's back and leaned her forehead against the cold glass.

"What color is that sea?" Zee asked her.

"What do you see?" Will asked from the table, bread in his teeth.

"It's indefinable," Hannah told her. "I've tried to figure it out in paint for years. It changes. You can only paint it as it is in one moment, in shape and color."

"You could teach me how to paint," Zee whispered. "But I want to paint it as it is always."

"You have to pick a moment and let it stand for always."

"What should we call it, how the sea is? I just don't want to be forgotten."

Hannah put her hand on the girl's hip and brought it against her own. "I don't know," she said.

Zee put her forehead against the glass, too.

She suggested, "Cerulean blue? Sapphire blue? Denim blue? All those things change in light."

"The name of faith in color," Hannah said.

"Would you teach me how to paint?"

"I don't know how."

"Do y'all want to go fishing today?" Will asked. There was oatmeal in his mouth.

Zee spun from the window. "Sure," she said.

Hannah looked at her and smiled. "Yeah, me too."

🦋 🦋 🦋

"We've been invited to Thanksgiving," Will said. His boots were wet. He sat on the floor, just inside the door, pulling them off. They tumbled away from him like puppies pushed back.

"What?"

"Mr. Eaton invited us to his house. It will be him and Zee and you and me and Zee's grandpa from the nursing home."

"I can't go," Hannah said.

"It will be fun," he said. "Zee's grandpa is a hoot."

"I can't go," Hannah said.

"You haven't been off the island since the end of the summer."

"I know. That was enough."

"We'd go slow in the boat, just like last time when we were searching for the dinghy."

"We can't leave the island alone, unprotected. You go ahead."

"You know I won't do that. Please, please won't you come?"

"Will, I'm just not in the mood. I know you can't understand it, but it's real."

"Well, it's just stupid."

He didn't speak to her for the rest of the evening. The light coming out of his room, from the single oil lamp at his desk, created shadows only a degree lighter than night. Light seemed to shift into darkness as if it lived there. His sulk overwhelmed the house, ballooned and expanded till it filled every vacant space. It forced baseboards from the walls, distorted windowpanes, filled the very pores of her skin, her nostrils, her throat. When she opened the front door, it shoved her outside into the cold and kept pushing at her spine till she'd stumbled all the way to the shore, where water lapped at her feet.

She'd made friends with Zee, accepted Zee, wasn't that enough? It was true that she hadn't done it on purpose, hadn't sought out her friendship. But the girl kept telling her secrets and every secret she told made Hannah tend to like her more. She told them as if she had no clue they could come back to torture her. And now she was going to teach Zee to paint. Wasn't that enough? Did they have to include the father, too? He already knew too much.

The black water, overwhelming but finite, reflected an infinity of stars, about enough to fill a cup if she picked them from the sky. Constellations undulated before her; crabs and lobsters clawed at them from below. She knew she could not step from point of light to point of light. It was far too treacherous. The sea and heaven were too deep. She looked up and the stars floated there now, too, just at the surface of her pupils. They slipped into her irises and disappeared, but she was able to blink them back again. She was so mad that fear wouldn't subside permanently, that it came in and went out like the tide. It wouldn't relent to rationalism or be overcome with food or sleep. It couldn't even be satiated by a glut of itself. It held its own through hunger and sickness and wealth and success. It was useless to say, "Today I will not be afraid," because bravado was only a parasite, could not live without fear. When fear killed you, bravado slunk away to another host.

Whenever she came out at night she always heard someone rowing. This eternal rower rounded her island, again and again, always just out of view, dusk to dawn. His oars left a green phosphorescence at the limit of her vision. Occasionally the boat seemed to slash through rockweed, scrape across granite. The rower's boots clunked against the thwarts then, as he shifted his weight to slide over the backbone of the world. It's just waves, she thought. They'll never stop coming.

🐚 🐚 🐚

The night before Thanksgiving, Will dropped his books on the stairs and dragged a chair from the kitchen to her worktable.

"What?" she asked. As usual, he watched her work without commenting.

"I've done a bad thing," Will said.

"What?"

"We need to clean up the house."

"Why?"

"I invited Zee and the two Mr. Eatons to Thanksgiving dinner."

She put down her scissors and began to rub at the dried glue between her fingers.

"That's tomorrow, Will," she said.

"I know."

"I don't have any goddamn food. I just ordered a little turkey for you and me."

"They're going to bring a big turkey. I told them we could cook it here. They're bringing stuffing and rolls and beans. We're supposed to make potatoes and a pie and some squash."

"You're not kidding, are you? I can't believe you did this without asking me," she said.

"You might have said no," Will said.

"I would have said no."

"So I was right."

"Goddamnit, it's not funny."

"I wanted to have Thanksgiving with you and Zee. She wouldn't have it without her dad and grandpa. You wanted to have it with me. This satisfies everybody, if you can get over it not being your idea."

"Will, God bless it, I used to feel bad about slapping you, but sometimes you just deserve it. This isn't fair. Why should you get everything you want?"

"I brought home stuff to make a pumpkin pie and I bought yams and marshmallows to make the potatoes."

"Yams and marshmallows?"

"We already have brown sugar and pecans."

"For what?"

"To make sweet potatoes."

"What are the marshmallows for?"

"You put them on top and melt them into the potatoes." He looked down at his hands, as if he were ashamed he had to explain this to her.

"I hope we can find a recipe," she said.

"We can still have Thanksgiving and we won't leave the island unprotected."

"You've embarrassed me by telling them I wouldn't leave the island. They think I'm crazy."

"Everybody in Stonington already knows you're a hermit."

"My mother used to make me hermits," Hannah said.

"What's that?"

"A molasses cookie with raisins."

"It sounds like a cookie an old person would like. Maybe you could make some for old Mr. Eaton."

"Why is he in a nursing home? Is it safe for him to come out here?"

"He forgets things. His health is OK, but he almost burned down his house because he forgot the stove was on. He can remember your uncle Arno, though. Old Mr. Eaton was a lobsterman, too."

"What does he say about Arno?"

"Just that he knew him. It's hard to keep him on track and sometimes he can't tell who you are, but he can tell all kinds of stories from fifty years ago. Zee says he'll get a big kick out of coming here. He hasn't been on the water in years."

"I want to know how much Zee's father knows about us."

"What do you mean?"

"He knows about the blue tender."

"I told him. But not about the gun."

"Does he know you're not my nephew?"

"No, no one knows. I told them my parents are both dead."

"If we're going to have people here, I need to know that kind of stuff. Which one of your parents was my sibling?"

He looked at her, puzzled, then said, "Oh, I get it. Let's say you were my mom's sister. She died of cancer when I was five. My dad died in a car wreck, let's say two years ago."

"I can't be your mother's sister. You have my surname. I have to be your dad's sister. What were their names?"

"Real ones, or made-up ones?" he asked.

"Whatever you prefer, but you'll have to remember them."

"My mom's name was Melody. My dad's name is Merritt."

"How old is he?"

"Thirty-eight."

"So he was my older brother. I think we should steer clear of family talk."

"But what would Uncle Arno be to me?" Will asked.

"He was my great-uncle on my mother's side, so he'd be your great-great-uncle, your grandmother's uncle."

"So how did I get to Texas?"

"Uh, your dad moved there from New York."

"From New York?"

"Yes, my immediate family lived in New York."

"That's funny. He wouldn't like being from New York."

"He's dead. It doesn't matter."

"I wish he were dead."

"You're going to have to start moving away from that opinion."

"Why?"

"Because he may show up here someday and I don't want you to kill him. If it comes to that, let me do it."

"Why?"

"I'll be more professional than you."

"Sometimes you are the scariest person I've ever met."

"He's still looking for you. Emily says he's sorry."

"I don't want to hear any more. I've heard it all before, from the horse's mouth. She'll believe him."

"How do you know?"

"She wants to believe everybody's good. She thinks I'm good."

"Aren't you? I think that."

"You've changed your mind since I invited the Eatons to Thanksgiving?"

"Oh, you're right. C'mon." She stood up.

"Where?"

"You're going to learn to bake a pie tonight. So tell me, how many sisters does your father have now, how old are they, and why didn't you come here right after he died and was the car wreck his fault and why didn't you ever visit me before this year?"

Will stood up, too, followed her. "I won't invite anyone over again," he said.

"Every time they bring up family, you switch the subject to fishing," she said. She looked into the bag of groceries he'd brought home. All the dishes they'd be contributing were orange. If she boiled a Thanksgiving lobster, half the table would be orange. There were still over forty pounds of Clementines left, too. She could decorate with those and the maple leaves they'd chased down. The two chairs in the bedrooms would have to be brought down. She didn't have five matching plates.

🐚 🐚 🐚

"Dad, this is Arno Weed's niece." Tom Eaton took off his father's coat.

"Arno Weed?" Everett Eaton asked.

"Yes."

"Didn't know the son of a bitch had one."

"Now, Dad, no foul language today."

Tom guided the old man to a chair. He didn't seem so old, although Will had told her he was almost eighty. He walked fluidly. His skin seemed healthy and bright. But his eyes lived in his face as if they were constantly looking for a way out. Tom Eaton pointed him toward a chair, but he didn't seem to recognize what it was.

"You want me to sit here?" he asked.

"Yes, Dad."

"Grandpa, this is Hannah, and my boyfriend, Will," Zee told him.

"Oh yes, I remember Hannah," he said. He smiled and held out his hand.

She was perplexed. Did he remember her from the time she worked on Arno's boat? Then the old man dropped his eyes and she realized he'd learned to lie about his memory. It wasn't polite to forget someone and so he'd lied.

Driftwood was weaving in and out of the legs and swinging coats.

"There's that dog again, too," Everett said.

"You know my dog?" Hannah asked.

"No," he answered. "I just know it's a dog. He just squeezed off a round on your carpet."

"Oh, Driftwood," Hannah said. The dog crossed quickly to the rug near the stove.

"I'll get it," Will said.

"He's got a bowel problem," Hannah explained.

Everett Eaton's eyes went wide. "Not me!"

"No, Dad," Tom said, "the dog. Zee, you want to help me with the groceries? We've still got a couple of boxes left on the boat."

"I'll help," Will said. There was another flourish of coats, and the dog jumped back up to twirl in the swinging coattails and scarves.

Hannah found herself suddenly alone with the old man. His hair was shaved over his ears, but when he took off his cap a bird's nest sat there looking as it if had been blown out of a tree in a storm. It was the color of bird down mired in bird shit. She felt herself peering over the edge, trying to see if there were broken shells there.

"Would you like something to drink, Mr. Eaton?" she asked.

"You got a beer?"

"Wouldn't you rather have something warm? I've got coffee and tea. Maybe some hot chocolate?"

"I'll have a hot beer."

"I'm afraid I don't have any beer."

"This is Arno Weed's house." He said this as if he'd suddenly recognized it.

"Yes, it is."

"Ask him. He'll know where the beer is."

"I'm afraid he died six years ago, Mr. Eaton. I'm his great-niece. I live here now."

"Arno Weed dead?"

"Yes."

"I didn't know it."

"That's all right."

"Your dog broke one off right there on the carpet."

"Yes, Will cleaned it up."

"Who's Will?"

"My nephew."

"I have a son," he said.

"I know, Tom."

"He's passed his whole life without an opinion. Not one opinion. His name is Tom. I named him after my uncle Tom."

She sat down across the table from him. He seemed to have forgotten the beer. She thought she wouldn't offer him anything hot either, at least until Tom got back.

"It came right out of his ass," he said, "and fell on the floor. It's a good thing he don't wear clothes. Maybe he should start wearing clothes. Is that why we wear clothes?"

"It's cleaned up now," Hannah said.

"I've lived my whole life downwind of the flatulent. And I only pass my own gas when the wind isn't blowing. It lingers, you know. I never had good gas timing."

She found herself nodding. "Yeah, I know. Sometimes, it's best to just get up and walk away."

"That works," he acknowledged. He brought his hands up to his cheeks. His fingers were short, the nails thick and blunt. Each knuckle bore off at a different angle, leaving diamond-shaped gaps between his fingers where cigarettes and pencils might fit. "My face is cold," he told her.

"You've been outside."

"I know that. You're a good-looking woman."

"Thank you."

"That's all right. It didn't cost me anything to tell you that. I tell it to every woman I see. They all like it. Men like it, too. Every boat I ever bought came with a fog huddled permanent round the pilot house."

"You've had a hard life," Hannah said.

"I have. You aren't Martha Stewart, are you?"

"No."

"Who are you?"

"I'm Arno Weed's niece, Hannah."

"Didn't know the son of a bitch had one."

"You didn't like him?"

"My uncle built his boat."

"*Break of Day?*"

"That's what he calls it."

The door swung open then with a blast of cold air. The dog came in first, followed by Zee, Will, and Tom Eaton. Driftwood carried a cake of sea ice. He dropped it near his water bowl and began to drink.

"We'll be walking to the mainland before long," Will said, and dropped a box of groceries on the Hoosier.

"Don't get your hopes up, Will," Tom said.

"Where are we?" Everett Eaton asked.

"We're out on Ten Acre No Nine, Dad. You remember it. Come look out the window." The two men stood at the fogged window. Tom had his hook on his father's shoulder. "You see our buoys out there. I fish about twelve traps out there."

"You won't haul anything there," the old man said.

"You always had traps here. We fished here for years before I left."

"You left for that girl and went to Jonesport."

"Yes, Dad. That was years ago."

"Where is she?"

"She's gone."

"Just like my wife."

"Yes, Mom's gone, too."

"Why are we here?"

"For Thanksgiving, Dad."

"Have we eaten yet?"

"No, Dad."

"That's good, isn't it?"

"It sure is."

"I don't smell anything cooking."

"I'll warm up the oven," Hannah said.

Will and Zee sat with the old man. Hannah turned from the kitchen occasionally to watch them. The old man said little, kept his eye on the dog, as if Driftwood were by far the most interesting thing in the house. When Tom started to prepare the turkey, Zee jumped up to help.

"It's all ready, Zee. I can do it. I just need to put it in the oven." Zee picked up the foil pan anyway.

Hannah said, "It's at temperature," and opened the oven door. Heat billowed out. Zee tried to get the turkey in but the wire shelf was too high. Before Hannah could reach an oven mitt, Tom's arm brushed by her own. He was reaching for the grate. "It's hot," Hannah yelped at him. She didn't have time to grab his arm. Then she saw the two hooks grasp the grate, draw it forth, then slide it back in, two notches lower. He moved out of the way to let his daughter place the pan and bird in the oven.

Tom turned to Hannah, holding his prosthetics up on each side of his face. "It didn't hurt," he said, and smiled.

Hannah dumped her breath from her chest. "Sorry," she said.

"That's OK, it took me awhile to get used to them, too. You know what the best thing has been?"

She was sure there couldn't be a best thing.

"I can fish in this cold water and my hands never get cold. I think it gives me a real advantage in the winter. It doesn't bother me near as much to fish in the cold as it used to."

"He washes the dishes in scalding hot water," Zee said. "You can hardly see him for the steam."

"My son lost his hands in an accident, too," Everett Eaton told them.

"That's me, Dad," Tom said.

"Yeah," his father said, uncertainly.

Hannah squeezed out of the kitchen between Tom and Zee. She tried to move without touching them. "I'm just going upstairs for a bit," she said, and avoided everyone's eyes. She found her bedroom and shut the door. She found her bed and sat on it. They were still talking below. She'd left adroitly enough, soon enough that she didn't think they could tell she was on the verge of collapsing. Perhaps Will could tell. That's why she hadn't looked at him. It had come upon her suddenly: there were too many people in the room. There couldn't possibly be enough oxygen to breathe. She felt trampled in her narrow kitchen. A few seconds alone and she could try again. There was a man with no hands in her house. The old man had forgotten his son was in the room with him, thought he knew two people who'd lost their hands. Obviously, he was handling the situation better than she, demented as he was. Her breath came in tatters.

The wallpaper beneath the window was beginning to curl at its edge: too much moisture over too much time. Large pink roses, oddly strung on a pale green vine rather than growing on stems or bushes, surrounded the little room. Vertical trellises separated each row of flowers. The wallpaper was mounted square to the planet, but the walls of the house weren't. The wallpaper had been hung long after the house had begun to lean. She wondered who made the decision eighty years ago to permanently fix the discrepancy, to try to straighten the house with paper and glue. It was as disorienting today as it must have been then. If she were ever to level the foundation and house, the wallpaper would lean. A conservator would remove the old paper carefully, level the house, then reapply the roses. They'd then grow parallel to the corners and door frames and windows. The room would seem square, even if roses didn't grow on vines. She thought she might go back downstairs now, having worked out this problem. Driftwood scratched at the base of her door. The crack beneath it was an eighth of an inch wide on the hinge side, a full inch beneath the doorknob. It needed to be that way so the door would open all the way. Still, there was an arcing sweep of wear on the pine floor. The door would have to be cut down a bit more.

She'd read somewhere that there were three things worth doing in life: making something new, caring for something old, and finding something lost. Her art was something new; the house was worthy of care. What had been lost? It was like asking what had been forgotten. You didn't know until you remembered it. She wouldn't know what was lost until she found it.

She changed her sweater before going down. The white one she'd had on before had been a ridiculous choice for a day of cooking and eating. It was her best sweater. She'd dressed for company. Now she put on her old navy blue cotton crew neck she'd worn on *Break of Day* back in college. She could push its sleeves up past her elbows and they would stay there. If the hem touched a hot oven rack it would smoke rather than melt. Besides, it was some sort of excuse for disappearing.

The dog preceded her down the stairs in order to take credit for finding her.

"Who's that?" Everett Eaton asked his son.

"Arno Weed's niece," Tom told him.

"I didn't know the son of . . ."

"Dad, no foul language."

"Had one," he finished.

Will looked cross. "What?" Hannah asked.

"The recipe for the sweet potatoes calls for brown sugar. I can't find it. I thought we had some. Zee wants to substitute molasses. Why does everything in Maine have to have molasses in it? It won't taste right at all with molasses in it."

"Brown sugar's in a plastic tub behind the oatmeal. It kept getting hard in the box."

"I still don't think we should put marshmallows on the potatoes," Zee said.

"Look, we're eating bread stuffing instead of cornbread stuffing. I haven't complained about that," Will said.

"It's just weird, that's all, marshmallows on potatoes."

"You wait, it's great," Will told her. "I'll eat it all myself if you don't want any."

"I've lived a life downwind of the flatulent," Everett Eaton said.

"I know, Dad."

"I'm on the losing end of life, not the finding."

Tom Eaton pulled back a chair for Hannah. He does that like it's his chair, Hannah thought. She sat down.

"Dad's been saying that since I was about five," Tom said.

Everett smiled at her. "I know your uncle."

"I'm afraid he passed away, Mr. Eaton," Hannah said.

"Arno Weed?" She nodded. "I didn't know it. But I forget things. Words are harder to come up with than they used to be."

"Tell Hannah about these islands, Dad."

"These islands used to be connected to the mainland, you know. Still would be if it weren't for the water. Sometime back a norther blew Deer Isle and Isle au Haut and the Merchants out to sea. It'll take a good blow from the south to bring 'em all back home." He put his hand over his mouth to conceal a smile. "My dad told me that. He said he wasn't waiting on a hurricane. That's why he cut stone. He said he was bringing the islands back a block at a time. Did you know my dad?" he asked her.

"No, sir, I didn't."

He worked for Old Man Goss, over at Crotch Island and all over these islands. He was a stonecutter. My father loved his work."

She thought of the blocks of cut stone cascading into the sea at Crotch and Russ and from her own island, huge blocks of granite like children's playthings, making the islands seem fragile and cheap.

"He loved cutting the stone, and moving it, and shaping it. He used to bring little chunks home to me and we'd carve on it with a hammer and chisel. We made a little tombstone for my dog. He talked about stone so it used to make me jealous. He loved his work and he died of breathing it. Stone dust in his lungs. It's called silicosis. That's the scientific name. He breathed stone. He told me you should die of what you love. I was eight years old when he died. He died a young man but I've lived to be an old man. But it's not because I've been careful. I was a fisherman my whole life. He cut a lot of stone from these islands and we buried him with lungs full of it. His chest was heavy. He's got island in him. He said if his share had been a long life he'd have brought all these islands back to the mainland, wind or no wind. He just knew these islands were only temporary."

"He was right," Hannah said.

"Who was?"

"Your father. I see it here every day, a little more erosion. The granite is harder than water, but the water's more diligent. That and somebody's digging the island up, destroying the ground cover and topsoil."

"Coast Guard have any luck with that?" Tom asked.

"No, at least I haven't heard back from them."

"Dad, somebody's digging holes on Arno Weed's island here. They're looking for something."

"What are they looking for?" he asked.

"We don't know," Hannah said.

"Arno Weed has lots of money. Maybe they're looking for his money. My son is in charge of my money."

"Well," Hannah said, "if Arno had money, he didn't leave it to me. And he sure didn't put it into his house or boat." She smiled.

"My uncle Haskell built Arno's boat," Everett said. "All of my uncles built boats. I didn't like to build boats. I liked to fish."

"I know you don't want to sell your boat, but if it's not too much to ask, I'd sure like to see it. I remember it from years ago, before I left, " Tom said.

"I'll stay here," Everett Eaton said. "I don't need to see one more lobster boat in my life."

They left the old man with Will and Zee, but took the old dog. There was at least two more hours till the button popped on the turkey, and the time had to be stuffed just like the turkey. On the way down the slope to the boat she asked him, "Why would your dad think my uncle Arno had money?"

"Old people think everybody has money but them. He accuses me of taking his money at least once a week. Some lobstermen do pretty well, but you'd have a hard time making them admit it."

"How's it going with you?" she asked.

"My fishing?"

"Yes."

"Oh, I can't fish anymore, not really. I used to be good at it. Had a nice boat, but it was only half paid for when I had my accident. Pretty much lost everything while I healed up. No, you have to fish fast to make a living of it, and I can't do that. I haul a few traps for peace of mind."

Hannah opened the door to the boat shed, held it open while he stepped over the threshold. She said, "But Zee thinks you're trying to get back into fishing full-time, and you're looking for another boat."

"She's a good girl. She knows I liked having my own boat, being in charge of something. I still get depressed about losing my hands sometimes, and she thinks a lobster boat will fix that. It's been hard, going from fisherman to floor waxer. I always had a lot of pride, and losing my self-reliance, being able to do for myself and my family, took a lot out of me. Look at this old boat."

She watched him move along the hull of the boat, his arms at his side, the hooks like tools he carried on the way to some job. She knew that when other men walked beneath a boat they often lifted one palm to the hull as if it were the smooth flank of an animal. That was lost to him.

"She's some dry."

"What do you mean?" She followed him around the boat.

"You could drain pasta with this hull. She's lost a lot of caulking. There's a pretty good check here in the stem and several along the keel. She's set in here and gone brittle. How long has she been inside?"

"Six years, since Arno died."

"He was a good guy, your uncle. Taught a lot of boys around here how to fish."

"He taught me," Hannah said.

"You fish?"

"For a couple summers during college. I was his sternman."

He tilted his head at her. "No kidding?"

"No kidding."

"Well, you got me beat then. I don't know a thing about art."

"You don't think *Break of Day* is salvageable?"

"Oh, I doubt it."

"But the water creeps up in here on big tides. It should be fairly humid in here."

"She might swell up. They built these boats out of cedar. But she'd need a lot of recaulking. And you'd have to go over her with an ice pick to check for rot. It's too bad. There's not many of her kind left."

"Do you want to see the cockpit?" She found it strange, this sudden desire she had that he be impressed with *Break of Day*.

"You lead the way."

He stepped onto the first rung of the ladder and lodged one hook over the rail. Hannah stood in the cockpit, looking down on him, unsure if she should offer her hand, unsure of her own hand. He climbed another step and looked for another place to lodge his hook. Hannah took her hand out of her pocket. Her fingers seemed weak and vulnerable.

"Here," she said. She held out her hand.

"I just need to steady myself a bit," Tom said. "My balance has gotten pretty good since the accident. Reach past the hook and take hold of my forearm."

She did as he told her. The hook curled in the cubital fold below her bicep. She took a firm grip and pulled. He was heavy. As he climbed aboard, his other arm flailed and his boot banged the coaming. She grabbed his coat with her free hand and rolled his shoulder. It was as if she'd pulled him from the sea. When he was finally standing, she let him go.

"I'm sorry, I'm sorry," he said. He looked down, arranged his coat with his hooks.

"It's OK," she said.

"I'm not very graceful." He looked up at her face finally, and smiled. "You ought to see me trying to thread a needle. I need a whole room. I feel like I'm tackling a buffalo."

It made her queasy, that he could joke so easily after that scene.

"Look at that radar set. Jesus, looks like it came off a battleship. You can get them an inch-thick now. And the Loran. Everybody's gone GPS. Arno always stuck with what worked. The guy was such an anachronism."

"He hardly used the instruments," Hannah said.

"No, my dad and all the other old-timers mapped the rocks up here." He touched his head with one hook. "Those that didn't are dead. Nice big cockpit. A little lean. These old boats weren't beamy and that made them quick. Did you know Arno used to race this boat?"

"No."

"Never officially, but when I was a kid you'd see him lined up with some other old shark on the Thorofare and they'd race back to the harbor. He used to change the engines in this thing every time he'd lose a race. Started out with a Chevy 6 then went to a Buick Straight 8 and finally a big Chrysler V-8. That's why the engine box sticks up above the sole like that. Engines kept getting bigger."

"I always tripped on that damn thing. He never said a word about racing."

"What's he got in there now?" Tom pierced the D-ring with his left hook and lifted the hatch. Hannah pulled the old blanket off the engine.

"I know it's a diesel," Hannah said.

"Yeah, a nice one. That's a Yanmar. That must have cost him."

"I know he took good care of it."

"There's your uncle's money," Tom said. "He knew where to put it. You could sell just the engine and get quite a bit for it."

"No," Hannah said. "I don't want to sell her. I come out here and sit every once in a while. I've changed the old house quite a bit since Arno died, but here it's just the same as it was." She sat down on the washboard, put her hands in her pockets. It wasn't what she wanted to say, but she needed to say something. "What are you going to do about Zee and Will?"

He sat down on the cap rail on the opposite side of the cockpit. "Is there something to do?"

"It seems like they've gotten very close very quickly."

"I think Zee's liked Will since the day she first saw him six months ago," he said.

"But Will's going off to college next year."

"So's Zee, if we can swing it."

"I'm saying they're very close. They see each other a lot. Don't you worry about how often they're alone together?"

"You mean sex?"

"Well, yes, sex and babies and your whole life changed."

"So you know they're having sex?"

"Yes."

"Good."

"Good?"

"Well, yes. I felt funny, you not knowing."

"Aren't you worried your daughter is going to get pregnant? It doesn't bother you?"

"I'm right here. No need to raise your voice. They're both too embarrassed to buy protection, so I pick up a box for them once in a while."

"What?"

"I buy their condoms for them."

"I can't believe it. You facilitate this?"

"Let's say I'm more worried about her getting pregnant than I hate the idea of my little girl having sex, which is a big hate. You can't remember as far back as eighteen? Nothing on earth is going to keep them in their clothes. Hell, sex was all I thought about when I was in high school. Zee was conceived spring term of her mom's senior year. I like Will, but I don't want him for a son-in-law just yet, much less do I want a grandson. Besides, everybody in Stonington thinks I'm a rounder now. You can't buy a box of condoms on Deer Isle without the news . . . well. Have you ever been in town when the bait trucks leave the commercial pier? They turn up that hill by the newspaper office and often as not a dozen herring will fall in the street. The seagulls are there waiting to pounce. Hundreds of them swoop down on those fish, then they fly back up to the ridges and dormers and wait on the next truck. They wait on me to buy a box of condoms like that. Everybody wants to know who's sleeping with the fella with no hands."

"I didn't know," Hannah said. "I mean I didn't really know they were sleeping together. I've been kidding him about it. I even made a joke about condoms."

"It's hard to get to know them. I just try to remember being eighteen."

"One of them's going to be hurt eventually," she said.

"Yeah, probably."

"It seems like . . . I mean since we have that knowledge, we should be able to . . ."

"What?"

"I don't know."

"To be able to stop them from being hurt?"

"Yeah."

"I don't think so." He thrust his arms away from his body but his hooks could not splay palm up in ignorance as his hands might once have. "But all the same, you watch out for them here, and I'll watch out on the mainland. Maybe they'll be one of those couples that reach a seventieth anniversary. Hey, I'm just happy they're not doing drugs. They aren't, are they?"

"I don't think so," Hannah said.

"That's good." He hid his hooks in his jacket pockets. "It's a good place to sit, this boat. It's like a porch."

"No, it's more private than that."

"Well, we're in a big building with lots of windows. Maybe it's like a church pew. Look at the dust motes in the sunlight."

"You're reaching," she said, because he was getting too close. It was a confession box, where she'd told Arno she was wrong for leaving early so many summers ago, where she apologized for not returning, where she confessed she was unloved and loved, where she doubted everything but her own art, her own existence.

"Well," he said, "my hands aren't cold but the rest of me is."

She stood to help. As he removed his prosthetics from his jacket, one hook caught in the pocket. He pulled and twisted. Finally, she stepped forward and held the fabric of the pocket lining back so he could pull free.

"Goddamnit," he whispered.

"There's no need to be . . ."

He finished her sentence, "Embarrassed? But I am. It's embarrassing not to have hands. You'd think I'd get used to it. But I wake up every morning and I'm surprised my hands are gone. I'm ashamed to walk into the kitchen without them."

"Stop," she said. "It's too much." She put her hands over her cheeks and eyes. It was horrible. She heard the steel knock against the wood of the boat's hull. Heard his boots on the granite. She could not see him.

They both said, "I'm sorry," at the same moment.

She climbed down and followed him back to the house. At the door, before going in, as they stamped their feet, she apologized again. "I can't even imagine my life without my hands. I've tried to since I met you."

"It was my fault," he said. He seemed to be waiting. "You'll have to turn the knob," he said.

"Oh, of course," Hannah said.

As she leaned across him, he said it again, "It was my fault. A sea came unexpectedly, as they do. My hand was drawn into the winch. I tried to free it with my other hand and it was drawn in, too. I was greedy. I wanted both hands, wasn't satisfied with the one. It was my fault."

She felt her own stomach twist as she turned the knob, and so had to release her grip. She brought her hands close to her body and covered one with the other. She looked up at him and squinted. This was why she kept the island inviolable, or why she had up to this point. The sun was behind his head, leaving his face in darkness.

"I'm sorry," he said. "But it's best to get it out of the way. Some people ask up front, but I could tell you weren't going to."

"It's none of my business," she said.

"It doesn't need to be a secret that we make mistakes. I just wear mine, and so I have to come to it sooner."

It was cold enough that she could see his breath coming from the darkness.

She didn't want to let him back in her house, but he was already on the island, his father and daughter already inside. It wasn't fair of him to include her. She hadn't asked. People like him wanted reciprocity, to be paid in kind for their secrets. Here's my misery, where's your torment?

"I don't have anything to share," she said.

"What?"

"Nothing that bad has ever happened to me."

He scratched his cheek with the tip of one hook.

"Oh," he said. Then he said it again, "Oh," as if understanding this time. "These aren't the worst things that've ever happened to me. I wasn't looking to trade. I mean I know you've lived out here alone for a long time and you don't really like people. I wasn't trying to get anything out of you in exchange for my hands. But I probably know more than you think I know. Everyone does. This little island isn't so isolated. It's more like one of those bell jars with an open clockwork inside. All of the lobstermen circle around it and watch the gears and hands move. We know you're not to be touched, but there's very little to surprise anyone after some study. After a while it's just something you pass on the mantel, something Aunt Beulah collected."

"I'm so interesting I've already been forgotten?"

"Well, you were never really part of the community so you weren't forgotten. They think of you as somebody who was left here by mistake, or came here by accident."

"I came here of my own free will."

"Of course you did. Aren't you cold? I'm freezing out here. Can't we go inside now?"

"Wait a minute. I make my living here. Making art out of this environment is much more sustainable than yanking fish out of it. You might find artists here long after the lobsters are gone."

"I don't doubt that the view will last longer than the fish. It'll last longer than us, too. Look, people talk, but if you were on every board and committee in Stonington people would still talk. It's something to do. You're not being singled out. In that way you're one of us. I grew up here. This place is in my lungs, too. But I left for a dozen or so years and it's like I fell back into town off a spaceship. Maybe it's just these things." He lifted his hooks and paused to stare at them. "I guess if I moved anywhere, the people there would be stunned. I've seen a couple of the girls I dated in high school on Main Street. They're polite, but you can see the relief in their spines as they walk away. I think maybe when I get comfortable with these things, other people will too. Maybe they won't. But I'll do one of two things: I'll either stick close to home for the rest of my life, or I'll always be on the move. Until Zee is in college, until my dad dies, I'll be around here. I know that. I'm just trying to get rid of all my secrets. That's just me. You may have good reason to hold onto things. I can smell something burning. Can we go in now?"

She turned the knob. They bumped against each other going over the threshold. Warmth clawed at her cheeks. Everett Eaton stood in the center of the living room, his hands held high over his head.

"Dad?" Tom said.

"Fire," Everett Eaton said, and pointed toward the kitchen.

Will and Zee were backing away from the stove with a Corning Ware pan in their mittened hands. Smoke billowed from the oven and fire erupted from the pan.

"Marshmallows," Will explained. "The marshmallows are on fire." They dropped the pan in the sink and threw a dishcloth over it to smother the flames.

"I guess we shouldn't have put it in the broiler," Zee said.

Will lifted the towel. "Boy, they sure are black and crispy. We'll have to scrape them off and try again. The potatoes look all right."

Smoke filled the house.

"Quarter-mile visibility," Everett Eaton said. "Fog in the wheelhouse."

"We're going to have to open the windows," Tom said.

"Windows have Plexiglas over them," Hannah said. "Just open the door."

Everyone put their coats on again and watched Zee scrape the burnt marshmallows out of the pan. Then Will replaced them. Zee smiled broadly and finally blushed.

"What?" Hannah asked.

Zee leaned over the counter and whispered into her ear, "It's the first thing Will and I have burnt together."

"Oh, please," Hannah sighed.

"What?" Everett Eaton asked.

"What?" Tom asked.

Why were Zee's secrets so endearing, precious as gifts, contagious? And her father's so debilitating? What could be worse than making a living with your hands and then losing them? Losing a child? Losing your religion?

🐢🐢🐢

It occurred to her that she met everyone as if their first words to her were the last lines of a novel. To know them she was forced to work backwards in their lives, to read the book from last page to first. Answers had little relevance without knowing the questions. Her artwork came to her in the same way: she realized each piece fully formed, and then had to work back to understand what it was she was painting or sculpting. The secret was to deconstruct an idea, not to build from a kernel. The stone within the bark was inspiration; the slow rise of sap beneath rock was the truth.

She wrote Gwen to say she was thinking of mounting a retrospective of her work in Stonington in the spring to raise money for the new art wing at the local high school. Nothing overreaching, just forty to fifty of her works presented in a white space. She asked Gwen's permission to sell a few pieces at the show. She'd also need a contact list of her past buyers to seek loans of the major paintings and sculptures. In addition to sales, donations would be accepted from those touring the exhibition. No doubt collectors from New York would visit, and Hannah asked if Gwen could help with advertising. She told her she hadn't chosen this course entirely for altruistic reasons. She felt it was time to see the body of her work in one place, to see where she'd been and where she might go.

Gwen wrote back to say it *"was a wonderful idea, but the costs of such an adventure, in shipping alone, not to mention the bonds that insurance collectors would require, would go far beyond the money brought in. You're too young for a retrospective at any event. Wait for a museum to underwrite an exhibition. For now, donate money, or donate a painting and send it to me and I'll sell it for the high school without taking a commission."*

It wasn't the answer she expected. She felt if the collectors received a personal request from the artist most of the details could be overcome. The sale of a single painting would pay for thousands in shipping, and perhaps the collectors would support insurance costs. She decided to find a space before contacting Gwen again. If there wasn't a suitable gallery available there was little use in pushing the issue. Besides, she needed to do some Christmas shopping for Will. It would please him that she was going ashore.

🏴 🏴 🏴

"We're going downtown?" Will asked.

"Downtown? Stonington?"

"Yeah, everybody at school calls it downtown."

"You're kidding."

"Nope. Maybe we could have lunch at the FF or the Harbor Cafe."

"What's the FF?"

"Fisherman's Friend."

"I do want to check around Stonington, but I thought we might go as far as Ellsworth, do some shopping at the L. L. Bean outlet."

"You have to help me get a present for Zee."

"I guess I could do that. What are you thinking?"

"She's getting her navel pierced. She wants a couple navel rings."

"I didn't know there were such things."

"All the girls do it now. Mr. Eaton doesn't like it, but he says it's better than a tattoo."

"Wait a minute, I do know there are such things. I've seen them in my art magazines. I didn't know it was a trend. I thought it was just an artsy thing."

"Well, not every girl does it," Will said. "Just the adventurous ones. You could get one."

She raised one eyebrow. "No thanks."

"Why not?"

"Will, I haven't even worn earrings in years."

"I don't see how you can make art without knowing what's going on in the world."

"I make it out of me. Every good artist does."

"It just seems like a selfish way to do anything."

"Well, there isn't any other way. I'm stuck with myself. I listen to the radio, read my magazines."

"But you really don't believe something till you see it, till it's close. You don't get the real details. You didn't even know where downtown was."

"There are things more eternal than fads and nicknames."

"Those things live in the present moment, and it's always eternal."

"Wow, Will. That was good."

"It was?"

"Yeah. Do you need underwear for Christmas?"

"I was hoping for something a little more exciting than that, Mom."

🐢🐢🐢

A few days after their shopping trip, the first heavy snow of winter fell. There was six inches of snow in the skiff, up to the level of the thwarts. Hannah and Will spent fifteen minutes shoveling it out of the boat before he set off for school. There was a thin skin of ice in the quarry that scraped against the granite as the tide fell. It broke into sheets as Will cut through it in the skiff. He turned and waved at the entrance, but not at her. Tom Eaton soon came into view and entered the quarry through the clearing in the ice Will had made. Hannah took his forward line.

"Invite me up for a cup of coffee?" he asked.

"Something wrong?"

"Things to talk about."

As soon as they turned toward the first ladder, Driftwood kicked up the snow in a darting circle and then shot away to cut them off at the pass.

"That dog likes the snow," Tom said.

"He likes any form of race, any form of hurry until he's ready to nap, then you can't get him to roll over for a scratch."

"Mind if I follow him around?"

"Oh, sure, go ahead. I'll go that way, too. I forgot about the ladders."

It bothered her to start out this way. They'd had a good Thanksgiving once they'd gotten back inside the house. The turkey and the sweet potatoes had come out all right. Old Mr. Eaton told stories, though he sometimes paused and asked where he was, or who he was speaking to. She'd shown Tom some of her current work and he'd been polite, even asked reasonable questions. He'd told her that if art put food on her table, it was just as noble as fishing. She knew he meant it as a compliment.

Driftwood ran back and forth down the trail between them and the house, each return trip a bit shorter, constantly reassuring himself that the destination and their progress toward it existed concurrently.

"He's beating down a trail for us," Tom said. "First snow's always special. Looks good on the ground. I tried to call you this morning, but couldn't get through."

She kicked the lowest clapboard on her house to dislodge the snow caked on her boots. "I don't leave the phone on. I just use it to call out." She held the door open for him and the dog. Tom sat at the kitchen table while she started coffee. "I hope it's not stale. We don't drink much coffee," she said.

"I don't taste it anymore. I just absorb it. I ought to make up some patches of the stuff to wear over the veins in my neck. My weekends are killing me."

"What do you do up at Jonesport?"

"I check on the summerhouses. I drive up a hundred gravel driveways, walk around each house, and make sure no windows are broken or pipes busted. If something's wrong, I call the sheriff or a plumber to come fix it. I get about four dollars per house after gas and oil. Friend of mine has this caretaking business. He lets me sleep over."

"Nice places up there?"

"Oh, it's not like Mount Desert, but there's some grand homes out on some of those points. Some of them only get used a couple weeks a year."

"Are there a lot of break-ins?"

"Not many. The only broken window I've found was made by a hawk. He flew right into it. I found him on the kitchen floor."

"How, I mean, how do you get inside the houses?"

"I've got keys." She didn't understand. "Oh," he said, "once I have a key in the knob I can twist the key and get in. The owners are more afraid of a broken window than thieves, anyway. Losing a TV wouldn't be much of a loss to them. You can't steal the view."

"No, I guess not. So what's up? Is something wrong with the kids?"

"No, but I got a call from Mr. Johnson this morning. Up to the salmon pens. His tender went missing again last night and I thought I'd let you know."

"It would be silly for them to use it again. They know I've seen it."

"You're probably right. But you can't count on thieves to be bright."

This made her smile. He went on. "I didn't see any tracks in the snow as we came down, and I circled the island in the skiff. Didn't see anyplace where someone had obviously come ashore during the night."

"They usually don't bother the island in the winter. The ground's too hard."

"You think maybe they're looking for Blackbeard's treasure?"

"No way."

"Blackbeard's treasure, some say he buried one around here," Tom said.

"I've read about that. It's a story some guy made up."

"It's possible to live inside a story. Some people live their whole lives there. These guys could be digging up every island between Monhegan and Swans."

"I just wish they'd find whatever it is and leave me alone."

"Well, I wanted to let you know."

"Thank you. I'm sorry you had to come out here."

"It's all right." He unclipped the coffee cup from his hook, but didn't immediately get up. "I wanted to apologize, too, when the kids weren't around, for the way I treated you at Thanksgiving."

"It wasn't your fault. It makes me uncomfortable that you've lost your hands."

"You see, you're the first person that's said that out loud. I know that was hard for you to say. I know you're uncomfortable. Everybody is. But I took advantage of you, telling you how I felt and how it happened. It just came bubbling out of me and I don't even know you. I think I must have done it because I know you're out here alone and I could confess to you and you wouldn't share it with anyone. I took advantage of you, a woman out here alone, just like these fellas digging up your island. I've been thinking about it ever since we were here and I wanted to apologize."

His hair had been tousled by the black watch cap he'd hung on the finial of his chair. His elbows were planted in the table, the prosthetics lying before him. Every line on his face spun out from his eyes as if engraved there by centrifugal force. His cheeks were still red from the ride out from Stonington.

"I was wondering," he said, "if you would let me come out and visit you once in a while. I know you don't like to leave here."

"I," she said, "I work here. This is where I work. It's enough for me just to think about Will. I don't have what you need. I can't even offer it. I came here to be alone."

"It just seems like there's only water between us," he said.

"I put it there on purpose. I'm sorry, it's not only for you. It's for me."

"You're right," he said. "I completely understand. But I won't go so far as to avoid you, if that's all right."

"No," she said, "please don't avoid me."

"You know, there's going to be some bad weather. There always is. I worry about Will out in his little boat. If he capsized in this cold, even if he was able to swim to a rock or one of the islands, the hypothermia would take him. It's all right for him to stay in town with us, even if it's a week or two at a time."

"I'd miss him," she said, unable to look at Tom.

"What if I talk to a couple of the boys that come in from Isle au Haut every day to pick up crew? Maybe they'd stop here on their way in and take Will to town. I'd bring him back out in the afternoon. He might have to get up earlier."

"But just on bad days."

"Right."

"Maybe that would be good. I could pay them. I could pay you."

"It wouldn't be so often that you'd need to pay anybody. It helps me to do things for other people. Makes me feel like I'm regaining some ground I lost."

"It seems like you're doing fine to me."

"I'm glad to be making a living again, but it ain't fishing. I used to fish. How'd you like to say you used to be an artist?"

"It would be hard."

"I'm sorry. It won't ever happen to you. You're not greedy."

She reached across the table slowly and touched the scarred steel at the tip of each hook. "They're just tools," she said. "I work with them every day. I love my tools, my pliers and screwdrivers and bones and brushes. I don't mind if you come every once in a while."

"I just want to talk," he said.

She decided to be as forthright and blunt as he'd been. "No," she said, "you want more."

🦑 🦑 🦑

She ate twelve oranges that day. She bought them now. Two for break-fast, two just after Tom left, and one each time she circled the island looking for the blue tender. She carried the bright peelings in her pocket on each trip till she arrived at the compost heap where she tossed them on the mound of snow. The contrast pleased her, summer's orange piquancy against winter's white resolve. The problem with her island, small as it was, was it had a far shore. She couldn't cover three hundred and sixty degrees by herself. After her fourth circuit, the dog stopped going along. She repaired two of her warning sculptures, hanging prop-slashed buoys from driftwood roots she'd jammed into crevices in the granite. She tied round stones in abraded warp and hung them from spruce branches, slingshots the wind could use when needed.

In the late afternoon, the sun came out and its sharp, slanting light made everything between her and the sun unbearable and everything between her and the coming night radiant in relief. Boats seemed to be spotlighted and the snow-covered islands seemed to glow from within. There was no heat, only light and reflection, allowing each spruce needle to become distinct, each snowflake to cast a shadow. It lasted for perhaps sixty seconds, not enough time to paint it. She felt the light leave her cheek and tried to gather it back with her hands.

The only thing that made her move from the cold spot she was standing on was the sound of Will's motor. It reverberated as he passed between Spruce and Millet islands. She saw him first, standing in the stern of the boat, his backpack still on, his hat and muffler covering his face. She met him at the quarry and tied off the boat while he tilted the outboard from the water.

"I wish you wouldn't stand up in the boat," she told him.

As he turned to her, his wake followed him into the quarry and the little boat wobbled. Will lifted his arms to steady himself. He smiled. "If you don't stop telling me what to do, I'm going to run away," he said.

"That's not funny. You always think you're so funny."

"OK, what's wrong with you?"

"The blue tender has gone missing again."

"No, it hasn't. Mr. Eaton met me at the dock. He said Mr. Johnson found it. It was still tied to the salmon pens, but it was sunk. All you could see of it was the painter."

"You're kidding me. I've been circling this island all goddamn day long."

"False alarm," Will said.

"I've lost an entire day. I didn't work all day."

"Well," Will said, stepping out of the boat, "you'll just have to live a day longer to catch up."

"If Tom Eaton hadn't come out here, I'd have been just fine. It's incredible how people can interfere with the smooth running of your life."

"People like me," Will said.

"Exactly," she said.

"Yeah, I know. I like standing up in the boat sometimes."

"You're going to fall overboard someday, Will. And you weren't even wearing your life jacket. If you fall overboard you're going to die. No college, no fishing, no screwing Zee. You'll be bawling into the water, thinking that goddamned Hannah was right." She was breathing hard, fogging the air between them. Her voice echoed in the quarry, tier upon tier, till it was swept away at ground level by the wind.

Will slipped his hands under the shoulder straps of his backpack. He opened his mouth to answer twice before he actually said something. "OK, I'll be more careful. But it's not screwing."

"I didn't mean it that way," she said.

"It's not even any of your business. That you should hold it over me for not wearing a life jacket is just . . . I don't know what it is. She likes you."

"I know she does. I like her, too. You have to promise me you're not taking advantage of her."

"That's so weird. Why aren't you worried about her taking advantage of me? She came after me. I didn't chase her."

"I don't know. I can only go by my own experience. Please don't hurt her."

He shrugged and looked up at the rim of the quarry. "OK," he said finally, "I won't fall overboard. I won't stand in the boat and I'll wear my life jacket. I won't hurt Zee or any other woman for the rest of my life, including you. I promise to make good grades and brush my teeth at least twice a day."

"GOOD," Hannah shouted, and shoved her fists into her coat pockets.

"You are exactly old enough to be my mother," Will replied.

※ ※ ※

Each Saturday afternoon before Christmas, Zee sat with her at the worktable taking lessons. They began with watercolor. They'd talk for a few moments, then Hannah would place a few objects on the table and step back. Zee was tentative at first, used a brush too small and color too thick, but soon she settled down to a faint pastel palette. It was soothing to Hannah to hear another brush in the studio besides her own. She'd forgotten the hushed tones of a classroom, the scrape of a fingernail across thick paper, a brush sloshing in water stippled by the metal ferrule ringing on the glass, a footfall stepping back from an easel, a sigh. There was a liquid sense of everyone around you sliding across life, immersed in slipperiness, gargling uncertainty. Half enjoyed it, half were simply trying to cling on. Hannah stood behind her, made suggestions, but before long she was jealous of the point of contact and began her own study. Zee made little burbling noises and yelps as she painted, as if she were finding baby rabbits sleeping in her shoes.

"What?" Hannah asked.

"The paint just goes where it wants to."

"Yeah, sometimes that's OK."

"It won't stay within the lines."

"There are no lines."

"There are in my head."

"Then you can manipulate them to conform to the paint."

"But my painting won't look like a milk carton and a lemon. Oh. Oh."

"What?"

"My lemon has a wake. It's supposed to have a shadow, but it's a wake. My lemon's a boat."

"Let me see. That's pretty, the way the yellow washes out. That's hard to learn to do."

"It was an accident," Zee said.

"I know. So was penicillin. You still own it. Make more accidents."

"That's how you do it?"

"That's how. You make enough of them till they accumulate into an entire picture. It took me about forty-nine accidents, and learning how to repeat them, before I made my first decent watercolor."

"I just want to get good enough to donate something to the school auction."

"We've got several months. You'll get there. I haven't told Will, but I was thinking about having a show next spring, too. There's that Green's Landing Gallery downtown. They don't usually open till July Fourth and so they're willing to rent the space to me for the month of June. I'd like to bring quite a few works back from New York and do a small retrospective. We could take donations for the school and maybe sell a couple paintings."

"You're going to donate paintings?"

"Yeah, I thought maybe a couple paintings and a sculpture."

"That would be great, Hannah."

"I'm going to need help staffing the show. Maybe a few students to sit in the gallery. Could you help with that? I can pay them."

"Sure. But I want to help, too. Who's going to set everything up, hang the paintings?"

"Me."

"You're going to go into town every day for a month?"

"No, just enough to hang the show. I'll let you and Will and the others run the gallery."

"You don't want to talk to the people coming in?"

"Not really. Not at all."

"Then why do you want to have the exhibition?"

"For me. To see my work again. It's never mattered to me what other people think of it."

"Really? Boy, all I care about is getting good enough so that someone else likes my work."

"For me that was always the easy part. The hard part is liking your own work."

"Why do it if you don't like it?"

"Because maybe someday you will."

"Hooey," Will said. He'd just come downstairs. "Hooey," he said again, crossing the room. "Nobody does anything unless they like it. They eat because they like it. They beat people up because they like it. They fish because they like it." He paused at the door to pull on his coat and heavy boots. He jammed his hat on his head and his gloves in his pockets and picked up his fishing rod as if all of these things had just been stolen from him.

"It's too cold to go fishing," Zee said.

"I'm gonna go fishing because I like it. Y'all can sit there and paint because you don't like it all you want to." He opened and slammed the door.

"I love him so much," Zee said.

"Yeah, me too," Hannah said.

"He told me you asked him not to hurt me."

Hannah put down her brush. "I did," she confessed.

"I could ask you to do the same for my dad, but I won't. I wouldn't want Will to stay with me because someone talked him into it. I'd want him to decide. All the same if you hurt my dad, I think I'd kill you."

"Zee, I'm not seeing your dad. We're just friends."

"I know. All the same. Between us girls."

"Between us girls, what?"

"He likes you. That makes you responsible for him."

"No, it doesn't."

"Yes, it does. He has something to think about now besides himself. You, like, saved his life and now you're responsible for his emotional health.

It's an oriental thing. He's all the time asking about you. It's wicked disgusting. I mean, you're both so old."

Hannah felt the skin on her forehead climbing, her jaw drooping. She didn't know which statement to reply to first. So Zee went on.

"I told him you probably weren't fertile anymore. You've been through menopause, right?"

Oh. It was a joke. Zee was pulling her leg. She was learning from Will. I can do that too, Hannah thought. "Yes, I have in a way," she said, tears forming in her eyes. "I lost a child years ago, a late miscarriage. They found cancer in my uterus. Most of my reproductive organs are gone." She lowered her face into her hands and sobbed for a few moments and finally paused to peek through her fingers at Zee. Zee's hands were clasped over her nose, her wide eyes separated by stiff fingers. "Got ya," Hannah whispered.

Zee sucked in a great draft of air and expelled it again around the words, "You bitch!"

"Takes one to know one."

"You just made up those tears out of nothing. How can I ever trust you again?"

"You'll trust me when you see your painting getting better. How do you feel about your dad being interested in other women?"

"Besides my mom?"

"Yeah."

"I guess it's good."

"You don't want him and your mom to get back together?"

"No. That won't ever happen. She couldn't deal with the accident."

"What do you mean?"

"She wouldn't let him come near her, that's all."

"Were they happy before the accident?"

"I guess not. I don't know."

"You know now. Did she love him the way you love Will?"

They'd both stopped painting. Zee swirled her brush in a glass of water that had become opaque. Beads of water on the exterior of the glass looked like they'd been painted there. Hannah watched as tears formed in her eyes.

"You shouldn't ask questions like that," Zee told her.

"Why not?"

"Because I don't want to admit I feel sorry for my dad. It wasn't his fault she didn't love him. You're right, I'm in love now and so I know my mom didn't love my dad."

"So, I guess it's best he's not with her anymore, and he's thinking about moving on."

"I know that," Zee said, wiping at the tears on her cheeks with the wet brush and transferring them to the dry paper where they weeped into the wake of the lemon. "Instead of being glad that he wasn't dead, she was mad that he was handicapped. She told me once that it was his hooks on the handle of the shopping cart that did it. The metal all looked the same. She's already met a guy. He's forty years old and he's got braces on his teeth. That just weirded me out, that she can kiss all that metal but wouldn't touch Dad's hooks. I don't see her much. She's crazy."

"You tell me secrets," Hannah said, "so I'm going to tell you one. I broke up with a young man once because I knew I didn't love him. I thought we'd both be better off. He killed himself a few weeks later."

"I'm sorry," Zee said.

"So I'm not so different than your mom. I hope you can forgive her someday. If you ever do, come and tell me. It'll make me feel better, too."

"You're not going to let my dad inside, are you?" Zee said.

"He doesn't need me and I don't need him. But we can be friends until he finds who he needs."

"How does it feel to have someone kill themselves over you?" she asked.

"I don't know yet. I still don't know."

"Maybe you'll need to feel that way about losing someone before you'll know."

"You and Will are a lot alike, Zee. You both learn so fast."

🦢 🦢 🦢

A week before Christmas, the sun was setting before four o'clock. Snow had come and gone twice, but ice remained, piling up on the dark foreshore, grinding against rock. When Tom Eaton visited he always brought his father. It was more comfortable with the old man between them. Like a dog or a child, he was there to allow them to avert their eyes, so that silences weren't wholly their own.

A reluctant half-moon rose slowly into a congealed sky. They watched its progress through the kitchen window.

"I could smell the onions growing in your garden this summer, out in the channel, when I pulled my traps," Tom told her.

Everett Eaton said, "Taking on a cargo of onions is a bad omen. You don't want to crew on a boat with onions on board. Same goes for dreaming of white horses. It's a bad omen. If we were to be abroad tonight you wouldn't want to sleep on deck in the light of the moon. If your shadows cross on deck, that's bad, too, and no way to undo it. I guess there are things I know that no one else on the planet knows, but they don't seem too valuable. Some secrets aren't worth knowing. They don't pay. They're like the coins of a previous government: you put them down on the counter and no one will take them. So they tend to become secrets forgotten, as near as anything can get to never existing."

"I'll listen to your secrets, Mr. Eaton," Hannah said.

"Who are you?"

"I'm Arno Weed's niece."

"Oh, you again? Well, I followed the light but darkness followed me."

"Oh, Dad," Tom sighed, "no more philosophy."

"I knew Arno Weed before he went bad. My uncle built his boat."

"What do you mean, Mr. Eaton?" Hannah asked. "My uncle wasn't bad."

"Some liked what he did, some didn't. He might have been drove to it."

"Drove to what?"

"He makes things up, Hannah," Tom said.

"I do not. Somebody's got my money, I know that."

"The nursing home has your money, Dad. When you're on Medicare they get everything."

"How can we get it back?"

"They promise to take care of you for the rest of your life."

"I just need a little spending money, for gum and cigarettes."

"You don't smoke, Dad."

"For gum and magazines."

"When I give you money, you lose it."

"I do not."

"Let's not argue in front of Hannah, OK?"

"When did she come here?"

"We came to her, you old fool. This is her house. We're on Ten Acre No Nine."

"Arno Weed's place?"

"Yes."

"He's a good fisherman. Where is he?"

"He died six years ago, Mr. Eaton," Hannah said.

"I didn't know it. We stick up just far enough off the surface of the earth that we're too easily scratched off. Did he drown?"

"No, he had a heart attack," Hannah said.

"Poor bastard. My uncle built his boat. Always worried about his taxes. When Spruce Island sold to that computer wizard, Arno's taxes jumped right out of the boat."

"They're high," Hannah said.

"I don't have to pay taxes anymore," he said. "I'm going to look out your window." He rose from the table and Hannah looked at Tom. He shrugged and smiled. They turned back to Mr. Eaton, who leaned over the sink and put his forehead on the glass. "Tide's coming in. The sky looks like a tub of margarine and the moon is stuck in it. We're all doing the same old orbit."

"Dad," Tom sighed again.

"Leave him alone," Hannah said.

"We're all doing the same old orbit."

"I've heard it a thousand times," Tom said.

"We're all doing the same old orbit. Even light has to travel at its usual speed. It took us so long to believe in science, that the apple would fall this time, too. Science is boring, so consistent. A boat rocks back and forth until it stops, but during the rocking isn't each moment still, too, isolated at its own pitch? Why must we let time and science describe everything? We should allow them no more importance than faith. To those who believe in time and science, fine. To those who don't, the moon rises and rises and rises, and the apple floats in midair, a moment at a time."

"That's beautiful, Mr. Eaton," Hannah said.

"What is?"

"What you just said."

"I didn't say anything."

"Are you ready to go home, Dad?"

"I've been ready since yesterday."

"He usually says, 'I'll be tired of waiting by tomorrow.' Maybe we'll come back out after Christmas. Weather's supposed to shut everything down for a while later this week. You and Will have everything you need?"

"Enough to last till May," Hannah said. She held the door for them as they stepped out into the darkness.

"Be careful," she said. "Good night, Mr. Eaton."

He waved at her. She heard him ask Tom who she was as they walked away. When Tom answered, Mr. Eaton said, "I think she's warm to me."

"Yes, Dad."

Then the old man asked him what happened to his hands.

🐚 🐚 🐚

Just when things were beginning to settle down, when she had everyone in their places and her work was returning to its old pace, the island had to be divided again.

She spent Christmas Eve and morning with Will, and then he took the skiff into town to spend the weekend with Zee. A deep cold had set in, and she made him call her from the dock when he arrived. It was the last she expected to hear from him for a couple days. He and Zee were going to drive over to Colby College to look at the campus.

Hannah told them the college would be closed, but Will said that was fine. They'd walk around and look through windows. It would be like looking at new cars after the dealership closed.

The wind blew while Will was gone. Ice piled up on the windward side of buoys, and Jericho Bay was empty of boats. The waves crunched when they came ashore as if they were full of gravel. Ice formed on the foreshore as the tide flowed, and was broken into shards as the tide ebbed. Snow seemed not to fall but to form in midair and hang there till the next gust of wind flung it over the house. Even though she was inside, Hannah put her back to the wind. The windows vibrated around her. She could hear the shingles on the roof lift and pop back down, like a deck of cards shuffled. Vapor crystallized on the Plexiglas storm windows in patterns that seemed to reveal the past scratchings of animals trying to get inside. She sat at her worktable, wearing the new wool sweater Will had given her for Christmas. Even with the propane furnace at full, and the woodstove smoking the ceiling, it was too cold to paint. She thought about laying her palette on the stove top, but finally picked up a pencil with her gloved hand and began to draw. She scratched at the thick paper, tearing at it with the sharp point of her hard pencil, trying to move among the rag fibers rather than on them. It wasn't long before she found the self-portrait, no line longer than a quarter-inch, the random scratches accumulating beneath her eyebrows and along one side of her nose. She worked into the paper, looking for the source of the deckle edge, each line a thin tear. Days later, when she heard footsteps on the brittle, ice-layered snow outside, she'd made more than twenty sketches. She'd ultimately given up the pencil, switching to an X-Acto knife, sculpting the paper so that only backlighting revealed her portrait, the cheekbones thick and dark, her lids almost transparent, her eyes swirling with individual red rag fibers. When the door opened, she swept all the portraits into a pile under her arms and looked over her shoulder. It was Will. There was someone behind him, swathed in muffler and blanket. Tom and Zee beyond. The wind had stopped blowing, and in its absence here were these people.

"I'm sorry," Will said. "We couldn't get out any sooner."

Her vision was blurry. Why was he apologizing?

"Are you OK?" he asked her.

"Yeah," she answered.

"It's been four days," he said. "I'm late. You never called to find out why. You never turned on your phone. I tried to call."

"Oh," she answered.

"We've got a surprise."

Tom Eaton closed the door. There were so many of them, so many coats and stomping boots. Driftwood was among them. Where had he been? They'd brought out one of Zee's friends.

"Oh, his water bowl is empty," Zee said.

Zee's friend came up beside Will. She looked familiar. She said, "Hannah?"

Hannah nodded.

Will knelt next to her, tried to look under her arms. "Hannah," he said. "It's your sister."

🦐 🦐 🦐

Her sister had already been in Stonington for three days. She drove into town, having passed Will and Zee on their way to Colby. She asked at the post office for Hannah and they'd sent her to Tom Eaton. She'd stayed with him till Will and Zee returned and the storm passed.

Hannah stood up from her worktable and found that Emily was an inch taller than she was. Emily hugged her before she was ready. She had on perfume. It wasn't perfume. It was her hair. It smelled of cut apples. When they released each other, Emily said, "Will said we looked alike."

"I must look awful," Hannah said, running her hands through her hair. It was tangled and oily. Then she said, "I didn't mean you look awful."

"You've been working so hard you didn't even miss me," Will told her. He was beaming, looking back and forth between them.

Emily's hair was brown and full, like her own. She had their father's teeth. Her eyes could have been Hannah's own. The self-portraits she'd been tearing at could easily be mistaken for Emily. An older Emily. As Hannah gazed at her, she cast down her eyes. Hannah suddenly thought she'd been mistaken. She'd only seen the reflection of her own eyes in

Emily's. Her eyes superimposed on hers. But when Emily glanced back up, Hannah knew she'd been drawing and painting those pupils for years. Emily seemed to recognize it, too, and wouldn't allow eye contact for longer than a moment. They're my eyes, Hannah thought. She immediately took charge. This was, after all, her little sister.

"Why are you here? You didn't tell me you were coming," Hannah said.

Will answered. "She came to see us. She just up and decided to come. She knew she would arrive before the mail."

"Before Federal Express?" Hannah asked. "Is Will in danger?"

"No," Emily whispered. She looked down and turned ever so slightly. Hannah recognized this gesture. She was looking off to the side. She was staring at the portraits Hannah had left uncovered. Hannah stepped back. She gathered the papers together as if they were individual feathers, as if they might blow away under Emily's gaze.

"I was just working here," Hannah said. "I didn't expect so much company."

Tom Eaton called across the room, "Where do you keep the dog food, Hannah? He's hungry."

"I keep it where I keep it," she snapped back.

"I'll get it," Will said. He looked over his shoulder at her as he walked away. He didn't understand.

"I'm sorry," Emily whispered. Then she drew both lips inside her mouth, shut her eyes. Her face became as taut and expressionless as a sheet of paper.

Hannah's first thought was to ask her what was wrong, but she overcame it. She reached out and took her by the elbow. "You look like Daddy," she whispered. Emily opened her eyes. She nodded. "Are you unhealthy?" She nodded again. Hannah glanced toward the kitchen. The men hovered over the dog. Zee stood with her arms crossed, staring back across the house at her. Hannah had never seen her so fixed, so adamant, as if she insisted some conclusion be immediately forthcoming. It was as if the sun had paused at the horizon without her permission.

"Listen," Hannah said to her sister, "I'm vibrating inside with fear. Promise me that Will is safe. You're not here to warn us about anything?"

"He's safe," she said softly. "I made sure of that. His father doesn't know where I am. I'm running from him, too."

"Did he hurt you?"

"Yes. Please don't tell Will."

"OK, but I can't stand this. I'm going to get rid of these other people. You look ill."

"I need to lie down."

Hannah took Emily upstairs to her room. Before she could shut the door, Will was there with Emily's bag.

"She can have my room," he said.

"We'll work that out later," Hannah told him. "I want you to go back into town with the Eatons. Take my car to Blue Hill and get the three of us something nice for dinner. Get fresh vegetables and a pork roast."

"I don't know how to do that. I've never bought a pork roast in my life. Can't we all go?"

"No, I want some time alone with my sister."

"Oh, are you OK, Miss Thomas?" he asked her.

"Yes, Will, I just want to rest. Will you ask Mr. Eaton to come up before he leaves?"

"Sure. I'll tell him now."

Hannah stepped into the hallway to let Tom in the room. The hallway seemed so small when they were in it together, as if they were two hands in the same pocket.

"Are you feeling sick again?" he asked Emily.

"Just a little bit. I wanted to thank you for putting up with me for all this time. I would have been lost without you." She sat on the bed. He crossed his arms and kneeled, his hooks protruding from his armpits as he leaned toward her.

"Nothing to it," he said. "I'll have another look at your car and if I can't do anything, I'll take it over to the garage for you."

"Thank you. It's always started before."

"Well, it's in Maine now. It wants to stay."

Hannah saw her smile at him. Emily reached out and put her palm on his cheek for an instant.

"Well, I'll let you know. If you need anything, Hannah knows where to find me. If you get tired of her cooking, I'll treat you to the Harbor Cafe or we can go up to Finest Kind again." He rose to his feet and backed out into the hallway. Hannah put both palms out flat to the small of his back so she wouldn't be crushed against Will's closed bedroom door.

"Oh, sorry, Hannah," Tom said, and hurried down the stairs. He tilted his head slightly when he reached the last step, avoiding the low ceiling, as though he'd built in this construction idiosyncrasy himself. It had taken Will three good whacks before he automatically ducked at the last tread. Even Arno had bumped if he put his cap on before going downstairs. She'd opened her mouth to warn Tom, but just as she'd started to yell, he'd tilted his head and swept under freely, only his hair brushing the blunt plastered edge. Then Emily called her name.

🦢🦢🦢

She hadn't seen her in fourteen years, not since their father's funeral. Emily was twelve years old then, a narrow child whose hands constantly toyed with her own knees and elbows. Her joints seemed to confound her, as if they unnaturally interrupted the smooth flow of her arms and legs. "It bothers me that you can feel the bones," she once told Hannah. Her dolls had no joints, only dimples. She pinched and jabbed and interrogated her knees till they glowed. At the funeral, Hannah and Emily's mother each held one hand to keep the girl from peeling the skin off her elbows.

Now, she sat on Hannah's bed, each elbow cupped soothingly in a palm.

"Can I get you some water, an aspirin?" Hannah asked

"No, thank you."

Hannah pulled the chair away from her desk and sat down. They listened to Will and the Eatons leaving.

"I didn't realize it would be so hard to reach you," Emily said.

"Emily, I don't mind that you're here, but you didn't mention anything about coming in your last letter."

"I've left my church."

"What does that mean?"

"It means I'm homeless." She made both these statements matter-of-factly, as if they followed logically. Her eyes were as listless as dead insects in the bottom of a white cup. Her face was dry. Flakes of skin were caught in her eyebrows. Her lips, chapped and white, remained slightly apart. "I think God loves somebody else," she said.

"You know I'm not religious, Emily. Why don't you tell me what's happened? Is this something you've come to after a lot of thought or did something cause you to leave? You're taking pauses between the things you say, but you don't seem so upset as you do tired."

"Hannah, I know we don't know each other, but I need someplace to stay for a while."

"There could be problems with that, Emily. Will's doing well here. I guess you know he is somewhat . . . I don't know how to say it . . . enamored with you."

"I know that. I never gave him any encouragement. I was his teacher and sister in Christ. I could leave in June or July."

"Why then? There must be lots of places that need teachers. It's midterm."

"It will take that long to have the baby." Emily clasped her hands between her thighs. The lids of her eyes covered half the pupils. Hannah thought she was either fainting or falling asleep. "I don't have any money. The church paid me with room and board and a little spending money for cigarettes and gum."

"I'm a little . . . I thought you were some kind of nun. Will said you practiced celibacy." She did not add, "And you smoke?"

"Yes, but God has made me pregnant."

"God did?"

"Yes."

"There wasn't another human being involved?"

"Of course."

"Where is the father?"

"He is a member of our church."

"Does he know you're pregnant?"

"No."

"Is it Will's father?"

"Yes."

"You're carrying Will's brother."

"His half brother or half sister. I don't want him to know."

"Were you raped?"

"No, I fell."

"You fell?"

"I fell."

"You felt sorry for this man and let him make love to you? Is that what happened?"

"For a moment I chose him over God."

"And now God won't let you forget it. So, why are you running?"

"Because this child needs some other father than Will's father."

"Where will you go after the baby comes?"

"I don't care," Emily said.

The island was covered with boulders, spalled and erratic, left by receding glaciers. They were part of the landscape but also separate, something obviously left behind, torn free from some other place and deposited here for the ages. It did little good to wonder what brought everyone here, so desperate. We're the Island of Misfit Toys, Hannah thought. We may never get off this island, either. She could put Emily in Will's room, move Will downstairs to the couch. What to do when Zee spent the night? She knew the island's defenses would have to be bolstered. He'll come now. He'll know why Emily left and he'll search till he finds both his children.

❦ ❦ ❦

It was quiet enough to hear the rain not just strike, but fall. The air hissed with the friction. There was thunder in the distance, rare in winter. Still it was muted, almost lackadaisical. Will was off to see Zee, and Hannah had just let Driftwood out to pee. She watched the dog work his way down to the foreshore, snuffle the dark seaweed. Steam rose when he relieved himself. Good dog, she thought. She was beginning to think she could expect no more of Emily. She'd been with them for a week and rarely left her room, only coming down to pee or nibble at toast. When Hannah asked her questions, she answered, "I don't know," or, "I don't care." But when she came down this morning she said she was feeling, "Without."

"Without what?" Hannah asked.

"I cheated on my marriage, but I thought He'd forgive me. Without."

"I don't even believe in God, Emily. It's hard for me to know what 'Without' means."

"It's the word that promises before it denies, gives, then takes away."

"You've been spurned in love."

"Do you think I'd be more like you if Daddy had lived? More confident?"

"He left my mother for your mother when I was nine. He certainly didn't make me feel confident."

"I miss him."

"Maybe dying is better than divorce in that way. I don't miss him. I learned to get along without him while he was alive."

"I miss God, too," Emily said.

"I can't help you with that."

"The painting of Will in my room: did I send him to the right place, Hannah? He's naked. What happens on this island isn't hidden from God."

"You're not so mild and meek, are you?" Hannah answered. "You're just as mad as you are sad. Well, I think that's good, but I hope we're not going to sit here and argue for the next six months over what kind of art God loves. Because I don't care. I only care about the kind of art I love. I'll get the painting out of the room so you won't have to look at it."

"It's just that it looks like him. Not Will, but his father."

"They look alike?"

"Alike like us."

"That's good to know. I'll recognize him when he comes. Will he come?"

"He may."

"You're not in contact with him, are you?"

"No."

"Did he beat you, too?"

"Only after I relented. He said I was weak to let him in. He was like God and the devil in one body. I couldn't understand how he could beat Will until he started beating me. I mean I knew he did. I saw the marks on Will's back, his broken arm. But I'd never been a witness."

"Or a victim."

Then she went silent again. And this pattern continued: a few days of silence followed by a ten-minute conversation. Hannah's work was rarely interrupted. When Emily came downstairs she did so in a robe and bare feet. The dog didn't raise his head. Even Will couldn't make contact with her.

"She acts like she's been sent to live among the infidels and heathens," Will told Hannah. "She wasn't like this at all at school. I asked her to help me with this paper I have to write over the break and she said she wasn't my teacher anymore. She's smoking cigarettes in my room. She asked me to buy her some cigarettes."

"I don't know what to tell you, Will," Hannah said. "You know her better than I do."

"She's your sister. I'll be glad when school starts again and I get my room back."

"She's not going back to teach. She'll be here for a while."

"Why not, I mean, why?"

"I think she's having problems with her faith."

"But why turn the cold shoulder to me? It's not like I'm going to judge her."

❦ ❦ ❦

Hannah began to go into Emily's room each morning after Will left for school. She'd already removed the Plexiglas from the outside of Emily's windows. Her sister would be up, or still be up, sitting at the head of her bed, wrapped in a mound of blankets. Hannah closed the door and opened both windows to let out the fetid air. Emily's hands protruded from the heaped blankets and held her Bible.

"We have to tell Will you're pregnant. You're showing already."

"You tell him," Emily said. Her voice was a mouse in a small cardboard box.

"It's not good for you or the baby: all this smoking," Hannah said. "What should I tell him?"

"That I'm pregnant."

"He won't believe in another immaculate conception."

"He doesn't believe at all. What have you done to him?"

"I didn't do anything to him. He didn't believe when he came to me. I want you to start putting on some clothes before you come downstairs."

"They don't fit anymore."

"You're not that pregnant, Emily. You need to start doing something besides sitting up here all day long."

"I'm having the baby," she said.

"That's not enough. There's chores I'm going to assign to you. You can refill the kindling box and wood box every day. Refill the lamps and trim the wicks. The ash drawer under the woodstove needs to be emptied every day."

"What are you going to tell Will?" Emily asked.

"That you're pregnant."

"He'll know who it was as soon as you tell him."

"Then we should tell him the truth. He's a good kid, Emily. You know that."

"I wish I hadn't sent him here, then I would have had a place to hide. Can you please shut the windows now? It's so cold."

"It'll be better once he knows," Hannah said.

"That little girlfriend of his already hates me."

"Zee? I don't think she'll feel so strongly about you when she finds out you're pregnant. I think she thought you were competition."

"I thought maybe her dad already told her."

"Tom knows?"

"He figured it out. He said his wife got sick when she was pregnant. Will said he's coming to see me this Sunday."

"He comes every Sunday," Hannah said.

❧ ❧ ❧

She heard something under the wind, beneath a dream, a faint but re-peated jostling of broken glass, as if it were being swept into a pile. It entered her dream when Tom Eaton began to sweep the length of a long, tiled hallway, pushing his severed hands along the floor past lockers and classroom doors. There was no blood. That's why he wasn't using a mop. The hands tumbled in front of the stiff brown bristles. Tom passed her without looking up.

She found the glass a few days later, scattered across the granite floor of the boat shed. At first she thought Arno's beer bottles had frozen and exploded. But why had it taken six winters? Then she found bits of fine brown glass embedded in the leading edge of *Break of Day*'s stem. The old boat had been repeatedly rechristened with beer. Someone had smashed each of the full bottles. The caps were still attached to the broken necks. They hadn't even bothered to drink the beer.

She swept up the dark shards with a stiff broom, often confusing the mica in the granite for glass. Arno's trash pit was just up the slope from the boat shed. She threw the bucketful of glass on top of all the other broken bottles and rusty tin cans. The pit was as deep as bedrock would allow. Arno had burned trash there for years. Old spoons and broken tools were embedded in fused masses of melted glass. Cans still held congealed lumps of varnish and paint. What looked like burned water hose writhed through the mound. It was the island's own little Superfund site. Perhaps this spring, she thought, with Will and Emily's help, she could dig out all the old paint cans and plastic garbage and bury what was left. The tin cans and saw blades would rust away, enriching the soil. The glass could stay till the next geological rumbling, when it would be completely reformed, or until global warming swept up the slope and the tide ground it back to sand.

She shook her head. You're too far into the future again, she thought. You should be concentrating on all that beer flowing down the granite into the ocean. She reached back down into the pit and retrieved the seven necks of the broken bottles. She could hang them from her warning sculptures. She knew every island in the archipelago had its own whistle, the ocean breeze filtering through spruce limbs and fissures in the granite. Ten Acre No Nine, with its quarry, already played a dimpled note that deepened as the wind rose, the same note a man's breath made across the hollow of a woman's neck. Perhaps these broken bottles would hum and mew, spin warning on the wind. Perhaps they'd cut the hand that reached out to silence them.

🐦 🐦 🐦

When she told Will that Emily was pregnant, he said, "He got to her then."

"You mean your dad?"

He nodded. "Then, once she'd done what he wanted, he told her it was all wrong. Somehow it was her fault. That's why she doesn't come out of her room. I felt the same way for years. You don't want to do anything for fear that even the right thing will be the wrong thing. That's why she asks every night if it's OK to set the table, like there could be some night when she shouldn't."

"She's worried that you'll be mad at her."

"Jesus," he said, "even Zee and I know to use . . ."

"Know to use birth control?" Hannah finished.

"Yeah," he said. "How did you know? Did you guess?"

"Tom told me."

"Mr. Eaton knows?" he shrieked.

"Yeah," Hannah said. "He buys your condoms."

"Jesus, Jesus, Jesus," Will whispered.

"You didn't know that?"

"No, I thought Zee was getting them. I can't believe everybody knows. Why hasn't he killed me? Why is he buying the . . . Jesus."

"It surprised me, too," Hannah said.

"How can I be at the center of everything and not know anything?" he asked. "Why hasn't he killed me?"

"He seems to think, and you can tell him if he's wrong, that you'd do it with or without the condoms."

"Uh, maybe," Will said. He grinned. "But I was going to start getting them. They're going to put condom machines in the bathrooms at the high school."

"I know. I read about it in the paper. The school board voted for them unanimously. Then they voted three to one to reinstate chocolate milk to the cafeteria. Somebody down there doesn't trust you guys with chocolate milk."

"Do you think Mr. Eaton knows I didn't know? I mean, I've been scared to death he was going to catch us for weeks."

"Well, I still wouldn't be too flagrant. Just because he's buying the con-doms doesn't mean he's overjoyed about it. I'd still be careful where you and Zee go parking. You might yet find a claw on your door handle when you come home one night."

"Very funny, ha, ha, ha," he said. All the same, a shudder twisted his shoulders and compressed his neck. "But it's not funny. He's not much bigger than me but have you seen his shoulders? The guy could twist me in half if he wanted to."

"I can't tell you how much it pleases me to see you writhing like this," Hannah said. "Here's something else: did you or Zee break all those beer bottles out in the boat shed?"

"No."

"Somebody busted seven full bottles of beer against *Break of Day*'s stem. Those bottles that were in the window."

"Miss Thomas maybe?"

"No, she hardly leaves the house."

"Mr. Eaton and his dad were out there last Sunday."

"I think it happened after that. They didn't mention any broken glass. But you can ask him when you see him next."

"I'm not asking him anything ever again," Will said. "So, you're not going to kick me out of the house or anything?"

"I got past that long ago. But if you ever do anything beyond giving her a kiss on the cheek in front of me, you'll be sleeping on *Break of Day* for the rest of the winter. So save your quarters for that machine. I don't want another pregnant woman moving out to the island."

"I hope Miss Thomas was careful about coming here," Will said.

"Me too. She said she was. She's just as afraid of him as you are."

"I'm not afraid anymore."

"OK."

"I'm not. If you've ever been trapped and escaped you'd understand. I know I'll never let myself be put under his control again. No matter what."

"Maybe he won't find us."

"I know he's already gone through everything she left there. If there was a scrap of paper with your name on it, he'll check it out. He's very thorough. I can't believe she let him get to her. I warned her again and again."

"Hey, that always works," Hannah said. "Will, I'm warning you never to make a mistake, or to be unhappy, or deluded, or poor. She says she did it because she felt sorry for him, but I think she was lonely, too. She was trying to solve her loneliness. I think she's found that when she's alone in a room with God she's still lonely. And when she reached out, she was punished."

"She shouldn't have felt sorry for him. That's when he beats you. He gets his way by wheedling and then when he gets his way he's humiliated because you let him have it. Hannah, he won't come here shouting. He'll come groveling."

"Will, what does 'without' mean?"

"They use it in our church to describe everyone outside the church. Did Miss Thomas use that word to describe herself?"

"Yes."

"They won't have her back then."

"Why not?"

"She's been excluded. She's the worst kind to them: one who was allowed inside, given the key, and refused it. She doesn't exist to them anymore."

"It just sounds cruel."

"They're scared to death of the people who leave them. We had a guy come back who'd been excommunicated. Everybody acted as if he weren't even there. He sat in the middle of the camp and cried. Some of the men started bumping into him and falling down as if he were an invisible wall. They carry everything they believe to its illogical limit. They don't handle snakes or see miracles or anything. There's no animal sacrifices or child molesting, unless you count me. It's just an isolated little place. Instead of water around it, there's a barbed-wire fence. There's about seventy or eighty people who live there. The men all go home at night. Everybody helps everybody, until you're without. I wonder if my dad is without now, too."

"Maybe you can talk to Emily about it. I'm worried about her. She does the chores I've given her but that's all. She doesn't seem to have any interest in anything. I've set up her first doctor appointment next Saturday. Maybe you can go with her."

"I can't believe she's pregnant. What are we going to do when the baby comes? She can't have it here on the island. We'll never get her to the hospital in time."

"Tom told me she can stay with him in town when she gets close."

"He knows about her being pregnant, too?"

"He knew before I did."

"Jesus."

🐢🐢🐢

On the third Sunday in January, Hannah found herself once again at the kitchen table alone with Everett Eaton, just as she had been the previous two weeks. Tom was upstairs talking to Emily. He usually spent more than an hour with her, the door closed.

"I know a song," Everett Eaton told her.

"Let's hear it," Hannah said.

He sang in a low, grumbling voice, as if he were slowly pouring gravel from one wooden bowl to another.

> *Away boys away, to Newfoundland today*
> *There's a fair wind at play*
> *And we've got to earn our pay*
>
> *Away boys away, into the deep blue,*
> *Your wives will cheat on you*
> *But the fish are always true*
>
> *Away boys away, there's hard work to come,*
> *You'll miss your children some*
> *But that's what for the rum*
>
> *Away boys away, around the tolling gong,*
> *We'll stop at Swan's for bait and song*
> *And take all their girls along*
>
> *Away girls away, we'll fish and fish all day,*
> *Yes, metaphor's the genteel way*
> *To say we'll fish and fish all day*
>
> *Away boys away, what can I say,*
> *There's no fish left in the bay,*
> *The sail and the song and the story's our pay*

Away boys away, the storms will rage and roll,
We'll pray for every body and soul,
But our boat will surely be holed

Away boys away, the horizon is our home,
Our headstones are the skipping rocks thrown
By our children into the briny loam

Away boys away, someday a chantey will be sung,
By every sweet girl's tongue,
We'll be forever young,
We'll be forever young

Away boys away, to Newfoundland today,
There's a fair wind at play
And we've got to earn our pay

He smiled when he finished, but the song hung in the air like smoke. "I've got a memory problem," he said. "But I can remember all kinds of useless information. I'd be living in my house if I hadn't forgotten that skillet of bacon."

"Do you know who I am?" Hannah asked him.

"Sure, I do."

"Who?"

"Same person you were yesterday."

"I'm Arno Weed's niece, Hannah."

"Didn't know he had one."

"Yes, but Uncle Arno's gone. He died six years ago."

"I didn't know that. Did the cancer get him?"

"No, it was a heart attack."

"That's a good way to go. Arno used a red buoy with a white cross. My uncle built his boat. I guess you're a rich girl."

"Why?"

"Didn't you inherit Arno's money?"

"He left me the island. I don't think he was rich outside of that," Hannah said.

"Oh, sure he was. He was tight. He loved beer, but would never buy a bottle. Wouldn't spend a nickel on his boat that wasn't necessary to keep it from sinking."

"He was a lobsterman like you, Mr. Eaton."

"Not like me. He was better. And I never was part of that other trade."

"What other trade?"

"He had the NoDoz concession around here for years."

"I don't understand."

"Aw, I guess it's a secret."

"Why should it be a secret?"

"What are we talking about?"

"The NoDoz concession, Mr. Eaton. Are you trying to say my uncle was a drug dealer?"

"Who was your uncle?"

"Arno Weed."

"No, no, Arno Weed didn't sell drugs. He sold those little pills so you could finish your work. Some didn't like it, but everybody knows Arno is better than them kids that used to come over from Rockland. We run them off. Arno was honest and he'd carry you over if you were short, just like the grocery. He never comes down hard on anybody. It all goes to his taxes anyway. Only way he can keep from selling out. These islands have gone up so much in value, you see. Maybe he loaned out all his money. He'd loan it back out to the fellas who bought from him. I know half of them didn't pay him back. Maybe that's why you're not rich."

"Are you sure, Mr. Eaton? He sold pills? I worked for him for two summers. I never saw him sell anything but lobsters."

"I never bought any. The younger fellas would work harder. They bought them. They'd run too many traps and have to stay out all night, sometimes two or three nights. They aren't consistent, the young fishermen. They'll work like hell and then lay off for a week, and then have to stay up two or three nights in a row again. They'd pay Arno in beer."

"Beer?"

"I saw it a hundred times if I saw it once: Arno would pitch across a little grocery sack and them boys would throw him back a bottle of beer."

"Those were sacks of vegetables, Mr. Eaton, not pills. Arno had a big garden."

"He never threw me a sack of vegetables."

"Did you ever throw him a beer?"

"There's no beer on my boat while it's working. But I'm not trying to convince you. Them boys that traded with Arno thought they needed the NoDoz. I tried taking one once and I had to stamp my foot all night long. My heart kept trying to escape through it."

"Who has the NoDoz concession now, Mr. Eaton?"

"After Arno give it up, the doctors around here caught on. There were too many backaches. Then they caught two fellas in a row complaining of kidney stones who'd rigged their piss samples by cutting their finger and letting the blood drip into the cup. Kidney stones are pretty painful. They give you their best pills if you've got kidney stones. I think those boys from Rockland worked back up this way. I don't know how it all works."

"Why did Arno Weed stop selling?" Hannah asked.

"That boy that drowned. He wouldn't sell no more after that. About half the folks around here got upset with him after that boy drowned. The Coast Guard found some NoDoz on the boat. Everybody knew Arno gave it to him. Then everybody else got mad at him for not selling anymore. Poor Arno had his warp in his wheel. Couldn't go back or forward. Later we found out that boy was on depressing drugs, antidepressing drugs. Things sort of died down after that."

"Your memory seems fine to me, Mr. Eaton."

"I can remember all the old, useless stuff. It's how I got here that baffles me. Where are we?"

"You're on Ten Acre No Nine Island. You're in Arno Weed's house."

"Do you know my son?" Mr. Eaton asked her.

"Yes. He's upstairs talking to my sister."

They both stopped talking and listened. Tom and Emily's voices washed through the floor above them in muffled waves, as if water were trying to imitate human voices. It surprised her. Emily's voice broke in long low sentences. Tom would speak a word or two, and then Emily would gather again and curl out at length till she spread so thin they could hardly hear her. No individual word of their conversation was discernible, nor did they seem urgent or concerned with time.

"How long have they been up there?" Mr. Eaton asked.

"As long as we've been down here," she answered.

"I don't have a sense of time anymore," he told her. "I remember when I was younger that I was against the passage of time. I didn't like it at all. Seemed like something was being taken from me. When I was younger I had to wait all day long for a sunset. Not anymore. Sometimes I see two or three sunsets in a row before I see a sunrise."

Everett Eaton put his finger in his eye and then wiped it off in the crotch of his pants. The surreptitious self-cleaning acts of his youth had turned into unself-conscious public habits in his old age: rubbing his front teeth with the flat of his index finger, pulling at individual hairs protruding from his nostrils, rearranging his testicles. Perhaps revealing secrets could be put in the same category. She didn't know whether to laugh or scream. The notion that Arno traded NoDoz to tired fishermen at sea for bottles of beer made her want to giggle. The idea that he sold amphetamines to addicts who may have died as a result left her digging into the soft wood underneath the tabletop with her fingernails.

"Do you smell bacon burning?" Everett Eaton asked her.

"No, Mr. Eaton, it's all right."

"Whenever I don't know where I am, I smell bacon burning."

"You're in Arno Weed's house."

"He's a good fisherman. My uncle built his boat."

🐚 🐚 🐚

"It costs my father little to lie," Tom Eaton told her. "He tells the nurses at the home that I took all his money. He's always told stories: big lobsters, invading icebergs, pirates."

"And you didn't inherit that from him?" she asked.

"No, mostly I listen."

"I've heard you listening."

"You have?"

"Yes, to Emily."

"Well, she's working through something."

"You don't seem to mind listening."

"No, it's interesting. She's in between two lives. She's like Zee in a lot of ways: not a girl, but not a woman either. I think she's so deeply ashamed she can hardly breathe. What did Dad say that was so upsetting?"

"Last week, when you were upstairs, he told me that my uncle Arno had the NoDoz concession. Do you know what that is?"

"Yes."

"Well?"

"He's gone, Hannah. What does it matter?"

"Someone's been tearing up my island for six years."

They were alone in the house. Emily, Will, Zee, and Mr. Eaton were out beachcombing, orbiting them at a distance of several hundred yards. She'd never seen Tom so uncomfortable. He sat in the big chair next to the stove and tapped the hot stove with the tip of one hook. The sound emptied the whole room.

"Stop doing that," she ordered.

He brought the hook to his lap and clasped it with the other hook. Then he released it, and this hook in turn clasped the other. The two hooks alternately bit each other, playing a morbid game of itsy-bitsy spider. He was more ill at ease now than he'd been when he told her about losing his hands.

"I'm sorry," he said.

"About what?"

"Arno did have the concession for a long while, I guess, before I left. It was the thing there for a while, to work on uppers. You could haul more, stay out longer. There were always dealers around, but they were controlled by who bought from them. Some of the older lobstermen didn't want the dealers around who also sold heroin and grass, so they set up Arno. He was the last fisherman who actually owned one of these islands. We don't lose our land in wars anymore, we lose it to taxes. It's nothing against you; you inherited your island. But the people who earn their living off the water can't afford to live on it anymore. Every lobsterman I know who hasn't inherited his folks' place on the sea, lives inland. The summer people own the shoreland now. Everybody wanted to see Arno keep this place. You have good seasons and bad as a lobsterman. It's not consistent enough to pay the taxes on a million-dollar piece of property."

"I thought he was giving people vegetables," Hannah said listlessly.

"He was. Arno always did that, long before the concession."

"But how did he pay his taxes? Did he sell the beer?"

"Sell the beer?"

"Your dad said he was paid in beer."

"Oh, Christ, no. The money was in the beer bottle."

Her gasp took wing like a moth that fell farther than it flew.

"What?" Tom asked.

"I worked with him, Tom, for a couple summers. The bottles he caught had beer in them."

"The money was usually in an empty bottle. They were easy to throw across open water, and if they fell in they floated for a while. Maybe they paid him some other way while you were here."

"There were a half-dozen of Arno's beer bottles out in the boat shed. A couple weeks ago someone broke them all open on *Break of Day's* stem."

"They thought there may still be a few deposits inside," Tom said.

"I can't believe it," she said. "He was so sweet."

"He was a good guy."

"He was a drug dealer, Tom, even if he did do it to save his home."

"Look, people thought they needed what Arno had. He only sold what they needed to stay awake, to make a living. They didn't think of it as dangerous back then. They didn't think of it as being addictive. It was just something they needed, like cigarettes or sleep."

"You've been in my house before," she said.

"What?"

"You've been here before, before I met you last fall. When you went down the stairs you didn't bump your head. You've been upstairs in this house long before I met you."

He sighed. "There was a season when the lobsters just weren't where they should have been. I had a new boat. Payments were coming due. I had to work longer hours. I couldn't do it by myself. I was falling asleep at the helm. I'd fall asleep between strings, the boat going full throttle. Arno didn't work in the deep winter. He wasn't out on the water. I came here. For a while there, he was sick. You had to go up to his bedroom. He wouldn't sell you anything till you kept him company for a bit. He was lonely."

"I want to know if you broke the bottles. Will said you and your dad were out there."

"I was showing Dad the old boat. I didn't break the damn bottles. I'm not the guy digging up your island. I haven't lived here for twelve years."

"I can't believe that a whole town would condone, would certify, a drug dealer."

"It wasn't the whole town. It was those who knew, like it always is. It's not like it was published in the paper or voted on at town meeting."

"Why have you left me in the dark for so long? You knew I've been afraid, that I didn't know what was going on."

"I'm sorry. I'm not proud of that year. I'd just as soon Zee not know about it. I've been looking for these guys, the ones digging. I thought I could handle it on my own. I haven't been here long enough to get back on the inside."

"So you think it's some of Arno's old customers looking for drugs or money?"

"Maybe. But I don't know. I've only been here awhile. You've been here for years. I didn't know if it wasn't some personal problem you were having with somebody."

"Like what?"

"Like an old boyfriend."

"That's not it," she said.

"No one?"

"No."

"Then you're more of a nun than your sister is."

"What a stupid thing to say."

"I'm sorry. Zee told me there was a man who died."

"That was in New York, not here."

"So that couldn't have followed you here?"

"What do you mean?"

"People think you're hiding something out here. You rarely come into town. You've been here for years and they don't know you. I didn't know that you weren't aware of Arno's concession. Some people in town think since you worked as his sternman you had to be in on it."

"I didn't know. He gave people vegetables; they threw him a beer. It seemed pretty straightforward to me. I thought it was funny when he suddenly stopped working his garden."

"He gave up the concession when Sonny Thurlow died. The Coast Guard found a bag of Arno's pills on his boat. Even though there were other drugs aboard, some grass and some prescriptions, Arno thought he shared some of the blame. Turned out Sonny was on antidepressants. When you mix them with uppers they can produce schizophrenic symptoms. People thought Sonny went crazy on that boat. The people in town who didn't use knew Arno sold to Sonny and they ostracized him for it. The guys who used were mad at him because he wouldn't sell anymore. He became more and more like you. He wouldn't leave the island much those last few years. Anyway, that's what I get from my old friends, from Dad. I wasn't here afterwards."

"They never found that man's body," Hannah said.

"No," he answered.

"I was here when it happened. Arno and I were out all night looking. Then he cut up his garden. I knew there was something wrong with him that summer, but I was preoccupied."

"With what?"

"A boy at Haystack. Arno and I finally had a fight over him and I went back to school. We wrote letters and cards afterward, but I never came back to the island until he died."

"And the Haystack boy?"

"God, he was Will's age. That was a long time ago."

"I don't remember. Was it me?" Tom said.

She looked at him and smirked. "No."

"I took classes there."

"He was from Hawaii."

"Oh, I guess it wasn't me then."

"What kind of classes did you take?"

"They had a program for island kids. Free tuition. I took a wood-turning class and pottery workshop. I still have a few bowls and pots. Only things I have left in the world with my fingerprints still on them."

She suddenly felt his hands on her upper neck, the back of her skull, the fingertips pressing against her headache there.

"It's hard to picture you there," she said, and rubbed her neck at the hairline.

"I wasn't very good. My pots were ungainly, like flat tires. Mostly I volunteered for construction projects. I helped rebuild some of the raised sidewalks. The viewing platform over the cove needed a new railing."

"But you met girls there, too."

"Yeah, my wife."

"You're kidding?"

"No, she was down from Jonesport. She'd won a scholarship for a weaving class."

"When were you there?"

"I think it was a few years before you. We just missed each other."

"What do you mean? We missed each other by years."

"Geographically."

"You mean, since we both stood on the same spot on the planet's surface several years apart we just missed each other?"

"Yeah, I guess, relatively."

"Relative to what?"

"All time and distance, I guess. And there's some of me still there at Haystack, and some of you still there, there in the past. You saw me in the past when I didn't bump my head going down the stairs."

"That's right. We just missed each other here in this house, too. You used to buy drugs in Emily's bedroom."

"I didn't have to tell you about that, about any of this," he said.

"Sure you did. You haven't kept a secret since you met me."

"Zee told me you tended to like people when they told their secrets."

"You know, you're not a normal father. Your seventeen-year-old daughter tells you everything."

"I know. Sometimes I wish I didn't know so much. It'd be easier to live on an island by myself."

🕊 🕊 🕊

Driftwood tried to lead, but found that he had to follow. Hannah often stopped and backtracked around the island, as if she'd forgotten or lost something. The tide was up and she didn't want to fight her way through the bracken just to make a circuit. The high water cut off beach access on the north side of her island, making it necessary to pull herself up a steep hill by roots if she wanted to make a complete circle. It was easier to stop and turn around, see the island counterclockwise. Arno had been on the island alone for six years after she'd left. She'd been here that long now. The dog bumped into the back of her knee and that leg buckled.

When they passed below the house, she saw Emily's face in an upper window. It seemed a distant mirror. Emily stepped back and the reflection was gone, replaced by a rectangle of sky. She knew the front door would not soon open. Her sister would not run down the hill to join her in pacing round the island. It was almost as if Emily were trapped within the baby, rather than the child locked inside her. She'd told her about Arno, and Emily had simply said, "So?"

Hannah hadn't known how to respond. She thought Emily would come down hard on the old man. If paintings of half-nude young men set her off, certainly drug dealing ought to earn a reprimand. Some commandment must have been transgressed. Hannah finally decided that Emily would cast no stones in her current state, that she thought pregnancy was a far deeper pit in hell than profiting from addiction.

She tried to find above her the rectangle of sky reflected in the window. It seemed impossible at first, but by determining the angle from her eye to Emily's room and following it back into the firmament, she thought she could make out the same shading of blue, the vault of heaven in a box small enough to understand it. Arno, what have you left me? Cells and shreds of Sonny Thurlow's body have been washing up here for twelve years now. That's probably his shirt hanging on my warning sculpture at the east end of the island, his shoes lodged in the seaward crevices in the granite. Someone's been turning the island over, like compost, ever since I came. No wonder the boats circle this island, Blackback gulls over another breed's rookery.

She'd gone up into the attic, pulled down the boxes of Arno's paperwork. There was nothing, not a statement, a receipt, a stub, from any time before the death of the lobsterman. But he certainly hadn't made himself rich. His bank records since that time showed he saved all he could each year and used most of that savings to pay his taxes. Everything else went for groceries and fishing equipment. She wondered what had been in the bottles: fives, tens, twenties? Perhaps there had been a little extra during the NoDoz concession, enough to buy a new engine, enough to hire a sternman, enough to take winters off. She wondered if he'd died just before he ran out of money, just so he'd leave the island to her unencumbered.

The water was too deep to see Arno's tombstone. The square stone cut with a flower was more than ten feet underwater at high tide. Arno had never moved it around to his grave site, and she hadn't yet either. His grave was unmarked, just like his little sister's. What were his instructions? Tie the stone to *Break of Day* at low tide, letting the buoyancy of the boat lift the weight of the stone as the tide rose, and slowly motor around the island to the boat shed. Then use the winch in the shed to haul it ashore, and the winch at the rim of the quarry to drag it farther up the island. From there it would be above the little cemetery and you could use log or pipe rollers to move it down to the grave. The stone must easily weigh half a ton. "Coax it," he'd said. They'd talked about it several times. "Use a lever to get a line under it. Borrow all the rope you can. Use a skid with the winch."

She said aloud, "It's going to be harder now, Arno. *Break of Day* won't float. The skid is rotten. Who'll loan rope to a dead man?"

Driftwood banked his head. There was a small green crab in his mouth. He held it gingerly, his lower jowls sagging away. The crab had both tiny claws buried in the dog's tongue. Hannah realized here that soon she would have to stick her hand in a dog's mouth, a mouth already occupied by an angry crustacean.

⸙ ⸙ ⸙

Emily continued to spend most of her day in her room, as if it were an island in the sea of the house.

"Would you like to go shopping?" Hannah asked her. "You could go in with Will. I'll give you the money."

"No," she said.

"Why not?"

"I don't want to be seen like this."

"Like what?"

She held her open hands beneath her stomach. "Like this."

"The people here don't care if you're pregnant, Emily. Isn't there anything you want to do, anything you're interested in?"

"I'm doing the chores you gave me."

"I know. I said anything you want to do. There are two bookstores in town. You could go in to the grocery and get the things you like to eat. Maybe Sunday you could take Will and Zee to the movies in Ellsworth."

"Tom comes on Sundays. I don't want to miss him."

"What about church? There are churches here, too, Emily."

"They won't accept me. I'm not married."

"That's ridiculous. Of course they will."

"If you don't have to leave, why do I have to?"

"You don't. But I have a life here, my work. The island interests me. You don't seem to have anything, not even your baby."

"I am held hostage by this baby. I'm like you. I wanted to live alone. It's not just that God loves someone else, or doesn't love me. It's that He isn't."

Hannah had been standing at the door to Emily's room, nauseous with the stale cigarette smoke. She stepped slowly into the room and sat on the edge of the bare mattress. Emily had drawn her blankets and even the sheets up around her chin. "You know it's too late for an abortion, don't you?" she said as calmly as she could.

"I know that."

"Emily, you're acting more like someone's died rather than someone's being born."

"I feel that way. God shouldn't have let this happen. I was working for Him. I'd rather believe a God like that doesn't exist, rather than believe in one who's flawed."

"You can't adapt your faith to this new experience? Most religious people I've met assume that God knows more than they do. It's the basis of faith, to trust Him with your life."

"What did that trust get me?"

"I don't know, Emily. I don't know what I'm doing, trying to get you to believe in God. I've never had any faith. It just seems like it's been your life."

"My life was based on false premises. I know that now."

"So what will the new premise be?"

"I don't know. Every woman for herself maybe."

"Can't we start with pants? You need some stretchy pants."

"I have my housecoat."

"Emily, you can't live the next five months in your housecoat."

"If you can live on an island for years, why can't I live in a housecoat for months?"

"Because you have doctor's appointments. And because this is my island. I'd like to inhabit it alone, even if it's only for a few hours."

"You let the dog stay all the time."

"The dog showed up here like me, unable to breathe anywhere else," Hannah said.

"I can't leave here. I can't breathe out there either. The doctor will know. They'll all see."

"See what?"

"That I've let someone inside me. That I've cheated on God."

"So did your mother, Emily. You need to concentrate on the baby now. What's outside, what other people think, what God thinks, isn't important anymore. I've made an appointment for you at the clinic in Blue Hill. Will's going to take you."

"As soon as the baby comes, I'll leave the island."

"And in the meantime? The doctors won't come out here, Emily. You can't have the baby here. I'm not a midwife."

"You could go in with me to the doctor's."

"I don't want to leave the island alone."

"You said the baby was what's important now."

"I did. All right. I'll go in with you. But we need to stop and buy clothes, too."

"If you go with me, they'll know I'm alone."

"What?"

"And Will is too young. Ask Tom Eaton to take me. That way you won't have to go."

"You can't pretend that Tom is the father, Emily."

"He won't mind. He likes me. I won't say he's the father. He'll just be there."

"Emily, you'll have at least five or six appointments before the baby arrives. He might not be able to take you every time."

"That's OK. But the first time's important. Why can't you let him decide? Why do you have to make up everybody's mind? You're not God, either. No one is God."

"I'll call him," Hannah said, and got up. Why should it bother her so, to be told she wasn't God? She understood that. All the same, she told the stair runners that her sister was a little bitch.

🐚 🐚 🐚

She was able to give up now, to some extent, the guilt she'd felt for not visiting Arno the last few years of his life. Even though he had invited her to return as his sternman, he'd never asked twice, and perhaps he really wanted to be left alone. She realized she was trading her guilt for his. Now that Arno was guilty, she no longer had to be. She was troubled by the thought that the island she'd inherited had been kept in the family through illegal means. But apparently the community had approved and even conspired in this arrangement for Arno's sake. It had been a strange twisting of the Chamber of Commerce's shop at home endorsement. The money had stayed in the town rather than gone ashore to Rockland, to turn over here at the grocery, the lobster co-op, the tithing plate. And Ten Acre No Nine stayed in the hands of a local fisherman.

But now the island was owned by an outsider. No one fished from its shores. Bit of irony there. They'd saved it for an artist. Perhaps they thought I'd be a fisherman, too. At least it wasn't sold. Every time an island or prime piece of shorefront sold at some exorbitant price, everyone's taxes went up. She wondered if that was why Arno didn't sell, why he permitted himself the concession. It would have been an odd compromise, to sell drugs to your neighbors to save them from higher property taxes. Who was using who? Where did the selfishness begin and end?

At any rate, since she'd arrived she'd paid her taxes honestly, by the sweat of her art. Perhaps by the time she died the stain would be washed off the island. Who would she leave it to? Her half sister's child, the Nature Conservancy, the town? A lottery among local fishermen?

All she wanted was to be let alone long enough to enjoy the view, and long enough she defined as the length of her life. By that time she hoped to be able to interpret the view as well. There had to be an answer for the beach, why the ocean met the land and lingered there softly licking for ages, as if the land needed soothing. The slow, gentle wearing of the world would lead all to one level. No wonder Noah built his Ark. There was no angel of warning required. He could simply watch the waves in their liquid lounging over rock and see what was coming. His wasn't a parable of the past but a warning for the future. The lobster had already prepared for the end of the earth. When the last of the molten rock cooled, and the last sand spit slipped under, the suspiration of the planet would sound as wave against wave and the faint, brittle burst of air breaking free from membranes of brine. In the meantime, there was her search for an idea, an understanding. She thought that perhaps she'd been working with solids too long, that a bowl of water might prove more satisfactory. She needed to take from the water just as the fishermen did. The stones she'd been sending to Gwen, like the ones on her windowsills, must be dry and dull by now. The sheen the sea left on a rock only lasted till the next wave.

🦤🦤🦤

He must have been thinking about his proposition for weeks. It was carefully reasoned, had endorsements from professionals, and there was proof of results from her own past. Will came home from school and sat down with Hannah at her worktable. He passed her his report card and began to play with a pile of Victorian dish shards. Hannah had been picking them out of the garden and off the beach for years. He reformed them, puzzle-like, into the shape of a two-dimensional cup and saucer.

"All A's," Hannah said. She couldn't help it. A warm flush filled her chest and cheeks. Her boy was so smart. She watched him with the shards, constraining herself from reaching over to fill in a gap with a piece she knew would fit perfectly.

"I'm taking a navigation and marine safety course at school now. It's a new program. Most of the kids in there already know the stuff. They've been fishing for years. Most of them have licenses already. I tell them it's like somebody from Mexico getting credit for taking Spanish. But I'm learning a lot."

"You get credit for taking English, don't you?" Hannah asked.

"I didn't think of that."

"You know Emily's going in with you tomorrow. Don't forget her."

"I won't. I'm just glad I don't have to go to the clinic with her."

"She doesn't bite, Will."

"I know. I wish she did. When people are as quiet as she is, something's up. You know, if you can't say anything nice about the people around you, don't say anything: she hasn't said much to me since she got here."

"Did you ask her about your dad, whether he is without, too?"

"Yeah, she said she didn't tell anybody anything before she left. He wins again. I hope somebody around there notices that all the people around him keep disappearing. Has she talked to you about her mom and your dad?"

"What about them?"

"She says it's their fault she's got troubles."

"How so?"

"Your dad died and her mom married that preacher."

"So they caused her pregnancy?"

"Seems like a pretty straight line, doesn't it?" He shook his head. "It's like she lost her faith in God and doesn't have any reason to fall back on."

"But you did?"

"I don't think I lost my faith. I don't think I ever had it. I remember lying in my bed as a little kid and chanting, 'I don't believe in Jesus, I don't believe in Jesus.' I think I was mad about something, maybe having to go to bed while it was still daylight. In the summer back home it's daylight till nine-thirty or ten."

"What do you want, Will?"

"What do you mean?"

"Every time you sit at my table and start playing with my supplies or tools, you're after something."

"I am not."

"OK, you want to glue those shards to some stiff paper? I like your cup."

"No." He put his palms on the shards and shuffled them like dominoes. "I was thinking about this summer."

"Yeah?"

"I could work at Billings again but my pay would be the same and I probably wouldn't learn much more. I thought I'd do what you did to earn money for college. I'd like to fix up *Break of Day* this spring and work her this summer."

"Lobster?"

He nodded.

She shook her head. "You don't have a license and they're hard to come by."

"I know. But Tom Eaton has a license. I could be his sternman. I think we could work out a better cut, since we own the boat. I mean, better than if I worked as a sternman for someone else on their boat."

"Did Tom put you up to this?"

"No, I haven't said anything to him. I wanted to talk to you first."

"Well," she said, "I guess that's the truth because he would have told you that *Break of Day* will never float again. She's too far gone."

"Actually, he told me she was gone, too, but that there's no wooden boat that couldn't be brought back if she wasn't rotten through and through. I did the ice-pick test on her."

"The ice-pick test?"

"You stick an ice-pick in her all over. It's not supposed to go in."

"And it didn't?"

"Almost."

"Well?"

"It went in an inch or two in a couple places, but some of the guys at school said you can just replace the bad wood. Hannah, I don't want to go to a state college. I want to go to Colby or Bates. They cost a fortune. It would help Mr. Eaton out, too. If it costs too much to fix the boat, I won't do it. If Mr. Eaton won't captain, I won't do it."

"I'll think about it," she answered, and they both went silent. After a pause of thirty seconds, Hannah pulled open the single drawer at her stomach. She took out a small clay figurine and handed it to Will.

"This," she said, "is the little dog you made when you were asking me if we could get the outboard motor repaired. I found it under your bed last week."

Will turned it over in his fingers. "I didn't make this. I squashed that dog flat and made a cactus out of him. This isn't even a dog. It's a cow, or a calf. It has hooves, not paws."

Hannah took it back. "I found it under your bed."

"Under Miss Thomas's bed," Will said, and smiled. "She's made a little graven image."

She smirked at him.

"If I were you," he said, "I'd put it back."

🐢🐢🐢

Hannah asked, "What did the doctor say?"

"He gave me a due date and I told him he was wrong. He was almost two weeks off," Emily said.

"How do you know?"

"There was only the one time."

"Oh," Hannah said. "I didn't know that. People are always getting pregnant in novels after only doing it once. I didn't know it happened in real life."

"He said it was unusual. Some people try to get pregnant for years."

"So did he tell you you're going to burn in hell?"

"No, he gave me some pamphlets."

"How's the baby?"

"He said it sounded fine."

"That's good."

Emily hung her coat on a peg by the door and took off the boots Hannah had given her. She had on a pair of black nylon pants Hannah hadn't seen before.

"Those look nice. How'd the shopping go?"

"I got these."

"Is that all?"

"Yes."

"I thought you'd get more. Something warm. You're always so cold."

"Tom gave me these." She took a half-dozen pamphlets from her bag and dropped them on the table, then a rolled up pair of sweatpants that she brought to her nose. "They smell like him. He smells good. He has lots of clothes like this. Have you noticed none of his clothes have buttons? Even his jeans open and close with Velcro."

Hannah nodded. Most of her conversations with Emily made her uneasy. "Did you make another appointment with the doctor?"

"Yeah. Tom said he'd take me to all of them. He got my car fixed, too."

"If your car was fixed, why didn't you just drive yourself? Tom works at night. He had to stay up to take you to Blue Hill. He sleeps during the day."

"I didn't know where the clinic was. You set it up. You asked him."

"I didn't know your car was fixed. He didn't tell me."

"He said he wanted to take me. I'm going upstairs."

"Why?"

"I need a smoke. You won't let me smoke down here."

She started up the stairs, carrying the sweats.

"Don't you want your pamphlets?" Hannah called after her.

"You read them," Emily said. "Pretend you're pregnant." She shut her door.

Hannah marched to the table and stacked and restacked the pamphlets.

Proper Nutrition
Financial Planning
This Hospital Cares
Choosing a Car Seat
The Time to Plan Is Now
Eating for Two

She was too furious to read them now. She'd read them later. The dog barked and she let him inside. Will was nowhere to be seen, but the door to the boat shed was open. When she began to put on her coat, Driftwood's hips swung with excitement. Segments of feces shot out to the left and right. Hannah flung open the door and screamed, "Out, out, out!" The dog fled. She picked up the turds and flung them into the snow where they sank quickly. Driftwood raced to each hole and dug wildly, chasing the disappearing, seemingly aghast that she'd thrown out something so valuable. His face was covered with snow. He stopped when he saw her approaching, spread his forepaws, barked, then raced in a tight circle, his haunches low and reckless. His joy in a face so loose—jowls, ears, and tongue repeatedly cast off but always miraculously returning—made Hannah realize her own face was drawn and starched. She bent down and rubbed snow on her cheeks. The dog moved beneath her to lick the snow from her chin.

"Come on," she said. "Let's go find Will."

Snow began to fall as she made her way down to the boat shed. The snow fell into the calm sea, the act of forgetting made visible.

Will was under the hull, picking at a seam with his pocketknife. Bits of hard caulking fell out, followed by strands of something fibrous. He looked up at her and grimaced.

"It's snowing again," she said.

"It's too cold to work out here," he said. "When will it warm up?"

"We're in February. You'll still be wearing a jacket in May."

"Back home the daffodils are already blooming."

"What did Tom say about your idea?"

"He didn't know. He wants to look at her again. He was worried that I'd be doing most of the work. You know, I think he told you *Break of Day* was too far gone because he couldn't fix her on his own. Some of my friends at school said they'd come out and help me. I've got three months before school ends to work on her."

"Then only three months of lobstering before school starts again," Hannah said.

"But I could come back every summer, Hannah, to work. I mean, if it was OK with you. I know you only signed on for the one year."

"I've never liked the idea of you on the water."

"I know, but it's the only way I can reach you, isn't it? You live on an island. I think I'm going to live on the ocean the rest of my life. I'm addicted now. When I drive inland I feel claustrophobic."

"I'm afraid you'll drown," she said.

"Me too," he answered.

"That's the one and only answer that would have worked with me, Will. OK. If she'll float again, make her float. But you have to promise me you'll never fish alone. Tom always has to be with you."

"Is it OK if I bring friends out to help work on her? Some of the guys at Billings might throw in a day or two."

"Yes, I guess. You draw people like flies."

He slipped his knife in his pocket, stepped from beneath the hull and suddenly picked her up. Her head banged lightly against the waterline. - "You were here first," he said, and he dropped her back down to the granite floor.

"Put me down," she said, after she was already down. "I wasn't here first. Arno was." She compared Will's face to the painting she'd done months earlier. His jaw had dropped, become more angular. His nose had narrowed and the hair on his cheeks had joined his sideburns. He should shave more often, she thought. "How does it feel," she asked him, "to have hair start growing out of your face?"

He stepped back and put his red hand against his cheek. His eyes opened wide in surprise. "Not there, too!" he cried.

"You are so sick," she said, and pushed him away with a palm-flat shove to the chest. "Let's go look at the snow falling into the ocean."

🐚 🐚 🐚

Zee held her mittened hands over the woodstove. "We've got that old stove out there red hot, but I can't tell that it makes a difference."

"Are you going to scrape on the boat with him all day or do you want your lesson?" Hannah asked.

"I want my lesson. He doesn't even know I'm gone. All he can see or hear is that boat. He talks with Daddy more than he does with me."

"He's pretty excited. I've got a project for you. Take these big sheets of rice paper and put a blue wash over them."

"The whole thing?"

"Yeah, I'm going to use them as backing for those self-portraits."

"I thought you were going to backlight those."

"I still will."

"They'll turn your face blue where the paper is thin."

"I know. I want to vary the wash over the sheet. Practice going from a thin, pale, almost transparent blue to a blue that believes it's black, as if you're painting the ocean from its surface to the deep sea floor."

"It will be as if your face is filling up with water," Zee said.

"Will you just paint?"

"OK, OK. Are these for the exhibition?"

"Some of them, but most will go to my gallery in New York. Have you found anybody to work for me this summer?"

"Not yet, nobody wants to commit just yet for a month-long part-time job. Everybody's hoping to work all summer. Will hasn't had any problem getting volunteers, though. All the kids in his marine class want to come out and help with the boat. Half of them are girls."

"Really?"

"Yeah, lots of girls fish with their dads now. It's not just the boys. And besides, Will is cute."

"Don't worry, Zee, you've got a tight hold on him."

"He wants to go to Colby or Bates. He'll get a scholarship, too. There's no way I can afford to go to one of those schools."

Something heavy dropped on the floor above them. Hannah pushed her chair back and called up the stairs, "You all right?"

"Yes," Emily answered.

Hannah listened for a moment and then turned back to the work-table.

"Don't she ever come down?" Zee asked.

"Not much," Hannah said.

"I thought I was going to have to kill her when she first came."

"Why?"

"Will acted like a frickin' idiot over her. And my dad, too. She let them do everything for her. Not once did she offer to wash a dish while she was at our house."

"Well, I won't defend her. I can't get much out of her either. As far as she's concerned, she's here to have a baby, period."

"All I care about is that Will's over her."

Hannah didn't know how much she knew about the pregnancy. She turned the conversation. "Will says your dad is going to quit the job at Jonesport so he can be here all weekend to work on *Break of Day*."

"Yeah, he's pretty excited, too. Thanks, Hannah. It's good to see him worked up again."

"I hope it's the right thing. I'm worried about them both. Can your dad swim without his hands?"

"He says he thinks he can."

"He hasn't tried?"

"He's never liked to get in the water."

"These fishermen work on the water their whole lives and never get in it."

"Do you ever get in your paint?"

"Never more than wrist deep."

"There's some painters that immerse themselves in paint and then roll around on a big canvas on the floor. I saw pictures. They're naked when they get in the paint."

"I guess that's some kind of point."

"There's a girl at school who's been to New York City and seen your artwork."

"Where?"

"At your gallery. She was there last fall. She said there was a bunch of rocks wrapped up with wool and leather, and some set like jewels even though they were just granite."

"That's my stuff."

"Why do you wrap up rocks?"

"To give them value or to show that they're already valuable, among other things. Somehow, placing something inside something else or finding it that way gives it a sense of worth. You crinkle some white tissue paper around an orange and it looks, smells, and tastes more intense.

You put a museum around a painting and it becomes priceless. That's why we wear clothes."

"I bought a twenty-dollar lipstick once. It was in a silver tube that rested on silver string in a gold box. Then they put it in a red foil bag. I used the lipstick all up one winter but the box still seems valuable."

"Sometimes the packaging is so ingenious or beautiful it shames and outlasts the product. That's not what I'm after. I want the rocks and the wrapping to seem whole, as if you could find them in nature that way. As if they weren't made. As if they grew, like a nut or a periwinkle."

"Immaculate conceptions," Zee said.

Hannah looked up from her work. "What a good name for the exhibition, Zee."

"Really?"

"I should have thought of it with my new brain."

"You can use it. It's just wrapped up in me."

❧ ❧ ❧

"For every action there is an equally harassing reaction," Everett Eaton told her. "You have to be careful what you push on, because it may squirt back. My dad used to tell me you better make sure that rock is going to crack when you strike it or it will crack your bones. He said that's why we have two long bones in our forearms: there used to be just one till some caveman hit a solid piece of granite with his club and split his one bone into a pair. Where is Tommy?"

"He's upstairs with my sister," Hannah answered.

"Where is his wife?"

"I don't know, Mr. Eaton."

"You're Arno Weed's niece."

"I am," she said.

"I'm not stupid, I just have a memory problem."

"What made you think of your father, Mr. Eaton?"

"He thought I'd be a stonecutter, but the trade played out. I still have his tools somewhere. Maybe Tom has them. He died when I was young. He breathed in too much stone dust. Coal miners get black lung, but stonecutters get silicosis. I don't know what lobstermen get in their lungs. I guess they get salt water. What do you do for a living?"

"I'm an artist."

"I don't know what artists get in their lungs," he said.

"Everything," Hannah said. "Fox hair, wool fibers, paint fumes, desperation, kiln smoke, sawdust."

"That sounds awful," he said. "I wouldn't be an artist for the world."

"Why not?"

"What awful spit you must have." Hannah raised her eyebrows as if a bug were crossing beneath them. "My dad used to spit out rocks. He said he could feel them on his teeth. One day there was some blood mixed in and he told us that was it. He started carving his own tombstone that day. They say you can taste it in your mouth: the moment you understand you're going to die. I've not experienced that flavor. Or maybe I have and I've forgotten it."

"I think you'd remember that, Mr. Eaton. I think it would stay with you," she said.

"Did you ever think about dying?" he asked her.

"Yes."

"That's all they talk about where I live. It's the favorite subject, dying and bowel movements. We had a fellow who turned a hundred."

"How old are you?"

"I don't know. I can't answer that question. The answer changes every year and I can't keep up with it. An answer's not much good if it only works for a year. I'm a hundred minus something."

"Me too," Hannah said.

"I wish I knew how I got here." He looked around the room.

"Your son, Tom, brought you out. You come here every Sunday afternoon. Do you want to sit by the window and look at the ocean?"

"You've got ocean here?"

"It's too cold to sit outside, but you can sit by the window."

"All right. I'll do that. I'm a good sitter. I'm not taking up your window, am I?"

"No, there's others. I'm going to sit over here at this table and work."

She watched from a distance as he carefully tucked the throw under his legs, as if he were hiding coins under the cushion. When he was satisfied he crossed his hands in his lap and looked out the window at the sea. He didn't seem to recognize it. Almost immediately his eyelids closed, but lay askew like a lid offset on a skillet. Glistening pink and white crescents lay alongside each other like two halves of a bean.

She thought there hadn't been this many people on the island since the quarry closed: Emily and Tom upstairs, Mr. Eaton down, and Zee and Will and four of their friends in the boat shed working on *Break of Day*. Ten people and a dog: it wouldn't surprise her if the island sank under the weight.

Once in a while, Zee or one of the other two girls came in to pee, but most of the afternoon, with Mr. Eaton asleep and the boys peeing on the rocks, she was free to work. Tom and Emily were quieter than usual. When he finally came down, Hannah realized that perhaps they weren't so quiet, that maybe she had been ignoring all sound. When he touched her shoulder, she could suddenly hear the wind, Everett Eaton's snoring, a hammer down at the boat shed.

"Oh, hi," she said.

"What country were you just in?" he asked.

"I was here. I tend to stay here."

He sat down across from her, but still watched his father. "When I was a boy I thought there was nothing he couldn't do. Then I got a little older and I was disappointed to find out he wasn't really God. But what you come to after a while is it's pretty amazing how close he got."

"My dad died when I was twenty. I never got to that third stage. You're lucky."

"You know, you knew your dad twice as long, but Emily misses him more."

"He died when he was still perfect for Emily. She misses a father in his first stage."

Tom said, "I've never met anyone more lost than her. It's like getting pregnant disproved the existence of God. And when you find out the thing you believed in above all else is false, nothing matters. It's like she's deep in a fog. She says she's come to a point in her life when she's decided to stop looking, has grown tired of searching. She wants to be found. I've been in that fog before, after I lost my hands. It's very calm and warm there, as if you're in the mouth of something sleeping. There's nowhere to go, sound comes from where it shouldn't, and straining to see ahead just serves to blind you. I don't know what to say to her. No one could have talked me out of it. The only thing I could offer was to tell her not to get used to it. If it's comfortable, it's wrong."

"Do you think she's in love with you?" Hannah asked.

"Oh no, there's no hope of that. I've got no hands. I'm harmless in her eyes."

"She waits the week out for your visits," she said.

"It's nice to talk to her. She seems sort of exotic, you know, from so far away, her accent. And it's like talking to myself after I lost my hands."

"Thank you for taking her into the clinic and going shopping with her. I was so tired of her housecoat."

"Well, I didn't go shopping with her. She had me wait in the truck while she ran in. She didn't buy anything so I gave her one of my old jogging suits."

"She bought a pair of black stretch pants."

"Not with me. She went into the clinic in her housecoat and pajamas. I gave her the sweatpants when we got back to the house. She said there was nothing in the store she liked."

"Tom, she brought home a pair of black stretch pants. The tag was still on them."

"I didn't see them come out of that store. She didn't even carry her purse in." He shrugged. "I'm going to wake Dad and take him down to the shed. I'll take all the kids home when I go so Will won't have to make the trip in."

"Did you quit the summer caretaking job?"

"Yeah, if it's all right, I'll come out next Saturday morning to help with the boat."

"Of course," Hannah said.

"I hope it goes without saying that I'll not let the boy suffer any harm. I want to thank you for the opportunity."

"It's Will. I can't say no to him. Being in love just makes me vulnerable. All that's left to happen is to lose. Look at Emily."

"Will said you always entertain the present as if it's already past."

He woke his father. As Tom put the old man's coat and hat on, Everett Eaton held out his arms and stretched his neck upward. He looked across the room at her and asked, "Did you finish your letter?" Hannah simply nodded. A nod always seemed to work with him. He told her, "The highest point of land on the island of Key West is the town dump, and there everyone will go when the sea rises."

Hannah looked at Tom. "There was a time when Mom and Dad went to Florida for a couple weeks every winter." Tom turned his father around to zip up his coat. "Did you see it then, Dad?" he asked.

"I thought I'd go first," he told Tom. "Your mother was younger and stronger."

Tom looked over his father's shoulder at Hannah and tilted his head as if he'd proved a point.

When they'd gone, she climbed the stairs. They seemed steeper than usual. This house was too small for a second story. The treads had too little run for their rise. Ascending to sleep was too hard, descending to morning too quick. By the time she knocked on Emily's door she was out of breath.

"Come in."

"I was thinking about turning things upside down," Hannah said, "having breakfast for dinner: bacon and eggs and toast."

"No bacon for me," Emily said.

"Could I have my change back from the dress shop? And you need to tell me how much the check for the clinic was."

"The check was for forty-five dollars. Your money is in the dresser."

"It's all still here, all three twenties."

"I didn't need it," Emily told her.

"How did you get the pants out of the store?"

"Under my housecoat."

"Why didn't you pay for them? You had the money."

"To see what would happen."

"What happened?"

"Nothing."

"This is happening, Emily. I'm confronting you about stealing the pants right now."

"Once again, you're not God."

"OK, Emily, have it your way. If God's dead, I'm the one who matters now. I'm next in line. This room smells like an ashtray. Everyone who comes in here comes out smelling like you. I'm not buying cigarettes for you anymore. If you want to eat, come downstairs and fix something. I'm sorry you're pregnant. I'm sorry you've lost your faith. Will says you were different in Texas. He says what you really believed in was being good, helping others, being part of a community. Those things are still valid, even without a God to say so. Just because He's dead to you doesn't mean His tenets don't have value. I swear I'm going to put you in the quarry cracking rocks."

"Stop preaching to me. Get out of my room."

"It's my room," Hannah yelled. "You're only gestating in it."

Emily pushed the covers off her lower body. She was naked but for the housecoat. She was so thin her belly seemed distended. She walked toward the door without pulling the housecoat closed. Hannah cut her off.

"Where are you going?"

"I'll go to Tom's. He'll let me stay with him."

"No you won't," Hannah said. She stood in the doorway.

"Get out of my way," Emily screamed.

"No."

"I have what he wants," she yelled. "He'll let me stay with him."

"You're not leaving. Close your robe."

Emily tried to push past her. Hannah put her shoulder between Emily's breasts and shoved her back into the room. They stood apart, breathing heavily.

"I stole the pants and nothing happened," Emily yelled.

"I happened. This is happening," Hannah shrieked.

"You painted a naked boy and nothing happened to you." Emily gathered her robe together with one hand and with the other reached out and struck Hannah on the bone of her cheek. It knocked her into a crouch. Emily stood over her, still holding the robe closed with one fist, but she did not look down. She looked at the doorway. Hannah turned. Will was there. His nose and cheeks were red with cold.

"That's enough," he said softly.

Emily let her robe fall open. She took its folds in both hands and opened it for the boy. "How's this, Will?" she asked. "Is this what you want? Even with my belly I'm better than her, aren't I?" She nodded at her sister.

Will gazed at her, then looked down at Hannah. She said, "It's OK, go back downstairs."

He looked at the floor between the sisters. "No more hitting," he whispered, and backed away.

When she heard Will reach the foot of the stairs, Hannah stood up and closed the door.

"I'm not so little anymore, am I?" Emily asked. "Will preferred me, Tom prefers me, and Daddy preferred me. I'm not twelve, like I was the last time you left."

"I don't know why you're so angry with me," Hannah whispered.

"Because I'm angry," Emily said.

"I've done nothing to Will. I painted a boy with his shirt off. That's all."

"He believed when he left home. We're a goddamned island of unbelievers. Why do people who come here lose their faith?"

"It's the other way around," Hannah said. "Only people who've lost their faith come here. Will only pretended to believe to get along with you and his father and the rest. I've told you before. I've taken nothing from him."

"It's this place then. The longer I stay, the worse things get."

"If you'd just leave this room," Hannah pleaded.

"Where then, once I leave? The island is no bigger. The mainland is no bigger. I'm trapped in this body. I can't get out of it. I'm going crazy in here. Everyone's being mean to me. No one's on my side. I just want to be left alone. I just want what I want."

She slipped back into bed, and sitting up, pulled all the sheets and blankets up around her torso. She formed the mound of bedclothes into a hive from which her gaunt face protruded.

"What do you want, Emily?"

"I don't know." She began to cry. She did not take her hands from beneath the blankets to wipe her face, so Hannah knew she'd cried often before. Her cheeks didn't itch with the tears.

"Do you want to talk with a minister?" Hannah asked

"No."

"A counselor?"

"You mean a psychiatrist."

"Anybody who can help you."

"Please just let me see Tom when he comes."

"Of course."

"I was so mad when Daddy died. I was so mad at him."

"Me too," Hannah said.

"I feel the same way now, but no one's died."

"You can get through this, Emily."

"No one's died. They just never were. How can you replace something that never was?"

"Can't you think about something small instead? Think about the baby."

"It's all I think about."

🐚🐚🐚

While Zee painted from a photograph of Stonington Harbor, Hannah drew rough sketches of lungs, preliminary drawings for sculptures. They wouldn't be finished in time for her spring show in New York or the Stonington exhibition, but perhaps by the fall. She had in mind a series: paired lobes in granite, coal, and blown glass filled with salt water. All these ways of dying were ways of living, too. The fourth set of lungs would represent her own. Although she knew its form, the materials yet eluded her. A thin gauzy canvas filled with used brushes, wads of crumpled paper, paint tubes squeezed flat? What did she breathe in everyday that would eventually be her undoing? How could she represent desire, a lack of understanding, loneliness and loss, daily absolved by her work? In the meantime, she made three sketches and left the fourth sheet blank. She wasn't worried about the granite, but what type of coal could be carved? And she'd have to find a glass artist who could take her model and make a mold.

"How is she this week, Hannah?" Zee asked. She lifted her brush from the paper and blotted it with a wadded tissue. There was a scattering of tissues with dark flat bottoms above the rectangle of watercolor paper, cumulous clouds threatening to rain on Zee's harbor.

"She seems better. Will brought her a stack of novels from the library. They move from one side of the bed to the other, so it seems like she's getting somewhere."

"Will told me she hit you."

"I wish people could keep a secret."

"I guess you can't hit her back. The baby, I mean."

"She's grief-stricken. Her faith was like a person who died and she's mad at it for dying. Maybe I deserved to get slugged."

"Why?"

"To the very core of my being I just want to scream, 'Get Over It' at her. I think that's because I don't understand."

"That's what I always wanted to yell at my mom before she left."

"Where is your mom, Zee? Your grandpa asks me all the time."

"Sometimes she's up in Jonesport, sometimes she lives with her parents, sometimes she's at a home in Augusta."

"What kind of home?"

"A home for people who sometimes can't take care of themselves. She loses things, and when she loses them it starts out like, 'I can't find my scissors,' and it goes on and on for days. Dad or Grandma would take her up to the home for a week or two. She'd come back and be fine for three or four months and then she'd lose something again. She'd run away, looking for it. When Dad lost his hands, she was gone for four months."

"Does your dad still see her? Is that why he took the job in Jonesport?"

"Yeah, and that's why he gave it up, too. She doesn't want anything to do with us."

"I'm sorry, Zee."

"I feel sorry for her. She doesn't know what she's missing. No pun intended."

"How are they doing out there?"

"I had to come in when they started in on the stem with that reciprocating saw. Will's using it on a ladder, and Daddy is telling him where to cut."

"Why are they cutting on the stem?"

"They found a pocket of rot just above the waterline. They're going to cut it out and splice in a graving piece."

"Won't that weaken the stem?"

"Daddy says it won't if it's not too deep. You should see Grandpa out there. He tells them how to do something, real detailed, then he looks out the window and asks, 'Where the hell are we?'"

"I don't know how he handles it, to never know where you're at or how you got there."

"He seems to be used to it now. It's as ordinary as knowing where you are and how you got there. Half the time he's smiling when he asks where he is, like it's a big joke on him. You'd think it'd make all three of us sad, but it doesn't. It's only sad when you think of the whole of it. In any one moment it's like paint: you can't keep it from running." She dabbed at her painting again.

"Do you look like your mom, Zee?"

"Yeah, but I wish I looked like Dad and Grandpa."

"She must be beautiful," Hannah said.

🐢 🐢 🐢

In the first week of March, a southwest wind brought warmth and acid rain to the coast. The snow that had lingered for weeks, turning gradually into a brittle crust of opaque ice, became porous and granular and at last liquid, indistinguishable from the present rain.

She'd managed to get Emily out of the house. They walked the perimeter of the island. Hannah peered into each crevice and catchall to see what had changed since the snow first fell.

"So we'll have spring now," Emily said. She kept her hands in her coat pockets, even when Hannah offered her a smooth stick or a shell.

"No," Hannah said. "This is just a respite. There's much more winter."

Driftwood kept approaching Emily to sniff her, but she wouldn't take her hands from her pockets.

"He knows something's up," Hannah said and tried smiling.

Emily turned away, took baby steps down the face of smooth granite that shelved into the sea. Hannah caught up with her, put her own hands in her pockets.

"Can you hate the dog, too?"

"Yes," Emily said.

The wind worked through the spruce at their backs, arrived tattered and spent.

"I was hoping you'd offer to help Will with his applications. He has to send an essay along with them."

"I thought you said his SAT scores were exceptional?"

"They are."

"He doesn't need me then."

"He's going to write about leaving his father."

"What would you have me do? Check it for facts?"

"No, Emily. He was reading through the list of proposed topics. He came upon 'How One Life Affects Another.' He's writing about you saving him from his father."

"I should have stayed out of it."

"Don't be ridiculous. You may have saved his life."

"Saved it for what? Part of me wanted him out of the way."

"I think you've given up on your faith too easily. Can't you adapt it somehow to include accidents, mistakes?"

"Yes, Hannah, it would be simple to adapt and conclude I'm ignorant and that God knows what's best for me, to conclude that the definition of faith is blind trust as opposed to understanding, but I think understanding is more valuable. Is it greedy to want understanding and happiness?"

"Yes, it is," Hannah said. "It is if you want it immediately. Give it time. Sometimes I walk around this island for weeks before something washes up and I understand what to do next. My overruling divinity is the water lapping at my feet, and I never know what it will cast up next."

"Everything you say is so exasperating. It's like you're slamming a cutlery drawer into my head again and again. Can't you just shut up? Can't you just let me solve it?"

When the cold returned, mud buckled, and the path down to the boat shed seemed root-ribbed, thin cover for hibernating turtles. Rocks rolled in their beds. Hannah rarely went down while they were all working on the boat, but during the week she checked their progress. The granite floor of the shed was covered with cereal flakes of paint scraped from the hull. Curled shavings and sawdust were rolled into an undulating mound where the tide crept under the big doors. Much of the hull had been sanded down to bare wood. The old caulking had been jerked from the seams with bent screwdrivers and horseshoe picks. It lay on the floor, too, gray and hard as flint. Long cords of bright white cotton wicking were being led into the seams. The graving piece had been epoxied into the stem. It looked as if they'd tried to repair a shark bite. Up in the cockpit, the engine's blanket, the one Arno had placed over it seven years earlier, had been removed. There were new water hoses and belts. They'd installed a new bilge pump. She thought Tom must be very careful or very nervous: the new pump was twice the size of the old one. She could see daylight through the seams that had been reefed out and were yet uncaulked. She wondered how many gallons per hour the bilge pump was good for, how long it would give them to call for help.

She reached up into the rafters and ran her hand along one of Arno's buoys. The Styrofoam had shriveled at each orifice. Coils of warp crumbled under her fingertips. The green water hose Arno had used to replace the split wooden handles on the bronze wheel had turned a pale yellow. The short pieces of hose lay on the sole, split open their entire lengths like dry seedpods. In their places on the wheel were newly turned and varnished mahogany spokes. No one had told her about this. Will must have made them in the woodshop at school. The bronze had been polished as well. She wasn't sure if she liked this. It told of more than a desire to catch lobster. Water hose had been fine for Arno. Somebody was already proud of this boat.

No one had said anything about changing *Break of Day's* name. How would the other lobstermen feel when they saw her out on the bay again? She couldn't decide if she should insist upon changing the boat's name or forbid it. She stepped into the wheelhouse, put one hand on the refinished wheel and the other on the worn bronze handle of the hydraulic pot hauler. It was Arno's station. She'd worked on the washboards behind him. How self-righteous he must have been, how desperate he must have been. Once *Break of Day* was floating again, the boat could be used to bring Arno's stone around the island. She thought he'd meant no harm to her. His grave had gone unmarked long enough. She knew who he was now.

※　※　※

She finally received from Gwen a list of the owners of her work. Only one of her major pieces was included. She sent queries to each owner to see if they'd loan their sculptures or paintings for the retrospective, and another letter to Gwen asking for a complete list. There were at least a dozen major pieces she wanted to include in the exhibition that weren't on the list. She was pleased to see that among her buyers was her alma mater, Bennington College.

At night she listened to the ice gnawing at the verge of the island. The ice scratched and clawed its way up the beaches as the tide rose, forming a bulwark when the water receded. The farthest extent of the sea left a frothing mark, a semipermanent solid wave. It was sharp enough to cut the dog's feet.

Almost every day Will or Emily rebuked the cold. "It holds on too long," Will said. "It's not fair." There were evenings when it was too cold to work on the boat, even with the stove roaring. Ice clogged the gap beneath the shed doors and when the tide rose, water was trapped inside and froze in a dark gray sheet beneath the stern of *Break of Day*. Will brought pieces of the boat inside the house to work on them. Eventually he ran out of detachable parts.

"What do I do now?" he asked her.

"Wait and plan," she answered. "Think about the summer."

"I don't think it exists anymore."

She pulled out the charts. "I can show you where Arno placed his traps," she said.

His hands came out of his pockets like live birds. He brushed his hair back off his forehead and swept crumbs from the tabletop. He found a pencil in his shirt pocket, and fought the inward roll of the chart with both palms as if it were a girl's blouse.

"I'll hold it down," he said. "You put an X on the spot."

She put a small X near Southern Mark Island. Another off the eastern shore of Gooseberry Island. Another between North and South Popplestone Ledges. She moved along the chart as the memory of each buoy surfaced. "Now, the lobsters move. You have to follow them. Arno knew how. I don't."

"OK," Will said. He seemed breathless with anticipation.

"What makes you want to fish, Will?"

"I don't know. It's fun."

"Why do some people look for adventure outside of themselves and others within?"

"You mean people like me and you?"

"Yes."

"I don't know. I feel like I know where I'm at. I don't know where the fish are and I want to find out. I like being out on the water. Maybe people like you don't know where they are."

"I'm right here." She leaned forward and put an X on Ten Acre No Nine. She slid the chart from beneath Will's palm and put an X on the bare table. "I'm right here." She put an X on her palm. "I'm here."

"You've picked a beautiful spot," he said, unsure.

"My uncle left it to me," she answered. "I get tired of the cold, too."

"When I fish, when I get the first bite, it's like I know a secret no one else knows."

She smiled. "I feel that way when I draw a line that I thought only existed in my mind."

"Yeah," he said, "like that."

"I want you to tell me that you're going to school."

"You know I am. I've applied."

"But you won't let fishing get in your way. You won't let Tom convince you to stay, to become a fisherman like him."

"What's wrong with him?"

"Nothing, but his prospects are limited."

"His prospects? He already is what he wants to be. He wants to fish. What have you got against Tom? Everybody likes him."

"I know. I do too."

"You always act nervous around him. He senses it. You should come out to the boat shed while we're working. You should see what he can do. In here he just sits with his hooks in his lap. Out there, well, he has all these tools that fit into the socket of his arm: hammers and wrenches and scrapers and all kinds of stuff. Hannah, he even has a fishing rod that fits into the socket so he can cast. It's like the world told him he couldn't fish but he's doing it anyway."

Driftwood slipped between them, rose up and put his front paws on the spread chart, leaving a pair of bloody prints.

"Oh, he's bleeding again," Will said.

Hannah sat on the kitchen floor with the dog lying across her lap. She rubbed Mycitracin into the cuts and slid white socks over his paws, taping them to the dog's fur at his knees.

"I can't believe he doesn't chew them off," Will said.

"He knows Hannah knows what's best for him, don't you, baby?" She kissed the dog on the snout between his nose and eyes. She looked up at Will and grinned.

"You've got hair on your lips," he said.

In late March, Gwen's return letter arrived in the same mail as Driftwood's new dog bed from L. L. Bean. Hannah opened and set up the dog bed first. The round foam bed was covered in a green and blue plaid. Driftwood's name was embroidered in yellow block letters. The dog seemed skeptical when she laid it down in front of him and urged him to climb in. While he sniffed around the edge of the bed, she opened Gwen's letter. There was no accompanying list.

Dear Hannah,

The remainder of your work was purchased anonymously. Due to confidentiality agreements, I can't give you a list of additional owners. I can, however, work as an intermediary to arrange the loan of your pieces for the retrospective. I think I can assure you of a good response. Let me know if you'd like to proceed. Don't let this upset you. My clients are often scrupulous about their privacy. Perhaps I should have told you sooner, but you were never interested in who your buyers were, only in your own relationship to your work, which is as it should be.

Love, Gwen

PS—I own two of your pieces. Did you know?

🐢 🐢 🐢

"I never felt like the fog was thick," Everett Eaton told her. "I always felt like I was thin. You know, so alone I was transparent. In a thick o' fog you're so wet you feel liquid yourself, somewhere between rain and pond. Your skin is just a suit, you know. We're 98 percent water. The only reason we don't puddle is we can't imagine it."

"How'd you cut your hand, Mr. Eaton?" Hannah asked.

He looked at the wound. "I don't remember. Looks like a three-day-old cut."

"Do you want a Band-Aid?"

"No, I like the air to get to a wound."

"Careful, Grandpa, she'll put a sock over your paw," Zee said. She sat across the room, twirling a brush in a glass of water. The clear water turned an opaque white, fog in a tumbler.

Tom had come in a few minutes earlier and told them to get ready to go home. It was Saturday evening, almost dark. Zee cleaned her work area and clipped her watercolor to a line to dry. "I liked it better when Daddy worked in Jonesport and I got to spend Saturday night here," she said.

"You can stay," Hannah said.

"No, I can't. We have to get Grandpa back for his medicine. And Dad doesn't like being at home alone."

"He's going to be at home alone when you go off to college."

"I know. It just breaks my heart."

"What breaks your heart, Zinnia Paulette?" her grandfather asked her.

"How handsome you are," she answered.

"Well," he said, "if I weren't born with my beauty, I'd've had nothing to speak of."

Hannah smiled and turned to Zee. "Zinnia Paulette?"

"Horrible, isn't it?"

"Do you blame your dad for it every minute of your waking life? I would."

"It's not his fault. Mom named me. And I changed it to Zee anyway. Grandpa can't remember anything, but he can remember my name."

He smiled as if he'd been complimented on his looks again.

"Put on your jacket, Grandpa. It's time to go," Zee said.

"Where is it?"

"Where it always is: on the hook by the door."

"First time I ever put it there," he said. "I don't know why you kids take such pleasure in hiding an old man's things."

"But we always find it for you, too, don't we?" Zee asked.

He took Hannah's jacket off the hook. "Is this it?"

"No, it's the big blue one."

"Oh, somebody stole my cigarettes out of the pocket."

"You don't smoke anymore, Grandpa. You quit four or five years ago."

"Well, I don't feel any better."

"Why are you so ornery this afternoon?" Zee asked him.

"I can't sit down and talk five minutes without being moved one place or another."

"I know, I know, but you like coming out here."

"Why do we have to go? This is my house."

"No, it's not," Zee laughed.

"I don't have any shoes on," he said.

"They're right here by the door, Mr. Eaton," Hannah said. "They were muddy so we took them off."

"It's mud season again?"

"Mud everywhere in the afternoon. It'll freeze up again by morning."

"I hate mud."

"Yeah?"

"Mud has followed me around my whole life."

Tom rapped on the door and stepped in. The wind that curled around him was warmer than usual.

"Ready, Dad?"

"Since before you were born."

"Well, let's go. Charlie and Sarah are already down by the boat. Will said to tell you he's going to work a bit longer, Hannah."

"OK, have you got enough life jackets for everybody?"

"Yeah, Will's friends brought their own. See you in the morning."

Emily came down the stairs as if they were built of cardboard boxes. "Bye, Tom," she said.

"See you in the morning, Em."

When Hannah closed the door on all of them and turned around, Emily was already gone. A loaf of bread was missing from the counter. Hannah walked up the stairs as quietly as she could and knocked on Emily's door.

"Come in."

The loaf of bread lay on the bed between Emily's feet.

"Why don't you come downstairs and we'll make dinner," Hannah said.

"This is enough."

"You can't eat only bread for dinner."

"I saw her digging a hole. From my window. Out near the boat shed."

"One of Will's friends? Sarah?" Hannah asked.

"The little girlfriend."

"Zee? Why was she digging a hole?"

"I don't know. Ask her. She was making a big secret of it. Looking around the corner. But I saw her from my window."

"OK, I'll ask her."

"Why didn't Tom come up to see me today? Maybe you didn't let him."

"No, I didn't talk to him much today, either. He worked on the boat all day with Will. It was a little warmer today. You could have gone down to the boat shed anytime, Emily, if you wanted to talk to him."

"He's probably worried you'll think he likes me."

"He can like you all he wants to."

"He does like me."

"Good," Hannah said.

"I'm just not sure if I like him that way."

"That's something for you to work out."

"I got up in the middle of the night once when I was at his house. There's a big hook on the back of the bathroom door. The harness he wears was hanging from it by a ring, the harness and the two pink plastic arms and the hooks. He must back up to the door and slide out of all that like a lobster molting. He must do that every night. He seems nice other than that."

"I'll warm up some stew. I'll send some up to you with Will later."

"You mean you'll send it up to the baby."

"The baby needs more than bread, Emily."

"I know that's why you're letting me stay."

When Will came in, long after dark, she waited till he'd taken off his hat and coat and sat down at the kitchen table. He sighed and laid his cheek on his folded hands. His breath blew salt crystals across the table-top. It pleased Hannah to see him have this relationship with her table, to find it a comfort and home.

"Why would Zee be digging a hole out by the boat shed, Will?"

He lifted his head. "What?"

"Emily said she saw Zee digging a hole. She said she was being sort of furtive about it."

"Oh, she was burying the chicken bones from your stew. She didn't want Driftwood to get them. Gosh, Hannah."

"I'm sorry. I'm paranoid."

"You sure are."

"I said I'm sorry."

"Gosh." He stood up and frowned at her.

"OK, Will. I get it. Stop saying, 'Gosh.' I can make amends, maybe. What do you think of this: it's getting warmer, warm enough maybe to put a heater in the granite house. The windows need caulking and the door should probably be rehung. What if we offer to let Tom and Zee and Mr. Eaton stay out there on Saturday nights? Your friends too, if you'd like. They'd have to use the outhouse. That way they wouldn't have to go back into town and load up again in the morning."

He looked at her with his mouth open.

"Well?"

"I can't believe you're offering that," he said. "That is so wicked cool."

"You said, 'wicked.' That's the first time you've used the word wicked," Hannah told him.

"It just slipped out."

"There's no furniture out there. They'd have to bring beds or sleeping bags or something. I don't know if it's OK for Mr. Eaton to be away from the nursing home overnight."

"You have to ask them," Will said. "It'll be better if you ask them."

"OK."

"Do you want some stew?"

"Yeah."

"Take this bowl up to Emily first."

"What if she flashes me again?"

"She won't. That was for my sake, not yours."

"When I was a kid, back in Texas, I used to dream about that, what she did. But it just made me queasy when it finally happened."

"So now you know what a naked pregnant woman looks like."

"Yeah," he said softly.

"So now you can imagine what Zee would look like if she was pregnant."

"She'd look like one of your sculptures, one of your stones wrapped tightly in pale wool."

🐢 🐢 🐢

She sat on Gwen's letter for three days before deciding it was unacceptable. How could 80 or 90 percent of her work have been purchased anonymously? She'd never heard of such a thing. Auction houses often reported major sales to anonymous buyers, but these were usually for single masterpieces, million-dollar works.

"I've been waiting for your call," she said.

"What's going on, Gwen?" Hannah asked.

"I can get your pieces for your exhibition. I can have them to you in as little as three weeks, by the first of May."

"I'd like to know why you can't tell me who owns my work."

"It's simple. I'm under contractual obligations. Why does it matter? Your work is being bought. You're being paid for it. You're one of the lucky few."

"Is it one person or many?"

"I don't know."

"You don't know?"

"I don't know who they are. It could be another dealer or a corporation. They work through a bank. I've already told you more than I'm allowed. But I've contacted them and they're willing to loan the work."

"Can you tell me the name of the bank?"

"No."

"Will you tell me where the pieces will be shipped from?"

"No. The only thing I'm allowed to do is sell to them."

"Someone must come in the gallery and look at the work before they buy it."

"Lots of people come in and look. Some buy on the spot. I have my suspicions. There are two different men who always come to your shows. They're both your age, maybe a little older. They never buy. Before the exhibition's over, I get a check. I ship off the work. Look, they're saying everything isn't immediately available, but they are willing to loan."

"Is there no way I can find out who owns my work, Gwen? This is ridiculous."

"I can't help you without risk of losing this contract, Hannah. I've signed my name to documents."

"You mean you might lose your commission."

"Yes, of course, and you might lose your patron. Under the terms of the contract, since they buy so much, I only take half my usual commission. People have a right to their privacy, Hannah. You of all people should be able to respect that. If you can create in seclusion, why can't the connoisseur enjoy it in private, too? After all, you've never allowed me to give out your address or phone number, have you? Many of your buyers ask to contact you and I turn them all down, don't I? And I've never asked why those letters I sent off to Texas had to come through me."

"What if I keep the pieces when they send them to me?" Hannah asked.

"I wouldn't do that. They're not yours."

"But someone would have to come after them eventually."

"I thought that was the last thing you wanted, someone visiting your island?"

"It was."

"Well?"

"They're my pieces, Gwen. I made them. I have a right to know where they live."

"No, Hannah, you don't. You gave them up to have your career as an artist. Do you want to have your retrospective or not?"

"How long has this been going on?"

"Ten years or more."

"Jesus, you should have told me long ago."

"You never cared, Hannah. This is the first time you've ever cared. I'm telling you now."

"Is the bank in New York? That's where I was ten years ago."

"Don't come here trying to understand this. You'd be wasting your time. I wish I had this kind of consistent patronage for my other artists, Hannah. You should be grateful for it."

"But to have one patron, Gwen."

"Many artists have gone a lifetime with one or two patrons. Not very many people have the courage and vision to stick up for a young artist, Hannah. The Medici supported some artists their whole lives."

"But it could end at any moment."

"Why would it?"

"I don't know."

❦ ❦ ❦

The air that inspired during relaxed, normal breathing was known as tidal air. It wasn't enough. She borrowed the antique tools of Everett Eaton's father, and with these and a power drill equipped with a masonry bit cut a flat, chest-sized slab of granite from the quarry. She used a lift, a natural fracture in the horizontal plane, as a guide, cracking out a stone uniformly ten inches thick. By the time she'd levered it free from the surrounding rock face, she was down to her shirt, though it was far from warm out. The freshly cut surface sparkled in the light, as if it were the sea in the direction of the sun. Drilling a line of holes four inches apart down the center of the slab, she cracked it in half with iron wedges and a sledge. The right and left lungs were separate now. She dressed down each stone with a five-point Bush hammer. The flying chips bit her lips and bounced off her protective goggles. The dust off each break was acrid as an electrical short. She thought it ironic, considering what she was making, that she'd forgotten her dust mask. When she'd removed as much excess rock as she could chance, she fought the two stones up onto a small sled and dragged them the long way out of the quarry. The strap dug into her chest and shoulders as she climbed up through the spruce, but once she reached the clearing, and the trail began to descend, she had to walk behind the sled and hold it back. It tended to pick up momentum over the grass. At the door of the house, Will and Tom both offered to help her carry the stones inside, but she refused their help and asked Mr. Eaton instead.

"How's your heart, Mr. Eaton?" she asked.

"I don't know," he answered.

"Can you help me carry these stones in? I'll get one end if you'll get the other."

He stood over the long pink elliptical rocks. "What are they?"

"Your dad's lungs."

"Jesus, let's get them out of the weather."

She'd ordered a pair of molded plastic medical-school organs for her models. The right and left lungs were not mirror images, having two and three lobes respectively. The models were light and extremely detailed. She wouldn't follow their exact contours because they were full of air. The lungs she would build would sag with the weight of accumulated stone dust, each alveolar sac packed with mica and feldspar. She'd already laid a heavy canvas on the floor. On this sat a driftwood-keel support, a 12"x12"x2' chunk of pine that had slipped from beneath a boat the day it was launched and floated away. Everett Eaton helped her lay the first plug on this timber. After the second stone was carried in and dropped on the floor, she raised a second canvas on a rope to a height of six feet to catch the chips that would otherwise fly across the room. The light of one window shone into her canvas corner. With calipers and a lumber crayon, she made preliminary notes on the stone. Then, with a lighter hammer and a chisel, she began to peck at the granite, as if she were a bird dislodging seeds from a dry flower. Only Tom was tall enough to rise up on tiptoe and look over the curtain. Will and Zee and Mr. Eaton peeked around its edges. Driftwood snuffled beneath the floor canvas, looking for an entrance. They all gave up, one by one. Obstinacy in a person was boring to watch. Emily came downstairs hours later to tell her the noise was like a drip of water, rain, the waves, incessant, and so she was going outside at last. When the door slammed, Hannah smiled, wiped the dust from her goggles, the blood off her knuckles, and smelled the biting end of the chisel. The stone was hard and rough, would rather be chewed than carved. She'd forced her out.

Through the week, as answers to her queries began to arrive, she took the rock to task with an automobile grinder and a diamond disk, and finally with rasps and files. Several of the owners of her smaller works were willing to lend them, as was Bennington College, who told her they actually owned two pieces and would be happy to send both. Her larger works from the anonymous buyer or buyers would be shipped in late May. They could be installed directly in the gallery, rather than first brought out to the island and then returned to the mainland for the show. She hoped there would be some clue to the identity of the buyer in the shipping papers or the packaging. Perhaps even the license plate of the truck or the driver himself could give her an answer. She'd thought about ransacking Gwen's office, but then thought she could wait her admirer out. How would he be able to resist the retrospective? She'd wait in her gallery for him. It was intriguing as well as disturbing, to think there was someone in the world waiting for her work, who actually caught it when she threw it off the island. It made the thought of Tom and Emily easier to bear.

🦋 🦋 🦋

Will and Tom spent an afternoon caulking the windows of the granite house. They stapled plastic over the back door and the access to the second floor. Then, rather than try to fix the leaking roof, Tom brought out a large tent and staked it out on the wooden floor. The tent flaps faced the granite fireplace. They set up three cots. Here Zee, Mr. Eaton, and Tom spent Saturday nights through the spring. Mr. Eaton tended a wood fire in the fireplace in the evenings. Often there was ice on the wood floor outside their tent in the mornings.

On Sunday mornings, Hannah made blueberry pancakes. She made Will's first so the blueberries could be poured on top. Everyone else wanted their berries in the batter. Even Emily came down to help with breakfast, setting the table and warming the syrup. Hannah put Everett Eaton on the bacon skillet. He stood over the bacon with raised fork, his nostrils flared like dogs yawning. Tom rested his hook on Emily's lower back when he reached over her to open a cabinet door. While Hannah cooked, the bathroom door was continually swinging. The outhouse had been forgotten. Everyone was peeing in her bathroom on Sunday mornings.

As they sat down for breakfast, Will cleared his voice and said, "Zee and I have a little announcement."

The table quieted. Tom continued to chew audibly. After he swallowed, he looked at Will and said, "Careful, son. It'd better be a very little announcement."

Will smiled nervously. "It's just that we've both been accepted to Bates."

"Will got a full scholarship," Zee said.

"Oh, Will, that's great," Hannah said. "Isn't that great, Emily?" she asked.

"It is, Will. You can start all over," Emily said.

Tom picked up his fork again.

"Daddy?" Zee said.

He looked up. "What, Zee? You've already been accepted at the University. You know we can't afford a private college. I don't know why you even applied there. It makes me mad, it does. To set yourself up for disappointment, with me as the mean old goat."

"I've got money I've been saving for school," Will said. "I won't need it now. And we'll make more this summer."

"That's out of the question, Will. Besides ridiculous. That school must cost twenty grand a year."

"Twenty-four," Will said.

"And you're going to come up with that twenty-four every year for the next four years?" Tom asked. "That's a hell of a promise, Will."

"Daddy, don't snap at him for offering to help," Zee yelled.

"I don't have syrup yet," Mr. Eaton told Hannah.

She passed it to him. "Careful, it's hot."

"That bacon's not burnt," he told Tom. "Stop yelling."

"Dad, Jesus," Tom said, exasperated.

"I could work while I'm in school," Zee said. "I could probably get financial aid. The counselor at school said that single-parent, low-income families qualify."

"Zee, why would you want to humiliate us that way, put yourself in debt, when you've been accepted to a school we can afford? You're going to school, not work."

"I guess I don't think it would be humiliating to go to a good school."

"That's not it at all," Tom said. "Let's be honest about it. You'd go to Purple Frog School for the Blind if Will was going there."

"So?" Zee screamed. "So? Like I didn't learn from you?" She slammed her chair back into the wall as she rose out of it. Everett Eaton stood up, too, a pancake in each hand. Zee left the house carefully, resetting her chair, pulling on her gloves, and closing the door softly.

Everett Eaton sat back down. "What'd I do?" he asked.

"It's OK, Mr. Eaton," Hannah said.

Everyone rearranged their utensils.

"Christ," Tom whispered.

"I guess I'll take her coat out to her," Will said. "She must be getting cold."

"When she gets mad, she's liable to forget her hands," Tom said. He looked up from his plate at Emily, snorted, and shook his head.

"I went to a state school," Emily said. "It worked fine for me."

Hannah slowly expelled the air she was going to use to speak. She waited till Emily was taking her bath, till Mr. Eaton was settled in the armchair with the paper. Tom helped her with the dishes. He handed her plates one at a time.

"The Purple Frog School for the Blind?" she said softly.

"It's very prestigious," he sighed.

"What did she mean when she said she learned it from you? I didn't think you went to college."

"I didn't. She wanted me to leave her mother long before I did. She thinks I'm a fool for lost causes."

"When I was her age I felt the same way about a boy."

"What happened?"

"I had a big fight with Arno. I told you. He was right, of course, but I was too humiliated and embarrassed to ever face him again. I never saw him again. I could help her, Tom. I was going to pay for Will's tuition. That money will be free now. I don't want them to blame us when they break up."

"It's too much, Hannah. You don't owe us anything." He put his hook down in the murky dishwater to retrieve a bread knife. "Zee always cuts herself on a bread knife," he explained. The cuff of his sleeve got wet.

"Do you want me to roll that up for you?" she asked him.

"I can't feel that it's wet, Hannah. It's all right."

"I know that, but it bothers me. Here, just let me . . ." She took the shirt at the wrist and tugged the cuff up a few inches, revealing more of the pink prosthetic arm. "There. Just because your shirt is wet doesn't mean I don't feel it on my wrist."

"She's not the student Will is. She'll be disappointed there."

"They accepted her. Obviously the school doesn't think so. It's the quality of people you're around in college, students and teachers, that can determine how well you do in life afterwards. Everybody at Bates will be as bright as they are."

"It's hard to believe she's two months shy of eighteen. She was just four yesterday."

"You know, it's only taken me ten months to fall flat on my face in love with Will. At least you've had the eighteen years."

She could see the reflection of the kitchen window in the drop of water on the end of Tom's hook. When the hook separated to pick up a dish or fork, the drop of water split and for a moment two tiny windows were reflected at the end of his arm.

"I'm attracted to women I know will leave me," he said. "It'll take me years to pay you back, but I will."

"She might surprise you. She could land some hundred-thousand-a-year job, and her school debt won't seem like much."

"None of those jobs on Deer Isle."

"I know. But at least for the next four years they have to come back here and work summers. We can make them pledge that."

"Like they're indentured."

The steel of his hooks left marks on the edges of her white plates. They both noticed this at the same time.

"I'm sorry," he said. "At home I've got some rubber tips."

Emily called Tom from the stairwell.

"Go ahead," Hannah said. "I can finish."

"Is it all right with you if I take her to the doctor's office again? She's getting too big to get behind the steering wheel comfortably."

"Of course. You don't need my permission."

"I know, but . . ."

"It's OK. All she does is talk about you."

"Thanks, Hannah."

When he'd left, she looked up and saw Will and Zee leaning against the boat shed, the morning sun pinking their faces. Zee was crying and Will was holding her. It made Hannah smile, to know that the crying was all for naught, and that the comforting wasn't. She dried her hands and sat in a chair next to Everett Eaton. He seemed to sense her staring through the newspaper and lowered it.

"Want to dance?" he asked.

🐦 🐦 🐦

Everett Eaton had told her that the only time he'd ever been able to dance was when his boat moved unexpectedly beneath him. "Then it was jitterbug across the deck to starboard, waltz back to port. On a lobster boat I could make you and Ginger Rogers swoon at the same time."

Break of Day was almost ready. She'd needed new batteries, but once they were installed, the engine started almost immediately. The bottom had been caulked and painted; the topsides were waiting on another warm day for the last coat of white. Tom planned a May 15th launch. During the week, Will repaired Arno's old traps. Many needed new heads. Emily offered to help with them if he would bring the traps indoors. It was the most active she'd been since she arrived. She sat on the floor with the trap between her splayed legs. Her protruding stomach pressed into the wire mesh, while her heels held the trap firmly in place. Hannah thought if she gave birth there the baby would be trapped.

All of Arno's buoys had to be repainted to Tom's colors, black rings over a yellow body. His colors reminded Hannah of bees. He'd rigged up a foot-powered treadle, belted to a lathe. While the buoys turned on the lathe, he held a flat brush to the revolving surface. Hannah wondered if she could somehow mount a canvas on a motor so she'd never have to move her hand to paint.

The granite lungs came off well. Each lung now leaned in its own corner, so that they seemed to breathe separately. She'd had to order a block of anthracite, hard coal, for the second set in the series. It would be weeks before it arrived. As soon as she'd shipped off the last of the pieces to her spring exhibition at Gwen's gallery, other works began to arrive from her collectors for the retrospective. Included with the pieces were letters of flattery and requests for catalogs if any were printed. She'd invited all the owners to the show, but most declined, citing the long trip to Stonington. They were pleased that their works could add the retrospective to their provenance.

In early May, for the first time in several months, she went ashore, and spent a day sweeping out the gallery and diagramming the exhibition. While in town she picked up her mail. There were several more pieces, each sculpture packed in layers of foam and cardboard. It was strange to see the old work again, some of it eleven or twelve years old. Sometimes the small paintings didn't even seem to be by her own hand. The stones she'd wrapped and sent away so long ago seemed to have lost weight.

She'd locked the door behind her. The gallery had been a general store originally. Large plate-glass windows fronted the street. When passersby saw her inside they would occasionally stop and press their faces to the glass and shield their eyes from the sun's glare with their hands. She felt then as if she were a bug at the bottom of a tumbler, unable to climb free. Tom came by in the late afternoon with a small crate. It was from Bennington College. FedEx had dropped it at his place. The town was so small that even FedEx knew they were friends. Tom walked around the empty gallery with his hooks in his pockets, gazing at the heavily abraded wooden floor.

"It's pretty, isn't it?" Hannah said.

"Mr. Pickering's counter was right here. That's why there's this swale in the floor. He had one of those big bronze cash registers. There was a meat locker in back. I used to come in here as a kid and shoplift candy."

"Ever get caught?"

"Just as I was going out the door he'd call my name and hit NO SALE on that cash register. Every time. That bell would go right through me. I can still hear it. A lot of fruit and vegetables went out of this place. Seems funny, empty. Seems like a funny place to sell art. They all wonder what you do. I guess they'll finally get to see."

"At first I just wanted to see it all for me, but the closer the exhibition gets the more I know I want everyone else to see it, too."

"Why?"

"I don't know. Maybe so Will will be proud of me. There are other artists here on Deer Isle. It might be nice to start a dialogue."

"A dialogue?"

"To talk."

"Then why didn't you say that?"

"Dialogue sounds less invasive. I don't know what I'm doing here. People have been looking in the window. It makes me nervous."

"Let them look. Maybe you're doing it because you're proud of what you've done. And maybe it's starting to make you nervous, having pride."

"Why should that make me nervous?"

"It shouldn't. I'd be proud if I could paint. Zee sure enjoys it."

"She's good, too, Tom. Has she said anything to you about majoring in art?"

"No. She's got that idea?"

"Yes."

"Where's the money in that?" he asked. Her eyebrows went to sea on the sudden waves of her forehead. "Well, you're different than most of them."

"She can teach or work in graphic design. It could lead toward architecture or industrial design, too. Listen, I'll not worry about Will becoming a fisherman if you'll not worry about Zee becoming an artist."

"I don't know if that sounds fair or if it's some kind of wisecrack."

"Me either. How did the doctor's appointment go?"

"The last two have been fine. She answers the doctor's questions, and even has one or two of her own to ask. I went into the clothing store with her this time and she bought three outfits."

"Did she pay for them?"

"Yes."

"That is an improvement."

"I had her pay for those pants, too."

"She didn't tell me about that."

"She didn't like it one bit is why. Didn't speak to me the whole way back home. Felt like I was in the truck with my wife."

"Well, she's over it now. She asked why you and Zee couldn't come out on Friday nights instead of Saturday mornings."

"Have to work Friday nights," Tom said.

"I told her."

"Do you see your wife, Tom?"

"No, not anymore. All the paperwork is long over. Her folks call me about her every once in a while, looking for her. I try not to think about her. Just hurt there. It makes me mad that she doesn't come to see Zee. Makes me mad that Zee won't go see her. I sound like a mad fellow to be as happy as I am."

"You are?"

"I am. You're a big part of it, too. I appreciate it, Hannah: the boat and Zee's tuition and everything."

"It's OK." She couldn't look at him.

"Well, I've got to get to work. I wish they'd outlaw black-soled shoes. Makes a hard life for a wax and buff man."

"Bye, Tom."

When he'd gone, she circled the wooden crate from Bennington twice before she found a crack for the blade of her screwdriver.

☙☙☙

The crate wouldn't pry apart. It was put together with screws having a star-shaped head. She left the crate and the other pieces locked in the gallery for three days, till she returned with her drill and the correct bit. In both instances she left the island in Will's care. He was allowed odd days off now as a graduating senior. More and more of his classmates were coming out to help with the boat and gear. The first thing she'd done that morning after Will had dropped her off at the Hagen Dock was buy a bottle of champagne to smash on *Break of Day*'s repaired stem.

For the first time in years the anxiety she felt upon leaving the island wasn't suffocating. Whether this was because someone she trusted was there to protect it, or because she finally knew what the people around her had always known, she didn't care. Will had arrived almost a year ago, and Emily had been with them for five months now. It seemed they had eluded Will's father. Will would be eighteen in a few weeks. She didn't know what the legal ramifications for her would be if his father showed up, but at least Will would be old enough to stand on his own.

The screws came out of the crate with a spiraling moan. Inside were two cardboard boxes packed in Styrofoam peanuts. In the first was a small sculpture, a granite popplestone into which she'd bored a hundred holes. These holes were plugged with smaller stones. She'd tried to make it seem as though the large stone had picked up the small ones as it rolled across a beach, her notion that with enough time anything was possible on the margin of the sea. There was a small matboard card included with the sculpture: "*Stanching the Flow*, Hannah Bryant, Purchased with Twyla M. Lyons Foundation Funds." The second box contained a small oil painting, a self-portrait of the back of her head and shoulders. It was one of a series of the side of things not usually painted, that included the back of a mirror, a refrigerator and a stretcher and canvas. Its attribution card stated: "*My Face*, Hannah Bryant, Gift of the Brighton Bank, Bennington, VT."

She knew of the Lyons Foundation. The family had endowed the school years before she attended. Their daughter had died while in college. One of Hannah's friends had been a Lyons Fellow. The family's lost daughter would never graduate, but in her name two students crossed the grass for their diplomas every year.

She knew the Brighton Bank, too. She'd had a checking account there as a student. It sat in a parking lot in front of a strip mall about a mile from campus. She lifted the card to her nose and inhaled deeply.

She'd left her cell phone on the island with Will, in case he had some emergency. So she had to use the pay phone in the parking lot next to the newspaper office. The administrator, who'd approved the loan of her pieces at Bennington College, told her she'd only been in her position for six months. She didn't know the circumstances or any details of the Brighton Bank gift. "But somebody there must like your work," she said. "They have two more of your paintings on the wall behind the tellers. You have to look at one for a while to figure out it's not a painting turned to the wall. The other one is the back of a refrigerator. I look at them every time I go in to make a deposit. I always feel like I can see through walls, like the refrigerator and painting are in the next room."

"Thank you," Hannah said. "The pieces you shipped arrived in perfect condition."

🦢 🦢 🦢

The weather turned mild. The sound of the sea seemed distant, as if it had moved inland. Everett Eaton lay slumped in her armchair, the paper across his chest.

"Wake up," she said softly.

He opened his eyes.

"Let's go for a walk," she said.

"Who are you?"

"I'm Arno Weed's niece, Hannah."

"Oh, you again."

She took his hands and helped him out of the chair.

"C'mon, it's a nice day."

At the door, he paused on the threshold and looked out to make sure he wasn't stepping off into some abyss.

"Have we eaten yet?" he asked her.

"Yes, you just had lunch."

"Where are we going?"

"Around."

"I don't get around so good."

"I know. We'll go around the easy way."

"I hear people working in that boat shed."

"Tom and Will and Zee and Driftwood are in there working on the boat."

"What boat?"

"Arno Weed's *Break of Day*."

"My uncle built that boat. That's an old boat."

"Watch your step here. It's muddy."

"Where are we going?"

"For a walk. We'll find a place to sit down. Doesn't it smell good?"

"Smells like it always smells."

She took his hand. "C'mon, we'll walk down to the beach."

"It's slippery down there."

"We'll go slow. Isn't it a pretty day?"

She led him down the slope, and they walked at the high-tide line among broken shells and polished pebbles, dry black seaweed. His hand was as soft as the old paper bags full of rusty nails in the boat shed. Their lips had been rolled back for access to the nails years ago. The sacks would never hold if anyone picked them up. They sat on the workbench like an arrangement of wilted and dried flowers, dark seeds at their centers. She found a slab of granite in the sun, raked plundered urchins and crab shells from its warm surface.

"Sit here," she told him.

"OK."

The ocean before them was still. The only movement was the tide working back in eddying currents. She looked out in search of driftwood. In a calm like this it was easy to spot, but the ocean was empty except for a thousand lobster buoys.

"It's just us and the water," Mr. Eaton told her.

"There's a crab," she said. A small green crab worked its way along the water's edge. As they watched it hide under a sheaf of seaweed, a single wave humped up and broke on the shore. They both looked up to see what boat had passed by. There was none.

Mr. Eaton turned to her and said, "A whale has shrugged somewhere in the deep lonesome." He lifted his shoulders and let them fall to demonstrate.

"Oh," Hannah said.

"It's time for a nap," he told her.

"You just woke up," she said.

"I did?"

"Yes."

"It's the worst part, not being able to remember you got some rest. It makes you feel tired all the time."

"Maybe you're tired because you're old," she said.

"Nobody told me that."

"That you'd get old?"

"That I'd be tired when I was old."

"Oh."

"One good thing, though."

"What?"

"If you're like me, I have a memory problem, sometimes you forget that you're old."

"What happens when you remember?"

"It's sort of sad."

She couldn't help herself. Her heart shrugged. "I love you, Mr. Eaton."

"Well, it's about time," he told her.

🦐🦐🦐

Sunday evening, late, after the Eatons had left, she packed her suitcase. She looked up and saw Emily's light leave through the crack under her door. It took the top step of the stairs in a streak then dispersed and mingled with the faint light from downstairs. Will was still up studying. She stepped across the hall and knocked on Emily's door before opening it.

"What?" Emily asked.

"I'm going in with Will in the morning. I won't be back till Tuesday evening."

"Where are you going?"

"To Bennington College, my old school."

"But Will has school tomorrow. I'll be out here alone." Half the room lay in shadow, half in the loom of the kitchen lamp. Hannah couldn't tell if Emily was lying down or sitting up.

"You'll be all right. It's good that someone will be here. I'll leave the phone with you. You and Will can make dinner for each other tomorrow night."

"What if he comes?"

"Who?"

"Who else?"

"It's been months. I think we're OK. You'll have the phone."

"You promise you'll be back Tuesday?"

"Yes, I promise."

"Why do you have to go?"

"I just have to."

"I'm not used to you being gone." It was the closest thing to a compliment Emily had given her since she'd arrived.

"How are you feeling?" Hannah asked.

"Like I'm too big to hide anymore. Like I'm bigger than this room."

The ride from the quarry to town in the early morning was choppy. Lobster boats were leaving the harbor in every direction at top speed, as if it were on fire.

"It's starting to get crowded. All the fair-weather fishermen are back at it," Will said. She held fast to the gunwale, her bag on her knees. The spray left white scraps of salt on her black jeans when it dried. When Will asked why she was going, she told him someone was collecting her art and she wanted to find out who it was.

"It's a secret?" he asked.

"Not until lately, not until I cared to know. Make sure Emily eats a good dinner tonight."

She dropped him off at school.

It was an eight-hour drive to Bennington. She hadn't been over the Deer Isle Bridge since, when? Since before Christmas. She was appalled by the rise in gas prices. The tolls on I-95 had gone up, too. She realized, shortly after crossing into New Hampshire, that she hadn't been by herself for this long since Emily had arrived. She was glad the bag on the floorboard was small, that she'd only be away for one night. She felt she was tethered to the island, the line stretching behind her always taut.

By the time she reached Bennington, the lobby of the Brighton Bank was closed.

She took a room at the Best Western. It was strange to watch TV without the surging background noise of a generator. There were two hundred channels. Not one was devoted to making art. Before dark she drove up to Bennington College. It seemed as if there were grade-schoolers visiting campus, until she realized they were undergraduates. They were Will and Zee's age. Had she been this young when she was at school here? It didn't seem possible. She'd been an adult. These were kids. She walked through the Barn and paused in front of the display of recent student applications, artwork on 5"x7" cards. It was all impressive work. She remembered when her own card was pinned here. It seemed less than promising compared to this new crop. She'd glued a mirror to the card and painted a small self-portrait on the glass. Anyone bending close to look at her would see their own two eyes, hugely out of proportion, on either side of her head. Her head became their nose, her shoulders their lips. They were immediately drawn into her work, became the work.

Down at the arts building she wandered through the studios and shops. The concrete floors were splattered in archaeological layers of paint. Her own drips were down there somewhere, all the paint that narrowly avoided art. She hadn't known she'd missed making art with others till Zee started studying with her. She'd been so worried here at school, about making a life as an artist, that she thought she'd overlooked the joy of becoming an artist on a day-to-day basis. She'd always been looking over her own shoulder to make sure she wasn't behind.

☙ ☙ ☙

Sitting in her car in front of the bank, waiting for it to open, she drew faint topiaries, then retraced her own languorous lines simply to enjoy the moment again. At the bottom of the page, her pen snuffled in the paper like a dog in short grass. There was something to be found there, or was it gone already? One by one the bank employees arrived and were let in by a security guard. They were all dressed so nicely, the men in suits and the women in conservative skirts and jackets. It had been a long time since she'd moved among people who dressed for the public. It seemed odd that her art was part of this façade, that it hovered over and approved financial transactions, usury, children's savings accounts, mortgages. It was ironic, and she was pleased to realize that her paintings were turning their backsides to commerce. Did her patron understand this? Did they see the joke? It was ten after nine. Hannah didn't know what kind of reception she'd receive. She tried not to make suppositions.

Hannah followed an elderly woman inside. She walked as if there were a large stone between her knees. It seemed to take them minutes to negotiate the two sets of entrance doors. "My legs have lost their minds," she told Hannah. "First I got to tell one to step, and then I got to tell the other. My legs have forgotten they're legs. If just one part of you stays hopeful, it can encourage the rest. Watch the tellers perk up when I finally make it inside. I've got more money in this bank than God."

Hannah smiled at her tentatively and thought about asking her if she was an art lover. One of the tellers did call out the old woman's name, and she turned to Hannah and winked before encouraging her knees onward. Hannah looked past the woman and found her paintings on either side of the old lady's head.

There was no one at the receptionist's desk in front of the president's office, no one protecting her. Hannah stepped up to the open door and knocked. The woman turned to her from a computer. Her face seemed nervous, as if it were about to emit a buzz. She looked out through the glass wall of her office to the empty receptionist's desk.

"I'm sorry," Hannah said. "There was no one there." The woman's long red coat was draped over her shoulders. Napoleon would wear it that way, Hannah thought. She was young to be a bank president.

"How can I help you?" she asked.

Hannah delivered her set line. "The paintings behind the teller counter: they're mine."

"I'm sorry?" the woman said.

She wasn't nervous. She was cold. The office was still freezing. Hannah could smell dust burning somewhere down the long passageway of the heater vent.

"I'm Hannah Bryant, the artist who painted the two works on your wall." She pointed. "You donated one of my paintings to Bennington College."

"What can I do for you?" she asked again.

How strange, Hannah thought. "I was wondering if you were responsible for buying them."

"No," she said. "They were sent down years ago from corporate headquarters, as I understand it." Hannah didn't respond. "We're just a branch. Is there some problem?"

"No," Hannah said. "Where is your headquarters?"

"In Syracuse, New York."

"But you donated one of my paintings to Bennington. It was part of this same series behind your tellers."

"Yes, a couple of years ago. We were short on wall space. We'd put in a new commercial window. One of our customers told us you were an alum."

"Yes," Hannah said. "I am."

"It's not that we didn't like it. There wasn't enough wall space."

"I'm not upset," Hannah told her. "Who would be responsible for sending the art to you?"

"I don't know. Would you like me to call up there and ask for you?"

"No, thank you. Could I get the address in Syracuse?"

"Sure. Why did you paint the back of the refrigerator and not the front?"

"If I'd painted the front of the refrigerator, you would have wanted to know what was inside it. There's a why behind any good painting. This was just a different kind of why."

It was a four-hour drive. She stopped at a country store in Albany for gas and a sandwich. Among the syrup and cheddar cheese and balsam were antiques: tobacco tins, cigar boxes, cobalt bottles, and feed sacks. She was surprised to see how expensive they were. The packaging retained its value even after the contents were gone: Christ's shroud, Mozart's skull, the raiment's of the Queen. Above the sandwich counter was a collection of vacant bird's nests and hornet hives. When the boy making her sandwich asked if it was to go, Hannah nodded. He put the sandwich in a Styrofoam box. It made her feel vulnerable. She wouldn't get home tonight. She was being drawn deeper into the mainland. The New York State Thruway had too few exits. It felt as if she were extending her hand and wrist into a dark hole. She'd have to take care not to grasp anything too large to withdraw. She'd have to be careful not to trap herself. She'd have to be able to give up anything she found in order to escape. She thought she'd given in to vanity.

The Brighton Bank was housed in a sprawling four-story glass building behind a manmade lake in a business park. A fountain gushed from the middle of the grass-fringed lake. There must have been five hundred cars parked some distance from the building, but she found a space for visitors close to the entrance. The foyer was vast, marble-floored. Light flowed into the hall from all sides and above. A receptionist sat at a large mahogany desk a hundred feet away. Between Hannah and the reception desk were a dozen marble pedestals, perhaps four feet high, lining both sides of the central walkway. On each pedestal sat one of her sculptures. The receptionist smiled at her from eighty feet. Her smile seemed like light under the door at that distance. Hannah wasn't sure anyone should be in that room. Behind the receptionist, mounted on a mahogany wall, was the largest panel Hannah had ever painted, *Ten Acre No Nine at Sunset*. The canvas was four feet tall and ten wide. The island hung motionless. The shallow water of the foreshore reflected the available light, and her home was surrounded and infused with gold, what lingered after a retreating sun. Before she knew it she had bumped into the long desk, her eyes still focused on the painting. The receptionist was speaking, but not to her. A tiny wire emanating from her ear vibrated along her cheekbone. Her hands played along a lit keyboard. The same gold light of Hannah's painting erupted from her fingernails when she pressed a button. She seemed like the vibrant mind of a bewildered creature, unable to keep up with sensory input. She spoke in broken sentences, without greetings, rebuttals, or good-byes.

Hannah's welcome was an affirmative interrogatory: "Yes?"

"Hello. I don't know where to begin. I live there," she said, and pointed beyond the woman.

The receptionist turned, but didn't recognize the painting as a place. "Where?" she asked.

There was a metallic tone, and the receptionist moved her fingertip to light.

Hannah looked back over her own shoulders. Men in suits swerved between her sculptures on their way to distant doors and hallways. They talked in animated tones or read as they walked, like the distracted choreography of a play opening.

"I'm sorry?" the woman said.

"I'd like to speak to the person who purchases this art," Hannah said.

"Hmm, I don't know who that would be. Let me call maintenance."

"I don't think maintenance can help," Hannah said. "Maybe someone who'd have the authority to spend large sums. Someone in management."

"May I tell them who's calling?"

"I'm Hannah Bryant. These are my sculptures. That's my painting behind you."

"Really? So you live on that island?"

"Yes."

"That must be nice."

"It is," Hannah said.

"Let me call Security."

"Why?"

"Don't worry. They know who to call when something goes missing."

"Oh," Hannah said. "Good idea."

"They don't put me here for my looks." She spoke to three people, each time explaining she had the artist standing in front of her who made all those rock sculptures in the lobby. After the third explanation, she said, "You go over to those elevators on the left. Go on up to the fourth floor. They'll have someone meet you at the door."

"I'm going to leave and you're just going to keep on pushing buttons, aren't you?" Hannah said.

"That's what they pay me for."

When the elevator door opened, she stood facing another of her paintings hanging in the hallway. There was no one waiting for her. She stepped back inside the elevator and went to the third floor, then the second. One of her paintings was on each floor. She pushed 4 again, and when the doors opened this time, a young man was waiting.

"Hi, I'm John. Are you Ms. Bryant?"

"Yes."

"If you'll follow me." He turned away, never having made eye contact.

"Can you tell me about my paintings?" she asked as they walked.

"I'm sorry, I'm just a functionary. They just asked me to bring you down."

"Down where?"

"To the investments department."

He led her through a maze of corridors, across two secretarial pools, to a richly carpeted vestibule.

"Please have a seat."

He disappeared through a heavy door. With each person she came to, she felt as if she were cresting another wave. The couches looked deep and soft and so she wouldn't sit in them. She'd have to struggle to get out of them should the door open suddenly. She already felt out of place in her jeans and sweater. Her canvas bag, splattered with oil and acrylic dabs, had no brass corners or combination lock. She opened it to see what comfort there might be inside: her wallet, a half-dozen stubs of watercolor pencils, most no longer than two inches, a sketch pad, a water bottle, and various paper clips, hair bands, a half bag of pretzels, two shells, and a stone.

There wasn't much here to fight with. It was at best a twenty-four-hour creative survival kit. A big watercolor would use up all the pencils. She stood in the center of the room for five minutes, ten, till she succumbed to the notion that she was, after all, happy to be forgotten.

When the door opened, Hannah was holding one of the cupped shells under her nose. The small round granite stone was in her mouth. She ushered it into her palm with her tongue. It glistened as if a wave had just slipped off its surface. The woman who came through the door offered a business card. She smelled of warm wool, a coat left to dry over a radiator.

"It's not my card," she said.

Hannah read it. *Michael L. Whatley / Vice President / Investments and Trust / The Brighton Bank.*

"I'm Margaret Storrel. Michael would like to set up a meeting with you in ten days or so," she said. Her two wrists protruded an uneven distance from her gray sleeves.

"I don't understand," Hannah said.

"He didn't expect you."

"I know. But this is the man who's been buying my work?"

"You'll have to speak with Michael. I'm afraid he's on vacation this week."

"Then how does he know I'm here?"

"I've just spoken with him on the phone." In Hannah's peripheral vision the couches seemed to tilt up on their bun feet and slowly move behind her, to block the doors.

"I drove twelve hours to get here. I can't come back in ten days," she said.

"He'd like to visit you in Maine."

"Really? After all these years?"

"Yes."

"Oh." She paused. "My work: it's all over this building. Do you work for Mr. Whatley?"

"I work with him. We both do the same work."

"But you can't tell me any more?"

"Michael wants to talk to you in person. We've been waiting for you to come." When she tugged at the cuffs of her sleeves, the furniture seemed to settle down.

"I didn't know I had a patron. I didn't know what to think about it. It seems medieval. I guess I can tell him that in person."

"Yes," she said.

"I didn't know I was supposed to come."

"He was going to find you soon, anyway. We're having a shipping firm in next week to pack everything up for you. You're having a retrospective?"

"Yes, in a small gallery in Maine. But I think I should have had it here. It would have saved on shipping costs."

"I'd like to see your other work. I have to admit I don't always know what's going on with your sculptures and paintings, but that doesn't seem to bother me. I'll miss them."

"Thank you. I didn't realize I've been missing them till lately."

"My grandmother says the world's level of love and every other emotion has to stay constant, and so when one person falls in love someone else falls out. So you and I will exchange being lonesome for your work."

"Thank you. That's sweet."

"Do you really live on that island in the lobby?"

"Yes."

"It must be nice to think you're going back there. Good luck, Hannah."

"This is my phone number." She wrote it down in blue watercolor pencil. "Don't let that get wet."

🐢 🐢 🐢

When she called the island to tell Will and Emily she wouldn't be back that night, Tom answered the phone.

"Hi," she said.

"Hi, Hannah. She's in the head."

"Is everything all right?"

"Yep, I'm stirring the soup."

"The soup?"

"Emily's making dinner for us."

"Emily is?" She couldn't keep the startle out of her voice.

"Yeah, onion soup, a pork roast, and cornbread. We started the winch engine today. Boat shed filled up with black smoke. Me and Will are still coughing it up. But she runs good. I think maybe we'll launch this weekend."

"You guys have gone too far without me."

"Hurry home."

"Why aren't you at work?" Hannah asked.

"I could ask the same of you."

"How's Emily?"

"Pregnant."

"Very funny. How's Will?"

"He's dirty, but happy."

"How's the island?"

"It's surrounded by water. You better come home."

🐢🐢🐢

She didn't need any encouragement. Will picked her up at the public landing the next evening. As she'd crossed Deer Isle Bridge almost all the uneasiness and vulnerability she'd felt for the previous three days ebbed away. The causeway between Little Deer and Deer was like the long, narrow jaw of a many-toothed creature. Anyone who followed her this way would have to make that dangerous passage. She realized she felt safer in Will's skiff than in her own car. Will was effervescent. Bubbles popped at the corners of his lips.

"We're going to launch Saturday, Hannah. Just for a couple hours. Then we'll put her back in the cradle and haul her out of the water again. Then we'll do the same thing the next day and the next, till she swells sound. We put this Slick Seam stuff in her. Tom says it will squeeze out as the planks soak up water. Every day we'll leave her in the ocean a little longer till she gets used to it again."

"Sounds like you're breaking a horse that's gone wild."

"We started the winch engine yesterday." His voice was at a high, vibrating pitch, about to fall off the edge of a table. He yanked back on the starter cord of the outboard, still looking at her. The cord snapped free of the motor. His clinched fist, unhindered by the recoil, struck her squarely below the left eye. She tumbled back between the thwarts and landed on her back, looking up at the blue sky, which quickly went wet and pale. Seagulls swam in the air.

"Jesus, Hannah," he said. He was leaning over her as the boat, engine running in neutral, drifted away from the float. "You all right?"

She placed her hand over her cheekbone. "Wow," she whispered.

"Jesus, I'm sorry," Will said. "The rope broke."

The skin of her cheek seemed out of place. She pressed it back down, drew it under her jaw. He helped her sit up. She opened her mouth twice, each time more fully. Then she wiped the water out of her eyes. "I'm OK," she said experimentally. Then said it again to reassure him.

"I've never hit anybody that hard," he said.

She rubbed her cheek as if it were some new fabric. "I guess we're even now," she said.

He smiled. "Guess so. It doesn't hurt so much as it's surprising, hunh? It's hard to believe the world was waiting to pounce on you like that. It'll be sore later." He started to giggle when he saw she was all right.

"OK," she said. "You sit in the bow. I'll steer."

"Sure."

"I'm serious." She shoved him off the rear thwart and threw her bag in his lap. She said the sentence, "Don't let that get wet," for the second time in as many days. Shifting the outboard into gear, she fired the throttle till they were planing between the moored lobster boats. She looked back to see her wake slap against them. It had been years since she'd sat here, low on the water, the power of motion squeezed in her fist. Water streamed from her eyes and seemed to freeze on her cheeks. She took the long way out, slicing between Bare and St. Helena islands and then turning east, passing Round and Wreck and McGlathery to starboard, Coombs and Ram and Spruce to port. Will bent down, holding his cap to his head, ducking cold spray and spring air. The throttle was wide open, the boat skipping from wave top to wave top, and she imagined entering the quarry at this speed, arriving home, thudding into the island like a bullet, flattening out, cooling down, extravagantly embraced. Or ripping into the shallows off the boat shed, the motor kicked away from the transom and the boat skidding up the spare granite slope and into the trees, buffeted by stones beneath thick moss and lichen and finally bursting out of the spruce into tall grass, a rain of splinters and ribs, skiff and human, an even layer of compost broadcast.

"OK, you can slow down now," Will yelled.

Her grip on the throttle relaxed. The boat slowed so quickly that the sea jumped over the transom and wet her from the navel down.

"What got into you?" Will screeched as he bailed with a cut-down Clorox bottle. The water, ankle deep, swirled around her feet.

"I'm just glad to be home, Will," she told him, and she gunned the boat forward a bit as Will pitched with the bilge scoop, so that his face caught up with the airborne water. He turned to her, the water dripping off his brow and nose.

"OK," he said. He picked up her bag and emptied it into the sloshing bilge. She screamed and dove for her wallet. And as he poured scoop after scoop of cold ocean onto her screams, she watched her watercolor pencils faintly paint a pale sea.

🐢🐢🐢

In early May there were days when the old house cradled the sun between the granite stoop and its worn blue door. Hannah opened the door and found Emily there, sitting on the warm stone. Driftwood sat between her legs, watching the sea. Emily riffled through his fur with one hand. Hannah bent down and handed her a cup of tea, rich with milk. She sat down on the weathered oak threshold and pulled the door closed behind her so she could lean against it. Her splayed legs extended beyond Emily's hips and she nudged her with the insides of both knees in a weak, tentative hug. During the middle of the week the boat shed below them seemed unusually quiet. Beyond, the tide was low, exposing ledges. Seagulls tore mussels loose from the tidal pools, took flight and dropped the shells on the shelving rock. The first time Hannah saw this, years ago, she thought it was an accident. But the bird repeated the process till the mussel cracked. Hannah reached out tentatively and touched Emily's hair. It was still moist from her bath. Emily leaned forward and turned slightly.

"What?"

"It's getting long," Hannah said. "I could braid it for you."

"No, let it dry."

"OK."

"You didn't come back when you said you would."

"No. I had to stay a day longer than I thought."

"Why?"

"I had to drive on to Syracuse, New York."

"Will said you found a bank that's buying all your work."

"Yes, a lot of it."

"Why do they do that?"

"I guess they like it."

"Do you feel funny now?"

"Why?"

"That you work for a bank."

"I don't work for a bank. I work for myself."

"If they pay all your bills, I'd think you'd call that working for them."

"They've never tried to influence my work, never told me what to paint or when to paint it."

"But they could. Maybe that's what they're coming here for."

"Emily, I haven't even known they existed. I can't be any other artist than the one I am, anyway."

"I was thinking this might make you understand what it's like to be under someone else's control."

"Like you were under Will's father's control?"

"No, like I was under God's control, and like I'm under your control."

"I don't want to be in control of you, Emily. You came here of your own free will."

"I had no other choice."

"So how is it my fault that you had no other choice?"

"Because I owe you now. Because you made it easy for me to come."

"So if I'd turned you away, I would have been off the hook?"

"You would have been no different than everyone else."

"It's so beautiful here, Emily. Why don't you let this place heal you?"

"This place drags me down. It makes me feel like I'm part of it, all the muck on the beach, the trees rotting in the moss. The whole island seems to leak, just like me. I want to be dry and light again."

"Can I touch your stomach, Emily?" The baby would be here soon. There was so little time left to try to be friends.

"What?" She twisted halfway round and looked at Hannah.

"Can I?"

Emily turned away, faced the foreshore again.

Hannah slipped forward, raised her knees. She put her arms under Emily's and let her palms fall flatly along the full swell of her stomach.

"It's as hard as a shell," Hannah said. Her chin rested on Emily's shoulder.

"It's my mistake," Emily said. "It's eating me from the inside out."

"You don't know what it is, Emily. Just like I don't know who you are. Give it a chance."

"I'm giving it a place to live, just like you're giving me one."

"You're the most complicated person I know."

"You're the simplest person I know. Everyone around you burns, and you still carve rocks and paint cave walls."

Hannah didn't know what to say, but knew she didn't want to move. She turned her head and placed her cheek on Emily's back. Wind came across the bay, shuttered the still tidal pools. All the airborne gulls stopped flapping and banked on the wind, caught it as if swinging aboard a dream. Then it was gone. The birds faltered, the tidal pools glazed over. Hannah held tightly to her sister's stomach, and listened to her heart's slow tide.

"How is your tea?" she asked.

"It's good."

🐚 🐚 🐚

It wasn't the fact that a bank bought her work that was so bothersome, but that her work was at home in a bank. She'd always thought of her paintings and sculptures residing in private homes, over mantels, not receptionists' desks. There was something unsettling about her paintings ceaselessly photographed before the slow shutter of elevator doors. The pedestaled row of sculptures in the busy lobby seemed like pylons on a test course. It was true her work had a larger audience on a daily basis. Perhaps more people saw them in a bank than would see them in a museum. But she thought that somehow the work had lost its repose, its contemplative intimations, and by its simple placement devolved to decoration. It was ridiculous, of course, a philistine's snootiness. Why couldn't art be appreciated in a workplace? Many of the world's great sculptures sat in front of businesses. Corporations built fabulous collections. In certain instances they'd led the way in modern appreciation. They commonly outbid major museums for iconic pieces.

Hannah left the phone attached to its charger for days. It was the first time she'd ever waited for it to ring. When it finally did ring, on Friday morning, her hands were suffocated in coal dust. She'd been working outside on the second set of lungs. The coal couldn't be chiseled. She was sculpting with a power grinder. Emily stepped out the door, held the phone up in the air. Hannah stopped grinding, dropped her mask off her nose. She took the phone and immediately began walking away from the house, away from the noise of the generator.

"Yes?"

"This is Michael L. Whatley, of the Brighton Bank."

"This is Hannah Bryant, of Ten Acre No Nine," she said.

"I'm sorry I missed you in Syracuse, Ms. Bryant. I'd like to try again."

"I didn't mean to invade your privacy, Mr. Whatley. I was so curious."

"No, it's perfectly understandable. I'd like to come to Maine and talk to you about your work. I thought I'd accompany the artwork, week after next, follow the truck."

"Sure. I could meet you at the gallery in Stonington. I really appreciate your loan, Mr. Whatley. We're trying to raise money for the local high school. I have to say I was pretty overwhelmed when I saw so much of my stuff at your bank. I want to thank you for your support."

"There's no need. The truck is scheduled to leave here early Monday morning. I think we should be there around six in the evening."

"You have the address?"

"Yes."

"Then I'll see you there, Mr. Michael L. Whatley."

"Good-bye."

She immediately dialed Gwen. "It's Hannah. His name is Michael L. Whatley and he's with the Brighton Bank. I just talked to him on the phone. He sounded tall."

"Tall?"

"He might have been in New York early this week. Did you notice anyone in particular looking at my work?"

"No, but I got an order in the morning mail. They're buying almost $30,000 worth this time: the self-portraits, four paintings, and several of the small sculptures."

"Gwen, I was there: in Syracuse. It's a huge bank headquarters. My work is everywhere: in the lobby, the hallways, the offices."

"So it hasn't gone on from there? I'd always thought some dealer was working through the bank for a client."

"Some of it is at their local branches. That's how I found out. There's some at the bank in Bennington."

"I'm glad it's all over, Hannah. I didn't like holding out on you. Year after year I expected you to ask. When it finally came, I felt more guilty than ever. Some of my artists have to know exactly where every piece goes. They feel like they want to know where their children are. It took you a long time to feel that way. What made you come around?"

"I don't know. I don't feel like they're my children. I wouldn't sell my children for any amount of freedom. I just wanted to see what the past looked like, whether I was remembering everything correctly. But when I left the bank I was happy to know everything was going to come back home, if only for a little while."

"Tell me what you're working on now."

"Well, right now, I'm covered in coal dust." She told Gwen about the lung series, asked her who could mold a glass lung to her design.

"So you're becoming an artist of social commentary now?" Gwen asked.

"No, I'm not trying to right any wrongs," Hannah answered. "I'm trying to show how we die of life."

🦢 🦢 🦢

"On the day Judy Garland died, a tornado touched down in Kansas," Mr. Eaton told her.

"She was in the movie *The Wizard of Oz*, right? She went up in a tornado in a dream," Hannah said.

"Some say it was a dream, others, no."

She'd pulled two rusty steel lawn chairs down through the grass to the boat shed. The chairs' tubular legs grumbled on the bare granite as they left the grass. The boat launching was behind schedule. The plan was to lower the boat on its wheeled cradle down the marine railway into a rising tide. As the planks swelled, the boat could be winched back up the ways with the aid of the rising water. Tom was unsure the old winch would pull the boat back up the beach and into the shed without some help. Two or three of his father's friends had told him they'd seen Arno run *Break of Day* up on the cradle and into the shed at full throttle, the propeller still turning as it broke the surface. Will, Zee, and three of their friends had cleared all the seaweed, mussels, and periwinkles from the rails and greased them with a gallon can of bacon fat. They'd intended to use petroleum grease, but Hannah had put a stop to that. She'd saved the ocean from one more contamination, but it was cramping her hand. She had a firm grip on Driftwood's collar. They'd caught him licking the length of both rails.

Everett Eaton put his hand under the dog's collar with Hannah's. "I haven't been to a boat launching in twelve years," he said. "It's come time again. You ought to do everything once every twelve years. That's about the life span of a dog. You ought to live a full and complete life every twelve years in case you're lucky enough to come back in your next life as a dog. Then you'll have had practice. You'll know just how to bark."

"You want to come back as a dog?" Hannah asked.

"If they won't let me come back as me," he answered.

"Tom and Zee tell me it's your birthday today."

"That's what they keep saying. I'd have preferred to wander along with the thought that any day could be my birthday, but now it's limited to just this one."

"So your birthday has made you sad rather than happy?"

"You're right. When did that happen?"

"It happens at age thirty," Hannah said, and smiled.

"Why are we sitting here?" he asked.

"They're about to open these doors and launch the boat."

"Whose boat?"

"Arno Weed's."

"My uncle built his boat."

"I know."

"Arno Weed is dead, isn't he?"

"He died almost seven years ago."

"I thought so. This dog might be him."

Hannah turned to him, turned away from the sea to Mr. Eaton and then to the dog. "You're the most unnerving person I know, Mr. Eaton."

"My wife called me 'Mr. Eaton,' too. It didn't feel strange that she wouldn't use my first name. But it felt funny when strangers called me the same thing my wife called me in bed."

"Would you like me to call you Everett?"

"If it makes you feel less comfortable, yes. I mean less intimate. I named my boat after my wife. When I retired from fishing and sold my boat, that fella fished her under the same name. Can't say as I cared for that. She might not like you calling me Mr. Eaton. This dog might be her."

Someone released the two stainless pins that held the shed doors closed. The doors swung open abruptly, as if they'd been holding back a sneeze for years. Will and Zee each chased down a door and wedged it open with stones.

"This is it," Will yelled.

The tall doors creaked in the light wind, unsure of their hinges. Spiderwebs, jeweled with sawdust rather than dew, were exposed to the sunlight, as was *Break of Day*'s transom. Fresh paint glistened in the light, as wet and slick as something just born. Hannah and Mr. Eaton stood up and walked toward the boat with the dog between them. They were trying to get a better angle. *Break of Day*'s escutcheon had been removed. Another, carved and gilded, was in its place. Tom walked out from beneath the hull and looked at Hannah.

"I told Will it was too fancy for a working boat, all that gilding. But we both liked the sound of it. And it's your boat."

They hadn't asked permission. *Break of Day* was now *Sweet Hannah*. Will and Zee and their friends came and stood beside her. They all looked up at the name board and back at her, as if there should be some resemblance.

"I carved it in shop, Hannah, and Zee gilded and varnished it," Will said.

"I thought it was bad luck to change a boat's name," Hannah said.

"It is," Tom said. "But it's worse luck to change it twice. We can't change it back now."

Emily stepped around one of the wavering doors, both hands splayed on her stomach. Tom trotted forward to help her navigate the granite beach.

"What do you think, Hannah?" Will asked. "It's OK, isn't it?"

"Who added the adjective?"

"Tom and I agreed to keep that a secret."

This made her blush with pleasure. She hid it by bending down and asking the dog what he thought.

"I mean, don't get the big head or anything," Will told her. "*Sweet Driftwood* was a close second."

"What did you do with the old name board?"

"It's under the workbench."

"I want you to nail it up over the front door of the house."

Will smiled. He turned to Zee and pinched her at the waist. "You were right." Then he and the other boys went back inside the noisy shed.

"What?" Hannah asked. "What were you right about?"

Zee said, "I told them you'd love it, that you'd love having a boat named for you."

"Why would you know that?"

"My father named his after me when I was little. I still think about it sometimes."

"They could have named this one after you, Zee. I don't mind."

"No, that's OK. One boat is enough." Zee reached up and put her hands over her grandfather's ears and whispered to Hannah, "I'm just glad it's not *Sweet Emily*."

Will and Hannah were aboard when two boys knocked big wedges from beneath the cradle. Tom released the clutch on the old winch. The steel cable between the winch and cradle slackened, but the boat didn't move.

Tom yelled up to them, "Jump up and down."

They couldn't jump too high or they'd hit their heads on the joists, but first Hannah and then Will took tentative hops, then began bouncing in earnest. Will's friends took their sledges around to the front of the cradle and began pounding on it just above the rails. When the boat slipped back three inches at once, both Will and Hannah fell on the cockpit platform.

Will burst out laughing, and with his cheek still lying on the platform, said, "I guess we haven't got our sea legs yet."

As Tom released the cable, the cradle and boat rolled slowly down the railway. Just before the rudder reached the water, Zee smashed the bottle of champagne on the stem at a point below the repair. As the boat entered the water, the sea seemed to accept her hull with cupped hands. The cradle remained on the rails and the boat floated freely. Zee stood on the bare granite holding a line tied at the bow. Tom emerged from the boat shed to the whoops of Will and his friends.

"She's floating, Tom," Will yelled.

"Open those hatches and see what's happening below," he called back. "Zee, don't let her float away from that cradle. Keep her right up over it."

Hannah opened the cockpit hatches while Will went below to look under the cabin sole. Water streamed into the boat from almost every seam. Immediately there was four inches of water in the bilge. Will came back up from below, his face olive green as Slick Seam.

"You named a sinking boat after me," Hannah said.

The bilge pump kicked on and a thick stream of bark-colored water shot from the side of the hull. The stern of the boat, pushed by small waves, began to swing away from the cradle.

"Keep her over the cradle," Tom yelled at Zee.

"I've only got her nose, Dad," she shot back.

Will called out, "It's really coming in fast, Tom."

"Put a line on that stern cleat and throw it to me, Will."

Will scrambled around the cockpit, but there was no line. The bilge stream coughed, spat, and halted.

"She's going to come up broadside on the rocks if you don't get us a line, Will," Tom yelled.

"There isn't one," Hannah screamed back. Just as she yelled, Will jumped over the side of the boat into chest-deep water. He pushed against the boat's hull, trying to push it back at the ocean. Tom sloshed into the sea alongside him and put his back against the hull and together they halted the stern's swing toward the beach. Zee waded in to her knees to hold the stem off the granite. Both Emily and Mr. Eaton waddled forward, their hands out before them as if they were about to catch something. While Tom and Will were able to hold the boat in place they could make no progress. Will's friends waded in, too, but the waves and current were just as strong as all four men.

Hannah leaned out over the starboard gunwale and told Tom, "She's really loading up, Tom. There's water everywhere."

"The bilge pump must be clogged. See if you can clear it."

Hannah stepped below into a foot of swirling water. She found the vibrating pump and lifted it and a section of hose clear. Chips of paint and a blue paper towel clung to the bottom of the pump. She pulled these away. The pump surged with noise and she plunged it back into the water. She climbed back out and looked over the side. Bilge water splashed on Tom's head and shoulders.

"You need to get her started, Hannah. We've got to get her nose off this beach and get her over the cradle again."

"You move forward, Will. Get away from the prop," she said.

"I'm OK."

"Do what I say or I'll let her sink right here," she screamed.

"OK, OK."

Hannah went to the helm and turned the key in the ignition. The engine turned once sluggishly, as if it were working in mud. She let the key spring back and turned it again. This time the diesel caught. She was immediately sprayed with a shower of bilge water. Water was up to the level of the crankshaft pulley and belts on the engine. As they turned they flung spray out the open hatch and over the helm and cockpit. Hannah popped the transmission into reverse and slowly backed away from the shore into deeper water.

"She's beginning to list, Hannah," Tom yelled, still hip deep in water. His hooks cupped his mouth as he yelled, as if they were still hands. She pushed the gearshift up into forward and advanced the throttle slowly, swung the stern around and headed back in. The boat was as sluggish as heavy chain. Will and Tom positioned themselves on each side and helped hold the keel between the rails. The bilge pump failed again, and the boat began to settle. Zee tied the bowline to the cradle, and her father slogged up the beach and into the shed. He threw the winch into gear, and slowly cradle and boat were dragged from the sea.

Hannah turned the engine off and the wild spray subsided. As the boat climbed the granite slope all the water inside the hull flowed back to the stern. Hannah went below to check the bilge pump again and found it clogged with more paint. She soon found her own throat clogged as well, the boat filling with smoke off the winch as it entered the shed. She climbed out of the gushing boat over the stern, and stood on the beach, dripping with Will and Zee. Tom came out of the shed, coughing and smiling.

"Same drill tomorrow morning," he said. "She'll swell up some today. We'll be more prepared next time."

Hannah left her hands on her hips. Water seemed to be flowing out of her namesake as fast as it had flowed in.

Mr. Eaton and Emily joined their leaking circle. Driftwood resumed licking the rails.

Hannah fixed her gaze on Tom. "You said she'd float."

"She will. Just not today."

"You have to believe she'll float," Mr. Eaton advised.

"I wouldn't get in it on a bet," Emily said.

"Can't we do something?" Hannah asked. "Maybe we should fiberglass the hull."

"You'll kill her if you do that," Tom said. "I should have been pouring buckets of seawater into her all along. Her keel and garboards are dry. But there's not much for us to do now but prepare a little better, get some line up on her. The rest is up to the old boat. She's wet now. She'll swell while we dry out. Two, maybe three more dunkings and she'll float like a cork."

"She has to drown to swim?" Hannah said. "I've never trusted that philosophy."

"Little better than a planter onshore," Tom said. "If you'll make the art, I'll get this boat afloat." Hannah's mouth dropped. He looked toward the water over the railway, as if he expected to see a hole in it, and tried to hide a smile.

Zee punched her father on the shoulder, hard. While he rubbed his arm with the plastic cuff of his hook, Zee turned him so the other shoulder faced Hannah. Hannah whaled it with her fist.

"Ha ha," Mr. Eaton whooped. "Ha ha. Best launching I've ever been to."

🐠 🐠 🐠

The tent pegged to the floor in the granite house was orange, and the fire before it shot light through the fabric and cast an amber glow over the entire room as if it resided in sunset. They didn't expect rain, so Mr. Eaton slept on a cot at the far end of the room. Zee and Will were inside the tent, asleep in a tangle of blankets and sleeping bags. Tom was walking Emily home. Hannah sat by the stone fireplace, waiting for him to return.

Their clothes had dried and they'd cooked mussels and hot dogs over an open fire on the beach. In all the years she'd lived on the island, she'd never cooked outside. She found it thrilling. Tom had been appalled when he discovered she had no ring of stones. "You've got to cook outside at least once a year to remain connected to the planet," he told her, and immediately began arranging a circle of popplestones. "I'll get some firewood," she'd said, and he'd told her, "No, you only burn driftwood in one of these." It seemed there was so much she didn't know. They laid too-long driftwood limbs across the stone circle, mounded smaller branches and boards within the rocks, till this heaped and gnarled structure resembled the skeletal remains of an ancient spider washed up on the shore. Tom lit the fire with the dry grass his father carefully pushed under the driftwood. Smoke, the same color as the driftwood, rose into the sky with the wandering curl and amiability of a feather's fall. As Hannah's clothes dried of salt spray, they soaked in wood smoke. Mr. Eaton and Will, neither of whom would eat mussels, approached the fire with hot dogs skewered on coat hangers. The dogs bobbed in the rising heat, wavered on their hangers, blackened in the fire.

"Did you burn the paint off those coat hangers before you cooked with them?" Tom asked.

Mr. Eaton looked at Will. They both looked at the dogs in their hands. Will reared back and heaved his into the sea. Mr. Eaton frowned and took a bite of his. Mustard and relish rimmed his upper lip. He chewed for a moment, then swallowed. "Little paint won't be what kills me," he told Will, "but you've just poisoned our lobster stock."

Tom slid a tray of mussels into the pot, and the pot onto the fire. By the time they finished eating, floating embers were being pinched out by stars. They lay on the smooth granite using stones for pillows. The tide seemed to be sliding out from beneath Hannah's body, the smoke and heat rising from her own mouth. Mr. Eaton began to tell them of a long dory row he'd made as a boy, from Deer Isle to Matinicus, when the mosquitoes struck. Emily pushed her body up from the rock as if she were breaking free of it for the first time.

"Little bastards," Mr. Eaton said.

They kicked the fire farther down the beach to make sure the tide would eventually douse it, and ran for the granite house. Here Tom and Mr. Eaton built another fire, and made tea over it, while Will burned marshmallows. He ate an entire bag of them before falling asleep next to Zee.

Hannah waited next to the fire, flicking bits of bark onto the hearth. When Tom came back from taking Emily up to the house, Hannah told him she wouldn't stay long. She knew he was tired.

"It's OK. I'm just thinking of that boat swelling up as we're sitting here," he said. "I'll think about it all night."

"Swelling up just like my sister."

"She's getting there too, isn't she? She looks good. She let me feel her stomach. Never felt anything so ripe."

"Yeah, it's so hard, isn't it? Like wood." She turned to him. He sat on the floor, his hooks hanging on each other around his clamped knees. He was looking into the fire. His black hair, sprigged with salt, splayed away from his forehead. He looked like Zee when she was concentrating on painting, yet he was relaxed, lost in the fire.

She didn't want to ask, but she wanted to know. "How?" she said.

"What?" He turned to her, but had to blink the remains of the fire from his pupils to see her.

"How could you feel her stomach?"

"Oh, I just put my cheek there," he answered.

"Oh," Hannah said. She looked into the fire too then, trying to decide who she was jealous of, Tom or Emily, and when she couldn't decide, she said, "Oh," again, aloud.

"What?" Tom asked.

"I saw something green in the fire. It flared up," she said.

"Maybe the salt in the wood. I've seen some driftwood burn turquoise. There's all kinds of minerals in the sea, I guess, and the wood soaks them up."

"You don't seem sleepy," she said.

"I'm wide awake."

"How're you going to work at the school at night and haul traps during the day?"

"I've put my resignation in for the end of the school year."

"You don't even know if the boat will float yet. How can you take such a risk?"

"I told you the boat would float, Hannah. Besides, I've got to fish. I'm no good at these other things. My life will be better as a bad fisherman than as a first-rate janitor. I'll need a good sternman, that's sure."

"What will you do this fall, when Will and Zee leave?"

"Hannah, you think way ahead, not just about your own life but everybody else's. I thought I was the only one thinking about the fall. I think I'll know what I'm capable of by then. Maybe I'll have proved myself to some of the other fishermen by then, and I can get one of them to come along."

A red ember popped out of the fire onto Tom's shirttail. He picked it up before it burned the fabric.

"You're getting good," Hannah said.

"I never forget they're not mine, but I'm grateful for them."

"When the boat floats . . ." she started.

"You haven't said the boat's name yet. You can't go on calling her 'the boat.' This boat will be my livelihood, my boss, my partner, my life. I'll miss the house payment, the grocery payment, the doctor payment, just so she'll have a fresh quart of oil. She'll save my life. Something that important isn't a thing and doesn't go without a name."

"Ok. When *Sweet Hannah* floats . . . it sounds silly . . . when she floats, I have a favor to ask."

"What's that?"

"Near the entrance to the quarry, underwater, there's a cut stone. It must weigh five hundred pounds. I want to put it on Arno's grave. He said I might pick it up with the boat, *Sweet Hannah*, I'll get used to it, and bring it around to the boat shed, then drag it up through the field with the two winches."

"Granite all over this island. Why's it got to be the one underwater?"

"He picked it out."

"He wanted to give you a challenge. So I guess you've forgiven him for the NoDoz concession."

"He was an old guy, all alone, trying to save his island. I wish he hadn't done it that way. I'm worried that he did it for me because he knew I was alone, too."

"Look, I haven't told you all I know. The guy that died, Sonny Thurlow, he was my friend. He was my best friend. I knew him all through high school and after. He took shortcuts sometimes. He was a good guy and didn't deserve to die young, but he took chances sometimes. No one forced him to take them. I never told Arno that. I should have. Maybe other people did. But I forgave him a long time ago. And I forgave Sonny, too."

"I'm sorry you lost your friend."

"I don't blame Arno. I'll help with the tombstone."

"Can I ask you something else, Tom?"

He nodded.

"Were you on drugs, too, when you lost your hands?"

"No, Hannah. It was a rogue wave. They were coming off the port quarter and this one was out of sync, from some other direction. I know you're supposed to be prepared for the unexpected, but I wasn't. I used to think it was premeditated, that no other wave could have made me lose my balance in just that way. But it wasn't directed at me, or even the boat. It was just out there. It wasn't coming for me, or even waiting on me. It was just out there."

She nodded uncertainly. Then said, "I believe the boat will float. *Sweet Hannah*, I mean."

"She's already become like my lungs," Tom said.

Mr. Eaton rolled over, cleared his throat. "Of all the things one must be put through, sleep is not the worst." He said no more.

Tom whispered to her, "He used to tell me that when I was little, when I didn't want to go to bed."

🐟🐟🐟

By the following weekend, *Sweet Hannah* rested on her mooring in the quarry. The old cedar planks had swollen, and the Slick Seam had burst through the red bottom paint in long pale bulbous stripes.

At breakfast, Sunday morning, Tom said, "We'll haul her out one last time and cut off the excess putty and paint her bottom again. I can't suffer that candy-stripe look."

Will, raking blueberries off his pancakes, told her, "The bilge pump only comes on every three or four hours now, Hannah. We're going to set out some traps later this week, after school."

"You've got finals next week, Will."

"I know, I'll be ready. I've already been accepted to college. I could flunk every course I've got now."

"Not funny," Hannah said.

"Are you going to eat your bacon, Emily?" Will asked.

She shook her head. "It's part of a pig," she explained.

Will swept it off her plate.

"That bacon's not burnt," Mr. Eaton protested.

"It's OK, Dad," Tom said.

"Look, these blueberries look just like you, Emily," Will said.

"Hey, Will," Tom said, "you want to eat those pancakes and the plate they're on in one bite?"

"Down boys," Hannah ordered. "You're on the verge of success here, don't spoil it."

"I was just joking," Will said.

"Leave him alone," Emily said. "I'm never going to eat again."

"I'll do the dishes," Mr. Eaton said.

"Sit down, Grandpa, I'll do them," Zee said.

"You can't tell me to sit down, little girl."

"You don't get all the syrup off the plates."

"Let your grandpa help," Tom told her.

Zee dropped the stack of plates into the enameled sink from a foot above it. Everyone at the table stood up except Emily. Zee turned slowly, the finger of one hand to her lips. "There's a pod of whales in the front yard," she whispered.

Everyone rushed the window. Four whales, six, eight, they couldn't tell. The tide was high and they surfaced just beyond the boat shed, moving along the shore.

"Minkes," Mr. Eaton said. "It's that time of year. Don't usually see that many at once. Herring must be schooling through here."

"There's a little one," Zee screeched.

"If you call ten feet little," Tom said.

The whales blew faint jets of spray as they cruised by. The dorsal fin seemed to come along ages after the snout surfaced. Their bodies were dark gray, black, blue black, the color of storm clouds.

"They sure are slow," Will said. Everyone leaned their foreheads against the glass and pivoted their heads as the pod turned the corner, rounded the island.

"I've seen 'em do twelve knots," Tom said. "Keep right up with the boat."

"They come to your boat?" Hannah asked.

"They'll surface on one side of you, then dive under the boat and surface on the other side. It's like one eye doesn't believe the other. Usually it's only one or two of them, though. Don't see them like that much."

"I've never seen them in that close," Hannah said.

"They eat herring?" Will asked.

"They'll eat anything," Mr. Eaton said. "They're gulpers."

"They're like you, Will," Emily said.

"Ha, ha. Can I bring *Sweet Hannah* around, Tom?" Will asked.

"Yeah, but I'll come along."

"Zee and I want a ride, too," Hannah said.

"We're just bringing her around to the railway," Will protested.

"That's OK. Do you want to go, Mr. Eaton?"

"Where?"

"For a ride on the boat," Hannah said.

"Are we going to the retirement home?"

"No, just around the island."

"I don't want to go around anything." He stood at the sink with Zee, drying plates. "There's some whales out there," he said.

Zee looked up. "Here they come again."

Everyone crowded the window once again. Except Hannah, who burst through the front door and raced the dog down to the shore. She could hear the whales' exhalations now, hear the water roll off their long, sleek backs. Small fish were breaking the water before them. Driftwood looked to sea and began not to bark but howl. The whales were swimming faster on this pass. They surfaced less, but their blows were more powerful. They were quickly out of sight, rounding the island as before. Hannah turned around, a grin locked into her jaw. Everyone stood just behind her. Grass was still springing up beyond them.

She clasped her hands and said, "That was so cool. I'm waiting to see if they come again."

"How'd you like to be a herring and have one of those after you? That's what it was like when I was a kid," Will said.

They all turned to him, and Zee slowly stepped behind him, put her arms around his body and hugged him.

"You'll be eighteen in a couple weeks, Will," Hannah said. "Then Zee will be eighteen a few weeks later. None of us will be kids anymore."

"Until this one arrives," Emily said.

"Jesus," Hannah huffed, "then we start all over again." She smiled.

They waited, but the whales didn't appear for a third circuit.

"OK," Tom said, "let's go for a boat ride. C'mon, Dad. You haven't been on a lobster boat in years."

Everyone but Emily walked in single file behind Tom up the hill toward the quarry rim. From there, looking into the channel between Saddleback and Millet, they could see the whales again. They followed the herring almost to the sloping granite shores of the islands before breaking off.

"They've got those fish trapped among these islands," Mr. Eaton said. Then he looked down into the quarry at *Sweet Hannah* and said, "We caught one."

"Christ," Tom said. "I looked at it and I thought it was the shadow of the boat."

Hannah sucked in an audible draft of air. There, hovering beside *Sweet Hannah*, four feet underwater, was a whale. His flukes pulsed and he circled the boat slowly, then paused alongside it again.

"He doesn't know how to get out," Zee whispered.

"He followed the herring right in," Tom explained. "Look, he's going around the boat counterclockwise. He'll never see the exit that way."

"I'd say he's twenty feet, Tom."

"Yeah, Dad."

They descended into the quarry by different routes. Zee and Will clambered down ladders, while Tom, Mr. Eaton, and Driftwood went the long way around. Hannah started down but turned and raced back to the house to tell her sister. Emily was sitting at the kitchen table when Hannah opened the door. She was on the cell phone. She put her hand over the mouthpiece.

"What?" Emily asked.

"Is it for me?" Hannah asked.

"No."

Who would call for her? Who was she calling? "There's a whale in the quarry. Come see."

"I'll be there in a minute or two."

"He might not be there then."

"OK, I'll hurry. It's a private call."

"You're not calling Texas?"

"No, of course not. Am I allowed to use the phone?"

"We'll all be at the quarry." She shut the door. Her short conversation with Emily had winded her more than the sight of the whale or the run down the hill. It was ridiculous to want to control every moment of her sister's life, but why was she now keeping secrets? She walked for a few steps, then broke back into a run.

Everyone stood on a ledge just above the water. The line of the whale's mouth turned up then down, giving Hannah the impression he was smiling and sad at the same time. His large eye was plainly visible. Long folds or pleats ran along his light gray throat and chest. There was a diagonal white band on the upper surface of each flipper. His head was flat and triangular, a wedge of pie.

"He's just sitting there," Will said.

"He doesn't know what to do," Tom said.

"Do you think the other whales miss him yet?" Zee asked her father.

"Maybe not yet. They're all feeding."

"He's looking at us," Mr. Eaton said.

The massive flukes pulsed again, roiling the surface of the water, and the whale rounded *Sweet Hannah* once again. All the water in the quarry swirled around behind him.

"He came in at high tide. We've got the ebb now. If he doesn't get out soon," Tom said, "he won't get out. How deep is the water here, Hannah?"

"It's forty or fifty feet deep in most places, even at low tide, but the mouth drops down to just a foot or so when the tide's out."

"Maybe I could chase him out with the skiff," Will suggested.

"You are not getting in that little boat," Hannah said.

"No, Will, he could swat that boat out of the water. And we don't want to panic him. He could stave in *Sweet Hannah* without even noticing," Tom said.

"You got yourself one fine whale weir here," Mr. Eaton said. "I've never had whale meat, but the Japanese prize it."

The whale made three quick orbits of *Sweet Hannah,* and water sloshed over the ledge wetting their feet. The skiff, moored along the ledge, bounced off its fenders. *Sweet Hannah* rose and fell on her mooring.

"Maybe we should call somebody?" Hannah asked.

"Most of the lobstermen have been to meetings where we learned about entanglement. These guys get caught up in warp every once in a while. But no one that I know has been trained in getting a whale out of your pool. I'll call the harbormaster. He should have the Center for Coastal Studies' number. They've got a disentanglement network."

Tom climbed out of the quarry and the rest moved up one level. It suddenly seemed quite plausible that if the whale built up enough speed he could skid up onto the lower ledges. They sat down, their legs dangling over a cut in the granite.

"He's so huge," Will said. "Look, there's a school of herring in there with him. They're swimming right in front of him. They're nuts."

"I don't think he's interested in food anymore," Hannah said.

The whale seemed to be testing his perimeter, swimming closer and closer to the sheer walls of stone. They could see the stark white of his distended belly as he swung around, the ridge line down the center of his flat skull. For the first time, he rose to the surface, his snout rising a foot or two into the air, the blowhole already spewing before it reached the air.

"He must have scraped his belly coming in, hunh, Hannah?" Will said. "The entrance is only eight or nine feet deep at high, and it's rough down there, all those shards of granite on the bottom. How thick would you say he is, Mr. Eaton?"

"Five, six feet, son."

Tom was back with Emily in minutes. He had the cell phone in one hook, Hannah's camera in the other. He dropped the camera in her lap. "Thought you might want a picture. I've called the C.C.S. They're kicking things into gear. We're not supposed to take any action, just to stand by. Al's coming out, though, Hannah. I thought it'd be all right."

"Sure," she said.

Within six hours there were twenty onlookers standing on different levels of the quarry. The harbormaster and several lobstermen were acting as a ferry service. A response team from the Center for Coastal Studies, a cetacean research organization, was on its way. In the meantime, representatives from the Stonington and Ellsworth papers were taking photographs and conducting interviews. The Coast Guard had dispatched an inflatable to keep boat traffic away from the mouth of the quarry. The same officer who'd questioned Hannah the summer before stood with an agent of the National Marine Fisheries Service. Members of the Island Institute, out of Rockland, were documenting the rescue effort. And finally, standing at the rim of the quarry, were a half-dozen of Zee and Will's friends, cooking hamburgers and passing out sodas. Occasionally the whale would make a slow circuit of the quarry, or surface for air, and everyone would stop talking and watch. At low tide there was little that could be done. The whale would have to be carried over the bar, and with each passing hour he seemed, to Hannah, larger and larger. The next high tide would be at 11:00 p.m.

At dusk the Coast Guard officer re-introduced himself. His southern accent had faded somewhat, just as Will's had.

"How are you, ma'am?"

"Well," Hannah said. She shook his hand.

"I was speaking with your nephew and he said the whale followed a school of herring in."

"That's right," she said, affirming Will's story and the nephew lie at the same time.

"When I first got the call I was at a loss. Our charts don't show the quarry as being open to the sea. How long has it been this way?"

"For as long as I can remember. I've lived here for seven years. My great-uncle lived here before that."

"Well, it's quite a little harbor, a hurricane hole if I ever saw one."

"It can be raging outside and the quarry won't have a ripple on it," she said.

"I was about to say it's a natural weir, but I guess somebody designed it that way. Do you get a lot of fish trapped?"

"They come in, but eventually find their way out. I'm hoping this guy will, too."

"Well, he doesn't seem hurt, just desperate, just tired now."

"Yes."

"Did you ever have any more problems with trespassers, the ones digging holes on your island?"

"No, not over the winter. I think back now and it seems like they came for the most part on weekends. I've had more friends on the island on weekends this spring. Maybe that's kept whoever it was away."

"It sure would be interesting to find out what they were looking for."

Hannah nodded. She'd forgotten she'd told him about the digger. And she realized she hadn't thought about the blue tender in months.

The response team arrived just after nightfall, and after determining that the whale seemed to be under no physical duress, decided to wait till daylight before taking any action. Perhaps the whale would free itself at high tide that night. They asked permission to pitch tents at the quarry rim. Tom, Zee, and Mr. Eaton stayed over Sunday night, after calling the nursing home. Through the night, Hannah walked up the slope and down into the quarry to check on the whale. Its great eye glistened in the moonlight. Phosphorescence streamed along its mouth and flanks as it surfaced. His exhalation sounded like trees whipping in the wind. As she knelt on the granite at three that morning, the whale rolled slowly, revealing his gleaming white belly, and she stopped breathing because she thought he was dying. But it was only a prelude to two quick orbits around the boat. He paused again between *Sweet Hannah* on her mooring and Hannah kneeling and the water around him seemed to shudder. For the first time she put her hand in the water with the whale. He was twenty feet away, but the water felt warmer than usual. The bones in her hand didn't ache. "You could stay here if you want. The herring would come to you. You wouldn't even have to chase them."

"It's against international law to keep a whale as a pet."

Hannah stood up quickly. It was one of the young men with the response team. "Hi," she said. "I didn't know you were there."

"I didn't mean to sneak up on you. It was my turn to check on him."

"He seems calm. He showed me his belly."

"They're just great, these little guys."

"Seems pretty big to me."

"Smallest of the seven rorquals, the great whales." The man's S's whistled; every word that started or ended with an S seemed as if it were escaping through a vent. "They're curious. They'll hang around your boat for hours, like they've got nothing better to do than look at you."

"I've been looking for the other whales all day. I think they've left him."

"These guys are usually loners. They'll come together to feed inshore occasionally, but out on the high seas they're by themselves. They were named for an eighteenth-century Norwegian whaler, a guy who flouted all the laws of his time about taking small whales. The Norwegians and the Japanese still hunt them. And they're supposed to be the Great White Shark's favorite food. So we need to save this one."

"Maybe it would be safer for him to stay here."

"Not enough room. He needs an ocean."

The last word the man spoke sounded less like a lisp and more like a Norwegian accent.

By 10:00 a.m. the next day it seemed the island was being stormed. A half-dozen skiffs were hauled up on the beach, three lobster boats were anchored off the stone pier. Two helicopters hovered high over the quarry, one each from Boston and Portland news stations. At eleven, high tide, three divers and an inflatable would attempt to coerce the whale into changing direction from counterclockwise to clockwise, in hopes that he would then find his way out of the quarry. More than sixty people stood on granite ledges at varying levels, all focused on the water below. Will's wooden skiff was hauled from the water up onto a flat shelf of rock. Tom wanted to take *Sweet Hannah* from the quarry but the response team was worried the sound of the engine and the prop reverberating in the enclosed water might spook the whale and cause him to hurt himself, if not against the rock then on the boat's propeller.

The small black inflatable entered the quarry and immediately the whale's flukes began to pulse. He raced around the quarry pool, his body canted into the turn, a whirlpool forming with *Sweet Hannah* at its center. The inflatable and the two men aboard were slammed up against a high wall and pinned there by the whale's wake. Their boat shipped water but did not capsize. After six or eight minutes, and dozens of circuits, the whale slowed and paused again, on the far side of the quarry from the inflatable, as if he were hiding behind the lobster boat's hull. The men raised the small outboard and rowed around the bigger boat toward the whale's head hoping to turn it. The three divers stood in water up to their knees on an underwater shelf of granite. They began to slap the water with their palms, while the two men in the inflatable dropped the flat of their oars onto the water's surface. The whale hovered, four feet down. His flukes swept. In an instant he shot forward, turned abruptly, and snagged the mooring line below *Sweet Hannah* and plucked it like a guitar string. The boat's stem plunged, green water nearly covering the forward deck, and then she popped back up as the whale came free of the line. The whale sounded to the depths of the quarry and remained there for twenty minutes. The water fell calm. The whale could be seen to a depth of fifteen feet, but held deeper.

"They're scaring him," Zee whispered to Hannah.

Mr. Eaton asked, "Has this ever happened to me before, Tom?"

"No, Dad."

"I seem to remember it somehow."

Will had helped Emily around the rim of the quarry. They'd all come together, weaving through the other spectators, to form their own knot in the human net spread over the quarry.

"He's coming up," Will whispered.

The whale did not breach but rose into view slowly, as if the water were pooling away from their own eyes rather than his. His snout lifted the sheet of the surface tentatively, and the ripple this caused lifted the rubber boat a quarter-inch higher. It was only six feet away. Slowly the long back surfaced a foot at a time, the blowhole gaping, the tall dorsal fin changing the direction of the wind rather than indicating its direction. The two men standing in the inflatable sat down. The whale moved away at an angle, as if it could slide through water as well as swim through it. Finally, it bumped alongside *Sweet Hannah's* hull, the whale almost as long as the boat, and nestled there in the shadow of the sheer.

"More like twenty-five feet, Dad," Tom said.

"I'd say twenty-six," Mr. Eaton said. "That's Arno Weed's boat."

"Yes, it is," Hannah said.

"My uncle built that boat."

"We know, Grandpa," Zee said.

"When that boat was twenty-six years old, Arno went back to my uncle and gave him an extra five hundred dollars. He told him he'd underpaid, didn't know he was buying such a good boat. Lots of my uncle's boats lasted twenty-six years. Arno was the only one who acknowledged that value."

"You never told me that story, Dad."

"I haven't told you half the things I know. Wouldn't have told you now if maybe that wasn't Arno down there in the disguise of a whale, come back to see his boat. He's dead, isn't he?"

"He's dead," Hannah said.

The three divers entered the water. They swam on the surface toward the whale until he sounded, then they replaced their snorkels with regulators, released the air in their buoyancy compensators and sounded, too. The water in the quarry was still again but for the divers' air bubbles bursting on the surface. They seemed to be working down along the walls of the quarry. Then, the streams of bubbles slowly began to converge beneath *Sweet Hannah's* hull.

"They're trying to force him toward the opening," Tom said.

"But he has to come up to go out," Hannah said.

Then they all noticed that the water in the quarry was circulating. Seaweed and flecks of Styrofoam swept around the boat in a counter-clockwise circle. The divers' bubbles seemed to spiral up rather than rise on a rope. The whale pumped to the surface as if born at the base of a tornado. He breached alongside *Sweet Hannah*, the forward third of his body to the flippers clearing the water. The splash reached up three tiers of granite and the people there turned their backs to the cold sheet of water as it fell. The inflatable worked its way around *Sweet Hannah* to the far wall. There they picked up two of the three divers, and turning, left the quarry. The whale hovered beneath the lobster boat. The third diver swam back to the ledge he'd left from. Men helped him from the water. One of the divers had been hurt. The wash of the whale's flukes had thrown him against the granite. He was having a hard time breathing. He'd swallowed a lot of seawater when the wash knocked the regulator from his mouth.

"He's OK," the diver told them. "But he's hurting." He looked up at Hannah. "You've got a load of lobster down there. I've never seen so many in one place. Food must wash in here for them."

The leader of the rescue team, John Woodson, was on a radio to the dive ship for five minutes. "They're taking him to the Island Medical Center. Think he just got the wind knocked out of him. It's more complicated when that happens underwater."

Someone asked, "What now?"

"We'll wait a bit. The whale's reluctant to swim toward shallower water to escape. There's a woman coming down from Canada to help. She'll be here in a few hours. She's with the Whale and Dolphin Conservation Society. They get these guys out of weirs up in the Bay of Fundy with some kind of net procedure."

The diver offered to try again.

"No, no one else in the water. If it's all right with you, Ms. Bryant, at low tide we'll try to clear some of that granite debris from the quarry entrance. We may be able to gain a foot or two of depth."

Another man asked if that shouldn't be cleared with the DEP or the Corps of Engineers.

"Holy shit, if anybody thinks they can get that paperwork through in the next four hours, go to it," John said.

Half a dozen area lobstermen started clapping.

"Ms. Bryant, do you mind if the entrance to your little harbor here is cleared of debris?"

"No, sir," Hannah said, smiling, "as long as I get to help."

"We'll need every pair of rubber boots and every strong back we can find."

At last, there was something she could do to help the whale.

"Did you hear what the diver said about the lobster, Hannah?" Will asked. "We can drop our first traps right here in the quarry."

"It's not enough in a day to catch a whale, Will?"

"I never wanted to catch a mammal. They breathe like us. It's bottom dwellers, water-breathers, that I want."

"Maybe you can get six of these guys to help carry the skiff out of the quarry. Then you can go to town and catch some hot dogs and potato chips, enough to feed all these people."

"Aw, Hannah, I'll miss something."

"No, you won't. This whale doesn't want to leave. You'll be back long before we start cleaning the mouth of the quarry."

As Will rounded up volunteers to lift the skiff from ledge to ledge, Hannah approached the diver, who sat among his equipment on the wet granite. Water still dripped from his hair and beard.

"Can I help you with anything?" she asked.

"No, I'm just trying to calm down."

"Was the whale frightening?"

"No, I dive with whales whenever I get the chance." He purged his regulator. A thin spray of water shot into the air. "But it was a little murky down there, a little like cave diving. When I reached the bottom I got a little disoriented because the bottom moved. It's a lobster pound down there. They're crawling over one another like they're in a restaurant fish tank. And they're crawling over a field of broken beer bottles." He looked at her as if for explanation.

"My great-uncle liked beer," she said.

"I figured somebody must. The lobsters have burrowed under them for homes. Lady, I don't know who has fishing rights in your quarry, but I'd say they've got an easy season ahead of them. Never seen so many lobsters in my life."

The time between high tide and low, six hours, never passed so quickly. The Whale and Dolphin Conservation representative arrived by seaplane. The pontoons of the radial-engined Beaver touched down in the calm water between Millet and Spruce, and taxied to Ten Acre No Nine, blasting the water it passed through, leaving a long tail of mist behind its rudder. The planed nosed up on the smooth granite beach and an elderly woman jumped out of the passenger seat, pulling a bright yellow flotation bag the size of a water heater from a rear compartment. Two men that guided the plane in helped turn it around, and it began its takeoff run from the beach itself, leaving the water without any reluctance, shaking off the water with a roar of release. The bespectacled pilot in the cockpit had spent less time on the island than anyone who'd ever bothered to arrive.

Hannah walked down with Mr. Woodson to meet the woman with the yellow bag. It took all three of them to drag the bag out of the water and up the rock.

"Bring a change of clothes, did you?" John asked the old woman.

"Get out of my way, John Woodson. Their mistake was sending a man to do a woman's job."

"What have you got there, Shirley?"

"My whale net." She stuck out a hand that Hannah thought she must have picked up beachcombing. Hannah shook it. "Shirley Langlais," she said.

"Hannah Bryant."

"This is Hannah's place," John Woodson said.

"I could see the whale as we flew over. Got a couple good pictures. I'll send them to you when I get them developed, Hannah."

"Thank you."

"How deep is that entrance to the weir?"

"About nine feet at high tide," Hannah answered. "But we're going to try to make it a foot or two deeper. There's some loose granite we're going to move out of the way."

"That'll help." Shirley Langlais stood on the beach with one fist in her pocket and one in her eye. Her eyes were pale green blown glass. Her hair was bleached blond, except the fresh half-inch of white at the roots. The skin of her face and neck was bleached too, driftwood high above the tide line. She wore green thigh-high rubber boots that seemed to be swallowing her in alternate gulps as she walked. "Is the whale injured?" she asked.

"We don't think so," Woodson said.

"How often does he surface?"

"Every five minutes or so."

"He's tired."

"Yeah."

"How long till high tide?"

"Eight hours. Do you want to do this at night? It'll be midnight."

"We've freed two from weirs at night in Nova Scotia. We had to work from boats. This looks like it might be easier. Can you walk all the way around that pool?"

"Yes," Hannah answered, "but at different levels."

"This whale is stuck on counterclockwise, Shirley," Woodson said.

"He may be diseased or injured if he'll only turn one way. We'll nudge him over to the entrance."

"What exactly will you do?" Hannah asked.

"We'll tie one end of this net at the mouth of your quarry, and then drop it around the inner walls. We'll run it through a ring on the far side of the opening and have a boat outside the quarry pull the net and the whale out to sea. The net has a large weave. You won't lose any of the herring in your weir."

"It's not a weir."

"You didn't design that opening?"

"No, and the only thing I collect from it is driftwood."

"Hunh," Shirley said, as if she'd never heard such a bad lie before.

"What are the dangers here, Shirley?" Woodson asked.

"It's possible the whale could become entangled in the net and drown. Some of our fishermen have had their weirs damaged, but I don't think that's likely in this case. Have you named him yet?"

"What?" Hannah asked.

"Have you given the whale a name yet?"

"No, that's not my habit, Shirley," Woodson said.

"I don't work with a whale I can't call by name," she said.

"I have an idea," Hannah offered.

"I've named eighty-seven whales," Shirley said. "I guess it's your turn."

"How about 'Shrug'? I have a friend who says a wave with no discernible source is caused by a whale shrugging in the deep lonesome."

"A name doesn't have to lug a story around with it," Shirley said, "but we'll use it." She set off up the hill alone, leaving Hannah with Woodson.

"She's quirky," Woodson said, "but she's rich and she loves whales and she knows them."

By 3:30 they were able to wade into the entrance and begin casting rocks into deeper water. Those rocks with starfish and urchins and mussels clinging to them were carried and set down in water of the same depth. Another crew set about hanging the big net around the inner walls of the quarry. *Sweet Hannah* was an obstacle. They'd have to get the whale on the far side of it and drop the net into the water from the boat's decks to avoid hanging the net on the mooring line. The granite debris in the entrance wasn't cut, but shattered. Arno must have used a ton of dynamite, Hannah thought. It was hard to believe a thunderstorm would have provided adequate cover for the blast. Zee worked alongside Hannah, rolling chunks of rock to the side of the channel that were too large to lift. There were fifteen or twenty volunteers working with them. Although the water was only a couple feet deep, everyone was wet to their caps. For more than two hours the deep ca-thunks of heavy stone dropping into deep water echoed off the quarry walls. When the cold became too much, they crawled out of the water and sat in the sun. Someone built a driftwood fire on an upper ledge, and people stood in their wet T-shirts before it, holding wet overshirts in the smoke to dry. Hannah looked up from her work, both hands holding shards of stone, and thought she saw Arno sitting on the quarry rim, watching over all the activity, but eventually the salt water dripped off her eyelashes and she saw it was Mr. Eaton, wearing Arno's old corduroy overshirt and one of the co-op's caps. She threw her rocks high up onto the near beach, trying to rebuild the island. As the entrance channel deepened, she realized she wouldn't be able to cut across here, take this shortcut around the island anymore without swimming. When they finally got down to solid rock, they'd lowered the channel by another twenty-seven inches. *Sweet Hannah* could enter or exit even at dead low now. The mounds of scree at each side of the entrance marked the quarry like pillars at the entrance of an estate. It seemed a fit portal for a whale.

Shirley stood on the bank and helped everyone from the water. She pulled Hannah up with both hands. "A stranded whale always makes for a party," she said. "That's why I always come."

"Are we ready?" Hannah asked.

"We're just waiting on the tide now. Dry off and get yourself a hot dog. I've been talking to Shrug. He likes small cod more than herring."

"He told you that?"

"No, I know that. I was talking to him. He wasn't talking to me. He's a whale."

"Oh," Hannah said.

"One of the response team said you were down here all hours of the night talking to the whale," Shirley said.

"Yeah, I was, I guess."

"I talk to them, too. Didn't want you to feel stupid, like you were the only one. He didn't talk back to you, did he?"

"No."

"That's good. I'd hate it if one of them talked to you while the rest of them gave me the silent treatment. You know, you can't count on him living."

"I can't?"

"No, I'm sorry. I didn't want you to count on it. Sometimes they're intent on leaving, whatever their reasons. Right now we all feel pretty powerful because we're deep in the endeavor. If we fail, it may not be your fault."

"OK."

"I find that the owners of property where whales beach themselves get depressed afterwards, rather than feeling chosen. I tell them a grave-yard is a sacred place. I've told you that now."

"OK," Hannah said. "Why do you name them?"

"Every leaf and stone deserves a name, so we can call it when it's gone from us. John Woodson's a good whale man, but he doesn't name whales because he doesn't believe in losing them. When he does lose one, he's bereft. He doesn't even have the name to put in his pocket then. I've been doing this for twenty-eight years. I've got a pocketful of names that I take out and call from time to time. Makes me feel better. I see the boat is named for you."

"Yes," Hannah said.

"Somebody loves you."

Water was still dripping from the brim of Hannah's cap when Will handed her a paper plate with a hot dog and chips on it.

"Thanks, Will."

He turned and pointed to the rim of the quarry. A man in a dark suit, carrying a briefcase, stood there, silhouetted against the blue sky. "I brought that guy out with me," Will said. "He delivered your paintings and sculptures while I was in town."

"Oh, Jesus," Hannah said. "I forgot all about it." She put the plate back in Will's hands. "And don't I look fine." She squeezed water out of her ponytail.

"Looks like a government man," Shirley said. "We could feed him to Shrug."

"He's my patron, a banker," Hannah explained. "I've never met him before." She pushed the hem of her T-shirt into her belt. "How do I look, Will?"

"Like you're about to feed," he said.

She looked down at her wet shirt. Her nipples were erect, plainly visible through the wet cotton.

"Here, take mine," Shirley said. She pulled off a chambray shirt and held it open for Hannah.

"Thanks, Shirley. Do you take donations?"

"I'll leave the Society's card with you before I go."

Hannah emptied the water from her boots then climbed the ladders out of the quarry. She held out her hand. "Mr. Whatley, it's so good to finally see you." He was younger than she thought he'd be. Perhaps her own age.

"Hannah Bryant?"

"Yes, a wet Hannah Bryant. I'm so sorry I wasn't in town to meet you. I was so wrapped up in the whale, I completely forgot. I'm sorry."

"I couldn't believe it when the boy told me. I hope it's all right that I've come out."

"Of course."

"It's my first time on the ocean. I got a little wet myself." He looked down at his black leather shoes. Pools of water surrounded them.

"Let's go down to the house. I can change and I'll loan you a pair of socks."

"Is there really a whale?"

"Yes. I'm sorry. He's on the other side of the lobster boat. Come around the quarry."

He followed her, ducking through undergrowth, using his briefcase as a shield. Hannah held back limbs so they wouldn't tear at his wool suit. His tie dangled away from his body, caught on brush. He had to stop and pull it free. When this happened again, he muttered, "Silly things."

"There," she said, "you can see him now."

The whale's right flipper almost touched *Sweet Hannah*'s hull. He seemed to rest no more than a couple feet underwater.

"Oh, my God," Michael Whatley murmured.

"Yeah," Hannah said.

"He won't leave?"

"He's afraid," Hannah said. "They're going to try to help him out late tonight with a net."

"With a net?"

"I know, it seems ironic doesn't it? Using a net to help him escape."

"I wish I could stay and watch," he said.

"You're welcome to. We could put you up on the couch. I'd let you have the spare bedroom but my sister's there. She's pregnant."

"Oh, I can't stay. I have to start back this evening. I've got meetings tomorrow afternoon. If we could sit down somewhere? I'll try not to take too much of your time."

She led him back down to the house. Tom and Emily were there. When she came back downstairs, after changing into dry jeans and a shirt, she found Zee, Will, and Mr. Eaton there, too.

"All of a sudden I'm more interesting than the whale?" Hannah asked.

"We were here first," Emily said, and nodded at Tom.

"Do you want us to leave, Hannah?" Tom asked.

Michael Whatley stood in the center of the room, barefoot, his briefcase hanging against his knees.

"You don't have to leave. Don't be silly."

"Actually, I do need to speak to you alone," Whatley said.

Hannah thought he should have said, "I'd like to speak to you alone," but simply nodded. Then she said, "OK, is that OK, guys?"

Tom got up from the kitchen table. "No problem. C'mon, let's go feed the whale that's in the belly of the quarry." They trooped out. Driftwood was the last out the door.

"Now," Hannah said, "can I get you something to drink? We've got tea and soda, or I could make some coffee."

"No, thanks. I could use those socks."

"Oh, geez, sure." She retrieved a pair of Will's gym socks. "There you go. They won't match your suit, but they'll hide your toes."

"Thank you." He immediately sat down and pulled the socks on, seemed to visibly inflate when his feet were covered.

"I don't know where to begin, Mr. Whatley. I was staggered when I went into your bank and saw all my work there. I was stunned to see so much of it in one place, and honored, too. Did you recognize the island as you were coming up on it?"

"How could I?" he asked.

"The painting over your reception area."

"Oh, yes, I see what you mean. No, I was more concerned about all the water around me. I've never been to sea on a small boat."

"Really? So much of my art is about the sea and this island."

He nodded uncertainly. She thought he was embarrassed by his fear of water, his wet feet. She took another tack. "You seem so young to be in such a position of responsibility. Is the bank your family's business?"

"Brighton Bank? No, I've only been there for a little over two years. I moved up from the City."

"I don't understand. Who's been purchasing my art?"

"I have, at least for the past two years. Before me it was Margaret Storrel, the woman you met at the bank."

"Really?"

"Yes, she held my position for six or seven years before she moved up. But I shouldn't say that I've been buying your work, of course." He opened his briefcase. "By the way, the landlord opened your gallery for us and everything's safely unloaded there. I need you to sign this item-ized receipt."

"Mr. Whatley, I don't yet understand. Who exactly owns my work?"

"That's why I'm here. You do."

"I do?"

"Yes, I'm sorry this procedure has seemed secretive. We, the bank, were charged with a trust, whose terms were laid out quite some time ago. Using accruing interest and dividends from a portfolio, we purchased and cared for your work for the past thirteen years."

"What trust? My father?"

He laid out a sheaf of legal documents on the kitchen table before her. "These funds, approximately $450,000, were put aside by Mr. Arno Weed, your great-uncle, I believe. Twice a year the proceeds from the investment were used to purchase your artwork from the Waashen Gallery in New York. Much of it was put into archival storage, and much, as you saw, we decorated headquarters and branch banks with. I'm afraid we couldn't get it all in the truck. I'll send the remainder next week. The work is yours without lien or hindrance."

Hannah covered her open mouth with both hands.

"I know this may come as a surprise. We didn't know how much you would already know. I'm sorry, also, to say the term of the trust is at an end. Mr. Weed directed us to stop all payments, and to direct the remaining funds to another party. It's important that you understand the bank will not purchase your artwork in the future. I'm sorry I can't be more forthcoming."

"I'm sorry," Hannah whispered, "I thought you were my patron."

"No," he said. "The bank was only an intermediary. Mr. Weed bought the work in your name."

He continued to speak, to ask if she had questions, but the waves seemed to drown out all other noise. She remembered telling Arno once that she wished she didn't have to sell her work to be an artist, wished she could keep everything. She even recalled telling him that the act of selling her art bordered on humiliation, like hawking her soul on a sidewalk. She was reminded of a woman she'd seen on an airplane who walked away from her seat laughing, and was brought up short by her attached earphones, which wanted the laugh back. So her career was not a career, her payment not even a stipend or a grant, but an inheritance, an inheritance most likely made up of drug money. Her years of work had been merely delirium, a drug-induced delusion. She had been no more successful than the friends who'd abandoned their careers after college, the friends who'd abandoned her because of her unusual success. How had she acted? She'd acted as if she'd deserved it all, that her own talent and hard work had made success possible, even probable. She thumbed through the paperwork, read but didn't ascribe meaning, until she saw Arno's postcard. It was addressed to her in his hand.

Dear Hannah,

Just wanted to give you a running start. I knew you wouldn't quit and I wanted to pay you for it. Go outside now, go to the island, and smell the foreshore for me. I miss it.

Arno Weed

Part Two

O f the hundred or so people on her island, she knew she was the only one who had no other place to go, knew she was the only one whose life was a complete and irradicable lie. It seemed now that they'd known this all along, allowed her to stand in the middle of her lie like a child in a street puddle. Everything in the room was tool and material to this lie, every seashell and sable brush, the accumulation of driftwood, stone lung, sketched bird. She felt if she held one of her self-portraits up to a mirror there would be no reflected image.

Mr. Whatley had left the house at some point. She was alone. She saw that there was salt on the table but could not feel it when she swept it onto the floor. What she thought was the sound of the sea was no sound, silence. She cupped her palms over her ears, but this made no difference. The world smelled like wet wood, or like wet without wood. She moved her tongue around her mouth and everything tasted the same. She closed her eyes and light was then absent, too, and all she felt was Arno missing not the foreshore nor the ocean itself but missing her, an all-encompassing lover's revenge.

She lifted her head from the table when Will came in. "I took him back to Stonington, Hannah. He said I should check on you."

"Who?" she asked.

"That banker guy. Are you OK?"

"Yeah."

"There's a reporter here from Ellsworth. He wants to talk to you."

"About what?"

"The whale."

"Oh."

"Should I let him in?"

"No, I'll come out. Tell him I'll come out."

He closed the door. Her clothes were dry. When did that happen? She slipped out the door without letting the reporter see past her into the house, where she'd been trying to make art. Will was striding away toward the quarry.

The reporter wore a solid black tie over a plaid, short-sleeved shirt. The shirt was working out of his pants, like a pack of dogs backing out from underneath a low fence. His face was awestruck. "I've just seen the whale," he said, smiling. "It's like a religious experience, wouldn't you say?"

"Yes," she said.

He wrote this down.

"Would you agree that the whale came to be trapped by accident?"

She nodded. He wrote this down, too.

"I was told this was Ten Acre No Nine Island?"

"Yes," Hannah said.

"And just to confirm, your name is Hannah Weed?"

"Yes," she said without hesitating.

🐚 🐚 🐚

Just after dark, the net was lowered around the whale. The moon tripped down the granite ledges and shattered on the water's surface.

There were dozens of small boats pulled up on the beach beside the boat shed, their painters crawling up above the high-tide mark, sucking the marrow from the island. The quarry was a crowded coliseum. Row upon row of spectators rose above the water stage, *Sweet Hannah*, and the whale. Children sat with their legs dangling over the granite; their parents stood above them with crossed arms. The only unnatural light came from the bright orange eyes of cigarettes, which seemed to peer from the stone in odd numbers, never simply a pair. Hannah stood with Tom on *Sweet Hannah*. The net crossed from the far side of the quarry to the lobster boat and circled back to the entrance. When Shirley called their names, they dropped their section of the buoyed net into the water. They gave the weighted bottom of the net two minutes to sink. Then another boat, beyond the quarry entrance, began to motor slowly to sea towing one end of the net. The whale was at some depth. The net seemed to catch once, then again. Hannah heard Shirley's firm voice, calling the towboat over a radio. She asked for a pause. The buoys strung along the top of the net glistened in the moonlight, a foot below the surface. The whale was now in the net.

"Proceed," Shirley said, "slowly." She repeated, "Proceed."

The pilot affirmed. The radio echoed in the quarry. "I am proceeding. The boat is not moving."

"More power," Shirley said. "He's in the net."

The net began to sing where it passed through a large stainless-steel ring embedded in a crevice at the quarry entrance. Then the net went slack and the buoys surfaced.

"Slowly," Shirley cautioned.

The net buoys plunged beneath the water again and *Sweet Hannah's* bow suddenly dipped. Hannah felt Tom's steel hook slip through the belt loop in her jeans.

"Hold on," he said.

The whale rose below the boat and *Sweet Hannah* rolled to starboard. Hannah lost her footing. The deck canted to forty-five degrees and the only thing that kept her from slamming into the coaming or rolling over it into the water was the hook in her pants. She hung from it like a loose sack of flour. She looked up and saw that Tom's prosthetic harness had broken, that his other hook was hung on the stanchion supporting the cabin. He hung by its straps with her. The boat finally slid off the whale's back and they scrambled to their feet. The whale's flippers seemed to be hung in the net. His powerful flukes beat at the water and *Sweet Hannah's* hull.

"He's caught on the mooring line or the prop," Tom yelled out. "Let go the net!"

When the towboat backed off, the whale drifted away from *Sweet Hannah's* hull, but remained below the surface.

"Can you see him?" Shirley called out.

"No," Hannah said.

Tom freed his hook from the stanchion, but the broken strap wouldn't allow him to wear it.

"Help me pull up the engine hatch, Hannah," he ordered.

She shone a flashlight into the bilge. Water was accumulating quickly there.

"We're holed," he said. "She's sprung a plank." Almost immediately the bilge pump kicked on and a stream of water bit into the dark ocean, leaving a phosphorescent wound.

"We're taking on water, Shirley," Hannah called out.

Tom screamed, "We've got to get this boat out of the quarry or she'll sink on top of the whale. We can't leave with that net in the way." Hannah was startled by the rage in his voice.

"We're not going to get the whale out of here without the net," Shirley screamed back.

"The whale was caught in the net, Shirley," Hannah yelled. "We think it hung on the mooring chain or the boat's prop. Maybe if we get the boat out of here we can sink the mooring and try again."

"It's about high tide," Shirley said. "We don't have time to haul the net and re-deploy it."

"Tell her we'll do it again in twelve hours," Tom said. He was breathing heavily.

"I want to do what's best for the whale," she said softly.

"Do you want the boat to sink?"

"Of course not, but I don't want the whale to die either," she whispered. He didn't respond. So she turned away and yelled, "What do you want to do, Shirley?"

"Let's try once more before we wait twelve more hours. He's been here too long already, Hannah."

"OK, go ahead."

"Do you want to come ashore?"

"No, we'll stay aboard," Tom said. "Maybe we can find the leak."

They heard Shirley give the OK to the pilot. The net buoys sounded, but the water remained calm. The engine of the towboat deepened as it took up the weight of the net.

"He's in that net," Tom said. "You can hear it in the engines. He's not swimming before it."

As the tightening net approached the mouth of the quarry and the shallower water, the whale surfaced. Its head lifted slowly and lay over the buoys, lolling back toward the inner pool.

"He's worn out," Shirley said. "Slow ahead."

But he would not turn. The net clung to his body from snout to fluke. He was broached to the open sea, broadside to the entrance. Each time they let slack into the net he turned toward the quarry. There was not enough width at the entrance to drag him through sideways. They worked for a half hour, an hour. Finally, Shirley relented.

"He's not leaving," she said. "He doesn't want to go. Release the net and haul it."

Tom had found the leak and stuffed rags around it, but water was already a foot deep in the bilge. Hannah went forward and dropped the mooring pennant off the cleat, and Tom started the engine. She rushed back to the cockpit. "Don't hit him," she said.

"He's been around boats before," Tom said.

The whale surfaced alongside. His blow sounded like a steam line bursting. The moon's light, shattered on the small waves in the quarry, suddenly accumulated on the glistening flank of the whale. The diesel engine filled the quarry with a resonant, deep hum.

"Slow ahead," Tom said, as he slipped the gearshift into forward. He turned the wheel hard over and then straightened out as he headed for the entrance. The whale dropped off astern. Hannah looked back, then put the flat of her hand on Tom's lower back, as if to urge him forward.

"What?" he asked.

"He's following us," she whispered.

Tom looked over his shoulder. The whale rode along the surface, water swirling over his back. He was fifteen feet off *Sweet Hannah*'s transom. As they approached the opening, Shirley backed away from the water's edge. Tom bumped the throttle up a bit.

"It's this big engine," he said. "Turns over so slow it sounds like a heartbeat."

They entered the channel and the whale did not balk, but followed them at the pace the boat set, in a long arc to the open sea, where he sounded, and was last seen off No Man's Island, heading slowly southeast toward deep water.

As they rounded the island in their sinking boat, bound for the railway and the boat shed, they heard cheering break from the quarry, echoing applause, sound erupting like a fountain from solid rock. Tom turned on the radar. The last they saw of the whale was a green pip on the screen as he surfaced.

"Hannah?" Tom said. "Don't worry. We'll make it."

She wiped her jaw, then wiped the spot again because the tear left an itch. She wiped with her forearm rather than her hand. "I'm not worried about sinking," she said.

"Oh," Tom said. He guided the boat through the dark, island-bound channel with his stump and hook. It was midnight, the boat sluggish in the sea. He cleared his throat and began to say something, then stopped, then allowed, "Was a good whale, wasn't he?"

Hannah cried, and cried, and cried, for everything that comes and goes.

❧ ❧ ❧

By morning the island was almost deserted again. The quarry seemed as empty as an overturned hand. Everyone who'd come to Stonington by car had been ferried ashore. Those who'd arrived by boat had gotten underway. Emily, Will and the Eatons had finally gone to sleep. Hannah stood on the granite beach with Shirley Langlais, waiting for her seaplane. Neither had slept. It had taken almost two hours to get *Sweet Hannah* in the boat shed the night before. Then there'd been the gathering of equipment, the pushing off of skiffs, the green glow of instruments reflecting off men's faces as they started their boats. It was daylight by 4:30, and Shirley waited impatiently, kicking stones off the swelling granite into the water.

"That's enough of that, Shirley," Hannah said. "I've only got so much island left. If we don't start kicking dirt uphill we're all going to be underwater."

"Oh, yes, I get your meaning: global warming, wave erosion. You're the old man who sleeps in his bathtub tied in the attic in 'The Miller's Tale,' convinced the flood is coming. Maybe you worry about too much for such a short life span. The miller became a cuckold while he worried about the flood."

"You save one whale at a time, and I'll save one island at a time."

"Got any children, Hannah?"

"No. You?"

"No, but I've got lots of money."

"Which is better?"

"Don't know. Told you I don't have any children. I know having money is good. You've got a nice place here. None of those sleeping people are yours?"

"Emily, the pregnant girl, is my half sister."

"You ever think about selling this place, you let me know. I'd let you visit anytime."

Hannah pointed up to the field. "Those are my people up there."

"But you could be an artist anywhere."

"I don't even know that I'm an artist here. The island is all I have."

"You'd have lots of money. Lots. I think I could hangar my airplane in the quarry. Make this an outpost of the Whale and Dolphin Conservation Society. You think about it. We'll be friends from now on. People who meet over a troubled whale become friends for life. Here he comes, finally."

"You never make small talk, Shirley," Hannah said. "You never talk about the weather."

"Who's got time for it?"

"OK," Hannah said. "I saw you kiss John Woodson in the wee hours of the night."

"Oh, that. We used to be in love."

"Then you stopped?"

"No, we didn't stop. And that's all I can say about that."

The plane came low from the northeast and landed in front of the island as if Shirley already owned it. The propeller blast flattened the corrugated sea while they pushed the net bag out to the airplane and loaded it in the aft compartment. They shook hands, and Shirley yelled, "Do you want a ride?"

"What?"

"Do you want to see your island from heaven?"

"No," Hannah yelled back. "I don't want to go that far away yet."

Shirley climbed aboard, and Hannah helped turn the pontoon. The roar of the engine was deafening; the blast rolled stones up the beach. When Hannah's hair fell back on her shoulders, she looked down at her rubber boots. They were awash. She felt as rooted to the rock as a barnacle. The plane left the surface of the sea and banked into the rising sun. Hannah watched it as long as she could bear.

Then, before anyone arose, she went inside and cleaned off her work-table, wiped it down with a wet dishcloth, as if removing evidence.

🐌 🐌 🐌

"The American Bald Eagle is a fisherman." Everett Eaton pointed at a speck in the sky over Jericho Bay. It was the first thing he said to her when she found him. He'd been missing for half an hour, since Zee and Tom woke and found him gone from his cot.

"We've been looking for you," Hannah said.

"I'm lost, but I didn't know I was missing, too," he told her. "Who's looking for me?"

"Tom and Zee, me and Will."

"Where am I?"

"You're on Ten Acre No Nine."

"Arno Weed's place?"

"That's right."

He shook his head and laughed. He sat on a smooth stone, with his back against a spruce tree. "I don't know why I thought to come out here."

"Remember the whale in the quarry?"

"Give me a clue."

They could hear Tom calling his father's name then, as he approached along the shoreline.

"Look at him," Everett Eaton said. "He's looking to sea. If I was out there, wouldn't be any use to call for me. Do you know my son?"

"Yes," Hannah answered.

"He has a new little girl. Sweet thing. His wife is used, though. I don't like how she treats him." He put his thumb and forefinger to his lips and turned an imaginary key.

"We're over here, Tom," Hannah called out.

He climbed up the exposed ledge of low tide, breathing hard. "Where the hell have you been, Dad?"

Mr. Eaton looked at Hannah, worried. "He's been on Ten Acre No Nine Island," she said, "and he still is."

"I swear, I'm going to start locking you up, Dad. I've been worried sick. You know you aren't supposed to go off alone. I thought you were drowned."

"I guess I would have gotten a better reception if I were dead," Mr. Eaton said.

"Jesus, Dad, you always turn things inside out."

"Well, I'm not drowned and you're mad. If I was drowned maybe you'd be happy."

"I'm not going to argue with you. Dad, have you been digging holes? Did you get the shovel out of the shed this morning?"

"No."

"What?" Hannah asked.

"There's three holes just above the high-tide line on the far side of the quarry," Tom explained. "They're all around a big spruce, dug to bedrock."

"I didn't do it," Mr. Eaton said.

"How would you know if you did or not, Dad?"

"I don't have any dirt on my hands." He held his palms up.

"Well, it's summer," Hannah said. "It's started again."

"Maybe you dug them," Mr. Eaton said, accusing his son.

"Tom held out his hooks. "I'm not very good with a shovel, Dad."

"The island was swimming with people the last couple of days. It could have been anybody," Hannah said.

"Whoever it was used your shovel," Tom said. "It's still there. C'mon, Dad. We've got to get Zee to school and you back home. I swear I'm gonna put a collar on you or one of those radio beacons they attach to endangered species to keep track of them."

"If I had a phone in my pocket, I'd answer it when it rang," he said. "You could call me."

"Dad, you're exasperating."

"No, he's not," Hannah said. "It's a good idea."

"Then *you* buy him a phone, and pay the bill every month, and maybe he'll remember to wear it, and maybe he'll remember to keep it charged up, and maybe he won't lose it so you need to buy him another one. Your answer to everything is to throw money at it, Hannah. C'mon, Dad." He turned and strode away. Mr. Eaton shrugged and scampered along behind him, leaving her standing alone on the corner of her island, penniless.

🐚 🐚 🐚

Three days after the whale left, Gwen called. Her voice seemed to buckle on every other syllable, as if she were slow-dancing on the hood of a car. She'd received a letter from the Brighton Bank terminating the relationship.

"What happened?" she asked.

Hannah left the house with the phone and sat on the granite stoop. She could feel Emily watching her leave, knew she heard Gwen ask, "What happened?" She didn't know where to begin. The silence lengthened, seemed to warp.

"Hannah?"

"I'm here," she answered.

Finally, she thought to begin with the ending, the conclusion she'd come to, hoping all the intermediate steps could be avoided. "I haven't been making art," she explained. "I'm not what I thought I was."

"I don't understand," Gwen said.

Hannah suddenly realized that Gwen had lost a good deal of her income, too, that she didn't know what art was either.

"My great-uncle," she explained, "the one who left me this island, was a drug dealer. He set up a trust for me with the profits. The trust bought my art, paid your commissions, with the interest and dividends it earned every year. That's why my sales weren't exactly the same every year. I should have realized my income followed the stock-market indexes, but it never occurred to me that my success depended on the Gross National Product. I thought it had to do with what I did here on the island. The trust was set up to last thirteen years."

"I'm sorry," Gwen said. "It's unbelievable."

"You didn't know then?"

"No. Family members often support their artists, but rarely do they want to pay a dealer's commission. I thought it was another dealer, a collector, a corporation."

"Arno knew I wouldn't have accepted his support," Hannah said.

"You didn't like him?"

"I did like him. We had a little falling out the last time I saw him. Then I felt guilty for not coming to see him after college. He knew I wanted to make it on my own. That's why he kept it a secret."

"I thought maybe you wouldn't accept it because it was drug money."

"I didn't know he was a drug dealer till a few months ago. I wouldn't accept it because his money was his money. I thought he needed it. Gwen, how much of my sales didn't go to the bank?"

"I don't know. Maybe 10, 20 percent."

"I won't be sending you anything this fall."

The silence emanated from the other end of the line this time, and Hannah took it as acquiescence. Then Gwen said, "But you'll receive the body of the trust now. You can't turn it down, Hannah. You weren't the drug dealer."

"I don't have that heroic opportunity," she answered. "It's going somewhere else."

"Where?"

"I don't know. The bank wouldn't say. To the town, some foundation, the lobstermen's co-op. I don't know and I really don't care. I'm glad it's not my responsibility."

"What about the art? Who owns it?"

"Well, I do. Most of it's already here. There's so much, Gwen. It's amazing: all the wasted wire and stone and glue and canvas and paint. I don't know what to do with it all."

"I thought you were having a retrospective?"

"I'm not going to embarrass myself any further."

"You could send some of it back to me, Hannah."

"I appreciate it, Gwen. I do. But we were both wrong. I thought I could make art and you thought you could sell it."

"Just because your art doesn't sell doesn't mean you're not an artist, Hannah."

"It's how I separated myself from the world, Gwen, how I deemed myself worthy. This man undermined my life. I haven't been supporting myself. I've been a kept woman. I've thought less of people all my life because they couldn't keep up to my standards, to my level of success."

"But you didn't know then," Gwen said.

"But now I do."

🐢 🐢 🐢

For the first time since she'd moved to the island she found her days as free as those of a dog. Yet even Driftwood seemed to have more purpose. Her legs felt weak, her hands useless. The dog moved ahead of her around the island, searching each fissure and pocket of gravel, dropping segments of feces behind nonchalantly, as if it were nothing to have eaten, to be able to imbibe and digest and defecate. He slept the moment his jaw rested between his forepaws. She'd never been more envious of a living creature. No artist or model or lover had ever made her more jealous than this dog, whose abilities so effortlessly matched his purpose. He was flawlessly artless.

She found crevices where the sun had cached and tried to sleep there, pour her body into the mold, but she did not fit. The stone was unyielding and her own bones too long and brittle. The body of a dead seal, curled around a stone on the foreshore, was more graceful than her own. The lie had entered her body and she felt false on the beach, like something dropped there, something manmade and so heavy the ocean couldn't wash it away. As she climbed over the ledge, her fingers began to atrophy and curl, to become almost unable to grasp. Shells and small stones slipped from her hands. Nothing seemed to have texture. The water was body temperature, which also meant it had no temperature, was neither warm nor cold. She found she had to twist her entire forearm to move her hand, to shrug with her shoulder in order to grasp. She finally abandoned the effort at rounding the island, and walked across the field to the house. Driftwood led the way. He rose up at the door and pushed it open with both paws.

Emily was lying on her empty worktable, flat on her back. Hannah hooked one hand over the other to mask the calcification in her knuckles.

"Are you OK?" she asked her sister.

"Yes. This seemed better than lying on the floor. I think it's a false labor pain."

"False?" Hannah said. "How do you know it's false?"

"The baby's not coming out."

"Maybe we should go in."

"It happened ten minutes ago, Hannah. If I have another one, we'll go in."

"You're not due for another month."

"I know that, but none of this has been on my schedule, has it?"

"I guess not."

"Why aren't you working? Why is this table clean? It hasn't been clean since I came here. You didn't work yesterday, either, or the day before."

"I'm taking a break."

"But you don't take breaks. You don't even let anyone around you take breaks. Tom says you miss the whale."

"The island seems so empty now. There were so many people here."

"But you like it empty."

"I know."

Emily sat up. When she swung her legs off the worktable, she placed both hands on each side of her stomach as if she were moving a box, something separate from her body. "I'm not sleeping anymore," she said.

"On purpose?" Hannah asked.

"Where are you? Why would I purposely not sleep?"

"I don't know," Hannah answered.

"I can't sleep because of the baby. It's uncomfortable."

"I'm sorry. Do you think about Daddy? I mean, that he would have been a grandpa?"

"No. Yes. Maybe he would have been ashamed."

"Daddy wasn't a religious zealot, Emily. He wouldn't have been ashamed."

"Did he ever touch you?" Emily asked.

Hannah walked away and stood behind the kitchen counter. "Why do you say shit like that?"

"Just to watch you flinch."

"He never touched you either, did he?" Hannah said.

"No, but your life was upside down for a second, wasn't it? That's how mine is all the time."

"I understand," Hannah said. "You don't have to explain it to me anymore. You don't have to hurt me because you hurt. I get it."

"How could you lose anything approaching what I've lost?"

"You're getting the baby in return."

"Why didn't you ever have children, Hannah?"

"There was no one else to share them with."

Emily got off the table and walked toward the staircase. She turned slowly at the first tread, and it was as if one of the erratic boulders on the island were turning. She paused in her turning, the great weight of her stomach wearing into the earth. She said simply, "Good answer," then continued up the stairs.

Hannah put her hands on the counter near the sink, and using the heels of her palms, flattened the fingers of the opposite hand. She tried

to think of what she had left, and found Will in the grooves of the washboard surface of the counter. He would be eighteen the following week.

☙ ☙ ☙

It wasn't as hard to physically move as it was to plan that action. No
direction seemed more desirable than her present position. It wasn't that
she couldn't roll over or get to another chair, but that she could not see
herself there. She was grateful that Emily rarely left her room. It made
Hannah smile to think of the two of them, stranded on each side of
the hallway, hanging onto the rafts of their beds. She dreamed of swimming to Emily's mattress with a line between her teeth, tying the two
beds together so they wouldn't be separated any further by storms.
Drowsiness overwhelmed her and only sleep seemed plausible, the only
way to leave where she was and arrive somewhere else without effort.
Once or twice Will came home early from school and caught her in bed
or on the sofa, but she was usually able to rouse herself before he arrived,
find her way to the kitchen and stand in it by the time he came home,
pretend she had just finished something or had just begun. She didn't go
far from the house for fear her hands would lock up again. She took aspirin every few hours to relieve the pain and stiffness. Even if she had the
desire to paint, she didn't think she could hold a brush for long. What
would be worse: her hand would grip the brush and never let go. She'd
carry it at the end of her arm forever, like a bird with a stick in its beak,
unable to find an appropriate place to weave it into the world. She'd
never be able to hide the fact she'd tried to be an artist. The brush would
be her embroidered letter, "A" for art rather than adultery, her sin pride
rather than lust.

☙ ☙ ☙

That weekend, while Tom and Will repaired the whale's damage to the
boat, Zee laid out her watercolors on the worktable and set up a still life:
her grandfather in a straight-backed chair.

Hannah sat across the room at the kitchen table. The breakfast
dishes had been cleared, and she was studying the wear patterns left by

the wrists of her ancestors on the table's worn edge. There, to the left of where a plate would sit, were grooves cut into the pine by a watchband. On the far side, gentle swales were pressed into the table rim as if some-one had pushed themselves up from the table for years with too much force. The edge nearest the wall was still straight and sharp. Here, at her own place, the rim was button-torn and wrist-wearied. Arno used to sit with his knife and fork in hand, his wrists in long khaki sleeves resting on the table's edge as he chewed.

"Sit still, Grandpa," Zee said.

"If you alphabetized my name, I would be called 'Eeerttv Aenot,'" he said. "That would have been better than the name I got."

"I know," Zee said. "You've never had anything good. Every boat you've ever owned had a fog huddled permanent around the pilothouse."

"That's right, little miss. I have accidentally wiped my ass with the long tail of my Sunday dress shirt too many times."

"Grandpa, gross!" Zee said. She turned to Hannah and grimaced. "Haven't heard that one before. Come look, Hannah. I can't get the line of his jaw right."

"What's wrong with my jaw?"

"It's hard to draw," Zee said. "Hannah, come look."

"No, do it on your own," she said.

"What's wrong with you?"

"Nothing. I can't teach you forever."

"O . . . K." Zee hung the two letters separately on a long clothesline. Then said, "How about just teaching me for the next five minutes?"

"If I come over there and draw the line for you, what good will that do? Just make it your own mistake."

"What does that mean, Zen master?"

"I don't know."

"Are you using saltwater to paint my picture?" Everett Eaton asked.

"No, Grandpa."

"We're related by water."

"Yes, Grandpa. Hannah, Will, and I only have half-days next week. We could help with the exhibition after school."

"I've canceled it," Hannah said.

"What?"

"You heard me."

"Why?"

"When they first installed that toilet in the Opera House, you had to wait for the applause to flush the toilet," Mr. Eaton said.

"Hush, Grandpa."

"In the Depression we had bugs in our flour and meal. My momma used to tell me the live boll weevils indicated freshness."

"Did you lose the space, Hannah?"

"No, I'm just too tired to deal with it."

"But you were going to give the proceeds to the school."

"Well, I'm sorry about that. It's very unlikely anything would have sold anyway."

"Will and I will help."

"I said I've canceled it. As soon as the boat is fixed, I'm going to bring everything out here to the island."

"Who's going to see it out here?"

"Nobody."

"Nobody, that's right."

"If it's any business of yours, I'll let you know, Zee."

"I don't understand," and Zee lowered her voice to a whisper, "you wake up today as Emily? What?"

"Can you just paint your picture and leave me out of it?"

"I can."

"OK."

"I've lived longer than I can remember," Everett Eaton told them.

"Shush, Grandpa."

🦐 🦐 🦐

"What would you have changed?" Hannah asked him.

Mr. Eaton had gone missing again and she'd found him on the far side of the island, sitting in a patch of dark blue mussel sand.

"I'd've had a better memory. I don't remember anybody, so I have to talk to everybody like they're an old friend. I know I don't remember anybody because everyone I meet tells me I don't. They wouldn't all be lying to me, would they?"

"Probably not," Hannah answered.

"I don't remember you. No offense."

"Arno Weed's niece."

"We've met before?"

"Yes and no. I've been a different person than I am now."

"Some people take offense when I don't remember them."

"It's fine with me. I'm glad you don't remember me from before."

"There's the other thing I would have changed."

"What, Mr. Eaton?"

"I would have had young brown foreign women wake me every morning by softly tearing orange rinds beneath my nose."

"That truly is something to regret missing." Hannah smiled.

"It is." He lowered his head.

"How long have you been walking this morning, Mr. Eaton?"

"I don't know, but I'm tired. This is one long stretch of beach."

"This is an island. You've been going round and round."

"Really? I didn't notice. I should have left a trail of stones, then I'd have known I came this way before."

"But the whole island is ringed by stones already," Hannah said.

"I guess lots of us have been this way before," Mr. Eaton said.

"Where were you bound for?"

"I was just walking."

"What's it like when everything always seems new?"

"I remember when new things once made me uncomfortable. I didn't want things to change. I didn't want my wife to die. All I know about now is I'm not unhappy. I probably shouldn't have been back then."

"Here comes your son. He went around the island the other way."

"I remember him. He cried a lot when he was a little boy."

☙ ☙ ☙

The whale had sprung a planking butt on *Sweet Hannah*'s port bow, and so the hull repair was relatively quick and simple. The boat was back in the quarry by Sunday evening and would be ready to fish the following weekend after Will and Zee graduated. In the meantime, the boat worked in art transport. It took six trips, two an evening, to bring all of Hannah's crated work from the Main Street gallery to the island. At both ends the crates had to be lowered and lifted to and from the boat with a derrick. Will and Zee ran the derricks at the commercial pier and on the quarry rim, while Tom and Hannah loaded and unloaded the boat.

"Zee says she doesn't understand why you're doing this," Tom said. "Not having the exhibition."

"But you do?"

"No, it's a way to ask the question."

"If you had to lobster in front of an audience, would you?"

"Maybe not." He hooked a strap tied around a small crate and swung the load over the boat, then signaled to Zee to lower it the rest of the way down. "Feels like it's got rocks in it," he said.

"It probably does," she told him.

"Send off rocks and they send back money. It's a good system."

"Your grandfather did it. He worked the quarries."

"Not the same. His granite didn't come back. It's still in a building or bridge foundation somewhere. Why are we taking this stuff out to the island when we're just going to have to send it back to that bank?"

"It's mine now. It won't go back."

"They want their money back?"

"No."

"Good deal. You can sell it again."

"No."

"Then I'm with Zee. I don't understand, either."

Her jaw clinched and she turned away from him.

"It's not necessary that I understand," he said.

When the first boatload reached the rim of the quarry and they began to trundle it downhill on carts and dollies, Hannah directed them toward the boat shed.

"But we'll have to put the boat back in there this winter," Tom said. "You could put it in the granite house."

"You and Zee and Mr. Eaton sleep there," Hannah said.

"But just for a few more weekends, till all the traps are out," Tom said.

"What about Emily?" Hannah asked. She set down her load and let Zee and Will pass on.

"What about her?" Tom asked

"Couldn't you work more easily from here? The boat will be here in the quarry. You wouldn't waste an hour every day coming out in the skiff. And Emily's here."

"We haven't talked about it," Tom said.

"I can put the art in the boat shed until you do, until you work things out."

"I have to live on the mainland, Hannah. I've got Dad and a house there."

"All I'm saying is you can continue using the house on weekends. I'd miss your dad. He likes coming out here."

"I worry about him falling in the water."

"I know. We'll be more careful."

"OK. For a while. We'll need to put blocks under these crates or the tide will get to them. They'll float out to sea in a storm."

"OK," she said, before he could finish. Then she said, "OK," again, thanking him for the idea.

☙ ☙ ☙

She did not give Will the small watercolor portrait of Driftwood for his birthday. She'd painted it months ago and now it seemed not the thing. Why she'd thought he would want to hang it in a college dorm room seemed a distant notion. Instead, she ordered a laptop computer and a printer. It cost a small fortune, but he would need it. The school said so. She cut the advertisement out and slipped it into an envelope. She wrote Happy Birthday on the envelope. She woke early that morning and left the envelope on his nightstand, then went back to bed. Will woke her again later, sitting down on her bed in the cup between her gathered knees and elbows.

"Hey, Birthday Boy," she whispered hoarsely.

He held the envelope in his hand. He held it between two fingers as if it were a small white bone he'd found on the beach.

"It won't come for a couple weeks. I ordered it yesterday," she said.

"Yesterday," he echoed. "You put a lot of thought into it, then."

"Is it not the right one?" she asked, and pushed herself up against the headboard.

"No, it's perfect. It's the one I would have bought with my earnings this summer."

"Now you don't have to," she said.

"Where's my birthday present, Hannah?"

"That's it."

"No, it's not. Where's my painting of Driftwood? Zee told me about it two months ago."

"The little gossiping bitch. I got you the computer instead."

"I want the painting of our dog, instead." He was dressed, ready to leave for school.

"He's my dog," she said.

"Hannah," he said, "I clean up just as much of his shit as you do. You know he's our dog. And why are you still in bed? I've had to eat breakfast alone all week."

"You don't have to ask about the painting for my sake."

"I'm not asking for your sake. It's my painting and my birthday present and I want it."

"OK, OK, OK," she said. She threw the bedcovers off, tugged her T-shirt down, and opened the closet into the eave. The painting had been gift-wrapped for weeks. She thrust it into his lap and got back in bed. "There."

Will stood up and tore open the package. The portrait was framed with bleached sticks. The dog held another of these sticks in his mouth. Will let the paper fall to the floor and held the frame in both hands at arm's length. "Ha," he whooped. "Look at him, Hannah. He just picked it up. He's so happy." He turned the painting toward her and shoved it at her as if she'd never seen it. "Now it's a happy birthday. I'm taking it to school."

"No, you're not," Hannah snapped.

"Why not? My dog, my painting. I'm late." He bent down, pinned the ball of her shoulder to the headboard with one hand and kissed her on the cheek. "Ha," he whooped again, and sang *Happy Birthday* to himself all the way out of the house. She sat as still as she could, listening to him go.

Emily was at her door then, leaning against the casement. She did not move lightly through the house anymore.

"You OK?" Hannah asked.

"Yeah. So he's eighteen now," Emily said.

"It makes me feel much safer."

"Why?"

"His father can't touch him now. He's his own man."

"Funny, I'm twenty-six and I don't feel that way. What makes you think a guy who beats women and children worries about the law or Will's ability to vote?"

"He can't legally force Will to return to Texas with him."

"No, so he won't do that. He'll just come and take what he wants illegally."

"You were calling someone the day I came to tell you about the whale. Who was it?"

"It's none of your business."

"It wasn't him?"

"Of course not. I'm not an idiot."

"I'm going to make Will a cake. Do you want to help?"

"If I see an egg crack open now I'm going to puke."

"It won't be long now, Emily."

"It's forever. Every minute is another forever. I can't see anything beyond having this baby."

"We could walk some more, encourage it."

"This island isn't safe. Too many places to fall. It'll come when it comes, just like the Second Coming."

"The Second Coming is a promise. This baby is a dead certainty," Hannah said.

Neither of them spoke for moments. Then Emily said, "Don't you ever get tired of hearing the waves?"

"No, I guess not. Maybe I don't hear them anymore."

"I hear every one. You'd think they'd just take a break."

"The kids graduate Saturday. You can get away from here for a little while. The school is in the middle of Deer Isle. I don't think you can hear the waves there."

"I could go to graduation and accuse every senior boy of being the father." She put her hand over her mouth but the laugh escaped.

"Maybe you should stay here, then."

"No, Tom wants me to go and see his baby graduate. They'll all think he's the father."

"Maybe," Hannah said.

"No maybe about it," Emily said, and turned back to her own bed. Her body filled the whole door frame. She slid into her room like a drawer into a desk.

☙ ☙ ☙

She'd known from the beginning that she was no artist. Brushes, pencils, and crayons had always fit her hand awkwardly, as if she were trying to fit someone else's teeth into her own mouth. Her admission to Bennington was an accident, her graduation as sure as any piece of driftwood's arrival on a beach once she'd been admitted. She'd tumbled along on her friends' shoulders, made partnerships in which she did all the work in trade for their talent. She'd gotten through by being jostled forward by the crowd. No professor ever singled her out for praise. No one saw promise. Her paintings and sculptures since that time were only ideas represented rather than conceived. She'd lost her friends not because they couldn't keep up, not because they were jealous, but because she was overbearing. So after she'd cried for two weeks, and slept between bouts of crying, she realized she shouldn't be upset. She'd known this all along. She'd only been caught. This was nothing new. She'd known she was no artist. She should be relieved.

What shamed her were the sculptures. She'd taken her materials from the island, which she'd always known wasn't innocent beachcombing or even scavenging. She'd stolen the stuff of this island, reducing its territory, shortening its life. Nothing had eroded its shores in the past six years more than her own hands. She'd sent away stone after stone, stick and shell and feather and bone, in this false trade of island for ego. She'd made the island an accomplice in the lie. She'd photographed the island's soul and shared it for profit. Here, touch this stone wrapped in lace. Buy the heat of an island sun within this rock. Caress this wave-worn branch, hold it in your hand, own it. It's not stolen: you paid for it. Nature didn't make it: I did. I don't sell souvenirs: I sell art. It's not the island: it's me. Lies. She'd been trying to make meaning out of beauty, but she'd only been clawing at its skin. At last she'd be able to leave the island alone. It didn't need her.

She began to make amends, to put things back. In the slow, waiting hours of the summer, while Will and Tom were at sea, she unraveled wool, peeled wire, and picked thread from sewn cloth. The beach stones fell free from their wrappings like grave goods. She realized she'd wrapped them to hide the fact they were stolen. She recognized each stone as it fell free, knew during the fall where it had come from, where it would be returned. The rocks were dull, lighter in color and weight than they should be. No living thing thrived on their surfaces. When she held them up in the sun they almost turned to gas. She put them back on the beach like a child replacing a stolen candy bar on a store counter. She left shells on flat slabs of granite where birds had dropped them years earlier, and cast sticks into thickets of beach iris and moss where they should have rotted long ago. She thought of Tom and the storekeeper who rang up No Sale as he left the store, and realized her own mind had been ringing as long as she'd been on the island, as long as she'd been mailing it away.

The island offered no thanks, but swallowed each rock and seagull bone silently. Wherever she dropped them, from whatever height, the stones and shells rolled to a perfect fit. Once the first wave washed over, they returned to island color, nestled into mussel sand, and began to accept the littoral-born life, barnacle seed, periwinkle suck, seaweed drape, every pore open to the storage of waste and egg, fetus or feces. The stones became clean again by returning to their cycle, by leaning into each wave.

What were you thinking, she asked, when you picked up a stone off the beach and let the sea encroach that much further, left yourself that much less room to stand? You were thinking about art when you should have been thinking about survival, keeping your head above water. Over the summer she crept around the island alone, apologizing with sticks and stones. She dismantled her small sculptures, burning the yarn and cloth and every other binding agent she'd used in Arno's pit of rusted paint cans and melted glass. No one noticed because she was careful to leave the shipping crates intact, and their contents blended into the island without seam or shadow.

The paintings remained. Having no desire to look at them, she left the crates standing on end in the boat shed. The canvases didn't carry the stain of being torn from the island, but they were embarrassing reminders of wasted years, so much time spent on such thin materials. They were vulnerable to every ravagement the environment could throw at them there in the shed, including being washed out to sea. That made her smile, the vision of her crated canvases like rafts at sea, washing up on some distant shore where they could be used for firewood or housing, where their passage would have at last made them as valuable as driftwood.

🐚 🐚 🐚

Tom and Will dropped their first string of traps directly into the quarry. Hannah, Zee, and Mr. Eaton stood on the granite steps as the traps were hauled for the first time a day later. *Sweet Hannah* was still tied to her mooring. As Tom worked the hydraulic pot hauler, Will brought the first trap aboard. It held a veritable hive of lobster.

"Oh, my fricking God," Zee yelled out.

Will popped open the trap and began banding lobsters. There was a keeper for every short. He called to Hannah, "At this rate we won't have to leave the quarry."

Mr. Eaton said, "I knew that damned Arno Weed had a secret."

Will tossed the keepers in a barrel on the port side, and threw the shorts overboard. The second trap held another three keepers, along with three females and six shorts. Will rebaited the traps and shoved them back into the quarry.

"How's he doing?" Zee yelled at her dad.

"He's some slow," Tom said. "You'd think a fella with two hands could work a little faster."

Will beamed. "Leave him alone," Hannah yelled over the water. "He's got cow hands. They take time to turn into lobster hands."

As they motored out of the quarry for their first day's haul, Zee turned to her grandfather and asked, "Don't you want to go along, Grandpa? I wish I didn't have my skiff business. I'd go."

"Not me," he said. "I forget why I don't want to go, but I know I don't. There must be something bad out there. The struggle's over for me. I'm here to relax. I've made it through to the far side of work and I don't mean to go back for my hat."

"Go back for your hat?" Hannah asked.

"I mean there's nothing in my past that I need," he explained.

Zee got back in the skiff she'd brought her father and grandfather out to the island in.

"Do I get in, too, Zinnia Paulette?" Mr. Eaton asked.

"No, Grandpa. You're staying with Hannah today. I've got to go to work. I'll be back out this afternoon. This is a Saturday, remember?"

"I remember."

As they took the long climb out of the quarry, Mr. Eaton asked, "Don't you have to work today, Miss?"

"What's my name, Mr. Eaton?"

They paused at the rim of the quarry. He looked into her face and then away and finally back. "I'm sorry, Miss. I don't know you."

"I'm Arno Weed's great-niece."

"That's right."

They paused at the oak tree with the embedded stone, the tree that had picked the rock out of the earth and carried it six feet into the air.

"Somebody put a stone in the fork of this tree like it was an egg in a nest," he told her.

"No," she said, "the sap lifted it up as the tree grew."

"No, it doesn't work that way. If it worked that way, every tree would be full of rocks. Ever seen a wire fence carried up into the sky? Plenty of those caught in bark. No, a tree doesn't push. It surrounds. Somebody, long ago, put this stone in the arms of this tree for safekeeping."

She took his hand and led him to the pressed-steel lawn chairs she'd already pulled through rising grass up to her garden. While he sat, she crawled through the soil she'd cultivated the day before, pitching out erratic stones and erratic shards of dishes.

"What shall we talk about today, Mr. Eaton?" she asked.

"What did we talk about yesterday?"

"Well, you weren't here yesterday, but last weekend you told me all about your lodge."

"I did?"

"Even the secret handshake."

"I wouldn't have let on to that."

She pushed herself off her knees and shook hands with him. His eyes pulsed.

"I won't tell anybody," she said.

"I've never had a woman shake my hand that way. You must've had something on me to get me to show you that."

"I've got nothing on you."

"I can't remember anything bad I've done. Oh, I took naps now and again, when maybe I should have been working, but my boy never went hungry."

"I'm going to tell you some secrets, Mr. Eaton."

"I don't want to know any secrets." He held up both palms.

"You'll forget them by this evening. You'll forget them before anyone else sets foot on this island. I've never trusted anyone with a secret as much as I trust you, except maybe the dog."

"A dog is a good secret keeper," he affirmed.

She went back to work, straining rocks and root nests from the soil. The ground was still cool from winter. At times she mistook her hand's shadow as that of a bird passing over. The stumps of her knees seemed to be able to find stones her fingers missed. She wondered if the ends of Tom's arms were as sensitive.

"I promised," she began, "to help send Zee to college, and now I won't be able to do that, at least not beyond her first couple of semesters."

"Zee, my granddaughter?" he asked.

"Yes."

"You shouldn't have promised."

"I know. I've lost my job."

"What is your job?"

"I thought I was an artist."

"Even if you had a job as an artist, they don't make no money."

"You're right, they don't."

"Have you told her?"

"No. If I tell, her dad wouldn't let her go to the good school she wants to attend."

"You mean her dad, my son, Tom?"

"Yes."

"You should tell him so she don't get her hopes all up. If you can't tell him, I will."

"OK," Hannah said. "You tell him."

"OK."

"OK, and tell him I don't know what to do with myself other than garden and look at the ocean and think about him and Will." The old man nodded, so she went on. "I was never lonely until all of you showed up. Tell him that."

"OK, I will."

"Tell Arno Weed that he shouldn't have loved me so much or so little, whichever it was."

"I don't see much of Arno anymore."

"I know. Also, I don't love my sister."

"You don't?"

"No. Tell them all I know it's my fault."

"OK."

"What am I going to do?"

"There's a piece of glass there by your hand. Don't let it cut you." He looked up then and down toward the house. "Here comes a strange dog," he said.

Driftwood parted the grass with his snout and put his head under the old man's hand. On cue, they both began to breathe heavily, as if it were a combined struggle against the air around them. When this passed, Everett Eaton said, "They say if you've had one good wife, one good horse, and one good dog in your life, you should die a contented man."

"Well?" Hannah asked.

"I never had a horse," he said.

"Me either," she said.

"I guess we got to go on living till we find us a pair of good horses."

"You've had a good life, Mr. Eaton."

"Yeah, but don't tell nobody. Somebody might take it."

"I don't know if I'm going to have a good life."

"Why not?"

"I keep going back after my hat."

"Oh," he said. "Don't do that. That hat sunk a long time ago. The bottom of the ocean is littered with hats. The wind blows them off your head for a reason. Why, there's lobsters living in your hat. You don't want it back. You want a new hat."

"You always know what to say, Mr. Eaton."

"Did you ever follow sports?" he asked her.

She shook her head.

"Me neither. This is going to be a big garden."

"I know. It's the biggest one I've ever had. Lots of people to feed this summer."

"My son won't eat a vegetable, except corn."

"I've noticed that. But he eats potatoes."

"Is that a vegetable?"

"Yes."

"It's sort of meaty, though."

"Yes. Do you remember what I asked you to tell Tom?"

"Sure I do."

"What was it?"

"To call his wife?" he asked.

"That's right," Hannah said.

"I thought it was. This dog's asshole is starting to pucker."

"It does that," Hannah said. "He doesn't know when he's going. He can't help it."

"Well, I guess it's better to lose control at that end rather than at the other, like me."

"I won't take advantage of you again, Mr. Eaton," Hannah said.

"Did you?"

"Yes, I'm sorry."

"Well, I don't remember it if you did. And forgetting is close enough to forgiving for me. I hope it is for you, too."

She pitched a small smooth stone across the furrows, and he caught it in both hands. Driftwood rose and looked back and forth between them. Mr. Eaton put the stone in the dog's mouth without letting him see it.

❧❧❧

She rose early to make Will's breakfast, and sometimes walked to the quarry rim with him to wait on Tom. In mid-June it was daylight at 4:00 a.m. and Tom usually arrived in his skiff by 4:30. She waited till they tied off the skiff and left the quarry in *Sweet Hannah* before walking back home. She took her time walking. She'd be alone with Emily till three in the afternoon when Will and Tom returned. The hours wilted one by one through the long day. She had nothing to occupy her hand or mind but the garden. Emily merely waited. They traded the binoculars back and forth, searching the sea for *Sweet Hannah*. The island sat in the calm center of a hundred swirling boats, boats like leaves in a whirlwind.

Distant and near, white on blue, they curled in upon their own wakes like dogs maddened by their tails. The snortings of their engines were disconnected from their gyrations, and arrived afterwards, as if the sound were being towed. Hannah and Emily knew the locations of Tom's traps within their view, but he hauled them on no schedule. The low, lean white boat with the yellow riding sail might appear from any direction, at any time of day. When they spotted *Sweet Hannah*, when they agreed this boat among the many was *Sweet Hannah*, their breathing became shallow and they ceased to speak and their breathing became one to facilitate the transfer of the glasses. On a clear day, even at a distance of miles, they could count the catch. Will would turn and pitch toward the barrel, or the short lobsters would leave his hands in a cartwheel against the sky, an undignified arc of returning to the sea. Following gulls descended upon the discarded bait like children under a burst piñata. The boat would then turn, the traps would trail off the stern, and the sound would come to them only after the spot in the ocean where the boat had been relaxed again. Hannah suspected Emily lied at times, saying she hadn't spotted the boat in order to hold the glasses longer.

"Let me see," Hannah said.

"I'm not through," Emily told her.

"Do you see them?"

"I don't know."

"Let me see." She took the binoculars. "That's not them."

"I told you so. What's wrong with you? Don't you have anything else to do?"

"Leave me alone," Hannah whispered. "I'm looking."

"You wouldn't leave me alone when I asked," Emily said. "I'm going to move into town soon, before the baby comes."

Hannah brought the glasses down to the level of the foreshore. The water swirled around the rocks like silk.

"I think that's good," Hannah said.

"Some people want other people who are flawed so they can change them, in the same way that God wants sinners. Do you think Tom is like that?"

"I don't know," Hannah said.

"I think his wife was crazy. I know he thinks I'm crazy, too."

"So if I were crazy, he might want me?" Hannah asked.

"You're not a crazy person," Emily said. "You're only sad. I go through life thinking there's something else I should be doing, something besides life, something more important than life. That's crazy, isn't it?"

"I don't know. Maybe what we do here isn't so important."

"See, something's wrong with you. It's come over you. Maybe you've caught it from me. You would never have said that six months ago. You thought everything you did was important, that nothing on earth was more important than what you did."

"Why didn't you just have an abortion, Emily?"

"He didn't want me to have the baby, but I wasn't supposed to kill it, either: God's Catch 22."

Hannah returned the glasses to her eyes so she wouldn't have to continue looking at her sister, her father's daughter, but the moment and the view seemed fixed, time moving on without it, like a drip of dried paint on the back of a closet door. Her sister's life and her own were as negligible as a periwinkle's on the foreshore. They could not move as quickly as the flowing and ebbing tide, nor could they always hold fast. The world moved through them as well as around them. Any decision was only that in name, a euphemism to describe moving along in a current of present culture fixed by time past. I will decide to become an artist, she had thought, but water thought otherwise, water and the moon and the wind and every moving creature and unmoved rock. My island is so small, she thought. I clung to this rock the way Emily once clung to the Rock of Calvary.

A yellow sail seemed to ride on the water in her eyes.

"Is that them?" Emily asked.

"Yes, no, I don't know," Hannah answered.

❧ ❧ ❧

An hour before they were scheduled to return, she began calling her own name over the VHF radio, "*Sweet Hannah, Sweet Hannah, Sweet Hannah.*" Then she'd release the switch on the mike and listen to static or the conversations of other fishermen she'd just walked over. Tom left the operation of the radio to Will. The slick plastic mike was difficult to operate with his hooks. *"Sweet Hannah, Sweet Hannah, Sweet Hannah,"* she called, as if she were offering herself to any taker on the airwaves, and often as not there was some wisecrack: "I'll take two," or "Sour Hannah's more like it," or "For Christ's sake, answer her or she'll not shut up." The interval between her first call and Will's answering might be moments or as much as a half-hour. If they were in the lee of Isle au Haut, the radio signals sometimes skipped over them. If they were in the middle of a string, they didn't stop to respond. If they were sinking, the radio was underwater.

If the interval lingered, Zee would check in with her to tell her she'd seen them off Mark Island an hour earlier or at the commercial pier in Stonington. If she hadn't seen them she called Hannah to break the static, as if it were the barrier, the opaque surface of water. As long as they were talking, the radio wasn't silent.

"What'd you do today, *Z To Go?*" Hannah called.

"Groceries most of the day. Passenger out to Merchants Island, and I took two day-hikers over to Crotch Island. I'll pick them up at four and then I'll come out to pick up Dad."

"I haven't heard back from them yet."

"I know. Guess they're having a good day."

"It takes half a second to pick up that radio."

"Roger that," Zee said. "Still, I can say Will's name while we're both sitting on the same couch and he won't hear it."

"It's just inconsiderate," Hannah said.

In late June, they decided to take their revenge. Zee finished early and brought balloons to the island. They filled fifty of them with cold water. Will answered their radio call and told them *Sweet Hannah* would be in the quarry in half an hour. They positioned themselves on each side of the entrance. It was low tide and *Sweet Hannah* would have to motor in slowly through the narrow channel. They stored their ammunition in brown grocery bags concealed in the rocks. The water burled between the women as they waited. Curling around starfish and urchins and over blue mussel beds, the sea resembled an active *Starry Night*, the old ultramarine oil wet once again, the night sky shimmering with the possibility of becoming fixed forever, this moment of waiting unchanging. They waited the half-hour and a half-hour more. While they waited, the water went slack, as if the world were pausing to remember what it had forgotten, whether it should go back. For a few minutes the water was still enough to mirror birds in flight, the stirring of individual needles on spruce trees, clouds turning inside out. Still they did not come. In the waiting, Hannah returned to all other unfulfilled waitings: letters that did not arrive, New York buses that did not show, never-ringing phones, sculptures that refused to find form. She'd spent years waiting for a way to resolve some dawdling canvas. The ocean promised arrival, wave after wave, but wouldn't commit to an interval. Waiting, unlike walking, was easy at first. Anybody could do it without trying, without even the knowledge. But at last it became impossible to maintain, intolerable as absolute balance. Zee reached her limit first. She rose, leaving the bright balloons in a niche in the rocks. Hannah didn't have to ask where she was going, but followed. They tried the handheld radio in the skiff first and then hurried down to the house to the more powerful base radio. To both calls there was no answer. They tried six different channels, repeating the call.

"Their radio could be broken," Zee said.

"That doesn't explain why they're not here," Hannah said.

Emily descended the staircase. She moved slowly, one hand on her stomach as if to hold it down, another in midair poised to catch something that would surely bounce.

"What?" she asked.

"We can't raise them on the radio. They're over an hour late," Zee explained.

Emily said, "It's a bright, blue, clear day. The water's calm. I'm sure they're fine."

"What an amazing moment you've picked to be sure about something," Zee said.

"OK, have it your way," Emily shot back. "They're sinking somewhere. We can't help them. We don't know what to do."

Zee slammed the mike down on the radio. "As soon as you have that kid, I'm going to kick your frickin' ass," she yelled.

"That's enough," Hannah screamed.

Zee picked the mike back up. "*Sweet Hannah, Sweet Hannah,* you on this one, Dad?" She released the key on the mike and dead air filled the room with a stifling silence punctuated by brittle sounds like the hard shells of bugs cracking underfoot. "Does anyone out there know where *Sweet Hannah* is?"

The radio popped, went silent, and then a distant voice asked for a radio check.

"It's five o'clock," Hannah said. "Most of the other fishermen are already in for the day. We should call the Coast Guard."

There were tears in Zee's eyes. "My dad will fricking kill me if I call the Coast Guard and he's all right."

"Well, he won't kill me," Hannah said. She took the mike from Zee, but before she could tune the radio to Channel 16, Will opened the door. Tom walked in behind him. They stopped and stood still among the three silent women, while the radio asked again for a radio check.

"You're coming in fine at Ten Acre No Nine," Hannah returned, and reached down and switched off the radio.

"What?" Tom asked.

"I told them you were fine," Emily said.

"Uh-oh," Tom said. "We decided to top up with fuel, and then I got to talking with some of the guys on the dock." He looked to Will.

"I guess I turned off the radio after I told you we'd be home soon," Will said. "That would be where I went wrong."

"You're both idiots," Zee said. "We've been waiting for an hour and a half. We were about to call the Coast Guard."

"You said you'd be here," Hannah said.

"Sorry," Will said. He hadn't moved since he'd stepped in the door. He looked to Hannah. "We had a real good day. While Tom was talking,

I walked into town and bought steaks." He held up the plastic bag they were in.

"Well," Hannah said, "I hope they taste good. C'mon, Zee, c'mon, Emily. We're taking the skiff into town to eat. I've had about as much as I can stand of this."

"Me too," Zee said.

"I don't want to go into town," Emily said. Both women turned to her. "OK, OK, OK," she huffed.

They left the men standing in the doorway.

Early the next morning, Hannah walked up to the rim of the quarry alone. Looking down, it was plain to see the paper grocery sacks hadn't held up through high tide. Red, orange, and pink water balloons were scattered across the pale ledges and lodged among the scree at the quarry mouth like bright roe.

🐟 🐟 🐟

It was easy enough to explain to them all that she was taking the summer off from art. By late August, Will and Zee would be at school, and Emily would be in town with Tom. The questions would stop. She'd have a year to sell the island then, and it would easily bring enough to cover Zee's tuition, anything Will might need, and enough to maybe help Tom and Emily and the baby, enough to pay the taxes, and enough. She'd call Shirley Langlais. It wouldn't be hard to let her have the island. She'd put it to good use, a center for the saving of distraught whales. Perhaps she'd let her join the effort. Or she could move back to New York. It would be hard to leave Mr. Eaton, who seemed to absolve all, to hold her blameless, not only in his forgetting, but in the present moment as well, when his mind held fast to her transgressions and was still able to pronounce no harm done that wouldn't pass. As for the island, it would still be here, wouldn't it, even without her? Even if she weren't standing on it, it would still resist the tide.

🐟 🐟 🐟

At graduation, she and Emily had sat on either side of Tom, as if they were his oars. He pushed through the ceremony staring straight ahead. Canned foghorn had been banned, so he blew a bosun's whistle in lieu of clapping when Zee crossed the stage. Everett Eaton sat next to Hannah, constantly turning in his seat, scanning the crowd. When Hannah asked him who he was looking for, he said, "I feel like some of these people are looking for me."

"Is Zee's mother here, Mr. Eaton?"

"She's here, standing behind the wind like she always did."

"Do you see her?"

"No."

She turned to Tom. "I thought Zee's mom might be here."

"I tried to contact her. No luck." He shrugged.

"So she doesn't even know Zee's graduating today?"

"I don't think she knows Zee's a senior."

"How can a person live so far away from their past?" she asked him, and he shrugged again.

A Billings student received more applause than most others when she crossed over. Big family. What could she do? When Will crossed the stage, she would have only her two hands. When his row stood and walked to the stage, she felt all the bones in her body dissolve. She wouldn't be able to clap now. As the names were read and Will stepped closer and closer to the short set of stairs leading onto the stage, her mind became oddly detached from her body. She turned hurriedly to search the crowd for Will's mother. There were so many smiling faces. She turned back and saw Will floating up the staircase in his robe, heard her own name mingled with his. He was searching the crowd, too, and suddenly she realized she should stand up, unsure if she were being chosen or was volunteering. His gaze found hers at last, and hung in the air over the crowd vibrating like a wet line pulled taut from the water. Here is love again, she thought, here is love, debilitating and transient. Will turned and waved and strode behind the stage curtain, leaving the auditorium empty. She sat down. Then she remembered she was going to look for Will's father in the crowd when Will had crossed the stage. But he, too, seemed to hide behind the wind. No one there looked like Will. Except, strangely enough, Tom. Both their faces were brown, burnt high on the cheeks. Both left their mouths open after they spoke, as if leaving open the possibility to take something back. Both let their hair hang over their eyes too long before brushing it away. It occurred to her that Zee had found a man that looked like her father. He was leaning over, talking to Emily. Hannah found herself drawing the line of his cheekbone, the shadow behind his ear, curl of hair at nape.

🏴 🏴 🏴

"Who is that on the boat with my Tom?" Mr. Eaton asked her.

"That's Will," Hannah told him, exasperated. "I told you that yesterday and the day before."

He looked at her as if she were lying, but said, "It's good to learn one new thing every day, even if it's the same thing you learned yesterday."

"What's my name?"

"Henna?"

"That's close. It's Hannah."

They stood at the quarry rim. Hannah waved to the boat as it left the harbor. Both Everett Eaton's hands were surrounded by pockets. "Aren't you going to wave?" she asked.

"I'm tired," he said. "It's been a long day. Hope, faith, optimism: the only things left to us once knowledge and research and discovery have reached their limit on any particular day. I'm tired. It's been a long day."

"It's 5:15 in the morning, Mr. Eaton. We just got up and had breakfast."

"Who found me?" he asked her.

"What do you mean?"

"When you go to sleep you never expect to be found."

Before Tom had left that morning, he had nodded at his father and told her, "Don't let him fall off the island."

She pushed the old man back from the quarry rim. He tried to smile through a yawn.

"What's so funny?" she asked.

"I'm just surprised that star has shown up again."

"What star?"

He pointed at the sun low on the horizon.

"Are you going to be like this all day?"

"Molly Haskell was the first woman on Deer Isle to wear long pants. Most of the fellas didn't like it. But I did. She kept her hip bone in her watch pocket. I always wanted to put my hand in that pocket."

"OK, that's far enough. Let's go for a walk. I can't keep up with your head, but I can walk as fast as you. Let's go."

"Two roads merged in a wood, and we, meeting there, decided to go on together," he told her. "That's Mr. Robert Frost."

"No," she said, "'Two roads diverged in a wood, and I—I took the one less traveled by.'"

"I like mine better."

They walked hand in hand down the worn grassy path to the shelving granite of the foreshore. He gave her hand a little squeeze there, as they watched the small waves trip blindly onto the rock one after another.

"Which way shall we go today, east or west?" she asked.

"Which way did we go yesterday?" he asked.

"I can't remember," Hannah said.

"Me neither. Let's go this way." He crossed his arms and pointed down the beach in both directions.

"Ha, ha, Scarecrow. Look, here comes Toto."

Driftwood rounded the corner of the boat shed with a pink tampon tube in his mouth. She pried it from his teeth. The plastic was faded on one side. It had been floating out there for some time.

"What's that?" Mr. Eaton asked her.

She looked at him and decided what the hell. "It's an insertion tool for a woman's sanitary device."

He looked at her with dismay. "What's a dog want with one?"

It was the first time she'd laughed since the whale left. She sat down on the granite and held the ache of laughter in, till tears fell off her cheeks. Mr. Eaton stood above her, looking out to sea. After a few moments, he dropped down on his knees to face her. "Do they wash up here once a month?" he asked.

She rolled onto the granite, felt barnacles push between her ribs. Now she could not breathe. He bounced on his haunches, looked at the earth, and said, "This ground under my feet feels old." A tear caught in the trough of her nose and balled cheek, pooled and trembled there. She could not roll over or sit up without it running back into her eye or into her mouth. Mr. Eaton had risen and was walking down the beach. He'd chosen a direction. She sat up, and the tear slid between her lips. He died that afternoon, long after their walk.

🐚 🐚 🐚

She'd left him in the sun, near her garden, in a lawn chair among tall grasses. She'd left him to fetch iced tea, left him with the dog and the sun and the tall grass. When she returned, she thought he'd fallen asleep in the chair as he often did, but he was gone. His hands lay cupped in his lap, his chin on his chest. The dog mouthed the ice cubes when they fell into the grass. She did not cry out yet, but looked from his suddenly too loose face directly to sea. She left her hand on his shoulder. His jacket was so warm. There was tea on her upper lip. She'd started without him, in the kitchen. When the sounds of gulls and waves returned, she tugged on his jacket a bit. You're missing this part, Mr. Eaton, she thought. She looked for some tree to sway, for a shag to pivot over the house, a single wave to reach up on the granite a bit farther than the others.

She walked up to the quarry rim to wait on *Sweet Hannah*, but Tom and Will and the boat were already there. As she climbed down to meet them, each level was warmer, the light more intense. The stone seemed soft, almost too soft to support her weight. She found herself unable to bend down to take the skiff's painter, and Will had to jump ashore to tie the boat off. Tom put his hook through the iron ring embedded in the rock and pulled himself onto the island.

"Tom," she said, "Tom." Without his arms, he smelled like rotten bait. He stood without understanding. Her own arms hung as useless at her side. They would not come up to hide her own face.

"What is it?" he asked softly.

"He's up in the garden sitting down. I just left him there a moment, a moment ago. He's still there."

"Is he gone, Hannah?"

Her face apple-rotted in a moment's fall, and she said, "Yes," and he opened his long insect arms and she stepped into them, saying she was sorry.

Later, after the sheriff had come and the body was ferried through the archipelago to Stonington, Tom told them, "I always thought I'd be with him when he died, with my hand palm flat on his chest so I could feel something going."

"But it didn't," she said, looking between Tom and Will and Zee and Emily. "I looked everywhere right away. Nothing else happened."

"But he was so alive this morning," Zee said.

"That doesn't matter," Emily told her. "What they told us at church: 'Almost saved means totally lost.'"

They sat in the quarry for more than an hour after the body was taken. The stone held the day's warmth long after the day was gone.

"We should have carried him into town aboard *Sweet Hannah*," Will said. "We should have gone with him. We shouldn't have let them put him on another boat."

Tom told him, "It's OK."

"I didn't think he'd die during the summer, Daddy," Zee whispered.

"It was his heart, wasn't it?" Will said. "He couldn't wait."

"I know it was the right thing to do, Hannah, bringing him out here. I'm glad it happened here," Tom said.

"I shouldn't have made him walk around the island with me. I needed to do that, not him."

"He never had any qualms about saying no. He wouldn't have gone if he didn't want to go."

"You can bring him back out here if you want to, Tom. We could put him here," she offered.

"No, he's already got a place up in Deer Isle next to Mom. That's where he wanted to go."

She nodded. Her eyes ached from crying. She sat next to Zee and held her hand. When the tissue Zee was using wouldn't hold more water, she brought the back of Hannah's hand up to wipe her cheek. It made them both laugh.

"I'm sorry," Zee said. "I thought it was my hand."

Hannah looked at the back of her wet hand. "Was it a tear or snot?"

"Gross, Hannah. It was a tear."

"Let's go, sweetheart," Tom said.

All three women looked up. Will held the painter as Tom and Zee stepped aboard the skiff.

"Be careful," Hannah said.

"I don't know when I'll be out tomorrow," Tom told Will.

"Maybe we could take the day off," Will said.

"Maybe. I'll think about it. I'll have to take the day of the funeral off, too. We don't want to get too far behind on our rounds."

"Lord," Emily said. "Farming lobsters is worse than milking cows."

"I could help Will," Hannah said. Both men looked at her. "I could," she said. "I've done it before."

"We'll see," Tom said.

As they walked back to the house they could see Mr. Eaton's chair, tipped over in the grass.

"Do you want me to bring it down to the house, Hannah?" Will asked.

"No," she said, "leave it there by the garden. I'm going to sit in it when I'm tired."

"Maybe I should have gone in with Zee," he said.

"Let her be with her dad. You made the right decision. I'm happy you're here with me."

"I'll stay in town after the funeral," Emily told them. "The baby's due soon."

"Maybe you should give Tom some time," Hannah suggested.

"It was his idea," she said. "Besides, I don't want to have the baby here. It could come early." She went inside the house, leaving them in the grass.

"Good," Will whispered. "I'll get my room back."

"Only for a couple weeks, till the baby's born," Hannah said.
"What makes you think she'll be back?"

🦞🦞🦞

She knew it was Everett Eaton's funeral, but it could have been Arno
Weed's. She was one funeral behind, and standing there at the grave side
it seemed Arno had just died, and Everett Eaton was yet to die. Somehow
the past and future were full of death and leaving. Perhaps some of the
old men standing here attended Arno's funeral, too, old men in off-color
suits and ties too wide or narrow, the same suits they'd worn to Arno's
service years earlier. They were fishermen, with facial creases so deep
lobsters could hide in them. They stood with their hands clasped before
their stomachs and looked not at one another, but at the sky. Mr. Eaton's
stone, already in place with his birth date engraved, was granite, but too
dark to have come from Deer Isle. The stone seemed to swallow light
rather than reflect it. Both Arno and Mr. Eaton had told her that Deer
Isle granite put forth more light than it took in.

Hannah stood with Emily, helping steady her in the wind. Tom and
Zee sat in folding chairs before the closed casket. The minister spoke for
a few moments, reminding them all that only the thief on the cross was
promised heaven, but he received this promise by making the simplest
of requests: remember me. He was sure that God remembered Everett
Eaton. Emily's knees buckled and it was all Hannah could do to hold her
off the ground before two of the old men helped her. They got her to
one of the folding chairs where she sat, resting her elbows on her stomach, covering her face with her hands. She sobbed softly.

That morning, Will had carried Emily's suitcase down from her room.
After Emily had gone down, Hannah pushed the closed door open and
stepped in. The bed was made, the floor swept. She pulled open one
drawer, then another. They were all completely empty. The closet held
four tilting hangers. Will was right. She wouldn't be back.

While Will brought the skiff around from the quarry to the boat
shed, they sat on the stone stoop and waited.

"I don't have a black dress," Emily said. "I hope this gray one is all right."

"It's fine," Hannah said. "Emily, you can come back. I mean, after the baby comes. We could find some way to get along."

"I don't think this island is big enough for both of us, not to mention three of us."

"It's supported families for centuries."

"Hannah, why didn't you ever draw me or ask to paint me?"

"I'm not doing that anymore."

"Before."

"I don't know. You look like me. I've been painting me and you for half a lifetime."

"It's vain, I know. But I always hoped you'd ask me to sit still, that you'd look at me for a long time, just me. The way you did Mr. Eaton and Will and Zee."

"I'm sorry," Hannah said.

"And now you're through with all that." Hannah didn't respond. "I know they all complained, but you made them feel special, made me feel jealous. It's the way you love somebody, Hannah, painting them."

"How do you love somebody, Emily?" Hannah asked.

The sound of Will's motor followed him around the point.

"I don't know," Emily told her. She pushed herself off the flat stone. Then she posed her answer as a question, "Maybe by leaving them?"

After the funeral, she and Will took Emily to Tom's house. He put her in his father's bedroom, where she slept through the reception. Before Tom would let Hannah leave, he brought her into the kitchen and showed her the blackened ceiling over the stove.

"You said you could help Will with the traps. I may stay here this week. Zee has her job. Someone needs to be here to take Emily to the hospital when the baby comes. She wants it to be me. I know it doesn't make sense. I should work the boat and you should live here with her, take her in."

"It's all right. She should have who she wants with her. Besides, you've got experience with this. Why did you show me the soot on the ceiling?"

"Oh," he said, "this is where Dad burned the bacon. I wanted you to see it before I painted over it."

"Why?"

"Because you loved him. Because I feel guilty about covering it up somehow. I didn't want to hide it from you."

"This was when you decided to put him in the home."

"Yeah."

"You loved him, too."

"Yeah."

"You'll call me when you go to the hospital?"

"Yeah." He reached up and ran his hook across the low ceiling, leaving a thin white trail through the soot.

*   *   *

Her foot broke loose from the granite as if it had been embedded there. Her shoe felt so heavy she worried she'd step through the thin cedar strakes of the skiff. For the first time in years, she was leaving the island unoccupied at regular intervals. She thought it was because she wouldn't permit Will to work alone on the water. But finally, taking his hand as she stepped down into the boat softly, she understood that she had to go to sea because she'd forgotten how to be alone. Emily was living with Tom now. Mr. Eaton was gone. Zee worked all day. If she didn't cover for Tom, Will would leave her on the island by herself. Driftwood seemed to feel the same way. When Will pushed the skiff off the ledge, the dog leaped over three feet of water, skidded across the center thwart, and fell over the far gunwale and into the water. He circled twice in the cold water before Hannah had him by the collar and dragged him back aboard.

"I'll row back in," Will said.

"No, let him come along. He doesn't want to be left behind," Hannah said.

"He's too old to go, Hannah. He'll fall off the boat. We can't watch him all day."

"Yes, we can."

"This is work," he said. "Not a picnic. We've got a hundred and fifty traps to haul today."

"Listen," she said, "I know you've been doing this for a whole six weeks, but it's my boat and I'm captain. You're still a sternman. You barely outrank Driftwood in my book."

"Why are you captain? You don't even know where the traps are," he yelled. "I don't know why you wouldn't let me get one of my friends to help out."

"You little shit," she yelled back. "I was pulling traps from this boat when you were what? Six years old."

"And your first decision as captain is to take along a dog that can hardly stand up and can't control his asshole?"

"Yes, it is," she screamed back. "What of it? I'll get one of your friends to help, and you can sit and wait on the island. How would that be?"

"That would stink," he said. They'd drifted out to *Sweet Hannah* during the argument. Will picked up the dog and lifted him over the washboards, dropped him to the afterdeck.

As Will tied the skiff to the mooring, Hannah started the engine. As he climbed aboard, she told him to cast off the mooring.

"I thought I'd steer," he said.

"You thought you'd steer and I'd haul traps? You thought wrong," Hannah said.

"But you don't know where we've laid the strings," he cried.

"Aren't you going to tell me where they are? Did you seriously think I'd fight the traps while you stood at the wheel watching?"

"I could've done it by myself," he said, and crawled up on deck to throw off the line.

"It takes more than six weeks to get your own boat," she yelled after him. Where had she heard the disdain in her voice before? She'd heard it out of Arno Weed, talking about all the sternmen he'd taken on. Little shit, she thought. Walking around in a bib and a gimme hat that smells like bait, thinking he's king of the world. Little lobster shit.

He returned along the port side of the pilothouse and jumped down on the platform next to the bait barrel. He pulled on a pair of blue rubber gloves and began stuffing herring into mesh bait bags. The dog put his front paws up on the barrel and sniffed.

"Get down," Will said.

"Now," she said, turning the wheel hard over, "doesn't it feel good to have somebody you can give orders to?"

She guided the boat out of the quarry, and Will said, "Off Colby Pup," without looking up.

Things didn't go well at first. She missed the first buoy and had to go round again. The throttle seemed obstinate in the lower range and so she kept having to bump it forward with the heel of her palm. Then she'd get beyond fifteen hundred RPM and the boat kept leaping and ploughing in, the throttle delicate as a mercury switch. When Will had two traps aboard, she found it hard to leave the wheel. The boat seemed like it wanted to broach. When she got to the second trap before Will finished with the first, she wasn't as good a judge of shorts as she once was. She threw a keeper back into the sea. Will's voice broke in despair.

"It's all right," she said. "We'll catch it again."

He handed her the brass gauge. "Use it," he told her.

The bait stunk, her lower back ached and her hair kept blowing into her mouth. It tasted of dead herring.

"We're too slow," Will said. "We've got to speed up between strings. We're not going to get done."

She looked forward but pulled the throttle back, as if it were the faucet handle on her kitchen sink and she was turning the water on full. The boat surged into reverse. She and Will and the dog all fell flat on the platform, the warp jerking underneath their bodies while they tried to climb out of the line before being pulled off the stern. Finally, she managed to slap the throttle, and the boat stopped trying to back down to the sea floor.

"Jesus!" Will called out when he regained his feet. "What was that?"

The boat waddled in a deep trough over a submerged ledge.

"I forgot where I was," Hannah explained.

He looked at her, rubbed his forearm, said, "I did that a couple weeks ago."

"You did?"

"I almost threw Tom overboard."

"Maybe, if it takes us a couple extra hours, that's OK," she offered.

"Yeah," Will said. "We're still getting the lobsters."

"It's better than me being alone on the island and you being alone out here."

"Of course, it is," he said. "Are you OK?"

"I was really expecting to go forward. I think I about pulled my thumb out of my hand when we didn't."

"I can get us to the next string while you nurse it."

"OK," she said, and stood behind him while he steered out into the bay. But the string couldn't be found. They crossed and recrossed the area, looking for either of the two buoys that marked the end of the string.

"It's gone," Will said. "That's another one."

"Another one?"

"Yeah, we didn't want you to worry. We've lost twelve traps now. Somebody's cutting the buoys."

"Still? I thought Tom handled that?"

"He thought so, too, but we've been extending our reach. We've been going back into grounds Mr. Eaton stopped fishing long before he retired."

"Maybe the other lobstermen will treat Tom better, now that his dad has died," Hannah said.

"I think they're mad at the boat and Tom for returning for their share long after everyone thought they were gone. Tom calls it the Prodigal Son Hate. Maybe they're mad at me, too, somebody from away taking a sternman's job."

"Will, you and Tom, you just fish when you're out here, right? You don't do anything else?"

He looked over his shoulder at her, leaving one hand on the wheel and one on the throttle. "What else is there to do out here but fish?"

"You don't come alongside other boats for a talk, or to exchange gifts?"

He throttled down, came alongside one of their buoys. "Exchange gifts? What are you talking about?" he asked. "Most of these guys barely have time to wave, much less gossip. They've got the radio for that." He frowned and his voice rose, "Exchange gifts?"

"Never mind," she said. Will led the warp around the davit block and dropped it down into the plates of the pot hauler. Water fanned out in an arc off the pulley. Hannah could see a faint rainbow in the mist.

"What, did they give you things when you were lobstering for Mr. Weed?" he asked.

"No, they ignored me completely. According to Arno, we'll have to die here before the locals will believe we're here to stay."

"I guess that would be proof," Will said. The first trap in the string broke the surface. Will reached out and brought the trap down on the washboard. "They're all shorts," he told her. She began chunking them back in the sea. "I don't know why we don't leave them in the trap with a fresh bag of bait. We're just farming." Seagulls descended on the discarded bait.

"What have you gotten Zee for her birthday?" she asked him.

"I ordered an assortment of egg tempera paints from that Blick catalog. They should get here pretty soon."

"Why is she working with egg tempera? Those paints are expensive. She's not that far along."

"How would you know? She says you haven't worked with her in more than a month. She's really good."

"I'm taking a break," she said.

"From teaching, too? I think maybe you're jealous of her."

"I'm not jealous of her, Will." But as soon as she said this she knew it wasn't true. Zee had her whole life as an artist before her, all possibilities open. She wouldn't spend the first fifteen years of her career working for a phantom. Her value could be tested on the open market. Favor would be granted on the basis of hard work and talent alone. How lucky she was. So Hannah corrected herself. "I am jealous. Not so much for her abilities as they are now, but for what she'll become. I'm jealous that she gets to go there with you."

The second trap brought a curtain of weed up with it. When they pulled it off they saw the trap had already been emptied. There was a jelly jar inside. The note in the jar read, 'You're trespassing. These are Sonny's grounds. Take the baby girl and leave again. That ought to be enough.'"

Will and Hannah both looked up, scanned the horizon for other boats. None were close by.

"What does that mean?" Will asked.

"I was going to ask you," she said.

"I guess Tom will know," he said. "That ought to be enough what?" he asked her.

"Enough warning?"

"What baby girl? Emily hasn't had her baby yet."

"I don't know, Will."

"Maybe this note's in the wrong trap."

"I wish Mr. Eaton were still here," she said.

"What do we do now?"

"We finish hauling our traps. Tom's not trespassing today. This is Arno Weed's boat. He used to fish here. I'm his niece. I've got rights, too. I've got to make a living somehow."

"Do you want to move this string?"

"No, let her fall off right back in the same spot."

🐢 🐢 🐢

She called Tom that evening. "We caught a jelly jar in a trap off Fog Island today."

"A jelly jar?"

"There was a note inside." She read it to him and waited. He didn't respond. "What do you think?"

"I don't know."

"Will said two more traps have gone missing. The pair south of McGlathery. Do you think it's those same guys you talked to before?"

"No," he said. "We came to an understanding. Once they learned who my dad was they backed off."

"Then who?"

"I can't be sure. It could be any one of a hundred boats."

"Who is 'Sonny'?"

"My friend, the young lobsterman who went missing. The one you and Arno helped search for."

"Oh, Jesus, Tom. They're not after you. They're after the boat, after me."

"No," he said, "it's me."

"But why?"

"I'd like to tell you about it." But he didn't.

"So?"

"I have to clear it with someone else first. I'll take care of this, Hannah. I promise. It's just a territory war. We'll lose a few traps. They're just testing us. My dad's dead. They think maybe I'll leave."

"Tom, sometimes boats get blown up in these territory wars. People get shot."

"Hannah, the whole fleet isn't out to get me. I've got friends out there. This is one or two guys. They'd rather fret about me working hard than work hard themselves."

"I'm not worried about the boat. I'm worried about you and Will. Maybe it's not safe for Will to be out on the boat with you."

Will was sitting at the kitchen table, listening to their conversation. At this he stood up and frowned at her.

"These sort are skulkers, Hannah. When they see I'm not leaving, they'll get tired of harassing us. I'll wear them down. But it's your boat."

"He's all I've got," she said.

Will frowned again.

"OK," Tom said.

"We're going to take a gun with us the rest of the week," she said suddenly.

"That's not necessary, Hannah."

"There's still a rack up forward, where Arno carried it."

"For Christ's sake, don't shoot a hole in the boat," he said.

"How's Emily?"

"She's fine. She thinks maybe the baby will be born on Zee's birthday. I don't have to tell you that doesn't thrill Zee. I haven't spanked her in ten years, but I think it's coming time again. She absolutely refuses to get along with Emily."

"I'm sure it's not all Zee's fault," Hannah said.

"Territory war," Tom sighed.

"And you're willing to wait the struggle out?" she asked.

"I'm stubborn as a compass," he admitted.

🐦 🐦 🐦

She wouldn't let Will touch the gun. She locked it into the rack with a bungee cord. Arno had built the rack so the barrel of the rifle pointed forward. If it went off, it would fire through the upper deck. This was important. He'd always kept the gun loaded, he'd told her. It was useless otherwise. Besides, she couldn't dislodge the old oxidized shell from the breach.

"We'll only have the one shot," Will told her. "That box of extra shells won't do us any good. The gun won't be able to kick the frozen cartridge out of the barrel once we've fired. Let me bring my father's gun."

"No," she said. "If the Coast Guard ever inspects us, they could trace that gun to your dad and then he'd know where we are."

🐦 🐦 🐦

The baby was born two days before Zee's birthday. Will and Hannah were at sea. Tom called Zee from the hospital and Zee radioed Hannah. They arrived at the hospital in Blue Hill an hour after the birth. Tom was in the waiting room.

"Well?" Hannah asked, still winded, still feeling as if she'd just jumped off the boat onto an unstable float.

Tom smiled. "Six pounds, six ounces. They're both fine. They're taking Emily back to her room. The baby is in the ward down the hall. They're giving her a bath. Emily said she smelled bad."

"What?"

"She told the nurses to wash her again. She thinks she smells bad."

"Does she? Have you been able to hold her yet?" Hannah asked.

"Smelled fine to me."

"Did she decide on a name?"

"Not yet."

"What's the baby look like?" Will asked. "I mean, does she look like Emily?"

"Looks like a baby to me, Will."

Zee yelled at them from down the corridor. "She's in the window, you guys."

Hannah peered through her own reflection down into the Plexiglas crib. The baby was tightly bundled and wore a white stretch cap. The bridge of her nose and lower brow were bruised.

"She's so tiny," Zee said.

"The doctor said the bruising will go away. It was just a tight fit," Tom explained.

Her hair was dark like Will's. She had the smallest cleft in her chin, so small it barely cast a shadow. Hannah had the thought she'd be impossible to draw. She was too round, too delicate, too beautiful.

"The bruise makes her look like she's scowling," Will said.

Hannah didn't know if Zee and Tom knew the little girl was Will's sister. She and Will promised Emily this was her secret to keep or reveal. So she didn't say the baby looked like Will, though she seemed a mirror image. She waited to see if anyone else saw it. Zee picked up Will's hand and squeezed it, smiled at him. Will didn't look at her, but continued to stare at the baby.

"How do you protect something like that?" he asked without turning to them. "The world's too dangerous."

"Look," Zee said, "she's opening her eyes."

Everyone leaned forward, put their brows to the glass.

"Look at that," Tom said. "Black as coal. She's a heartbreaker. What do you think, Aunt?"

Oh, she thought. That's me. "She's gorgeous," Hannah said. "Her eyes are as dark as the quarry at night."

"It's impossible to name something that's so pretty," Tom said.

"Hmph," Zee said. "You named me."

"No, your mom did that, if you'll remember. I've always thought you were too beautiful to name."

"Fit of jealousy narrowly avoided," Zee said.

A nurse told them Emily was back in her room and could receive visitors, but by the time they got to her door another nurse was placing a No Visitors placard outside the door.

"I'm her sister," Hannah said. "Can I go in?"

"Perhaps later. She's resting and doesn't want to be disturbed."

"When can we see her?" Hannah asked.

"Let's give her a few hours. We'll bring the baby back down in a few minutes so they can have some time together."

"But she's OK?" Hannah asked.

"Yes, just tired."

They sat in the waiting room, watched the baby go by on a cart. At six, they left the hospital and had a celebratory dinner at the Subway inside the local market. Finally, at eight-thirty that evening, a half-hour before the ward would close for the evening, Hannah was allowed to see her sister. The baby had gone back to the pediatric station.

"Little chip off the old block, isn't she?" Emily said.

"Maybe you could think that she looks like Will instead of her father."

She lay propped up in the bed, watching TV. "It's nice to watch TV without a generator in the background."

"Have you gotten to feed her yet?" Hannah asked.

She didn't look at Hannah. She looked at the television. "I fed her with a bottle. I'm not working yet." She laid her forearm across her breasts.

"What did the doctor say?"

"That sometimes it comes late. I feel tender anyway. It's just as well."

"Can you see Will and Zee tonight?"

"I'll see them later. I'm too tired."

"The nurse said you might be released tomorrow evening."

"Yeah. You know I can't go back out to the island, right? It wouldn't be good for the baby. I'm going to stay with Tom. He takes good care of me."

"Of course," Hannah said. "I can visit you and the baby there, can't I?"

"Sure. If you need to."

"I want to."

🕸 🕸 🕸

The next evening, Zee showed up at the island. It surprised Hannah because she thought she'd be with Will, who was helping a friend repair a boat shed on Little Deer Isle.

"I'm tired of listening to guys talk about boats, you know?" Zee said.

They sat on a ledge in the quarry, the sun settling uneasily onto the pointed tips of spruce trees above them.

"And I couldn't go back to the house because Emily's moving back in tonight. Daddy's putting them in my room."

"That doesn't seem fair," Hannah said.

"She said the sun comes in Grandpa's room too early in the morning. I got so mad I told him I was going to move out here with you and Will. That didn't go over. He said I was only going to be home for another month and it wouldn't kill me to sleep on the futon in the living room or in Grandpa's room. Jesus, tomorrow's my frickin' birthday and I don't want to live in my own house. I know she's your sister and I'm sorry, but it's like every time she opens her mouth I want to whale on her."

"She's not staying in your dad's room?"

Zee shook her head. "No, she's too much of a control freak to do that yet. She just soaks up all the concern Daddy has and he doesn't get anything back. He promised me he'd never let this kind of thing happen again."

"What do you mean?"

"He used to let Mom come home, time after time. I'm her daughter and I could see it was hopeless. It's like he's one of my dumb girlfriends at school, mooning over some guy who, it's so obvious, doesn't give a shit. What did you do to your arm?"

"I cut it on a trap," Hannah said.

"Will says y'all are catching up."

"Yeah, but it's killing me. I haven't hauled in twelve years and it's different now. My hands just ache. I don't remember my hands hurting so. I told him I needed a couple days off. You said, 'y'all.'"

"I did not."

"Yes, you did."

"Will you come in to my birthday party tomorrow?"

"I don't think so, but I've got your present at the house. Do you want it now?"

"Of course."

They pushed themselves off the granite and climbed out of the quarry. The wind and the dog met them at the rim. Mr. Eaton's chair had been blown over and they made a detour to the garden to right it.

"I can't wait to get to school," Zee said. "I don't think I'll miss Grandpa as much there. I hope they work me like a dog."

"It'll be up to you, how hard you work," Hannah said. "There'll be all sorts of distractions, people I mean. I don't want to tell you not to work hard, but you should have some fun, too. I know you'll do well."

"How do you know?"

"Because you already work hard. You worry about everything. I can see it in your face, that little knot between your eyes."

"I don't mind work. I don't mind studying. I'm not a natural at anything, so I don't mind worrying. I hope I don't drive off all my teachers, the way I drove you off."

Hannah opened the door and they stepped inside. On the kitchen table, wrapped in torn trap netting, old bait bags, and a pink bow, was Hannah's backpack easel. Hannah said, "I thought about ordering you a new one, but then I thought this one might make it easier to paint, what with paint already all over it. When it was new, with all that nice mahogany and gleaming brass, I didn't want to get paint near it. But now it's broken in."

"I thought you stopped teaching me because you thought I wasn't any good," Zee said softly.

"No, I stopped teaching you because *I'm* not any good."

"I can't take your easel. You use it around the island."

"I want you to have it. There's paint and brushes inside, too."

"Why won't you tell us why you've stopped working?"

"Because it's embarrassing. Because I'm ashamed. Why does anyone keep secrets?" she asked. "It's just obvious that it's time to stop. I'm glad that you're picking up the brushes, so to speak. And it's not just that I'm disappointed in myself because I had too much pride. You're going to be disappointed in me, too, because I have a promise to break. The money won't be coming in the way it used to, since I'm not working. I can still help with your tuition this year, but probably not after. You might have to switch schools next year."

"Go to a different school than Will? Is that what you want?" Zee asked. "You're breaking us up?"

"Of course not. I'm helping you go to school with him, remember? The money just won't be there next year."

"But you promised."

"I know."

"You shouldn't have done that. I thought at least that much of my life was in order."

"I'm sorry, Zee. I'm going to try to come up with the money, but I wanted you to be prepared if I can't."

"How are you going to come up with the money if you aren't willing to work?"

"I don't know."

"Why won't you just work?"

"It's none of your business."

"You know why Emily accepts so much pity? Because somehow she thinks she deserves it. She's full of pride. And people don't keep secrets because they're ashamed. They keep them because they're too proud."

"Look," Hannah sighed, "I'm going to try to sell the island. Emily's gone, Mr. Eaton's gone, you and Will are leaving."

"Sell the island? Are you some kind of idiot? If you aren't an artist anymore, this island is all you've got. I'm not eighteen yet and even I can see that."

The dog moved uneasily between them, curling around the chairs and their bodies. Hannah didn't answer. Every bit of her story that she released made her more fatigued. Nothing she suggested anymore seemed to be heralded or even accepted. Even Driftwood seemed to feel sorry for her.

"So where are we?" she asked the girl.

Zee stamped her foot. "Think of something else," she ordered. "If you sell the island, I won't take the money." She took a pocketknife from her jeans and cut through the netting around the easel, then yanked one of the straps over her shoulder. "If you're abandoning ship before there's a hole in the boat, I'm taking this." She put her arm through the second strap and pulled the easel onto her back. Hannah thought it a curious life preserver.

In self-defense, Hannah blurted, "You've never lost anything."

Zee stopped at the door and turned back to her. "What?" She took two steps back toward Hannah. Her thumbs were already hooked under the shoulder straps, easing the load. "What did you say?"

"You don't know what it is, to lose your way of life," Hannah said.

Zee paused, then shifted the weight, brought it higher on her back. "I lost my mom," she said. "It seemed like a way of life." She turned and left.

❧ ❧ ❧

She didn't go to Zee's party, and Will spent the night in town. It was warm, and so she left the window open when she went to bed. The dog hadn't followed her into the room but slept on the rag rug in the hallway in case Will should come home. The wind through the window lifted the pages of a book on the dresser as if it were tired of reading. She'd slept late that morning, and had a long nap in the afternoon, so she lay there listening to the wind and the water work at the island. She heard Mr. Eaton's steel chair tump in the wind and fall into the grass, and heard the shells on the foreshore capitulate under a heavier wave. She could sense swells rolling in from the deep ocean and parting among the islands, the archipelago like chunks of meat thrown down to momentarily interrupt the charge of dogs on the mainland. The planet was warming, the ocean rising. So giving up the island now was only a prelude to its entire loss anyway. Before long no one could have it. It would simply be more water. And what if it weren't so, what if the water was falling, the ice forming again: before long the island would be only more mainland, as valueless and unsafe as a continent. She did not think of a place to go, but only of being gone. Here, she'd been Arno's cormorant, catching fish she'd never get to swallow. I can leave here, she thought, and save myself the way Will and Emily did by leaving home. She couldn't be Tom, who was as patient as an empty bucket. It didn't seem possible to return to art with a handicap, to go back in the water when you'd almost drowned there. The waves ceaselessly chided the sand, and the wind never seemed to lose its way. What Arno said once over a crossword puzzle, "A three-letter word defining eternity? Ah: NOW."

🐚 🐚 🐚

She was still awake early that morning when she heard the skiff enter the quarry. The morning had gone still. She could hear the skiff's motor choke off and heard the wake the hull made as it coasted alongside *Sweet Hannah,* and heard Tom and Will board the boat. The diesel came to life like something weary pushing over a heavy stone. She heard voices, amplified by the trumpet of the quarry, squelched by the boat's wake and exhaust. Will and Tom were finally fishing together again. So she was surprised when Driftwood rolled out of sleep and barked at the door, when she heard someone knock. It wasn't 5:00 a.m. yet, the sun still beneath the second-story window. She pulled the thin sheet she'd lain under all night around her as a housecoat and went downstairs. She looked out the kitchen window before opening the door. It was Tom.

"Will's out alone?" she asked.

He stepped inside. "No, Zee's with him. They're going to haul a few strings and then come back for me."

"What is it? Is the baby all right?"

"Yeah, sure. Everybody's fine," he said.

She wrapped herself tighter in the sheet. "Do you want to put some clothes on?" he asked.

"Are we going somewhere?" she asked.

"No, I just thought . . . I'm going to sit down at the kitchen table. Is that all right?"

She followed him there and sat down. "What?"

"We had a surprise visitor yesterday evening."

"Who?"

"That same banker who came to see you when the whale was here."

"He didn't call me. Does he want to come out to the island?"

"No, he was there to see us. He showed up about an hour after Zee's birthday party. She wasn't at home and the guy sat on my couch for over an hour till she and Will got back. You didn't tell us when he was here that first time that he took your livelihood with him when he left. I mean, about Arno not buying your work anymore. He was surprised to find out we knew you, that Will and Zee were dating. I told him it's a small village. You could have told us. Zee feels awful. She said she yelled at you when you told her you couldn't pay her tuition."

"I don't understand," Hannah said. "Why should he come here to tell you this? It's none of your business."

"Well, he didn't tell us your side of it. We figured most of it out. Like I said, he was surprised we were friends."

"Then why was he here?"

Tom brought both hooks from his lap and laid them on the table. He sighed. "I've known all along that it wasn't right to keep things from you, but I didn't know it was wrong. I think I was coming to it by and by, but now there's no time left. It's here. I haven't told you things because I thought you'd treat Zee and me differently. You'd have suspected us, our intentions. Maybe you would have thought you owed us something. You don't. We never thought that. We don't know what happened out there. Zee only knows her father died fishing. That's all I know. Only the sea knows more. This banker, Mr. Whatley, was here to give Zee a bequest on her eighteenth birthday from Arno Weed. It's the same money he bought your art with. It was just as much of a surprise to us as it was to you. Arno left her over $400,000. Now she's full of questions."

"Who are you?" Hannah asked softly.

"I adopted Zee, married her mom. We looked alike, Sonny and I. We were good friends. I told you. He had no family. Sonny's parents were gone before Zee was born. He had no brothers and sisters. Zee doesn't tell people she's adopted. She hadn't even told Will. She's only known me as her dad. Lots of people in town know who she is, of course. She doesn't know about the drugs her dad used, or any connection between him and Arno, so she doesn't understand this bequest. She wants to talk to you but I wanted to tell you about this first. I was going to come to it on my own by and by, but it's caught up with me."

"She's not your daughter?"

"She'll argue with you about that."

"But you said you met her mom at Haystack."

"I did, when we were young, and then she married Sonny. When he died, I took over. I took them both back to Jonesport, where she was from, to get them away from here. When Zee's mom and I divorced, Zee and I came back home."

"Why didn't you tell me?"

"Zee doesn't want me to tell people she's adopted. She isn't worried about herself. She's worried about me. She wants me to know she's mine. I'm sorry about all this."

"*Sweet Paula,*" Hannah said.

"Yeah, Sonny named his boat after Zee. Her middle name's Paulette. Danny Haskell has Sonny's boat now. She's *The Green Goose*. He may be part of my fishing problem. There were several guys that were friends of Sonny's, who were also in love with Zee's mom. Old hurts all the way around."

"When were you going to tell me?" she asked.

"When your sister came. You know, when I was interested in you. Emily sort of sidetracked me. I remember you, Hannah. I was on the commercial pier one day and you walked right past me with your suitcase like I wasn't there. I didn't reach out and grab you because you were leaving, like all the summer people here leave. I had hands then, too. I didn't know we'd meet again, on the other end of this. I was just waiting for you to get off Arno's boat so I could go down and buy from him. I was standing there with Sonny. You were this beautiful girl and all we were thinking of was the drugs."

She looked up from her fists that clinched the gathered sheet at her breasts. "I need to get dressed now," she told him.

"Is it all right if Zee comes to see you?"

"No," she said.

"You're right," he said. "I'll tell her what she needs to know. We weren't after this money, Hannah. We didn't even know it existed. She feels awful. We don't want you to sell the island."

"You should leave now." The pity in his voice was rising up in her own throat. When he left, she dropped the sheet and bent over the kitchen sink and vomited a waking night of bile.

🐚 🐚 🐚

She was confused. Was it safer to stay on the island or to leave? Safer to rework and shore up her warning sculptures or abandon them? There seemed to be overwhelming odds for failure. The island was too small to defend and the world too large to hide in. There must be someplace where the wind didn't worry the water so, where waves weren't cease-lessly lapping the land. But where else could Arno Weed's niece blend in as well as she did in Arno Weed's house? The idea was to be invisible, unnoticed, to live in sleep.

Will woke her that afternoon.

"Hey," he said, "Wake up. It's three o'clock. Why are you still asleep?" He brought her a T-shirt and a pair of jeans, draped them over her sheet-clad legs. He opened her top dresser drawer and took out a clean pair of socks, pitched them at her. "Do you want some coffee or a Coke or something?"

"No," she answered.

"Why are you still in bed? You sleep too much."

"I'm tired. I helped you fish for the last week. I haven't done that kind of work in a while."

"You look like Emily used to," he said.

"She's my sister. I'm supposed to look like her."

"I'll go downstairs while you put on your clothes."

She let him go. Then she didn't. "Hey, come back here! What right have you got to be mad at me?" she yelled.

He returned and stood in the doorway. "I'm not mad at you. I'm mad at them."

This took a moment to sink in. "What? Who?"

"My parents, your parents, Zee's parents, everybody in the past. Zee spent the day on the boat with us. She's mad at everybody, too, especially Tom."

"But why? It was my uncle who killed her father. He was the drug dealer."

"Tom told her that they were friends. That they used together, that he never once tried to get him to stop. And he told her that he loved her mom long before her dad died. He said your uncle was just an old man that everybody trusted. Before him the drug business was always dangerous, people getting beat up and houses burned. He told Zee it was Sonny's own fault he died, unless some of the fault was his, Tom's. How did he let his best friend go out in a working boat while he was high? He'd never let me do that, and Zee knows it. All this cut-trap business stems from it, too. He kept telling me he didn't know why we were losing traps or who was after us. And so now they've got all your money, and Zee said you're thinking about selling the island."

"It's not my money, Will. It was Arno's and he wanted Zee to have it. He wanted a little three-year-old girl without a father to have it."

"And that's another thing: I've been with her for months now and she never tells me she's adopted? What's that? Isn't that kind of secret supposed to be ours and not just hers? It's like she didn't trust me, like neither of them trusted us."

"You didn't say any of this to them, I hope?"

"No, I didn't say anything all day. It was too much. They were locked up with each other. We were out there and Zee hadn't said anything for a while and then she asked Tom, 'Where?' 'Where what?' he said. 'Where did my father die?' And he turned around in the middle of the ocean and took us . . ."

"Off Grumpy Ledge."

"Yeah," Will said.

"I was there, too, on Arno's boat, helping search for the body."

"He took her to the spot where the boat, *Sweet Paula*, was found circling. We stopped there and Tom shut down the engine. We sat there awhile and then Zee asked her dad, 'How long after the empty boat was found did you start thinking about Mom?' He told her, 'Right away. Even before the searching was over.' Nobody said another word the rest of the day. It just creeps me out that we fish in that spot every day. They never found his body, Hannah."

"I know," she said.

"You're not going to sell the island, are you?"

"I don't know," she said.

"Please, don't. Zee has all the money she needs now for school."

"I just have enough savings to last a couple years. The taxes are high, Will. Maybe I should start again somewhere else, like you and Emily. I need to learn a trade."

"You have a trade. You're an artist."

"I thought so, too, but not one, apparently, that can make a living without her relatives buying her work."

"But your work maybe never had a chance because your uncle bought it all up. That bank guy told me to tell you they've found a couple more of your pieces they'd overlooked. He's going to ship them to you."

She sighed. Everything came back to you, no matter how old or how far away. Nothing could be buried without time and the wind eventually uncovering it. She finally looked up at him and said, "Don't be mad at anybody, Will. You've got your secrets, too. Does Zee or Tom know that the baby is your little sister?"

"I don't think so," he said. "But that's Emily's secret, not mine."

"Yeah, but you see how people get caught up in other stories."

"We're like porpoises in a tuna trawl," he said.

"No," she answered. "We're like tuna in a tuna trawl."

"Why can't you be an artist again, Hannah?"

"There's no point in catching lobster if no one wants to buy them."

"You and I could fish, Hannah. It's your boat."

"You're going to school."

"But I could stay. I could stay here and fish with you."

🐚 🐚 🐚

It was a relief to get Will out of the house each morning, to be beyond the question, "What are you going to do today?" She tried answering truthfully: I don't know. But he didn't want to accept that answer and so she'd lie and say she planned to work in the garden or gather driftwood or pile rocks against erosion. But just as the garden started to produce, she'd given it up and let the island take the soil back. She let the cucumbers and zucchini and okra grow too large, and tomatoes hung on the vine till they split. Gray limbs and boards piled up in the quarry and on the beaches. There seemed little reason to cut and stack it against the winter, when the boat shed was full of packing crates. Her only exercise came from disemboweling her sculptures, debarking the stones, and then scattering them on the foreshore. She often carried a large rock halfway around the island, stumbling over other stones along the way, to find the place she'd originally stolen it from.

She felt the island was on a regular patrol, that instead of living or even hiding there, she was imprisoned. It was August, and every lobster boat was in the water and they circled Ten Acre No Nine continually, on constant guard. Yachts and kayaks produced a constant constraining wake that ceaselessly hemmed the beach. When she found kayakers in the quarry or a family picnicking on her shore, she turned away rather than run them off. She felt like the last missing bird on every watcher's list. She wondered how she'd made the guidebooks so quickly. There must be signs posted on every buoy from Eastport to Kittery, this way to the island of the failed artist.

She found some comfort in the warmth of the sun, lying bare-chested in the tall grass or in the furrows of the garden with the dog lying beside her. Each skin cell on her stomach seemed to tremble with increased sensitivity. When a single blade of grass tilted in the wind and cast a shadow over her body she could draw it with her eyes closed. She felt the razor-thin shadow scrape across her navel and thump from rib to rib as if it were a boy running a stick along a picket fence. When a bird passed between her chest and the sun, she knew which of its wing feathers was missing. The warm wind moving over her body didn't seem to require inspiration. Her lungs lay dormant. The air inspired under ordinary circumstances was called tidal air, as if breathing were controlled by the moon. Here the sun and wind held sway, the world breathing without so she wouldn't have to exert and support herself. It was so pleasurable, to melt into the island, to be so graciously absorbed.

The dog always woke her when *Sweet Hannah* returned to the quarry. Hannah sat up, buttoned her shirt. While her blurred vision cleared, she brushed the island from her hair. It was plain she'd forgotten how to be alone, and that a small island was no place for someone like her. She was good at being alone once, but now it was only something else she'd lost.

🐝 🐝 🐝

For weeks she received no visitors, nor did she invite them. Will worked with Tom every day. Their catches were improving, especially those in the quarry. There were now a dozen traps placed there. The lobsters funneled into them. It couldn't last, Will told her. The lobsters would soon begin moving off into deeper water. When Hannah asked if they'd lost any more equipment, Will told her no, that things seemed to have settled down. It was only a week now before he would leave for college. Hannah had mail-ordered new school clothes for him from L. L. Bean and Eddie Bauer. His computer had arrived, too. He picked up her mail now and bought their groceries. Zee had given up her delivery job. Hannah hadn't seen her since the day she'd left with her easel on her back.

She wanted to go into town to see the baby, but knew there was no welcome there. Everyone would be uncomfortable. There was too much past between them now. There was too much shame on her side, too much compassion on theirs. Emily had the right to be as remorseless as Hannah had been with her. They'd both lost their religions, and Hannah knew she was bearing her loss no better than Emily had. But overwhelming all was the fact that her uncle had a part in killing Zee's father, and there was no way to undo that, no way to pay for it, even though Arno had tried. No matter how long she lay in the sun, this wouldn't burn from her body. This time Driftwood gave her no warning, other than the thumping of his tail in the grass. She opened her eyes. Zee was standing above her. Hannah pulled her shirt together and sat up.

"Does that feel good?" Zee asked her. "I mean, having your shirt off in the sun?"

"Yes," Hannah said softly.

"I didn't mean to sneak up on you. I checked the house first."

"It's OK."

"Can I sit down, too?"

Hannah nodded, shifted in the grass. The dog sat up and looked to sea. There was a lobster boat not far offshore. It pivoted in the water and as it turned left a small whirlpool behind it, a hole in the ocean.

She looked at Zee, who was beginning to raise the hem of her T-shirt. Zee paused and asked, "Is this OK?"

Hannah nodded. Zee pulled off her shirt and spread it on the ground, then unclasped her bra. The skin of her breasts was translucent, so pale it held and reflected the sky and sea. Her nipples were the same color as her hair, but opaque, Clementines under clear ice. Zee lay down, left her knees raised. Hannah looked to sea again, then lay back down in the grass, too, and opened her shirt.

"Do you have any suntan lotion?" Zee asked.

"No."

"I'm afraid I'll burn pretty quick."

They lay there without looking at each other.

"I don't know what to say," Hannah finally said.

"Yeah, me neither. Do you lie out like this all the time?"

"Whenever I get a chance."

"You look really brown. This is the first time I've ever done this," Zee said. "Is it against the law?"

Hannah giggled. Then she said, "I don't know. Maybe."

"Wouldn't they like to walk up on us now, all of 'em?"

"Who?"

"I don't know. All the fishermen."

"It would scare them to death, couple of mermaids like us."

"It does feel good. They go without their shirts all the time. It's not fair."

"No."

"We're not very far along as a species, are we? I mean, we don't know how to treat each other. I haven't asked anybody else's opinion. I wanted to ask you first, Hannah. Am I supposed to give this money back to you? I feel guilty about accepting it."

Hannah sat up, buttoned her shirt. "I can't talk to you with my tits hanging out. Put your shirt back on."

"OK. I think I'm burnt already."

"Look, it never was my money. I didn't know it existed. It was my uncle Arno's. It was never anything I expected or was counting on."

"But the bank used this money to buy your art."

"Yes, that was Arno's gift to me. He wanted to give me a head start as an artist. He was always trying to give me money I didn't earn when he was alive. He got his way in the end."

"But I didn't earn the money, either."

"I guess he thought he owed it to you. What did your dad tell you about all this?"

"It's taken him weeks to get it all out. He said your uncle sold amphetamines. Some of the fishermen bought them from him so they could work longer hours, stay up all night. He said my biological father may have died because of them. Did you know my dad?"

"No."

"He died when I was three or four. I can remember him a little, but a couple years ago I realized all my memories were associated with photographs in Mom's album. So maybe I don't remember him, only the pictures. I always knew I was adopted. My dad was such a good dad that when I was ten or so I decided to just treat him as my only dad, my always dad, as a gift to him. That's why I never talked to you or Will about it. Do you know that when Will was ten he decided not to believe in Jesus? That's early. We'd both made up our minds. It didn't seem like I was keeping something so important from you both. But it seems important now, doesn't it, like I was spying when I was here on the island."

"I never thought that," Hannah said.

"You weren't part of the drugs, were you?" Zee asked.

"No, I was pretty naïve. He did it right under my nose."

"So my dad was a buyer and your uncle was a seller."

Hannah nodded, not knowing which Dad she was referring to.

"So all three of them were wrong, and it didn't involve us."

"All three of them?"

"Both my dads bought from your uncle."

Hannah couldn't tell if Zee was asking or telling. She said, "I guess it involved us in that your father was trying to make a living, to feed you and your mom. And my uncle was trying to save this island for me."

"I did some research on the pills. The amphetamines, they impair your judgment, and they can be addictive. They can cause euphoria and depression and hypertension. And there's idiosyncratic reactions: aggression and paranoia. Nowhere in the encyclopedia does it say they catch more lobsters or that they drown people. I think it's because they can't do those things. None of it had anything to do with us," Zee said. "You and my dad may never be able to get along. That's OK. But we can."

"I want to," Hannah said.

"Our parents' lives don't have to be ours. We're new, right?"

"Yes," Hannah said, but felt "no" was more truthful, thought the die was cast before they were both born.

"Did you know my father was my father's best friend?"

"Yes."

"That my mom was leaving my dad when he died?"

"No," Hannah said.

"She was leaving him. I didn't know that till three years ago, when she told me she was leaving again like she did with her first husband, and whatever happened wouldn't be her fault, just like it wasn't her fault the first time. So it might not have been the warp around his ankle, or the euphoria or the aggression, but maybe the depression. I asked my dad this week if Mom was leaving my first father for him."

The rims of her eyelids went raw, and tears started.

"What did he say?"

"He said no. But I'll never know, will I?"

"Sure you could know," Hannah said. "This is the place where it all happened. It was only thirteen or fourteen years ago. You could ask people. You could find out if you wanted to. Or you can decide to trust your dad."

"I ask myself what kind of idiot would let himself get snared in warp and jerked off a boat, and I think the same kind who'd let both of his hands get chewed off in a winch."

"Accidents, Zee, accidents."

Zee wiped at her cheeks with her bra. "Cheap-ass bra. It's nylon. Won't even soak up a tear. I'm really sorry I yelled at you about not working."

"It's OK, you didn't know. I didn't tell you."

"Will's treating me like I'm from another planet."

"We've always known he was too good to be true," Hannah said.

"We've been waiting all year on Will's dad and instead mine turns up."

"Yeah."

"I don't know what to do with all this money, Hannah. I wanted to buy Daddy a boat but he won't let me."

"Use it for school."

"But what will you do?"

"I'm OK. I have some savings."

"I know your uncle bought your work, but you're still an artist. It's OK to be an unpaid artist. Most of them are. I am. Join our ranks. You could still work."

🐚 🐚 🐚

They sat in the quarry on the last Saturday of August, with Will's suit-cases and computer stacked around them. Zee was on her way in her skiff to pick him up.

"How long is the drive?" Hannah asked.

"I think about three hours, depending on the traffic," Will said. "Seems like a long time ago, when she first brought us out here."

"She told you not to look at her butt."

He looked up at her through his black lashes, through the three white ones, and smiled. "I can't believe I never figured out Tom wasn't her dad."

"I just thought she must look like her mom," Hannah said. "Did you see the baby when you were in town yesterday?"

"Yeah. She's growing. Her little fingernails grow about an inch a week."

"Has Emily named her yet?"

"She's still just 'the baby.' I think she likes me."

"All the girls like you, Will."

"No, it's something special. She knows I'd do anything for her. She knows I'm gonna be around for a lifetime. It's between me and her. The same way it's between me and you."

She took his hand and leaned into his shoulder. "I'm going to miss you, sweetie," she said.

"I was going to come back on weekends to help Tom and see you, but he's already taken on another sternman."

"You come home at Thanksgiving. You'll have homework on week-ends. It won't be as easy as high school. I'll look forward to Thanksgiving. It will be good to have it on my calendar."

"You could drive down and see us," he said.

"Oh, you know me. There's the dog to pick up after, the island to protect. Who did Tom take on?"

"Aaron Casey. He graduated with me. He's in love with Zee. I think that's why he took the job."

"But Zee will be at school."

"I know, but I understand. Working with her dad, you're close to her, too. Maybe that's why I never figured out she wasn't his: because they're so much like each other."

"When you see him today, I want you to tell him to start mooring *Break of Day* in Stonington. It's silly for him to come out here when you aren't here."

"You mean *Sweet Hannah*."

"It's always been hard to say."

"It was his suggestion, to change the boat's name. You're going to have to make up with him someday. He's living with your sister."

"I'm not mad. They need to have their life. I'm glad there's water between us. Maybe we all got too close."

"Zee can't wait to go to school, to get out of the house, and I swear Tom feels like she's leaving forever. Like we won't be back at Thanksgiving. Have you thought about what a wild year it's been for him? He's back fishing again, he lost his dad, Zee's moving away, and now he's adopting a second little girl."

"He's adopting Emily's baby?" Hannah asked.

"Yeah. It takes awhile, but he'll be a dad again just as Zee's leaving. What will that make me to him? I wouldn't be his stepson, would I?"

"I think only if you wanted to be."

"That wouldn't be so bad, hunh?"

"No," she said.

"You've let the driftwood pile up in here," he told her.

"It will give me something to do this fall."

The sound of Zee's motor began to echo in the quarry. Will stood, released her hand. "Where's that dog?" he asked. Then he cupped his hands around his mouth and howled. "Driftwood," he yelled, "Driftwood!" The dog appeared at the rim of the quarry, both ears perked. "Come down here. I'm leaving."

The dog took his accustomed long route down, jumping from ledge to ledge, and Will met him from below. He hugged the dog at shoulder level, Driftwood kneeling on a ledge four feet above the one Will stood on. Hannah couldn't help herself. As Zee motored into the quarry, she had to put her hand over her mouth. Will let the dog go, and pitched his bags and boxes down to Zee in the skiff. He turned to Hannah. "What?" he asked.

"Go hug her, you idiot," Zee ordered.

"I was going to," he snapped.

He opened his arms, smiled at her, then dropped them. She walked toward him slowly, still holding her cupped palm over her mouth, and put her chin on his shoulder. She felt his arms around her, but she saw only Zee standing in a blur of ocean. She finally had to take her hand from her mouth to breathe.

"You be good," she said.

"I will, Mom."

She waved them out of the quarry, holding onto the dog's collar. She couldn't tell which of them, her or the dog, was keeping the other from jumping into the sea.

🐢 🐢 🐢

As early as the first week in September, the leaves began to float up on-shore again, oak and maple and birch from the mainland. Among them, undulating yellow from point to eraser, was a pencil. She picked it up and put it in her pocket. It would burn as well as any driftwood. The archipelago seemed to sigh out of the summer and loiter into fall. The yachts had returned south, and kayakers rounded the island as if looking for anything they might have left behind. As she walked around the island with the dog, waiting on winter, she realized there was almost no sound that water could not imitate. Was this memory? Did the ocean record everything and spew it back out indiscriminately, chord and held note, and sewing machine and song, and leaf's fall and dying breath and bell? Or was the water working it all out on its way to complete silence?

The seaward coast of the island was smooth and bare, sloped and spare. The leeward coast was humped and more vertical. The islands had yielded to the sea what they'd had to: so much granite into sand, but they'd held much of themselves in reserve. They'd be islands to the very last wave that washed the last barnacle under, till the tide lost its significance because all was beneath water all the time. An island's life was abrasion, water sanding rock, and time was on water's side. But bird shit was on the island's side, and grass seed and anything that feeds and lives and dies there, taking lunch from the water and sky and leaving it in the crevices of the granite so ice couldn't form there and split the rock further. It occurred to her she shouldn't burn the driftwood any longer, but should let it pile up, reinforcements sent out by the mainland to fend off rogue waves and the winter surf. The island knew what it was doing without her. Away boys away, there's a fair wind at play and we've got to earn our pay. She tried to remind herself she was not alone. Half of us in this world are the lesser loved.

🐢 🐢 🐢

The new delivery boy for Bartlett's Market was the newly retired harbormaster, the same man she'd chewed out a year earlier when he told Tom about Arno's boat. When she tried to tip him after he unloaded her groceries and mail, he held up the flat of his palm and told her, "I'm doing this to get out of the house. I was retired for two months. Like to have killed me. Haven't caught any more whale in here lately, have you?"

"No," she said, "just the one."

"News is you've talked to some of the realtors in town about selling this place. Trying to come up with a price."

"Yes," she said.

"Shame," he said. "Hate to see year-rounders go."

"Hmph," she snorted.

"Well, I know," he said. "Islanders don't associate much because we know you won't stay. We don't know you'll stay until you die here." He smiled a creased smile.

"Was my uncle Arno Weed a pirate or a Robin Hood?" she asked him.

His smile went into his wallet. "I guess it depends on who you talk to."

"I'm talking to you."

"He never took anything from me or gave me anything but a wave. But he knew I was one could look after myself. He was one like that, too. He was a good dancer."

"What?"

"He used to travel all over to dances, up and down the coast. You examine the floor of your place. The wear goes in a circle around that old stove. Years and years ago we'd come out here and dance. High times."

"Really?" she said.

"We never know enough about each other," he said. "See you next week."

❧ ❧ ❧

The following week he dropped off more groceries, a package from the bank, and an envelope he told her was taped to the outside of her post office box. She carried everything back to the house, then opened the box first. Another of her wrapped sculptures, wool and copper wire around an egg-shaped stone. It was dusty, as if it had lived in an attic. She put it aside to unwrap later. The note that had been taped to her box was written in a neat hand.

I'm here in Stonington. I would like your permission to see my son, Will. Can you meet me at the Harbor Cafe tomorrow at noon? I'm sorry but I only had your box number and this is the only way I could think to reach you short of coming to your island unannounced. Your phone number isn't listed. I've been looking for my son for so long. I know your sister sent him here. Please.

She immediately went to the door and locked it. "Permission." "Please." Will said his father would come pleading. It was plain he didn't know Emily was in Stonington. He was after Will. He knew Hannah lived on an island. He must not know where Will was, or he wouldn't bother with her. What would happen if she didn't show up at the cafe? He'd stay in town, perhaps find out about Tom and Emily and the baby. Or he'd get a boat and come to the island. She'd have to deal with him alone, without the protection of witnesses. The house warped in the wind and she turned to each window in rapid succession to see if anyone was looking in. Bowing grass, curling waves, spruce nodding.

She called Tom. Emily answered.

"He's there in town," she said, "with you."

"Who?"

"Will's father. He left a note with my mail. He wants to meet with me tomorrow at noon at the Harbor Cafe. I don't think he knows you're here. The note doesn't say anything about you or the baby. He's here for Will."

"Tom won't be back for another couple of hours. Can't you keep us out of it, Hannah?"

She paused for a moment. "What?"

"For the baby's sake."

"I wouldn't tell him you're here. I wouldn't tell him about the baby. Tom could just be there with me. You've made me afraid of this man."

"You should be afraid. Get the police to help you."

"There are no police in Stonington, Emily. I'd have to get a sheriff to come down from Ellsworth."

"If you get Tom involved, Will's father will eventually find out about me and the baby. The police will find out, too. He'll have rights to the baby."

Hannah hung up on her sister.

🐦 🐦 🐦

She crossed through the Merchant Islands in the skiff, going all the way around Crotch Island and entering Stonington Harbor from the west. Somehow it eased her mind. If Will's father was watching . . . perhaps he didn't know which island was hers. As she tied up at the town float she scanned Hagen Dock above her. A few kids kicking gravel into the harbor, and a couple sitting under the Muir statue. Hannah wore sneakers, jeans, and a sweatshirt. She carried no purse, and had taken everything out of her wallet except her driver's license, the key to her car, and enough cash to buy her own lunch.

She'd thought about leaving, taking a bag and driving to New York. If she were gone for a few weeks, he'd tire of waiting for her and leave. Let him ransack the house and island. She would remove all trace of Will and his whereabouts. But she understood finally this wouldn't work. Will's father would just return, or he'd nose around till he found Emily. If he was diligent, he could simply go through back issues of the local paper. Every high school senior's plans were listed under their picture in an article that came out at graduation. She had this chance to divert him, to tell him Will didn't want to see him, or at least to tell him Will had left and she didn't know where he was. She wanted to see his face anyway, to see how much he looked like Will.

As she walked up the dock and into town, she put her hair in a ponytail with a rubber band. But then decided this would be too easy to grab and let it loose. She was thirty-five years old, for God's sake: it was time to have short hair, hair that couldn't be yanked or torn in a fight.

The summer rush of tourism was over, so the Harbor Cafe wasn't crowded. It occupied half of the lower floor of a Second Empire Victorian on Main Street. A bay window leaned over the street. A woman her age sat in the window. Hannah stepped inside and scanned the booths. She was five minutes early. Two couples occupied booths on the outside wall. Four fishermen sat in the booth behind the stone oven. In one of the large booths across from the cash register, a lone man sat. It was Tom. He'd been there for a while. His food was already before him. When she started to walk toward him, he nodded at one of the empty tables in the center of the restaurant. She sat there, with her back toward him. The waitress brought a menu and pointed out the specials on the board. Hannah ordered water. She waited with her elbows on the table, leaning forward. She looked past the woman in the bay window to the street. A single man came out of the bookstore. He stood on the sidewalk and opened a pack of cigarettes. The woman in the booth leaned forward into her line of vision and Hannah lost sight of the man momentarily. His hair was dark. A child came running up to him. Again the woman in the window was in her line of sight. She was getting up. Hannah stood to look over her shoulder at the man in the street. He walked behind a car and stepped toward the restaurant. The woman was standing near her now, but off to the side. She was carrying her glass to the counter to get it refilled. She was speaking. Hannah turned to her, annoyed.

"I'm sorry?" Hannah said.

"Are you Hannah Bryant?"

"Yes," Hannah said, still looking over the woman's shoulder at the door. The man would be there at any moment.

The woman said, "Thank you for coming. I'm Will's mom."

❦ ❦ ❦

Hannah dropped into her chair. The woman sat across from her. Hannah looked into her face, trying to recognize her. She was too young to be Will's mother. Her hair was mousy, not black. Then she smiled again. Will's smile was in her mouth. She'd painted that smile, those teeth. She knew them. Will said his mother was seventeen when he was born. She was so young.

"Is Will's father with you?" Hannah asked abruptly.

"No, I haven't seen him in more than ten years," the woman said. "I haven't talked to him."

"You're here by yourself?"

"Yes. I've been looking for Will."

"You left him with his father when he was young," Hannah said.

"Yes. Things are better now. I started looking for him when I realized he'd be graduating from high school. Is he still here with you?"

"No," Hannah said. "How did you find me?"

"When I left Will's father I ran to my sister in Victoria. When I found out your sister ran from him, too, I started looking for you. Your sister was Will's teacher. Everybody at that church thinks your sister sent Will away and then joined him. But when I got here yesterday, the first person I talked to said Will lives with you."

"Who was that?"

"A girl who went to school with him. She works at the market."

"You went to Texas, to the church, and you didn't see your husband?"

"He's not my husband anymore. I've been married to another man for four years now. I have two little girls. They said Will's father had been gone all summer. They didn't know where he was. But I pieced together what happened. I talked to the women there and Will's classmates. Is he here? Can I see him?"

"He's not here. He's at college," Hannah said.

The woman leaned back and put the back of her hand to her mouth. Her eyes began to water, and Hannah could hear her breathing through her nose. She started to cry openly, and finally, from behind her hand, said, "He's still smart."

Hannah felt the sockets of her own eyes hardening, aching. She nodded.

"I shouldn't have left, I know it, but I thought he'd kill me. I was so afraid."

"I don't know your name," Hannah said.

"Rachel. I'm Rachel Vent, now."

"I've been so afraid his father would come after him," Hannah said.

"He didn't come after me."

"But you seem to have found me so easily," Hannah said.

"It wasn't easy. It took me a month to find out Emily even had a sister. Then I had to track you down. How is he? Is he . . ." She was crying again.

Hannah turned and looked at Tom. His head was tilted. A knife and fork were suspended in his hooks. He looked back at her as if she were sitting with a movie star. She turned back to Rachel.

"He's fine," Hannah said. "He's about four inches taller than me. He's handsome. He's kind. He loves to fish. He has a girlfriend. He's at Bates College. You could be there before dark. Do you want me to call him and tell him you're coming?"

Rachel stood up as if to leave, and then sat down again. Hannah gave her another paper napkin. "I'm sorry. I'm nervous. Can you show me on the map how to get there? I'll find him."

"Are your little girls with you?" Hannah asked.

"No, they're at home in Victoria with their father."

"I'll show you how to get there," Hannah said.

"He's been living with you this whole year?" she asked.

"Yes," Hannah said. "We're good friends. I mean, he's a good boy."

"Has he ever said anything about me?"

"Only that you left when he was young."

"Thank you for taking care of him," Rachel said. Hannah shook her head slightly. "Things are different with me now. I married a good man. He's a doctor. We have a house on Vancouver Island. I don't know if I need to ask your permission. I'd like to invite Will to come home for Thanksgiving. He likes to fish?"

"Yes," Hannah said. "You don't have to ask me."

"Don't worry," Rachel said. "He may hate me."

🦐 🦐 🦐

After walking Rachel to her car and highlighting the route to Lewiston, Hannah returned to the cafe and Tom's table. When he popped open his hooks, the utensils clattered onto the plate. He looked at her without asking and she said, "Will's mom."

He nodded slowly. "That's sort of a relief. I haven't fought anybody yet without my hands."

"I didn't think you'd be here," she said.

"I'm not, if you get my drift."

"OK." She pushed the condiments from the center of the table to the wall. "It was Will's mom. The note wasn't signed. I just assumed it would be the father."

"It's OK."

"She's married again, to a doctor in Victoria, British Columbia. She has two- and three-year-old girls. I made her show me pictures of them to prove she wasn't lying."

"Why did she come now?" he asked.

"She said it took her ten years to get over the loss of her son, to get brave enough to find him again."

"I've never seen a face at once so full of fear and excitement. Well, good for Will, right?"

"I guess."

"Sure."

"These people from our past, we never seem to be able to escape them. They keep turning up."

"Yeah, but only the ones we weren't finished with."

"Zee said you won't let her buy you a boat."

"No. Some people already think I was overpaid as a result of that accident. Besides, if it's all right with you, I like the boat I'm using now. I was thinking I'd start paying you a monthly rent. I know you don't want to sell her."

She shook her head. "It's good for her to be in the water. That's enough. You have a new sternman?"

"One of Will's friends. He's slow, and he's afraid of these." He lifted his hooks off the table an inch or so and dropped them again.

"I wish it had been Will's father. It just kept building up in me, how much I wanted to fight, to physically hurt someone."

"Didn't you want to fight his mom?"

"Of course not."

"Hard to tell by the clinched fists and the jawline."

"I don't have anything against her."

"Just that you've been his mom for a year and now here she is. She could have come last summer and you wouldn't've had the year. Zee and I would never have met you."

"Let's get to something you know about. How's the baby?"

"Fine. It takes me awhile to change a diaper, but I'm getting the hang of it."

"You change diapers?"

"Of course, I do. I can put a band on a lobster's claw, I can certainly change a diaper."

"I didn't doubt that you could."

"But that I would?"

"That Emily would let you."

"She lets me."

"How is she?"

"Better, I think. She never got her milk. That bothered her. But she's exercising, and she reads a lot. I don't think she's as mad at the world as she used to be. Are you going to call Will and warn him his mom is on the way?"

"No, she asked me not to. She wants to see if he remembers her. She wants to look on him from afar before she approaches him."

"Like our parents do to us now," Tom said.

"Our parents are dead," Hannah said.

"I like to think if I remember them, they're watching over me."

"I know mine left a long time ago."

"Time's nothing to them, for all we know."

"For all we know," she said.

"I have a bone to pick with you and afterwards I won't bring it up again."

"What?"

"You have no right to sell the island," Tom said.

She looked at him as if he'd told her she had no right to breathe, and then something overtook her, as if it were on a faster wind, and she lowered her head, and said, "Of course, Zee should own it. It should be hers."

"No," Tom said, obviously annoyed, looking across the restaurant because he'd said it too loudly. "You have no right to sell it because the first guy who sold it, whoever that was, had no right. And whoever bought from him had no right. If you have anything to pass on, it's something like caretakership. You pass that on when you're too tired to go on, just before they bury you. It's not yours to sell. Arno Weed didn't sell it."

He got up from the table and walked out.

જ઼ જ઼ જ઼

She left the phone on for a week, repeatedly checking the charger and her voice-message system, but Will didn't call. She thought he'd call. In early October, the dog vomited on the couch two days in a row. He'd eat but couldn't seem to hold down his food. When she tried to get him to follow her around the island, he wouldn't go out of sight of the house. On the morning of the third day, when he wouldn't get off the couch, she called the Veterinary Hospital in Deer Isle and made an appointment. He was able to walk up to the quarry rim with repeated encouragement, but finally she had to put him in the basket and lower him down to the skiff with the derrick and winch. She laid him on a blanket in the bottom of the boat and talked to him all the way to Stonington. She felt no need to make complete sentences, only wanted him to hear the sound of her voice. "Cormorant," she said. "Seagulls over St. Helena. Slow Blue Heron on the pocket beach. Pink buoy. Driftwood in the bottom of the boat. Good dog. Mr. Eaton. Arno Weed. My mom, Catherine Elizabeth Bryant. White dinghy. Lobster boat with turquoise trim. Sticks. I love sticks. Is there anything better than a stick? Rocks, too. You can throw rocks, stack them. *Break of Day*. The moon over Stonington. Good dog. Such a good dog. That's the truth of it, dog of mine. So many white birds. A well dog would chase them from the sky."

The vet pushed all four fingers of one hand into Driftwood's abdomen and the dog bared his teeth but did not growl. The nurse drew blood from a foreleg, and they asked Hannah to leave the room while they took X rays. Finally, the vet asked her back to his office.

"How old is Driftwood?" he asked.

"I don't know. He washed up on my island a little more than a year ago."

"Well, we know he's elderly, don't we, looking at his teeth and the gray on his muzzle. I want to keep him overnight before taking any action. Have you noticed if his stools are hard or soft?"

"There hasn't been any stool. He can't keep anything down."

"I think he has a blockage in his lower intestine. It could be a particularly hard stool or something else he's eaten, perhaps a bone. I can feel something very hard there and he's sensitive. It's inflamed. I'll give him a diuretic to try to break it up, then we'll wait on these tests and the X rays, but I think we'll need to go in and see what it is. It could be a lump or cyst, in which case I'll need some direction from you. How far do you want to go?"

"As far as we need to," she said. "I'm afraid I waited too long to bring him in."

"We'll keep him here tonight. Can you call in the morning? I'll be here at 7:30."

"I'll be here at 7:30, too."

"Ms. Bryant, he's an old, old man, even if he comes through this."

"OK," she said.

She lay that night listening to her empty house. Without Driftwood's breathing, his fidgeting foot, she could hear the very nails contracting within the wood. She thought she could hear the glass in the windows ebbing. The clapboards rolled down the exterior walls, lapping like waves. Tom had used the same periwinkle blue on *Sweet Hannah*'s trim as she'd used on the house. This color ran around the gunwale of the skiff, too, and gloved the grips of the oars. She didn't have to row because the dinghy was being towed by *Break of Day* on a long painter, so long that at times it disappeared in the peak of wave between the two boats. *Break of Day* was moving so quickly that Hannah thought she'd be pulled through the back of a wave. But the waves, coming in off her stern, lifted her boat and then she'd skid down the far side, so swiftly that she often overtook the bigger boat, surfing alongside on a taut tether. It was fun. She could hear her own laughter. There were people in *Break of Day* who looked worried. She supposed it was possible, if the waves were just right, to end up in the cockpit of the lobster boat. Birds raced her, seagulls formed up off her oars. As the waves built, the painter popped, flinging off spray. Her boat seemed to leap from wave crest to wave crest, a gravestone skipped. She gripped the oars, but the dinghy was moving too swiftly to dip them in the sea without losing them. At last the ring on the stem gave way and the painter looped forward into darkness and the waves were free with her. A mountainous wave slid beneath and she shot forward, rising. She could see *Break of Day* far below, racing before the big wave. Spindrift trailed off her spread oars and hung there, like cobweb then lace then feather, and she found the oars bore weight like wings, and at the crest of a wave, when there was only foam beneath, she dipped her oars and the boat took flight and she dipped again and the boat banked and glided down the front of the wave, mere inches off the water. There was only the sea and speed and she rowed on the air, banking up and laying out and it didn't seem day or night or dangerous only effortless, as if she were painting this rather than living it, her brush gliding, as comfortable in oil as in air, sweeping along through chiaroscuro wave, lifted by a tireless hand, her whole body wet with paint, her life immersed in vivid color where the very wind was a brushstroke and a leaf's fall a flame.

She woke at five. The house was as she'd left it five hours earlier.

The vet operated on Driftwood at nine that morning. There was a one-inch chunk of Styrofoam in his intestines, a piece of the lobster buoy Hannah had seen him chewing on days earlier. The vet brought it to Hannah in a jar of water. It floated on the surface and still retained a slash of red paint. It was one of the dog's favorite pastimes, gnawing an entire buoy down to the long plastic bone at its center. Hannah had used the Styrofoam fragments to aerate her garden for two summers.

"You can take him home tomorrow," the vet said. "He'll be sore for a few days and you'll have to watch that he doesn't pull his stitches out. But I think he'll be OK."

For the rest of the day, she stayed on the mainland. She had breakfast in Stonington at Connie's, then left her car there and walked into town, past the ball field and the old school, past the Opera House where the last movie of the season was showing that night. The town pitched steeply into the sea, built on the stepped granite ledges of an old quarry. Even though women had been hauling in topsoil for over a hundred years, the granite still reared up between houses and under garages, erupted from gardens and spilled out onto the sidewalks. The old houses were unusually square and solid because their foundations were the bedrock itself. She walked from one end of town to the other, to Billings on Moose Island where Will had worked his first summer, and all the way out Indian Point Road to Ames Pond. It seemed like everyone in town had used the summer to prepare for winter. The old Congregational Church had large new insulated windows facing the sea. At the John L. Goss house on Church Street, three handsome young carpenters were finishing off a new tin and copper roof. On Greenhead a fish house was undergoing a Victorian restoration. Things were clearly winding down, but it had been a busy season. On Main Street, a couple of the glass storefronts near the road were covered with plywood to protect them from the snowplows to come. The restaurants had already posted winter hours, and most of the galleries were closed. The summer population of 2,500 had dropped to a little over 1,000. Only the fishermen and the retired remained, a few artists. But even the lobstermen were already retreating, beginning to pull their traps and stack them in sideyards. Everyone was moving toward the stove, toward a source of heat. She walked past Tom and Emily's house and saw that they'd ordered at least two cords of firewood. It was stacked neatly near the side door. A faint plume of blue smoke rose from the chimney. A single seagull stood on the peak of their roof, as if on guard there. Tom's truck was parked on the commercial pier, his skiff on *Sweet Hannah's* mooring in the harbor. Hannah stood on the pier, near the harbormaster's open window and listened to his VHF radio. It was early afternoon, and the lobstermen were coming back in, throwing end of days at each other across the airwaves. It seemed just yesterday that she'd come here and thrown her bags down to Arno. She'd listened to this same radio a year later, listened to Arno berate the Coast Guard, describe an empty boat turning in a tight circle. She wondered if it had been Tom who jumped from one racing boat to the other, as if leaping from one horse to another, an Old West hero.

🐚 🐚 🐚

She picked up Driftwood the following morning. He sat up and wagged his tail when she came in the room. When the vet's assistant opened his cage he stood and walked stiffly out. The lower half of his torso had been shaved. In the middle of this bald patch, a line of black stitches closed a long pink wound, hell's zipper. His shaved skin was mottled. There'd been these faint, pale clouds under his fur all this time. It was as if a rent in the sky had been repaired.

"Poor baby," she said, and tucked her face into his neck.

"He had a little soft dinner last night and a nice little BM this morning," the assistant said.

Driftwood waited unsteadily as Hannah paid the bill, sniffing her sneakers and along the baseboards of the waiting room. He jerked back once, looking under his armpit, as if he'd been bitten by a fly. She spread a blanket on her front seat and he was able to climb into the car unassisted and lie down. As she drove back to Stonington, the dog would whine softly for a moment, reach back and lick his wound, then lay his warm chin on her thigh.

"It's OK," she told him. "We're going home."

She pulled down to the public landing in the car, so the dog wouldn't have so far to walk. Luckily the tide was in. The gangway wasn't too steep. There were a couple of skiffs tied alongside hers, and a large white yacht at the end of the floats. She only noticed it because she'd never seen such a big boat so far inside the harbor. If it were low tide, it would be grounded out. She tied Driftwood off with the bitter end of the painter to a cleat on the float, then returned her car to the ferry landing. As she hurried back to the dock, she thought she'd need to order more firewood. She'd need to keep Driftwood warm over the winter. And better food. Maybe a new, larger dog bed.

When she reached the ramp leading down to the floats she saw an elderly couple stepping off the yacht. They walked down the floats slowly, pulling a two-wheeled cart. Driftwood began to bark at them, and Hannah hurried down the gangway. She was worried he'd frighten them off the pitching floats, or pull a stitch in his excitement. She was on the float when the old woman yelled, "Charley!" to warn her husband about the barking dog. The old man had a cane. He raised it and Hannah screamed, "No!" but his expression was wrong. He wasn't frightened or mad or defensive. She arrived at the dog just as the old man did, and then he dropped to his knees and said, "Charley!" too, and then she understood it wasn't the old man's name, but the dog's name. And before she could say no again, both the old man and his wife were hugging the dog, tears in their eyes, their hands moving over his face, their hands in his mouth and the dog shivering in recognition. They hadn't even noticed Hannah. She stood over the three of them, her knees and ankles fighting for balance on the suddenly tilting float. "Good old Charley," the old man said.

She thought to say, "Be careful, he has stitches," and they looked up at her, squinting. "He's just come from the vet," Hannah said.

"This is our dog," he said. "We lost him last summer on our way through these islands."

"This is my dog," she said.

"We lost him. We backtracked for miles searching for him," the old woman said. "Where did you find him? Thank you so much. We were sure he was gone."

"What's happened to Charley?" the man asked. Driftwood lay on his side, licking his stitches.

"He had a blockage in his intestines," Hannah explained. "Do you live around here?"

"Oh, no. We live on our boat in Miami. In the summer we live on the boat in St. John. Bring the boat up every spring and go back south every fall. Where did you find him?" he asked.

Hannah pointed to the islands. "I live out there. He washed up one day."

The old man looked at his wife, who sat on the float with Driftwood's head in her lap. "We thought he went overboard up near Mount Desert. We circled and searched for three days. Put signs up all over Northeast and Southwest harbors, Bass Harbor. You've had him all this time?"

"Yes," Hannah said. "I put ads in the local paper. No one answered them."

"It's like a gift from God," the old woman said. She was wiping tears out of the wrinkles under her eyes. "I don't know how we can repay you. We've had him since he was a puppy. He's twelve years old now, my little lost dog. Look, Dale, she even gave him his shots. He has new tags."

"It's amazing," he said. "We just stopped here to pick up some groceries. We wouldn't have stopped if it hadn't been high tide. The boat's too deep for this harbor at low. I'm going to show you our album." He turned and scurried back along the floats. Hannah bent down and touched Driftwood's wound. How beautiful it was, like a bolt of dark lightning.

"He's going to be all right?" the woman asked.

"The vet said so," Hannah said.

"I guess you love him, too," she said.

Hannah nodded.

"We've had him so long. We raised him. Dale talked about another dog, but I just couldn't." She held the dog's head in her hands.

"His name is Driftwood," Hannah said.

"He's Charley to us."

The old man returned with a photo album. There were pictures of Driftwood as a puppy, asleep in a baseball cap, and at their marina in Florida, aboard their boat.

"We still have his box of chew toys on the boat," the old man said. "Neither one of us could throw them out. What's your name, young lady?"

"Hannah Bryant."

"I'm Dale, and this is Mary. Hannah, this is difficult, a difficult situation. Mary and I, we have resources. I mean a reward, as such, and all the expenses you've incurred over a year and a half, food and licenses and the veterinary bills."

"He shouldn't travel," Hannah said. She couldn't look the old man in the eye. His eyes were too pale. She watched the woman's hands move through Driftwood's fur again and again. She couldn't look at their faces. They looked like the damned dog, gray-muzzled and mottled skin, ears too large.

"No, no, I guess he shouldn't. We could take him across the bay to Camden and get a slip there for a week or two, till he heals enough to travel."

"I don't know," Hannah said.

"Let me write you a check, dear. You don't know what this means to Mary and me. He's like a child to us. We're so grateful that a good person found him."

The floats took a boat's wake and undulated beneath them. As the float settled, the old woman stood up and hugged her. "Won't you have dinner with us tonight? We'll stay here for the night if you'd like. You don't know us. You might not trust us."

"No," Hannah said. "I have plans for the evening." She reached down and took the skiff's painter off the cleat, pulled the bitter end from the dog's collar. The old man had his wallet out.

"No," she said.

"It's not money," he said. "This is my card. My address at the marina in Florida and in St. John. You come see Charley anytime. We come through here twice a year. We'll stop with him if you'd like."

She handed the woman the sack with the dressings and antibiotics. "The vet said canned food for the next ten days. And to make sure he doesn't pull out his stitches."

"Are you all right, Hannah?" Dale asked. "This doesn't need to happen so quickly. Mary and I are retired. We have time to make this transition."

Hannah bent down and took the dog's ears in her hands and lifted them to a point. The next to last thing she said to him was, "I've always loved you when you look like this."

She hugged him and climbed into the skiff. The boat and the float wobbled with the transfer of weight. The dog stood, moved to the edge of the float as she started the engine and backed the boat away. He looked up the float and down, shook his head and yawned uneasily.

The last thing she said to the dog: "Stay."

🐟 🐟 🐟

Cried all the way to the island, the wind pulling tears across her temples and into her ears. Thought, so that's the last of them, they've all come and gone, and there isn't an aloneness to even return to, because she wasn't there anymore. She didn't want to find it even if she could.

She called Shirley Langlais and left a message on her answering machine. "I've been thinking about your offer. I'm ready. Please, get me off this island."

🐟 🐟 🐟

The leaves were banking up on the island's beaches once more, low, fragile bulwarks, a defense too easily breached. She had the thought she might rake them farther inland before the next storm took them out to sea. But there were too many for one person. She wondered if trees were once born with one large over-arching leaf, a sail that allowed trees to travel, but were so repeatedly shredded by the wind, so often snapped, that they learned to tear themselves apart at the seed, tearing along interstices to form smaller leaves in the image of the once whole tree, smaller leaves that could be sacrificed to the wind and the fire and the bug to save the one life, the one life forever stationary. She has seen them, the shadows of trees at night, the ancestral leaf whole in shadow, as it once was. Idiosyncratic reactions. Will was an amphetamine. Emily was an amphetamine, and Tom and Zee and Arno and Mr. Eaton and the whale and the damned dog, all. This was only the same euphoria that Sonny Thurlow found off Grumpy Ledge, line looping round his foot and ankle, hugging his calf and thigh, wrapping his body in a warp of loss. Too depressed to be found, too idiosyncratic to float, a performance enhanced by love. He's here, she understood, washed up on the granite as surely as the leaves, co-op cap and button and skin cell, impaired judgment, daughter, best friend, shrug.

She walked around the island day after day, waiting to leave. Walking faster with each circuit, she made the island smaller and smaller to prove it couldn't support even one life. She threw driftwood back out to sea and kicked sea wrack and leaves down the shelving granite and into the water. Her warning sculptures had become so intertwined and elaborate over the years that it took days to dismantle them. The knots that bound driftwood branches and boards were weather-knuckled, and the barkless wood had worked its way into the cracked granite as if it had grown there. All the ornaments that swayed on frayed warp, the bird and seal skulls, the slashed buoys and eviscerated urchins, the Clorox bottles and plastic flip-flops, deck brooms, nylon bait bags filled with the delicate, fibrous skeletons of herring, all this she laid out within the littoral so the tide could take what it liked.

Within hours of lowering the last warning sculpture, when she lay exhausted and asleep on a stone slab, her fingernails split and her knees bruised, Will's father arrived. She saw him first, Will himself it seemed, in a bright yellow plastic rental kayak, a few hundred yards offshore. She climbed up the bank into the brush and trees, and followed him, in a tighter orbit, around the center of the island. He was moving closer in a slow spiral. She paced the island as if caged, always looking out. He passed the house and she moved through it, as if she were only wind, picking up Will's gun and two shells. She could see him clearly now: Will, but shorter hair, broader chest and shoulders, Will as driftwood, debarked, raw. He was tentative with the kayak, unfamiliar with the way

it worked in tide and current. As his gyre tumbled, she saw he was working toward the mouth of the quarry. He'd found it. The gun was loaded.
She'd pulled back both hammers. When the bow of the kayak was ten
feet from shore, she stepped out of the brush and held the gun level. He
stopped paddling, but the impetus carried the boat on. She waded into
the cold water and put her free hand on the dolphin-like nose of the boat
and shoved it back out to sea.

"If you want to reach my island, you're going to have to get wet," she
yelled.

The kayak bristled in the water. If he'd been better with it, he could
have been on her in two strokes, ramming the bow into her chest as she
stood in the waist-deep water. Instead, he dipped one end of his paddle in
the water and flipped a splash of water at her face, even though the gun
was pointed at him.

"You look like your sister," he told her.

She didn't answer.

"That's my gun," he said. "I've got the other half of it here with me."
He opened a bag and showed her the steel barrel of the shotgun she
held. "So you'd know I was his father."

"He's not here," she said.

"But he's been here, hasn't he? You've got my gun."

"He's not here. He's eighteen. He can do anything he wants."

Whether it was the cold water or her fear, small ripples emanated
from her thighs. She was shivering.

"Now, I'm going to give you this card," he said. It landed in the water
facedown. She could read the card even though it lay facedown in the
water, read its gothic letters as they reflected on the pale granite below,
the letters ensnared in an undulating net of shadow and the letters read,
RUN. The current that ran around the island began to take the card
slowly between them.

"I'll get it," he said, and turned the kayak and pulled forward two
strokes. She stepped back, but it was too late. With the third stroke, he
brought the seven-foot spruce paddle out of the water, over his head, and
with the added length of his arms and lunging from the kayak, brought

it down on her arm holding the shotgun. Both long bones broke at the wrist. The gun slid into the water and down a steep ledge, and he was in the water with her, trying to free his legs from the kayak. The pain in her arm was effervescent, tiny bubbles breaking on the surface. She could see points of bone straining at the skin. She struggled from the water to the shore, up the bare granite and into the brush. Her hand looked so odd, hanging on the end of her arm like a loose sock. By the time she came out of the brush and into the trees her skin began to scream, as if it were being shredded. She tried to hold her hand but it shook loose, wouldn't be comforted. The pain began to come out of her mouth then and at first she moaned, then began to scream. She ran through the spruce, around the quarry rim, and down through the grass to the house. Ran and stopped. Ran and stopped. The hand demanded it. She had to stop or it promised to drag her whole body down. The marrow of all her long bones seemed to course toward her wrist, to empty into another body distant from her own. Her house looked strange, the door on the wrong side. The phone was not to be found. Arno's gun was still on *Sweet Break of Day*. Will's father pounded on the door, and she slipped out a window, dragging her hand behind her on a long rope. The boat shed seemed a hundred yards farther from the house than it should have been. It ran before her. She caught it by the doorknob and locked herself inside, hid among the crated paintings till they began to smoke. The building was on fire. The big doors were so rotten, the grain so rife with herring, she was able to kick through them. In the smoke that billowed out after her, she ran mistakenly into the ocean. Will's father was behind the boat shed, a box of matches in his hand. He seemed surprised to see her. He'd left his paddle leaning against the house. She'd have to run around the entire island to get to it before he did, but this seemed possible. She was so mad. He'd burned her paintings. Then he had the kayak paddle again, its blades made of shark fins. She stood between the house and the burning shed in tall grass. Mr. Eaton was worried the bacon was burning. She raised her good arm to fend off the blows. *Sweet Break of Day* was in the bay, roaring around the island and turning in to the boat shed. Her white bow wave was as long as a fence in a field. Tom was aboard. The boat did not stop at the mooring or the beach but slammed ashore, the huge red and white hull sliding up the gravel beach and shelving granite and into the grass between Hannah and the finned paddle. The force of the landing knocked Tom overboard. He fell beside her and handed her Arno's gun because he couldn't get his hook inside the trigger guard. The one bullet only. Will's father walked around the boat. There was bottom paint in his hair where the keel had parted it. She could see the dimple forming in the end of the verdigris cartridge, the slug born from the long womb of the barrel and entering the man's body as if it had been waiting years to kill him.

"We've killed Will's father," she told Tom.

He took off one of his prosthetics and gave it to her. "For your arm."

When she woke, the island was as she'd left it, except the tide now had her by the calves. She was wet from the knees down. Well, he can come now, she thought. There won't be anybody here. Her wrist ached from lying on it. She thought, you are the absolute queen of melodrama. Your life isn't anything other people haven't lived before.

🦋 🦋 🦋

There remained Arno's headstone. She thought of it on the spring tide, the lowest of the season. She'd found the stone once before, remembered it two to three feet below water at low. She rowed the skiff out of the quarry to the granite scree on the back side of the island, where all those stones, large and small, unfit to ship to Boston or New York, were tumbled into the ocean. They'd made the island broader but less high. She was surprised to find the stone only a few inches below water and the tide was still falling. It was perhaps three feet by two, and sixteen inches thick. Carved in relief on its broad flat surface was a single flower but it was so encrusted with barnacles, she couldn't tell if it was a daisy or a rose. There was a hairline crack extending diagonally across the stone, perhaps the reason it had been abandoned. She dragged the skiff ashore and waded across the jumble of rock to the headstone. It sat at an angle, resting on fragments of granite. She'd brought a line and an old buoy to tie the stone up and mark it till she could borrow *Break of Day* to carry it around the island to the boat shed. There were gaps under the stone, but not a clear enough passage to snake the line beneath it. She couldn't hold her hands under the water long enough. It was too cold. She sat down above the water's edge, above the stone, and kicked at the sharp scree beneath it. She was surprised at how loose the assembled rock was, like gravel on a path. It had lain there too long to be so unstable. She kicked enough stone from beneath the slab to pass a line underneath. She had to put her cheek to the water to reach all the way beneath the big rock. Farther down the incline, in deeper water, there were other carved stones resting on the granite debris: the wing of an eagle, a Doric column, acanthus leaves. She finally got the line around the stone, tied a knot with the bitter end, then took the free end around the stone in the other direction, as she would tie a ribbon around a gift. She didn't want the headstone to slip free when it was lifted. If she dropped it in deep water, she'd have to hire a diver to go after it. She sat back up and kicked at a chip under the near corner and it gave way easily, so easily her foot slid beneath the stone. Before she could stop her own skid over the little shards she'd kicked out the debris on the far side, and the headstone settled on her ankle and calf like a car falling off a jack. She could feel barnacles biting into her skin for a few moments, but then the leg went numb. She put her free foot against the stone and pushed till the tendons on the inside of her thigh began to tremble. The water was at her hips. The falling stone had left a smirk on the surface but now it was still. There was no current. The water was at low. She tried prying at the debris under the far end of the slab that she could reach, but it was as if it had been mortared in place now, as if it had filled the last gap in a solid wall. She looked to Spruce and Millet islands across the channel but there was no one onshore. She couldn't even hear a lobster boat, then realized it was Sunday. Her nose was approximately two feet above the surface of the ocean. The tide would rise ten to eleven feet over the next six hours. She had approximately an hour to get someone's attention. If she had a stick, she might pry the stone off her foot. There was none within reach, but maybe one would float up. She kicked at the stone again, cursed it, then yelled out. Seagulls answered. How completely stupid this was.

Shit, shit, shit, shit. It wouldn't even be considered a suicide, just an accident, a stupidity. No one would realize she was unhappy enough to leave her life of her own free will. No one killed themselves by putting their foot under a big rock. Just another fricking idiot dying in the granite. The buoy she'd brought to mark the stone floated by, still tied to the line. It was one of Arno's old buoys, old enough that it had a three-foot stick through it rather than a piece of plastic. She jammed the stick alongside her calf, under the stone, and used her knee as a fulcrum. She bent forward, got both hands on the stick and pushed. It snapped immediately. Shit, shit, shit, shit. She realized her calf was squeezed to the thickness of the tibia. The skin seemed as rigid as sheet metal. Why didn't it burst? The water was at her crotch now, unspeakably cold, obscenely forward. The skiff was ten feet away, nose in the scrabble. She retied the buoy to the line and threw the buoy into the skiff. But the buoy was shaped like a bobber, designed to roll off passing boats, to shed props and line, even seaweed. Each time she managed to land the buoy in the boat, it pulled free with the least tug. She managed to pull the stern a few inches closer while the water climbed her groin, slipped under her belt. She couldn't believe this was happening on a Sunday. Any other time the wakes of passing boats would lift the skiff off the beach and carry it to sea while her back was turned. The water was as dumb as wax. Seagulls seemed to be mired in it. When the water reached her navel, there was no denying it, she had to pee. She held and held and then thought, what are you doing? What the fuck are you doing, why not get rid of it now so they won't have to deal with it on the stretcher or the autopsy table? Allow yourself this last pleasure, this last release, and so she did, she peed in her pants, peed into the ocean and it billowed around her bottom warmly, filtered through her jeans and appeared for a moment as a yellow wash of heat before joining the sea. The skiff jostled a bit on the rising tide, the added volume of urine. Her arms ached from throwing the buoy, but she tried again and again. At last it bounced off the middle thwart and rolled under the aft thwart. She began to pull slowly, then stopped. She saw the lone wave at a distance. It came around both sides of the island at once, lifting birds a few inches, a single

wave twisting buoys on their warps an inch this way, an inch that. It was
Mr. Eaton's whale, shrugging, and she waited for it to arrive, watching
seaweed appear on the horizon momentarily, watching buoys spin and
loll. When it reached the stern of the skiff, she brought the line taut, and
when the wave lifted the bow a fraction off the beach, she pulled. The
boat slid into the sea. She dragged it slowly through the water till it
rested above Arno's stone. She knew now it was only a question of ratios,
of time and weight. She threw the line over the center of the skiff, laying
it in the open oar locks so it wouldn't slide along the gunwales. Then she
passed it beneath the slab again, between her ankle and the slab, forming
a loop in one end of the line and passing the free end through it and
pulling down with all her might, tugging the skiff as deeply into the
water as she could before tying the line off. Breathing hard, she tried to
calculate if the hull would hold a volume of water whose weight was
greater than the stone's. If it would, if it did, the rising tide would lift the
boat, and the boat would lift the stone off her leg. If it didn't, the boat
would simply sink. The water was just beneath her breasts now. She
watched the line slowly stretch, Arno's headstone acting as an anchor.
She began to shiver. There were thin, flat stones nearby. She slid two
beneath her butt, but the bones in her leg wouldn't let her go higher. If I
had my razor knife, she thought, I could cut through my pants and knee,
leave the leg here. Another wave caught her by surprise and the boat's
hull slammed into her body. She felt the skin of her calf tear where it met
the granite; the pain broke through like light from an opened door. The
line over the skiff went stiff, but the stone did not rise. Instead, the tide
crept higher and higher up the side of the hull. The strakes began to
moan under the strain. They were only thin cedar held together by copper rivets and habit. The line was squeezing the hull like half a lemon.
She added up all the things that could go wrong: the age and weakness of
the rope itself, the weight of a cubic foot of stone versus a cubic foot of
water, her own height and relative proportion of her body (if she were
only taller, or her torso longer than her legs). When the water was at her
chin, she took a sharp bit of stone and began to write Will a note on the
hull of the skiff, telling him where the dog was. She didn't want him to

think he'd disappeared. But she found herself unable to compose. A sentence would require more reach, more boat than she had to write on. So she began to scratch a little drawing of Driftwood into the paint, a profile, his long ears alongside his jowl, his tongue lolling to a curl. And beside the drawing she simply wrote, 'OK.' The boat was almost down to its gunwales. Another four or five inches and water would begin to pour in over the stern and she'd sink. When the water reached her mouth, she was able to rise up a couple more inches by jamming her free foot under her thigh. She felt no more pain from her leg. And she was used to the cold water now. She couldn't understand why anyone would die in it. It was almost impossible to resist grabbing onto the gunwale of the boat to try to pull herself up, but she knew if one cup of water rolled over into the boat, it would be one less cupful of granite it would be able to lift. She took her foot from beneath her thigh, dropped down below the surface and tried to kick the headstone into deeper water again. She kicked until her lungs began to burn and then climbed to air. Her own splashing kept her nose below the surface and finally, realizing this, she settled, and let the water around her settle and she was able to breathe at last, her nose and eyes and forehead rimmed by the water. The gunwale of the boat was only a couple of inches above water. She could almost see over the boat. Another wave would roll into her. It was useless to scream. The sky was so blue. Birds flew over as if swimming in slow motion. Some portion of her body had been in the water for an hour now. But she didn't think of hypothermia, only of how tired the ocean was, how old and tired. She let her head drop below the surface again, held her breath. Driftwood was there, scumbled in saltwater, happy. It wasn't such a bad little drawing. She reached forward to touch it with her fingers but it grew distant and she began to cry because she couldn't touch it, work on it, make it a little more like him. The saltwater burned in her nose and her own tears obscured her vision and the water in her mouth tasted like old olives and at last the stone drifted off her leg, scraping across the bone of her ankle, and she shot up on her one good foot, the water draining from her hair and mouth and ears. She crawled out of the sea and up the bank, up above the high-water mark. Her shoe was missing, the sock gone, too, and blood ran freely now from punctures and scrapes. The bone inside the flesh felt fibrous, like bundled reeds rather than a single hollow shaft. But it didn't seem broken. Each of her toes bulged with pain. She looked back for the boat. It was carrying the stone to deep water, slowly, as if in state.

🍃 🍃 🍃

She was still on driftwood crutches three days later, when she saw a man walking slowly along the shoreline, stooping from time to time, turning over rocks. It was Tom. He crossed below the boat shed and the house and continued around the island. It took her fifteen minutes to get up to the quarry. *Sweet Hannah* was on the mooring, Tom's skiff at the landing. She waited another fifteen minutes for him to make the circuit and enter the quarry from the shore. When he saw her, he seemed surprised. He climbed out of the quarry and sat with her on the winch cover.

"I didn't think you were here. The skiff's gone."

"Yeah, I lost it."

He pointed at her wrapped foot and waited.

"I was moving Arno's headstone. I should have waited for help."

"Are you OK?"

"Yeah. It's sore, but it's getting better. What are you doing here?"

"Looking for my grandfather's lungs. The kids told me you were putting your sculptures back on the beach."

"I think too much rock has been taken from this island. I'm just putting it back where it belongs. I won't send away another stone, no matter how carefully it's wrapped. The rocks are more valuable here than anywhere else."

"Where are they?"

She lifted her chin. "In that niche on the far side of that big shelf, where I cut the stone out to carve them."

"Do you think there's any way we could get Boston and New York to send back the stone when they're through with all those old buildings?" Tom asked.

She smiled.

"Have you sold the place?"

"No, I've put that on hold for a while. That old lady, the whale lady, Shirley, even she tried to talk me out of it. She told me if a rich lady like her wanted it, it was too good to give up."

"So are you working?"

"Not yet. I did a little drawing of Driftwood. I don't know if I'm confident enough anymore."

"That would seem like the perfect time to begin," he said. "That seems like the only honest state an artist should reside in. If you're confident you can make some art, maybe it's not art. If it's going to be art, it should begin in uncertainty, shouldn't it?"

"Would you think of yourself as a fisherman if you didn't catch any fish?" she asked him.

"Yes, I did," he said.

"I don't know. I've got to find a way to make a living if I'm going to stay here."

"Hannah, don't let the world determine what you do by the amount of money they're willing to pay for it. The world wouldn't miss me if I stopped being a fisherman, but I would. That's how Arno Weed was able to live out here alone. He loved his job. You know, as hard as those last six years must have been for him, he still fished until he died."

"You think about other people's problems a lot, don't you, Tom?"

"Don't have to think about my own that way. Have you talked to Emily lately?"

"No. How's the baby?"

"Fat as a cod. Have you talked to Will about his mom?"

"No. He didn't call for a week, so I turned off my phone. I don't want to talk to him, either."

"Why not?"

"Driftwood's gone. I was in town a couple of weeks back. We ran into the folks who lost him. An old couple on a big white yacht. They said he jumped overboard when they were motoring through. They even had pictures of him as a puppy. You should have seen them, Tom. It was like they'd found their lost child."

"And you let them take him?"

"Yes. He's so old. They'll take him to Florida for the winter. It would have been hard on him here. The snow and ice cut his feet. All last winter he crawled under a rug because his own coat is so thin. We were in town to get a chunk of lobster buoy out of his belly. They must be good people. They took him with twenty-three stitches and all."

"I'm sorry, Hannah."

"Sometimes it hurts so much, I go stand on a rock at the beach and call out his name. I just yell his name as loud as I can at the ocean."

"Zee was with Will when his mother showed up."

"Yeah?"

"She said the woman was almost afraid of him."

"Why?"

"Because he looks so much like his father."

"Is he going to Victoria for Thanksgiving?"

"No, I think maybe that's why he hasn't contacted you yet."

"What?" she asked.

"He invited his mother and her husband and his two half sisters to the island for Thanksgiving. He thinks you'll probably kill him."

She nodded.

"You can call him on Zee's new cell phone. It's the first of Arno's money she's spent outside of her tuition. She calls me twice a day. Will's always with her. Do you have a pen?"

She felt her jacket pockets. "No, yes." The lead was dull, most of the yellow paint weathered away. She picked up a pale leaf. "Go ahead."

"That pencil drift in?"

She looked up and smiled at him. "Yes."

"You're alone on an island, a pencil washes up on the beach, and you haven't used it to save yourself?"

🐦 🐦 🐦

She looked up from her worktable a week later to the sound of a horn. *Sweet Hannah* was in the bay. Tom was towing something.

She'd been working on a portrait of her sister in pencil. He blew the horn again. She opened the door. He stepped out of the wheelhouse and pointed at the thing he was dragging. He cupped his hooks around his mouth and yelled, "I'll bring them around to the quarry."

He's bringing me flotsam, she thought. It looked like crates or palettes some ship had thrown overboard. She hobbled up to the quarry and took the long way around to the granite landing as Driftwood would have. As *Sweet Hannah* entered the harbor, she could see it was her skiff being towed, or rather the bow and stern of her skiff. It looked like someone had cut the boat in two with an ax.

Tom yelled, "She washed up on Isle au Haut, bow and stern a hundred yards apart. I'll come alongside and we'll drag them out."

They worked without speaking to each other.

When the fragments were up on the ledge, he said, "This boat wasn't just lost, Hannah. What happened?"

She'd finally caught up with Will and Zee the day before. They told her Emily had been gone for over two weeks. She'd left the baby with Tom.

Hannah didn't answer him. They were both still breathing hard from dragging the boat from the water. Instead, she said, "I want to think that she left to protect the baby. If Will's father, if he finds Emily now, he won't find the baby."

He sat on the coaming of the lobster boat, his feet on the granite. "I'm sorry I didn't tell you. I thought maybe she'd come back, but I know she's gone now."

"Where?"

"I don't know."

"Why?"

"I think she missed being in love with God, even if He didn't miss her. When I told you she was reading a lot, it was her Bible. She wouldn't name the baby. It was just a matter of time. I think she decided to give God a second chance."

"But what about you?"

"I know she needed me, even if it was only for a while. I always knew she'd go, didn't you?"

"No. I don't understand why people come and go," she said. "Who takes care of the baby when you're not home?"

"Mrs. Hutchinson, Al's wife. She's just two doors down. She's been a real help."

"Why didn't you bring her to me?" She started to cry before the sentence was out of her mouth.

"Emily left her with me."

"I know, but . . ."

"That's not the reason. I didn't want you to think you had to take over. I find it difficult to think of letting the little girl go and I'm afraid that's what would happen if I brought her to you, even though I know that's the right thing to do."

There were smooth granite pebbles in her hands. She'd picked them up as he'd spoken, warmed them in her hands. There were tiny bits of pink feldspar in them, flecks of black mica. She put one in her mouth. It tasted of salt and seaweed. It was the tiniest of islands, awash in the ocean of her body, and she toyed for a few moments with the idea of swallowing the small stone, and then she did. It was there now, in the bowl of her stomach, but she could not separate it from the other minerals in her body, couldn't tell it apart from liver or bone or brain cell or the feeling of being in love.

She offered, "You come, too."

🦋 🦋 🦋

Working from the pencil sketch, she brought a blue shadow into her sister's portrait. Letting the brush linger along her cheek was almost like holding it in her own palm. The baby was finally asleep. She slept in Arno Weed's cradle near the stove. Hannah was able to reach it with her toe to rock it gently from time to time. The cradle's rockers rolled in the worn hollows of the wood floor, in the path of Arno Weed's dancing. For moments at a time, she confused this child with the one that lost her father at sea fourteen years earlier. And confused her own image with the one she was painting. Out of sheer habit her brush swept up into her own face. Impasto built up to almost sculptural levels as she repeatedly recognized her own features and painted over them. After days of work, she felt she'd finally floated up out of her sister's eyes and was able to look back into them to see her own reflection. She put the painting away for the baby.

While Tom fished, she raised the two ends of the old skiff to the quarry rim and dragged them through the grass to the graveyard. She dug shallow depressions on each end of the row of graves, and let the bow and stern settle into them. Then she filled the interior with soil and planted bulbs. Somewhere between Ten Acre No Nine and Isle au Haut, the weight of Arno's stone had become too much for the little skiff and the line had ripped through the strakes, cleaving the old boat in two. She liked to think Sonny Thurlow finally had a headstone. For Arno, she'd have to find another stone, some piece of the island left behind a hundred years earlier because it was somehow flawed: a wing, a column, a keystone. The broken boat rode the crest of the island. In the overturned soil she found a small shard of mirror in the shape of an artist's lung.

In the evenings, after the baby was asleep, before they went to bed, she helped Tom out of his prosthetics and rubbed cream into the skin of his flaking stumps. His forearms and wrists were so pale. "Next summer," she told him, "these are going to get some sun."

He came home in the late afternoons, washed the salt from his face, kissed the baby, kissed her. He repeatedly found flecks of paint on Hannah's cheeks or brow, and since he couldn't remove them with his hands, he locked a small sable brush in his hook and painted her face. He straddled her in her worktable chair and ran the brush along her chin, through her eyebrows, flattened out the ridge of her nose; when the brush curled through the whorls of her ear it was too much, and she hid it in the flannel cloth covering his chest.

She carried the baby outside the house and introduced her to individual seagulls, to erratic boulders, her favorite hidden irises, the quarry, the red leaves of blueberries, the cold, the distant view. She kissed the baby's hands repeatedly.

🐢 🐢 🐢

As they washed dishes after supper, a week before Thanksgiving, Hannah looked up and saw Zee digging in the old trash pit down by the boat shed. She was down on her knees, her hands thrashing through the broken beer bottles. She and Will weren't supposed to be home for another three days.

"It's Zee," she said, and nodded out the window. "What is she doing?"

Tom looked up, through the flowing glass. "That's not Zee," he said. "It's her mom."

The woman stood up, lifted a shovel, and drove it into the shattered glass.

"Is she looking for the money?" Hannah asked. She took hold of both of his hooks beneath the dishwater.

"Let me go. I need to go down to her."

Hannah followed him. When Zee's mother saw them coming, she dropped to her knees again and began burrowing into the glass with her bare hands. Tom began to run. He picked her up out of the pit from behind, and she screamed, "No, no, no, Tommy. He's here." Blood ran down her wrists and hands. She squirmed in his arms, turned and beat on him, the blood stippling his face.

"He's not, he's not," he screamed back at her, and carried her down the foreshore and into the high tide. They both fell headlong into the water, separating as they fell. The woman screamed when she rose up above the surface, and Tom yelled, "This is where he is, out here." They both stood in water to their waists. Hannah realized she was wet, too. She looked down and the water swirled around her hips. She'd followed them in. Zee's mother wrapped her arms around her own body and began to cry. Tom held out his arms. She moved to him and he picked her up and carried her out of the water.

🐚 🐚 🐚

"After Sonny died, I tried to get her away to Jonesport but she always slipped back here," Tom told her. "I didn't know why. I didn't know she was coming out to your island."

They'd gotten Zee's mom into dry clothes and he'd taken her to the state hospital the night before.

"She never got over losing Sonny. I don't know. Maybe she was crazy before he died. Maybe that's why Sonny was so wild, caring for a crazy wife."

"But she was your wife, too," Hannah said.

"I almost went crazy, too." He went to the crib and picked up the baby. He sat down next to Hannah and said, "Pet her face for me." She reached across his lap and stroked the baby's head while the child looked at Tom.

"She was leaving Sonny for another man, not me. She was sure Sonny committed suicide because of her affair. The guy wouldn't have her afterwards. So I married her. That other man is still around, bitter and torn. He's with her at times. He cuts my buoys when it wells up in him. I'd always loved her, since before she married Sonny, but I knew her heart was coiled up in the past with Sonny and this other man. So I realized I was there for the little girl, for Zee. I asked her if she dug all the holes and she said no. If she'd said yes I might not have believed that either, I don't know. Hannah, all the things we live with that are repaired badly."

He didn't continue.

It seemed to her his long-hidden heart was suddenly revealed, as exposed as a bird's nest in winter.

"Rest," she said.

🐌 🐌 🐌

"I was thinking we should give her a name before the kids get home," Tom said. He was putting on his coat. Hannah stood with the baby over the woodstove. The intense cold had finally arrived. It blew in over Canada and across the Gulf of Maine and under their very door. Tom was taking *Sweet Hannah* into Stonington to pick up Will and Zee. The rest of Will's family would arrive Thanksgiving Day. The baby opened its mouth as wide as she possibly could and fell suckling on Hannah's cheekbone. It felt good. Hannah turned and did the same to the baby's cheek.

"OK," Tom said, searching around the room, "where are my gloves?"

She dipped across the swooning floor on socks, pressed his back against the door with her own and the baby's body.

"I was thinking: Lily," he said. "Lily Bryant Eaton. Could you call her that name for the rest of your life?"

"Lily," she said, and she shrugged, and felt her shrug billowing out through the physical world, turning leaves, swaying dry grass, lifting birds on the wing and the loose ears of dogs. The baby cried softly, and Hannah bent down and kissed her crying lips. Such a beautiful face. She looked like everyone she'd ever known.

Epilogue

for Margaret Ryan

That winter, the cold returned as it hadn't since 1935, when the Merchants were ice-bound to the mainland and Isle au Haut. Stonington Harbor froze around the pilings under the shops and the ice reached out across the Thorofare to Crotch and Russ, to Spruce and Millet and Ten Acre No Nine. At the crushed floats of the Public Landing, the dog saw no reason to stop at the splintered lumber. He jumped down to the solid sea. The elderly couple stood at the top of the gangway shouting him back, but finally she said to the old man, "Let him go." And the dog, too, knew they'd all had enough of pleading and shouting. The brown stains left on the teak deck of their yacht didn't smell like he was sorry or blameless. They smelled like him. He didn't know how they got there. He found his place in the world without cause and effect. And a single boat took no time to round. He'd become accustomed to wandering. He'd run away from the marina too many times. The way to the island seemed both familiar and odd, as if it were his own tongue swollen. He defecated without knowing it, on the run. The sea was humped and jagged, but firm. He'd always wanted to run behind the boats and now suddenly he could, though there were no boats around. When he reached the quarry, the cold seemed to break, the granite beneath to shift. But this much of the way he knew. He raced the long way around the quarry. His feet were bleeding from the sharp ice, but she would put socks over his paws, lay him beside the fire. He scratched at the door. He heard footsteps inside. The past was far from over. His tail whipped the world behind it into a frenzy of expectation.

Suggested Topics
for Discussion

1. Why is Hannah so driven to have complete solitude on the island? How does she change with the arrival of her numerous visitors? Is she happy alone at the end of the book? Consider the beginnings of Hannah's artistic career. When does Hannah become a loner?

2. How do Hannah and Arno resist or accept the impermanence of the island? Discuss the meaning of the holes that have mysteriously appeared on the island.

3. How does Will challenge Hannah's solitude? How are they similar to and different from one another? When does Will first call Hannah "Mom"? How are Hannah's feelings toward her young guest affected by being in her mid-thirties and single, without children of her own?

4. Early in their friendship, Tom asks Hannah, "What are you hiding from?" What, if anything, do you think she's evading? Is everyone who comes to Ten Acre No Nine hiding something? In what context do they reveal these secrets to each other? How is each of the characters vulnerable? What happens when truths come to light?

5. What effect does Hannah's sister Emily have on our perceptions of Hannah? Do Hannah and Emily like each other? What are the similarities and differences between the two sisters? What does Hannah discover through coming to know her sister after all these years?

6. What do you think about Hannah's thirteen years as an artist on the island? What does Hannah think about them? Trace the different kinds of art Hannah makes from early in her life through her last art projects in the book. What does the novel have to say about being an artist, isolated or within a community? Would "Immaculate Conceptions" have been an apt title for Hannah's art retrospective? Was Arno's gift to Hannah truly a gift?

7. By the end of the story, Hannah, Emily, and Tom have each faced a significant loss. What has each of them lost, and what made it important? What comes next? How do Emily and Hannah grieve? What are the costs and (if any) benefits of each character's loss? What new experiences are possible?

8. Shirley, who arrives to help rescue the trapped whale at Ten Acre No Nine, says she names every whale she tries to save. What is Shirley saying about the nature of love and the risk of loss? Discuss the importance of names and naming.

Acknowledgments

I began this novel in the spring of 2001 and finished it in the spring of 2003, six months after I moved to Stonington, Maine. I'd been traveling there by old boat for almost ten years. It is a beautiful and endearing place, and like everyone else who's moved to Deer Isle, I hope I'm the last. I was in the mood to write a happy book in 2001, and feel lucky to have found the place I'd imagined. I'd like to thank Anne and Maynard Bray, without whose help my marine terminology would have sunk this novel. Anne Czarniecki has shepherded the book through a difficult editing process, mostly due to my lost computer disks. I'm grateful. Graywolf Press and Fiona McCrae continue to be supportive, without which support, Reader, we would not have met. My big black Lab, Molly, died during the writing of this book. Since a writer was her only hobby, it seems appropriate that her spirit survives in his book, in Driftwood. And Isabelle – she knows.

Pocketful of Names has been typeset in Weiss Antiqua, a typeface designed by Emil Rudolf Weiss (1875–1942), a German poet, painter, calligrapher, and type designer. Book design by Wendy Holdman. Manufactured by Sheridan Books on acid-free paper.